Libraries,
Erotica,
PORNOGRAPHY

Libraries, *Erotica,* PORNOGRAPHY

Edited by Martha Cornog

ORYX PRESS

The rare Arabian Oryx is believed to have inspired the myth of the unicorn. This desert antelope became virtually extinct in the early 1960s. At that time several groups of international conservationists arranged to have 9 animals sent to the Phoenix Zoo to be the nucleus of a captive breeding herd. Today the Oryx population is nearly 800, and over 400 have been returned to reserves in the Middle East.

Library of Congress Cataloging-in-Publication Data

Libraries, erotica, and pornography / edited by Martha Cornog.
    p. cm.
    Includes bibliographical references and index.
    ISBN 0-89774-474-8
    1. Libraries—Special collections—Erotica. 2. Libraries—Special collections—Pornography. 3. Libraries—Special collections—Sex oriented periodicals. 4. Sex oriented periodicals—Bibliography--Methodology. 5. Pornography—Bibliography—Methodology. 6. Sex oriented periodicals—Censorship. 7. Erotica—Bibliography--Methodology. 8. Pornography—Censorship. 9. Libraries—Censorship. 10. Erotica—Censorship. I. Cornog, Martha.
Z688.E76L53   1991
025.2'73067—dc20   90-46102
                                                               CIP

To Tim, indeed.

Contents

Acknowledgments

Any book is a collaborative work. I wish first to thank my contributors for putting up with me as an editor. I was delighted to obtain as contributors some old friends, some others whose work I have admired from afar for years, and still others who came highly recommended. Thanks to all. And thanks especially to two whose work in sexuality early inspired me: Gershon Legman and Bob Rimmer.

Two other individuals have been enormously helpful and supportive. The first is Sanford Berman, Head Cataloger at the Hennepin County Public Library in Minnetonka, Minnesota. His other friends and correspondents in the library world will not be surprised to learn that this book was originally his idea, and that he provided feedback and advice to me during every step of the project—from suggesting contributors to reviewing chapters. The second is Ken Garson, Information Science Librarian at the W.W. Hagarty Library, Drexel University. As a Drexel alumna, I naturally used the Hagarty Library to research this book, and met Ken in the process. He soon took a personal interest and provided me with regular and invaluable assistance in obtaining background information and materials.

And, indeed, my husband Tim last and first. His warm support and critical judgment enabled and assisted me in persevering with this book for over three years and in shaping it as I wished. From him I learned concentration and single-mindedness. Thanks, and love.

Contributor Profiles

Evelyn Apterbach is a reference librarian and bibliographer in the areas of History, Jewish Studies, and Library and Information Science at Queens College of the City University of New York. She has coedited two other annotated bibliographies entitled *Future Librarianship: Technology and the Profession* and *International Students and the Library*, both published by the Library Association of the City University of New York (LACUNY). I invited Apterbach and her coauthors' contribution after attending the LACUNY 1987 Institute, for which it was prepared.

Vern L. Bullough, Ph.D., R.N., is a SUNY Distinguished Professor at SUNY College, Buffalo. He is the founder of the Center for Sex Research at California State University, Northridge, and a past president of the Society for the Scientific Study of Sex (SSSS), where he had been a genial and sharp witted example to me in my work with the Society. An historian, he has written extensively on the social and cultural aspects of human sexuality. Among his books are *Sexual Variance in Society and History, Women and Prostitution, The Subordinated Sex, Sexual Practices and the Medieval Church* (with James Brundage), and over 30 other books including major bibliographies on homosexuality and prostitution. He has also written over 200 scholarly journal articles, plus numerous popular articles.

Martha Cornog. I have held a variety of positions in libraries and the information industry over the past 20 years. I have published articles in *Information Today*, the *Journal of the American Society for Information Science*, the *Annual Review of Information Science and Technology, The Serials Librarian, The Indexer, The Journal of Sex Research*, and *Maledicta*. I coedited *Abstracting and Indexing Services in Perspective*, coauthored (with Timothy Perper) several teachers' guides for sexuality texts, and served on the board of directors of the American Society of Indexers and the Society for the Scientific Study of Sex. None of this was as difficult or engrossing as finishing this book. I hold an M.A. in Linguistics and an M.L.S. in Library Science, and am currently employed at the American College of Physicians.

Adam Halicki-Conrad is Assistant Professor and Bibliographer in Economics and Business, Sociology, and Urban Studies at Queens College of the City University of New York. He was formerly Head of Reference with the Library and Documentation Center of the International Labor Organization in Geneva, Switzerland; Head of Acquisitions for the Russian and East European area studies program in the Graduate Library of the University of Michigan; and Economics Specialist and Reference Librarian in the Economics and Public Affairs Division of the New York Public Research Libraries. In addition to the annotated bibliographies, *Zero-Based Budgeting* and *Wilderness Preservation, Planning, and Management*, published by the Council of Planning Libraries, he contributed to several bibliographies published by the Library Association of the City University of New York: *International and Comparative Librarianship, International Students and the Library*, and *Future Librarianship: Technology and the Profession*. I invited the contribution of Halicki-Conrad and his coauthors after attending the LACUNY 1987 Institute, for which it was prepared.

Christine Jenkins is a school librarian who has been active in the American Library Association's Feminist Task Force for a number of years. She co-chaired and facilitated the FTF's discussion meeting on feminist librarians' responses to pornography and the feminist anti-pornography movement, which was held at the 1985 ALA annual conference.

Bill Katz, Ph.D., is Professor at the School of Information Science and Policy, State University of New York at Albany. He is author of the two-volume *Introduction to Reference Work*, and of *Magazines for Libraries* and *Reference and Online Services: A Handbook*. He edits a magazine column in *Library Journal*, which I have enjoyed for many years, and has edited *The How-to-Do-It Manual for Small Libraries* as well as a series of how-to-do-it guides published by Neal-Schuman Press. He is also Editor of *The Reference Librarian* and *The Acquisitions Librarian*.

Gershon Legman is the world's leading authority on erotic literature and folklore, as well as a marvelously witty letter writer, with whom I've been fortunate enough to correspond for over 20 years. He is the author of many books on these subjects, including *Rationale of the Dirty Joke* (and its second volume, *No Laughing Matter*); *The Limerick; The Horn Book: Studies in Erotic Folklore and Bibliography; Oragenitalism: A Practical Manual*; and *Love & Death: A Study in Censorship*. He has also written a great variety of articles, introductions, and commentaries to other authors' works. He is currently preparing for publication Vance Randolph's *Roll Me in Your Arms* and *Blow the Candle Out!*, a two-volume manuscript collection of "Unprintable" Ozark folksongs; and his own Memoirs of the New

Freedom, *Peregrine Penis: An Autobiography of Innocence*, of which several chapters were published in 1989 in *Libido: The Journal of Sex and Sensibility*.

Will Manley has been a public library administrator for 18 years and is currently Director of the Tempe (Arizona) Public Library. He is author of *Snowballs in the Book Drop* (1982) and over 100 articles in national, regional, and state library publications. His forthright and more than a little satiric column, "Facing the Public," which inspired me to invite his contribution, has appeared for over nine years in *The Wilson Library Bulletin*. He holds a B.A. from the University of Notre Dame and an M.L.S. from the University of Denver.

Elizabeth M. McKenzie is Director of Public Services for the School of Law Library, St. Louis University, St. Louis, Missouri. Formerly, she served as Information Specialist for the Kentucky Department for Environmental Protection. After receiving her J.D. from the University of Kentucky College of Law, she practiced law for two years with Central Kentucky Legal Services, before earning an M.S. in Library and Information Science at the University of Kentucky. She is a member of the Kentucky Bar Association, the American Bar Association, the American Association of Law Libraries, and the Mid-America Association of Law Libraries. I invited McKenzie's contribution after reading her insightful article "Libraries and the New Censorship" (*Public Library Quarterly*, Spring/Summer 1986).

Mimi B. Penchansky is Associate Professor at Queens College of the City University of New York. She has worked there for the past 25 years as a reference librarian, serving at various times as Interlibrary Loan Librarian, Head of the General Reference Department, and, currently, as Head of the Online Search Service. She holds degrees from Queens College (English Literature), Columbia University (Library Service), and New York University (Media Ecology). As a member of the American Library Association Social Responsibilities Round Table, she compiled and edited several editions of *Alternatives in Print: An Annual Catalog of Social Change Publications*, as well as several bibliographies for the Library Association of the City University of New York. I invited the contribution of Penchansky and her coauthors after attending the LACUNY 1987 Institute, for which it was prepared.

Timothy Perper, Ph.D., is an independent researcher and writer in sexology, anthropology, and biology—and my husband for 10 years. He is the author of *Sex Signals: The Biology of Love* and of numerous technical papers, and coauthor of *A Descriptive Dictionary and Atlas of Sexology* and several guides to sexuality texts. His over ten years of research into American courtship and flirtation was supported in part by a grant from the Harry Frank Guggenheim Foundation. He has been Associate Editor and Book Review Editor of *The Journal of Sex Research*, and has published science fiction/fantasy stories in *Analog* and *Oziana*. He is currently doing research for a book on music and sound synthesis for the eclectic amateur, tentatively titled *Alarms and Diversions*.

Gwendolyn L. Pershing has been employed since 1985 as the Head of Information Services at the Kinsey Institute for Research in Sex, Gender, and Reproduction, Indiana University, Bloomington, Indiana. Her responsibilities at the world-renowned Institute include answering questions from scholars, media, and the public, as well as researching the questions for the nationally syndicated Kinsey Report. Several years ago, she participated in a panel on information resources for sexuality professionals that I organized at an annual meeting of SSSS. Previously, she held the position of Head of the Medical Science Library, Indiana University Libraries. She received an M.L.S. from Indiana University in 1984.

Robert H. Rimmer is the author of 14 novels, including his most recent *The Oublion Project* (1988) and *The Harrad Experiment* (1966), which kindled my fascination with sexuality in 1968. His novels have sold more than 10 million copies. Many of them propose what he calls entopia, or achievable utopias, and offer unique approaches to premarital and postmarital interpersonal and sexual relationships, including legalizing bigamy and group (corporate) marriage. He was President, Relief Printing Company, for over 20 years, holds an M.B.A. from Harvard Business School, and served as First Lieutenant, Air Transport Command, in the China, Burma, and India Theatre during World War II.

David Steinberg has been active in the California and national feminist men's movements for the past 12 years, leading workshops on men's roles, fathering, male sexuality, and "Pornography, Erotic Imagery and Sexual Fantasy." He co-created and performs in *Celebration of Eros*, a multi-media erotic theater presentation that has toured nationally since 1985. He is the author of *Erotic by Nature: A Celebration of Life, of Love, and of Our Wonderful Bodies; Fatherjournal: Five Years of Awakening to Fatherhood; Beneath This Calm Exterior; Welcome, Brothers; If I Knew the Way . . .; Yellow Brick Road;* and *Doing Your Own School*. During a panel at the 1987 American Library Association conference, Steinberg spoke of the need for "quality" erotic materials and his attempt to meet that need as editor of *Erotic by Nature*, which encouraged me to invite his contribution.

Daniel C. Tsang is a Social Sciences Bibliographer and Lecturer at the University of California, Irvine. He is the American Library Association Social Responsibilities Round Table representative to the Board of Trustees of the Freedom to Read Foundation. He serves on the editorial boards of the *Journal of Homosexuality* and *Paidika* and he is also a Research Associate at the Center for Research and Education in Sexuality at San Francisco State University. He compiled *The Age Taboo: Gay Male Sexuality, Power and Consent* (1981), published by Alyson Publications and Gay Men's Press, and reviews lesbian and gay periodicals for *Magazines for Libraries*. He is a former Chair of ALA's Gay Book Award Committee. In his spare time, he runs Lavender Archives. I have known Dan over several years for his presentations at SSSS on homosexuality and intellectual freedom.

Foreword

The volume that these words come before or introduce is written largely, though not entirely, by librarians and is directed largely, though again not exclusively, toward an audience of similar composition. The exclusion consists of such persons as have a special, or professional, interest in writings and other forms of publication that have to do with sexuality, in particular with representations of an explicitly sexual nature, representations of sexual activity and representations that are either intended to create or that reputedly create sexual arousal in those that read or see them. These materials extend over a vast field of printed and graphic or visual matter, and the volume that follows touches in one way or another on many parts of that area.

One of the central problems that recurs in many of the essays in this volume bears upon certain structural conflicts in the vocation or role of the librarian. On the one hand, the librarian works for and is in some sense the agent of a local or specific community and is hence implicated in the values of that community and in their reproduction and transmission through the books and other materials that are in his or her charge. On the other, the librarian is also involved in and attached to another larger and more abstract community of literacy and of values. This second community also believes in books, but tends further to endorse strongly the value of freedom of choice, and regards variety and plurality as moral and social goods. The structural conflicts in the librarian's role or vocation are frequently called into play and dramatized by the presence of sexually explicit material, particularly when that material moves into the realm of circulation within the library's complex system of relations. This volume traces in a variety of ways, among different themes and subtopics, developments and changes that have occurred during the last 25 years or thereabouts in how libraries and their related communities or social contexts have learned to deal with and negotiate, if not solve, some of these conflicts. In this sense, this volume has the value of a kind of historical report; it brings the reader up to date on what has been happening in recent decades in those special institutions in our communities in which reading or visual materials and the larger publics come together.

The story that these essays generally tell has to do, by and large, with a generally increasing liberality or liberalism of view within the universes that libraries make up and serve. That enlargement has not been without its disputes and troubles, as when, for example, the concerns of certain feminists over the way women are represented in some sexual publications came into conflict with the regard in which most librarians have come to hold freedom of speech and the freedom to read. The conflicts in this instance concentrated in two apparently liberally oriented groups that came into opposition over whether the value of the freedom to possess and circulate materials depicting women in certain ways outweighed the damage that might be done ultimately to women by these materials. The damage, it was argued, was wrought by the effects such representations would create in the minds, attitudes, and ultimately actions of those who read or looked at them. Another, less serious, series of episodes has to do with the fate of *Playboy* in local libraries; what happens, mostly to the physical body of the magazine itself, when the monthly is freely circulated within the walls of the library, and what happened when the Library of Congress was "discovered" to be subsidizing the circulation and distribution of *Playboy* in braille. This latter story, in particular, makes for amusing reading.

Most of the contributors to this collection of essays subscribe to the belief that the librarian's primary obligation or responsibility is to books themselves and to the general idea of unhindered public access to them. Few of them adhere without modification to the older notion that the librarian is primarily the custodian of either traditional or communal or literary values. And in the light of recent decisions by trial juries in Cincinnati and Florida, it seems that these writers are in accord with developing moral opinion in the country at large. That is to say, they seem closer than many of them appear to believe they are to some current social consensus on what latitude of freedom of expression is appropriate, if not perhaps in community libraries, at least in public museums and in musical recordings. At the same time, one of the questions that, at least for this reader, remains to be discussed has to do with budgetary choices and priorities. In view of the severe constraints on purchasing allowances in libraries, one has to ask: What books or other material are not being acquired when the kind of sexual material discussed in this volume is bought by one's local or campus library? I do not know the answer to this question, but raise it as a matter that might be worth thinking about.

This volume will inform the reader about how some librarians (and people with related interests) who are essentially libertarian in their views currently think about a number of problems that have a long history to them. It makes for an interesting and valuable account of historical changes in certain opinions on important matters, and although I do not agree with everything that is asserted in each of the essays in this book, I think that the work as a whole is well worth reading.

Steven Marcus

Libraries,
Erotica,
PORNOGRAPHY

CHAPTER 1

For Sex, See Librarian: An Introduction

Martha Cornog and Timothy Perper

A CURRENT DILEMMA

Why a book of essays on libraries, erotica, and pornography?

In April 1988, according to the records of the Ellensburg, Washington, Public Library, a patron borrowed a cassette recording of Isaac Asimov's *The Robots of Dawn*. "The Good Doctor," Asimov is called among science fiction fans, and to others he is known as the author of hundreds of books explaining science to the lay reader. Furthermore, he is the father of the friendly talking robot of modern fiction and film.

But this library patron was not pleased. *To what in the book do you object?* asks the borrower's complaint form submitted on April 20, 1988 for *The Robots of Dawn*. "Sexually oriented material with no socially redeeming quality," reads the response. *What do you feel might be the result of reading this book?* the form continues. "Recent studies show that psychological damage may be caused to young people." *Is there anything good about this book?* "Nothing."[1]

Now here we do not have such a work as might be titled *Sex Slaves of the Astro-Mutants* or even—as one might imagine SF romance novels—*Martian Rapture, Passion's Planet,* or *Starship Mistress.* Certainly, Asimov is no drooling lecher or shambling pornographer with notions of depraving the young and innocent. *What would you like the library to do about this book?* says the form. "Do not permit children under the age of 18 to borrow it. Or preferably withdraw it from the library."

Withdraw it from the library. In that phrase, we encounter the focus of the censor and the dilemma of librarians. The issue is not about acquiring *Sex Slaves of the Astro-Mutants* (say) nor about shielding sensitive children from viewing clinical material on sadomasochism. The issue about censorship is far broader, for it touches millions of purchasing and access decisions made daily by librarians: in one form or another, sexuality pervades our entire experience and much that is written or portrayed today.

Fiction, perhaps, attracts more attention than nonfiction—fiction that, like *The Robots of Dawn, Forever* by Judy Blume, or even *In the Night Kitchen* by Maurice Sendak, contains a sexual depiction as an integral part of its characters' tale. The great censorship court cases have been fought about fiction: *Lady Chatterley's Lover, Ulysses, Madame Bovary.* Mention *erotica* or *pornography* and most people will think of fiction, but many other types of writing concern sexuality in more or less direct fashion and have drawn the censor's attention, thereby bringing problems to the library. The Kinsey reports, *The Joy of Sex* by Alex Comfort, and the books of Masters and Johnson have all been controversial. Likewise, censorious attention has been drawn to books on erotic art, AIDS education, and even dictionaries, e.g., the *American Heritage Dictionary* with its definitions for *fuck* and *shit.* Today, these are all essential information sources, and yet each has attracted the censor's eye.

Also essential are vertical file holdings on current topics, as all librarians will agree. But how many libraries set up a file in the mid-1980s on a phenomenon variously called *gerbiling* or *gerbilization*—the alleged practice of inserting a live and wriggling gerbil into the anus for sexual stimulation? The gay press actively denied rumors attributing the practice to gay men, with vigorous research and careful documentation (e.g., Avicolli 1986; Broderick 1986). But where could general readers satisfy their apprehensions about these rumors save from the library? Yet, probably few libraries dared to respond to this particular need-to-know, although the print material exists.

All sorts of material involve sexuality, with varying degrees of global interest and relevance to library patrons. Libraries in coastal states could, and perhaps should, carry directories of nude beaches. Many communities have local utopian groups, whose sometimes avidly pro-sex publications belong in the community library—*Kerista: Journal of Utopian Group Living*, published quarterly in San Francisco, comes to mind. What of political and social satire? Underground "comix" provide both, plus considerable entertainment value—and, because of their explicit sex, were targets of court actions for years (Estren 1987). And what of collections of bawdy songs, limericks, locker-room tales, and other examples of the irrepressibly erotophilic, if anonymous, folk who do *not* find sex utterly without socially redeeming value?

Nonprint media, too. The Ellensburg Library complaint about *The Robots of Dawn* concerned a cassette version of the book, and the well-publicized case of braille *Playboy* and the Library of Congress is discussed in detail in Chapter 9, "A Case Study of Censorship? The Library of Congress and the Brailling of *Playboy*." In Tallahassee, Florida, a photographer was asked to remove five pictures from a library exhibit because of complaints about their "intimacy [sic] and provocative nature" ("Photographer Removes Exhibit" 1990).

In short, we are talking about thousands of books, magazines, print and film media that are routinely bought, read, viewed, or listened to by millions of people. Likewise, censorship and the related issues it raises for libraries potentially involve all writers, from John Updike through Masters and Johnson, from Gay Talese and Erica Jong through Judy Blume and Maurice Sendak—and, as readers, from you to us. Seen in that numerical background, censorship is no small problem, socially, culturally, intellectually, or economically.

So, we reach some basic and difficult questions: what does it mean when this patron of the Ellensburg Public Library says *withdraw it from the library?* How should librarians respond to such efforts—forestall them? yield to them? prepare court briefs? give up? What criteria of quality exist for judging the value of a book concerned somehow with sex? How should a library process and protect such materials? How have scholars and readers used such books?

These issues have not arisen suddenly in the last decade or so of librarianship. For much of this century, librarians have had to deal with them, although in both stereotype and, often, reality, they have decided to avoid sexual materials as much as possible. A brief historical sketch of the problem since the 1920s will show how librarians have viewed sexual materials and how the library literature has addressed the issues.

AN OVERVIEW OF THE PAST

> Our present state of mind in regard to it is so chaotic, and subject to change, that there would be no use in trying to record it. (Feipel 1922a, 857)

Thus wrote a librarian nearly 70 years ago in response to a survey by Louis Feipel (1922a, 1922b) about "questionable" or "objectionable" books in public libraries. And just what kinds of books are these, that they cause such chaos?

> The term "objectionable book," as used in the questionnaire, was understood to cover "suggestive" fiction of the type of which many examples from authors of repute are but too well known, books honestly or otherwise offering physiological information, [and] the classics which are usually grouped in book-catalogs under the heads of Erotica, Facetiae, or "Curious," including unexpurgated editions of such works as the "Arabian Nights." (Feipel 1922a, 857)

Today, Feipel's delicately worded prose sounds arch and coy, but there is no mistaking "'suggestive' fiction," "physiological information," "classics . . . head[ed] . . . Erotica, Facetiae, or 'Curious.'" In the changed terminology of the post-1960s era, these terms all mean "sexually explicit."

However, perhaps the censors' efforts have been sufficiently successful that today we do not recognize Feipel's references. The *Arabian Nights,* or *A Thousand and One Nights*, far from being a collection of children's stories suitable for animated cartooning, is a folktale collection of Eastern Mediterranean (Levantine) origin that dates back at least a thousand years and is probably far older. Many of its stories are openly erotic, and Legman (1964, 222, 387, 459, 463) argues that they were the ultimate source for many, if not all, European joke books (often themselves erotic) from the 17th century onward. In 1885, Sir Richard Burton, collaborating with Leonard Smithers, produced a 16-volume translation for private circulation by the Kama Shastra Society (Walton 1964, 8); approximately a decade later, Smithers edited a 12-volume illustrated "library" edition of the work (Hyde 1966, 186–187). These were rare and costly works, but were of some renown in the United States; for example, in 1894 they appeared in a court case involving the bankruptcy of a book publisher (Kendrick 1987, 174). In 1922, the very name *Arabian Nights* elicited a sense of oriental erotica and the forbidden. (For a recent critical discussion of how European and American erotic fantasies of the 19th and early 20th centuries became firmly lodged in Levantine settings, see Kabbani 1986.)

Moreover, Feipel's allusion to "authors of repute" was very likely a reference to James Branch Cabell, whose *Jurgen*, published in 1919, provoked scandal and legal turmoil for its sexual allusions. "A very naughty book," an admirer is supposed to have said (Loth 1962, 169). However, it was deemed "free from the evils accompanying suggestiveness" by the judge who ruled it noncensorable in 1922 (Loth 1962, 170). Still, for most readers, *Jurgen* dealt less with the fantasy world Poictesme (rather reminiscent of Piers Anthony's modern-day and immensely popular Xanth) than with *sex*. And, despite legal judgments, the opinions of chic and trendy readers, and widespread critical acclaim and testimony, *that* caused the problem. Books about sex were objectionable in libraries and to librarians.

The Librarian as Censor

Things have not changed much since 1922. The librarian's state of mind about sex books is still "chaotic." And in the public stereotype, librarians still "object" to sex books. In one cartoon from the great 1960s satirist Gilbert Shelton, a neo-Nazi virago booms to the counterculture hedonist Fat Freddy, "[T]he library of the state university does not contain any 'FUCK BOOKS.' And as a matter of fact, the state university will NEVER contain any 'FUCK BOOKS.' Now GET OUT" (Shelton 1971, 13; see page 6). In another cartoon, published in *Playboy*, a voluptuous young woman behind the circulation desk is approached by an eager young man who ventures, "Under 'Sex,' the card catalog says, 'See Librarian'" (Sneyd 1982).[2] The two librarians, both women, differ in appearance and social style, but both restrict sex books: the first through not purchasing them, and the second by keeping them behind the desk. Even during the preparation of this book, a librarian friend commented about the project: "Libraries and erotica, eh? This should be a slim volume. Good luck."

However, since 1922, immense social changes began to result in public availability of materials about sex previously found only in costly and imported privately issued editions of the "classics," in books "restricted to the medical profession" or "issued for anthropological purposes only," or in poorly printed, flimsy, but popular ephemera such as the "Tijuana bible," an eight-page illustrated cartoon depicting famous characters (e.g., Popeye) in various explicitly drawn sexual adventures. In 1922, most librarians responding to Feipel's survey bought only a few "objectionable" books, selecting only the highest quality according to "prevailing and accepted literary and aesthetic canons" (Feipel 1922a, 858). Those chosen few were kept "segregated from the general collections" and circulated only "thru application at the reference desk and the information desk" (Feipel 1922a, 858; 1922b, 908). It is clear that Feipel's librarians saw themselves as custodians of public tastes and morals.

But, external to the libraries, both morals and reading habits were changing. Also in 1922, Lee Alexander Stone, M.D., "Late Official War Department Lecturer and Instructor to Troops in Social Hygiene and Venereal Disease Control; Major M.C.U.S.R.; . . ." (the list continues for 14 lines) published *Sex Searchlights and Sane Sex Ethics: An Anthology of Sex Knowledge*, which contains among its 777 pages *two* complete chapters explaining the then illegal techniques of birth control and contraception, and *strongly* urging their legalization for use for family planning purposes. He quotes Margaret Sanger with approval and describes how, in 1920, the Peace Society of Milwaukee, led by its "lady-president advocated a 'bride's strike' and [urged] the refusal of married women to give birth to children until future wars were made impossible through disarmament" (Stone 1922, 142). It is not Lysistrata: it is the voice of feminism and the peace movement, heard in prophetic words immediately after World War I. Stone's book also contains a sentimental, but remarkable, introductory "Letter to Dorothy," opening "My Dear Little Girl, This is your twelfth birthday. . ." and saying "Fortunately, you are living in the 'Age of Woman'; therefore, I may say to you—amount to something.

The Fabulous Furry Freak Brothers, copyright © 1987 by Rip Off Press, Inc. Used by permission. (For a catalog, write P.O. Box 4686, Auburn, CA 95604.)

Vow to be more than a parlor ornament, vow to do something that will place your name among the annals of the blessed" (Stone 1922, vii–viii). And yet, we suggest, one would have been hard pressed to find a library in 1922 that contained the work of this retired Marine Corps physician and humanist.

Stone was not alone. In 1926, Th. H. Van de Velde, M.D., published a book destined to become perhaps the best known and most widely reprinted work on marital sex ever written: *Ideal Marriage: Its Physiology and Technique* (the Random House edition, copyright 1930, 1957, and 1965, lists slightly under *fifty* printings between 1941 and 1970). Yet, his 1931 *Fertility and Sterility in Marriage: Their Voluntary Promotion and Limitation* contains the warning "This book, because of its scientific character and because of the legal restrictions placed on its distribution, is available only to duly licensed physicians on their written or authorized order." Not fare for the public library!

But three writers were to change the face of sexual writing, and they, perhaps more than any others, brought sexuality to a vast reading public: Bertrand Russell, in *Marriage and Morals* (1929), Margaret Mead, in *Coming of Age in Samoa* (1928), and, of course, Sigmund Freud. Russell's urging of the companionate, loving marriage, Mead's open discussion of the lifeways of another people, sexuality included, and Freud's powerful, unrelenting examination of sexuality all became the very stuff of educated discourse (and fad!) in the 1930s and 1940s. With them, material previously kept locked in the private collector's cabinet or hidden under the medical librarian's desk potentially became the property of anyone who could read. It would be an interesting, although very difficult, research topic to determine how frequently in the 1930s and 1940s libraries—public, academic, and medical—received requests for these books, and how they were handled; but probably such data are next to impossible to gather today. Even so, one can speculate that if Feipel's librarians were bewildered, so were the librarians of the 1930s when confronted with a request for "that book by the lady anthropologist about sex in Samoa."

Yet, after World War II, again there was a change: "1948 will go down as the year of the K-bomb: *Sexual Behavior in the Human Male*," wrote Roger Bristol (1949). Curious "to discover what librarians do when faced with books that are too hot to handle," Bristol polled 11 libraries in the Boston area about the Kinsey report and about Norman Mailer's then-controversial *The Naked and the Dead* (1948). "Do they or don't they? How do they justify their decisions? And if they do buy them, how do they solve their 'handling problems?'" (Bristol 1949, 261). Of the 11 libraries he surveyed, four rejected Kinsey, five Mailer. After describing interviews with the librarians involved in these pro and con choices, Bristol drew a conclusion:

> So far as the library is concerned, the basic conflict seems to be between two conceptions of the librarian's job: (1) maintaining taboos of society, and (2) providing wide variety of community fare, even including material personally repugnant to the librarian. (p. 263)

This theme of dual and conflicting allegiances to different ideals of librarianship will appear over and again in the essays in this volume, and there is no question that Bristol's perception is accurate, even today. And yet, notwithstanding its accuracy, Bristol's comment raises a subtle problem about consonance between a library's ideals and society's ideals. In Feipel's 1922 report, his prose rings true about the mores and taboos of his time. Social custom was clearly against the open distribution of "objectionable" books, at least among the lettered classes that formed the libraries' clientele. Library ideologies about such books thus fit comfortably together with ideologies external to libraries.

But, by 1949, when Bristol was writing, disconjunctions were beginning to appear between the Feipel-like library ideology of restricting acquisition and access to books on sex, and rapidly relaxing external standards that were making sex a commonplace in writing, film, and social discourse. By 1949, it was beginning to sound old-fashioned to speak globally of "society's" taboos against sex, for no longer did "society" have a monolithic view of sexual morality. Nor, we may assume, did libraries have as narrow a clientele as they might have had in 1922: if nothing else, the GI Bill of Rights brought thousands of World War II veterans to college and into contact with academic libraries. Cultural diversification of library clientele was an important emerging factor in Bristol's 1949.

Furthermore, libraries were starting to touch what historian Paul Robinson has called the "modernization" of sex, a society-wide secularizing transformation that brought sexuality from the domains of privacy, religion, and the demimonde into the domains of commonplace existence and everyday, virtually public occurrence (Robinson 1977, 188; for a more detailed analysis see Perper 1985, 212–253). In brief, if Feipel's librarians could depend on cultural consensus for supporting their stance against "objectionable" books, that consensus was rapidly fading in Bristol's time, as a result of both diversification and secularization. Consonance was becoming assonance, if not yet cacophony.

Nowhere, perhaps, is this theme better illustrated than in Sidney Kingsley's dramatic and very popular 1949 play *Detective Story*. Set in New York City and played with rapid-fire realism, it concerns Police Detective Jim McLeod, a man of rigid and strong morality, who discovers—and is destroyed by the discovery—that his beloved, seemingly virginal wife Mary had had an illegal abortion before they met, performed by a physician whom McLeod has himself just arrested for murder because of a patient's death. As his wife leaves him, McLeod—hate-filled and bitter—tries to disarm a gunman and is killed.

In the 1949 performance, McLeod is a tragic figure: the tragic hero who upholds his view of morality in a world where all morality is changing, even though doing so destroys him emotionally and physically. Thus, *Detective Story* illustrates an important aspect of writing about sexuality in the Korean War period. McLeod's inflexible rectitude is no basis for living one's life in the real world.

And yet there is a subtler reading of the play, equally compatible with the script if not with a 1949 audience's reactions. Mary's abortion has permitted her to become McLeod's wife, because her child-free condition and untarnished reputation allowed him to believe that she, as his *wife*, must be and is "immaculate" (p.179). He cannot accept that she has had another lover, and that his own "love" for her is a delusion made possible only by the abortionist he so hates. He can only blame her, reject her, and yet beg her to stay with him. When "stronger than he, at last" (p. 200), Mary leaves him, McLeod's world is crushed, and his death follows virtually as retribution brought by his own hand.

It is not a morally simple play, because, no matter what reading one adopts, the point is not merely the loss of moral fixed points for sexuality, but a vision of the *uselessness* of older sexual-moral codes, for women and men both. And, given *that*, what were librarians to do? *Detective Story*, played on Broadway to large audiences, could not be (figuratively at least) locked up behind the circulation desk, although it concerned a topic about which traditional "decency" once remained utterly silent. In a real sense, therefore, the quandary faced by librarians from the 1950s onward was of maintaining the traditional standards of decency and silence about topics that were generating a lot of noise outside.

Bristol himself was well aware of this contradiction. He opens his essay by observing that "It is no news to librarians that the climate is changing" (Bristol 1949, 261). Moreover, he comments on the irony of restricting adolescents' access to Kinsey's work when the Kinsey report itself documented the sexual knowledge and activity of adolescents.

Nor was the contradiction restricted to adolescents. Bristol cites *Library Journal's* review of *The Naked and the Dead*: "The language employed is very strong and *so accurately reported* that it probably will offend many and may create problems in handling" (Bristol 1949, 261; italics added). Translated, this sentence seems to say that sexual *truth*—i.e., accurate reporting—is itself offensive and by itself can create "handling" problems. A similar problem existed for the

Kinsey reports (1948, 1953): by virtue of their seemingly endless and incontrovertible tables of statistics, Kinsey and his co-workers were documenting a series of sexual truths that morality sought to deny existed.

And this was indeed a major change, which lies even today behind much of the debate about sexuality materials in libraries. In Feipel's time, it can be argued that no one denied that people did immoral things: after all, Societies for the Suppression of Vice, to say nothing of Anthony Comstock himself, flourished on proving that vice was rampant—particularly masturbation, prostitution, and pre-marital unchastity. The moralists' point was to restrict vice and prevent its spread, for example, by making sure that libraries did not purchase "objectionable" books. These patterns of sexual activity were found by Kinsey too, yet differently labelled. Kinsey's work attributed sexual activities formerly characterized as "vice" (and pre-sumably engaged in largely by a deviant subclass) to a wide cross-section of *average* people in society—making vice seem normal, as his moral critics charged (Geddes and Curie 1948). Thus these critics, including many uncertain librarians of Bristol's 1949 Boston, could only wish to deny the existence of these sexual activities—and of Kinsey's reporting them.

So it is probably not true to say that librarians in 1949—or now—wanted to enforce "society's taboos." A single "society" with monolithic taboos no longer existed. But, unable to accept easily either the diversification of society or the secularization of sex as described by Kinsey and others, librarians sought refuge in preventing information about sexual activity (vice or commonplace) from spread-ing too far. It was, in brief, a *strategy of denial and avoidance* that Bristol's librarians were enacting, rather than a *strategy of morality* such as was familiar in Feipel's time. And perhaps nothing proves that point better than *The Naked and the Dead* itself, for its so accurately reported language was the language of millions of Ameri-cans who had served in World War II, and who had seen atrocities, sexual and otherwise, that made adolescent masturbation seem virtu-ally polite by comparison.

Times they were a-changin' indeed, and, in Bristol's report, we hear for one of the first times the voice of the ostrich, head in sand, and a new voice that led, in part, to a then radical alternative of providing library clientele with what they want, no matter how "re-pugnant" it might seem. In this, Bristol's report captures a crucial moment in library history, poised between the conviction that the old ways—suppression of vice by publicizing its horrors—were socially mandated and culturally inevitable, and at least two new ways—the suppression of *information* about sex, seen as vicious, and a growing, countervailing trend to open the libraries to all material, sexual or not, and thereby serve a new morality captured best, perhaps, in the slogan "Ignorance is the worst form of violence."

And in the following years, more and more reasons appeared to sharpen this conflict between "protecting" the clientele and "serving" them, even if they had repugnant needs. The literary and intellectual movements of the 1950s, notably the Beat Generation of poets and writers, were underlain by a different cultural calculus than that which formed the basis of Cabell's Poictesme and *Jurgen*. In a world built upon Freud, Mead, and Kinsey, arising as a compound of the Great Depression, the Nazis, the Holocaust, and perhaps above all, Hiroshima and Nagasaki, it became hard to retain innocent and childlike faith that Good Shall Triumph, and that a chaste and virtuous world of family, hard work, and sexual purity would prevail. And then, in 1961, came another sexual and reproductive bomb: the birth control pill, followed soon by "The Sixties."

With them came an explosion of fiction and nonfiction dealing explicitly with sex, including small press titles, magazines, and solid, scholarly works such as Masters and Johnson's epochal *Human Sexual Response* (1966). No longer could sexual "physiology" be restricted to books ordered solely by physicians! And, caught up themselves in the public culture shock, librarians found themselves in a deepening quandary. Writing about an avant-garde, stick-it-to-the-middle-class literary "little magazine," Milwaukee librarian Don Dorrance described an episode of the period: "I had quite a fight with our trustees over indexing *Fuck You!* . . . Anyway, we finally settled on a compromise: I could index *Fuck You!* as *F--- Y---*, if I kept it off the open shelves" (quoted by Clifton, In Press).[3]

The quandary and confusion among librarians in the early 1960s about sex materials were well illustrated by Broderick's (1962) and Moon's (1962) surveys. They circulated lists of "controversial" or "problem" fiction and nonfiction titles to public librarians, asking which items were purchased and why. (Sixteen of the 20 fiction titles, and five of the 24 nonfiction titles, had been selected as "controversial" because of their sexual content, an interesting change of euphemism from the word "objectionable.")

Practices and responses among responding librarians varied widely. A few libraries bought all the books on the lists, but many bought few or none. Moon observed about books rejected that "much more common than judgments on literary merit or quality were judgments on content, assessments of moral values or taste, with a protective attitude toward a public described with alarming frequency and condescension as 'unsophisticated'" (Moon 1962, 490). Sometimes librarians chose not to purchase certain titles *because* they were controversial—whether the topic was sex, race, or politics.[4] A few comments, however, uncovered those rare librarians who "balanced their collections without second thoughts about 'demand'" (Broderick 1962, 3378) or controversy:

> We don't buy all of it [current fiction]. We don't necessarily like, or have to like, what we do purchase. But we do select sufficient to reflect what is being written in our day. (Moon 1962, 488)

> We attempt to add a variety of fiction, providing a wide field of choice to our patrons. (Moon 1962, 489)

Some librarians reported a double standard whereby "problem" books were selected only if they were of higher quality than uniformly acceptable items.

> In effect, I suppose our practice is this: a book with a harmless theme designed principally to entertain and characterized by a style ranging from trite to mediocre to fair is judged less vigorously than a book addressed to a serious, challenging or controversial theme. (Moon 1962, 489)

Among these 1960s librarians, we still hear the custodial voices of Feipel's 1922 or Bristol's 1949 respondents, but they are mixed with newer voices stressing the importance for library acquisitions of patron need and free intellectual access.

The Librarian as Anti-Censor

If, by 1965, the focus within the profession was shifting towards assuring patron choice among a wide variety of materials, the shift only increased the chaos. By now, assonance had become discord and even violence. Librarians were assumed to be fairly open-minded about purchases and circulation of *all* kinds of material, so long as it did not lack "social values" and was better than "marginal taste" (Lacy 1965, 474). It was *"public"* pressure that might be the source of censorship (Lacy 1965, 474; italics added). At least in part of the library literature, which reflects the profession's view of itself, a transition was being made from librarian as rightful and proper censor to librarian as guardian of "the freedom to read."[5] At least some of the specialized sexuality libraries described in later essays in this volume owe their existence to precisely this change in emphasis. One might suggest that the change arose because at least some librarians were seeking an ideological or theoretical basis for liberalized collection/access policies in precisely the changes in politics and morality that were occurring outside of libraries; at a minimum, the view was emerging of the library as a flexible, *responsive* institution rather than one embedded in rockhard traditions of the past.

The change was not without its influential critics. Kathleen Molz, editor of *Wilson Library Journal*, observed that

. . . with the determination of the *Ulysses* case, the librarian found in the temperate wording of the decision a more proper and rational focus [than aesthetics] for his [*sic*] own book selection policies . . . It may seem unfortunate, . . . for pornography is essentially an aesthetic, not juridical, problem. (Molz 1966–1967, 97, 99)

In this, Molz too is attempting to secure library collection policies in a bedrock of principle that exists external to the quotidian realities of filling out purchase forms: for her, however, this bedrock is not an unquestioned *moral* sense, and is certainly not a sense of being able to trust judges, but lies in *esthetics* or *taste*. Thus, she is sure that "high pornography," e.g., *The Story of O* or Genet's *Our Lady of the Flowers*, is a "subcultural literature" (Molz 1966–1967, 101). Likewise, she is sure that ". . . the strongest opponents of the *inherent* tawdriness of much modern fiction should be the academic or literary critic" (Molz 1966–1967, 100; italics added). Thus, she can conclude that ". . . it does not lie within the responsibility of a public library to indulge every vagary of human taste" (Molz 1966–1967, 101–102).

And yet, sadly perhaps, there is no universal standard of taste. Indeed, taste is notorious for its fluctuating, faddish, and often foolish shifts. Tawdriness inheres less in a work of a writer or artist, and more in critics' and audiences' reactions to it. Accordingly, Molz' hopeful evocation of eternal verities and standards of truth and beauty provides a genuine standard for purchasing only to those who share her own tastes—and, if they do not, what *then*? To be sure, Michelangelo is a standard of artistic greatness; does that deny a place to modern art in museums? Hence, esthetics and taste have often proved a weak reed upon which to base purchase decisions, because the standard Molz adopts—and, in one form or another, it is probably widespread among traditionalist librarians—only serves to separate the library and its holdings from a public whose tastes have been nurtured on other art forms, including, perhaps, "high pornography."

It was this sense of separation from the public—of history passing the library by—that led radical critics of library collection policies to propose, and sometimes to implement, "alternative collections" concerning minority groups, labor union history, sexual minorities, women's history, and a variety of other "non-central" aspects of the American social scene. If the eternal verities and esthetics dictate Michelangelo, radicalism dictates printing a literary magazine called *Fuck You!*

In brief, by the late 1960s and early 1970s, the battle was joined. Was the library a bastion of good taste, mandated by its traditions to uphold the view that libraries were "those houses of high culture located around the corner from Elm Street" (Molz's apotheosis of the traditional library, with which she ends her essay, page 103)? And, if so—runs the radical retort—by what kind of madness have we elevated Babbittry and small-town parochialism into the arbiter and adjudicator of *all* that is written in America?

Whose interests are served by the library? What principles underlie its purchasing of its collections? Who, exactly, is in charge here, and of what? In 1971, Bill Katz had one answer:

> A viable collection should include at least a scattering of titles which [the librarian] finds offensive and disturbing. Relatively uncontroversial titles are hardly going to do this, but neither are they going to represent the broad gamut of opinion possible in a country with a democratic heritage. . . . Why shouldn't the larger public libraries have a section devoted to pornography? . . . The proposition may be justified on two counts. First, a pornography collection would tend to blunt the censor's interest in other, possibly more exacting and controversial areas of the library. Second, and more important, it would be a move toward the future before the future caught up with and passed the library. (Katz 1971, 4061, 4064)

Katz' argument depends integrally on two ideas: first, that library *holdings* should represent the range of writings produced in a diverse nation, and, second, that the library as an *institution* should move with the times. Implicitly, however, his argument also depends upon the conclusion of the 1970 Commission on Obscenity and Pornography that sexually explicit materials were not harmful. Molz, speaking for the opposition, could counter only by referring to traditional values and to traditional taste: the library as the small town House of Culture.

Accordingly, one sees in the 1970s a gradual diversification among librarians themselves, as new ideals of librarianship—responsiveness to public needs and flexibility in acquisition policies—slowly emerged. Differences in opinion about what books to buy had become clashes of clearly stated viewpoints and visions: in brief, purchasing and access decisions were becoming ideologized.

A Diversity of Views

This diversification among librarians is documented in a survey conducted in the early 1970s by Nolan Pope. The results, aptly published under the title *Sex and the Undecided Librarian*, showed that university librarians were more liberal about buying sex materials than were public librarians, who in turn were more liberal than school librarians (Pope 1974). Men librarians were generally more liberal than were women librarians. Furthermore, social science librarians were more liberal than those in the humanities, who were more liberal than those in the sciences.

In an ideologizing context, it seems possible that different ideals of librarianship underlie these differences. Apropos of Molz' image of the library on Elm Street, are these differences due to greater Babbittry among school librarians, women, and those in the sciences, or to adherence to solid American virtuousness? Perhaps, but another possibility is that these differences also reflect different usage patterns among, say, the clientele of academic, public, and school libraries. It is also quite possible that the differences reflect differing reactions of various segments of society to the secularization of sex. University libraries serve an intelligentsia with more liberal attitudes overall. For public librarians and school librarians, however, it is another matter. Their clienteles are very diverse within themselves—and to serve one subgroup may often alienate another. So these librarians may simply resort to the simplest conflict-free path of serving the most conservative of their communities, thereby to alienate none.[6]

Even so, such matters do not fully explain the sorts of differences Pope (1974) was reporting. It was the librarians *themselves* who were sometimes conservative, and that conservatism is not explicable solely by pointing to, say, usage differences between university and other libraries.

This is not the place for a thorough discussion of why people differ in sexual, moral, or political liberalism and conservatism. Cultural factors, personality variables and history, as well as temperament, all play their roles, and suffice it to say that such differences are real and can affect career choices or attitudes within a career. There are then several reasons why at least some librarians might be drawn to traditional values, particularly in sexuality. First, one can speculate that people drawn to the small-town public library, either as librarians or as its users, may be relatively more comfortable with its conservatism (or, if you prefer, its solid base in tradition) than inner-city radicals, say, who might want very different things from a library, if they use libraries at all. Second, librarianship was a respectable profession for women to enter at times in American history where the norm, if not always the fact, was the woman as home-maker and the man as bread-winner. If so, again we can speculate that some women librarians came from social or family backgrounds conducive to accepting tradition, including components of traditional sexual morality with its "decent" silence about matters like abortion, masturbation, or even pre-marital sexual activity. Such people would find it natural indeed to try to *maintain* standards of taste and decency, very much along the lines Molz (1966–1967) describes. It follows then that the "conservative" librarian, woman or man, is not an anti-progress reactionary, but someone who genuinely and deeply believes that standards *do* exist or, if they are weakening, *should* exist.

So it is not surprising in Pope's 1974 survey that *every* category of sex materials listed on the questionnaire elicited a "would not purchase under any conditions" response from at least 13 libraries (of 718 responding) even though the rejected works include some that seem relatively innocuous by "modern" standards, e.g., a slang dictionary containing "dirty words," a book about venereal diseases with no illustrations, and a sociological study of prostitution. Pope concluded that the "[r]esearch indicates that librarians gave strong support to the concepts of intellectual freedom and open access to information, but do not necessarily implement these concepts in their libraries" (Pope 1974, 184), a position we above called "the strategy of denial and avoidance." It therefore seems that one can firmly believe in the freedom to read while still believing that standards of morality and decency should be observed. Nonetheless, the result appears to be self-inconsistent, and, without doubt, it generates conflicts that bothered (and bothers) a good many librarians, particularly in the absence of a cultural consensus on sexual morality existing outside the library. Librarians were undecided indeed.

Thus, Hawks (1975) maintained that pornography is not explicit sex but "uncaring sex," but could add that "[t]o me, censorship is pornographic. . . . The library, above all others, is no place for censorship" (p. 189). On the other side, Flanagan (1975) took up the cudgels for a viewpoint championing the librarian as custodian of quality in society:

> To refuse to impose some values in the world of ideas and information, and on the means of expression—to undertake as the Introduction [of ALA's *Intellectual Freedom Manual*] advises, to provide all points of view on all questions—is to avoid doing what professionals in other fields actually do, that is, to avoid judging what is conducive to human growth and what is not. To "give 'em what they want" . . . is to avoid constructive judgment. (Flanagan 1975, 1889–1890; see Berman 1981)

However, individuals on the other side of the intellectual freedom issue could easily reply that Flanagan's argument is most seriously flawed because his assumption that librarians are able *professionally* to judge what promotes human growth comes close to genuine hubris. For example, in psychology, it is a matter of intense debate among trained experts whether or not certain forms of childhood sexuality (e.g., masturbation) are a necessary component for adult sexual health. Here, Flanagan's argument slips deftly from professional evaluation of scholarly or scientific content, which librarians cannot usually do unaided except when it comes to books on librarianship, to moral judgment, which presumably any citizen, librarians included, can and do make all the time. Yet it does not follow that because a person went to library school, he or she is better equipped than anyone else (parents, for example—or behavioral scientists!) to judge what promotes overall human growth and development. Flanagan's argument, then, distills itself into the use of slogans, e.g., *We want to promote human growth*, that cover so much territory and are so vague that they can numb critical thinking while simultaneously soothing the worries of people who are afraid that "this sexuality stuff has gone too far." Once again, one is left with the powerful impression of uncertainty and unclarity in the librarian's mind about what to do with sexuality materials.

One response to the uncertainties and doubts was that articles and books on libraries and sex began to appear with greater frequency. In 1979, *Library Journal* published a Special Report containing "Bibliographic Control of Sex Research Materials" (Walker 1979), while, in 1978, Woods categorized and deplored U.S. censorship attempts from 1966 to 1975 that involved educational institutions, over one-third centering on sexuality materials. In 1980, an astonishingly pro-sex article appeared in *Canadian Library Journal* entitled "Pornography in the Public Library, Are Librarians Ignoring Its Role?" (Wertheimer 1980). A year later, Haworth Press published *Sex Magazines in the Library Collection: A Scholarly Study of Sex in Serials and Periodicals* (Gellatly 1981), a valuable and eclectic overview of the challenges of acquiring and processing sex-related magazines in libraries.

However, perhaps the most important change in the 1970s was the emergence, from roots in the 1960s and before, of ardent feminist criticism of pornography. This movement made a crucial connection between pornography and violence against women, and served as an impetus to hundreds of articles and books debating whether or not pornography, in general, had any social value at all or was instead the source and proximate cause of rape, among other crimes. With this, the debate about sexuality materials in libraries took a new turn, because now it was possible to refer to a coherent body of theory and writing when discussing the pros and cons of free or open access to magazines, books, and films about sexuality (see McKenzie 1986).

On the other hand, feminist critiques of pornography were tied to a specific theoretical vision of the relationship of the sexes, and were associated in the public mind with other feminist goals. Accordingly, feminist writing could not, and did not, attract universal or even widespread public acceptance, with the exception of feminist attacks on pornography. In that arena, there was sufficient apparent goodness of fit between feminist criticisms and traditional moral stances that individuals who did not support feminist goals in other areas could support them when it came to suppressing or restricting the publication and distribution of sexually explicit materials. From that, there arose the well-known 1980s "uneasy alliance" between feminists, often radical in their views of society, and extreme conservatives, who yet could agree with what they perceived as the "feminist" critique of pornography.

Independent of such alliances, an important result of feminist writing on pornography was the emergence of a new language for talking about sexually explicit materials. First is the distinction, often very hard to make, between *pornography* and *erotica*. (See Chapter 3,

"Words, Libraries, and Meaning.") As defined by feminists, the former seems to have broadly to do with exploitation, while the latter seems to concern loving sex. But beyond that, the distinction has been remarkably elusive. Second, by introducing the phrase "violence against women," feminist language allowed individuals to refer to an existing cultural consensus when condemning pornography. Since no one *favors* violence against women, this concept promised to achieve what Molz' (1966–1967) effort, say, could not: it is not a matter of taste, that most volatile of things, that lets us condemn pornography, it is a matter of preventing violence that does so. Feminist thinking, then, seemed to provide a solid bedrock foundation upon which to build a new moral vision that condemned sexually explicit materials and yet did not seem stodgily old-fashioned or hopelessly repressive.

We are not suggesting that feminist anti-pornography writing of the 1970s and 1980s was *intended* as a vehicle for producing consensus about this single issue of sexual morality. Indeed, one sometimes feels that there are people who use feminist language and yet have never read feminist writing at all. Instead, we are suggesting that a particular feminist insight, generated as part of a far broader critique of society and sex, could conveniently be isolated as a nucleus or kernel around which to re-center existing, if uncertain, sexual moralities. Above all in this re-centering is the concept that pornography is actively and dangerously *harmful,* not merely distasteful or ugly or morally offensive.

Nonetheless, no simultaneous consensus could be developed for defining the term *pornography.* Justice Potter Stewart's famous remark, ". . . perhaps I could never succeed in intelligibly doing so [defining pornography]. But I know it when I see it" (*Jacobellis v. Ohio,* 378 U.S. 184, 197, 1964, quoted in Feinberg 1983, 120), went far to undermine whatever consensus was forming around the issue, for it offered neither legal nor moral definition. Once again, we return to taste, esthetics, and therefore confusion. (Later attempts to define *pornography* in relation to harm, e.g., the Dworkin-MacKinnon Minneapolis anti-pornography ordinance, encountered equally severe problems; see Chapter 8, "The Feminist Attack on Pornography: The Minneapolis and Indianapolis Porn Ordinances.")

Nor did it prove easy to determine that pornography, whatever it is, actually causes harm, whatever that is. By adopting the "totality of evidence" criterion, the 1986 Commission on Obscenity and Pornography tried to circumvent a growing body of scholarly evidence exculpating sexuality depictions *per se* as harmful (see, e.g., Baron 1990; Donnerstein, Linz, & Penrod 1987); but their efforts only increased the controversy by awakening liberal critics to the weaknesses in the report (see, e.g., "The Meese Commission Exposed" 1987). There remained only an ill-defined *sense* that somehow, something about pornography was harmful, but it was proving increasingly elusive to locate the harmful content, so as to cordon it off legally and otherwise. In consequence, and despite the efforts of feminists, the debate was thrown back to ill-defined generalities about taste, esthetics, and personal moral judgment and preference.

Paradox and Consensus: 1980s and Today

By the beginning of the 1980s, however, it appeared that at least some librarians believed that sex was a respectable heading in the catalog (e.g., Walker 1979; Gellatly 1981). Furthermore, there were strong indications that public opinion concerning those "objectionable" books in libraries was changing. In 1981, White discussed one of the findings of the 1970 Commission on Obscenity and Pornography, that 76% of a sample of American adults believed that librarians should keep "objectionable" materials off the shelves. Librarians felt, as Lacy (1965) pointed out, that public opinion was a barrier to the freedom to read and a reason for librarians to tread softly in acquiring sexuality materials. Thus, Woods and Perry-Holmes, in a 1982 study of 63 "controversial" items in libraries, found that responding librarians often did not purchase the items for fear of community objection, controversy, or "flak." However, when White (1986) analyzed questionnaire results from four General Social Surveys, conducted in 1976–1982 by the National Opinion Research Center, he found that overall a majority of Americans opposed removing books by controversial authors from libraries and favored the availability of pornography to adults and sexuality information to teens as well as to adults. Large minorities took the opposing view; and when respondents were segmented by age, religion, geographic region, and education, categories having a majority for censorship tended to be from the South, to be age 60 or older, or to have less than a high school education. But still later, Carpenter (1988) reported results of a survey in a southern state, North Carolina, in which a majority of 55% agreed that pornographic materials should be protected by freedom of speech and the press. A larger majority, 72%, felt that "any adult who wants to have pornographic materials should be allowed to" (p. 27). America *was* changing, despite the conservative image projected so strongly by the Reagan administration.

But there is a complexity within these changes that eventually leads to a paradoxical and curious consensus where one might least expect it. Although the cultural center of gravity was shifting somewhat to the left, or at least in liberal directions, at the same time American culture was becoming intensely factionalized, with vocal and politically often eager minorities vying with each other for control of the public mind, and therefore of legislatures and judiciaries. One example was the Dworkin-MacKinnon anti-pornography ordinances, brought to the city councils of Indianapolis and Minneapolis in 1983–1984. These sought to make the possession, distribution, and/or exhibition of sexually explicit materials a civil rights violation on a wide variety of grounds, including the doctrine of harm to women. However, the Indianapolis ordinance was not upheld by the courts, and the Minneapolis ordinance ultimately was not passed. In these two cases, liberal contest of the ordinances was strong, equally vocal, and ultimately effective.

And yet in this debate, and in others like it later in the 1980s, an apparently ineradicable and historically quite radical consensus was emerging, if in a paradoxical place. In fact, one can argue that it dominated the seemingly conservative 1980s. Consider, on the one hand, that a keystone of traditional sexual morality, for example the attitudes of Feipel's 1922 librarians, was that certain, perhaps most, sexual topics were to be treated with silence. One did *not* speak of masturbation, abortion, or group sex publicly. In fact, much of the history of sexuality writing reviewed above was designed to break these conspiracies of silence. But there *is* another hand, and here we encounter the paradox. During the 1980s, a number of sexual topics dominated much of American political and moral debate. And through this debate itself, a perhaps unforeseen consensus has come about. It has come to be perfectly proper to speak and write about sex in ways unheard of in previous decades.

However, a distinction is needed. By politicizing sex—not merely secularizing it, but actively bringing it to the forefront of American politics—advocates of various sexual moralities, rights, and viewpoints needed to find print vehicles that would, each hoped, rally the voting public to their own side. And that is the paradox: by thundering denunciations of homosexuality, say, the denunciator is uttering words that were once themselves utterly taboo. A central aspect of America in the 1980s was to debate sex, loudly, publicly, and often.

The list seems endless. There is pornography itself, brought forcibly to the attention of American citizens by no less than the United States government in both the 1970 and 1986 Commissions, as well as in the endless debates those reports spawned; AIDS, which became a subject of terror and deep concern to millions while simultaneously providing seemingly infinite copy for magazines, newspapers, and television shows; the reappearance of the condom, both as a birth control technique and an AIDS preventive; abortion, already hotly debated before the Supreme Court recently made its continued discussion inevitable as a states' rights issue; sex education courses in high schools, which created local political fervor and brought subjects to open debate that perhaps some people had never thought to hear discussed in public; child pornography cases, which, unlike other issues, generated real moral consensus; the singles scene, which has produced book after book, magazine article after magazine article, and advice column after advice column on How to Find the Ideal

Mate (or sex partner); personals advertisements, spreading like brush-
fire in the back pages of elegant magazines; rock video, which is often
as sexually explicit as one can get and avoid an X rating; sex videos
themselves, to say nothing of the explosion of R and X rated films,
which do not condemn the material so labelled as much as identify it
for the convenience of the consumer; premarital cohabitation, become
virtually the norm for the urban middle class; scandals gleefully
publicized by all concerned documenting the sexual peccadilloes of
political and religious leaders; media-gathering rock stars, who, like
Madonna or Michael Jackson, are sexiness personified for their fans;
daytime television soaps, in which the details of sexual liaisons and
misalliances are the very stuff of the plots; daytime television talk
shows, with topics ranging from transsexualism through homosexuality in the clergy through finding a sex partner; and finally—last but
not least!—the saturation bombing of the American consumer with *It*,
that old fashioned term for sex appeal used to sell virtually anything
from automobiles to zoos, all without including the efforts of popular
sex educators, like Dr. Ruth or the pages in *Playboy* magazine devoted to recording, and pillorying, various anti-sex rulings, statutes,
and hypocrisy at large and in general.

And in this, there *is* consensus, because one can argue that in the
1980s, talk and writing about sex represented *the* dominant cultural
event. But perhaps because it is so obvious, it can be easy to miss the
significance of such discourse. It is not "about" proving one morality
or viewpoint right and another wrong; it is about words, media atten-
tion-getting, publicity, and even sales. Upholders of *all* viewpoints
agreed on one thing: the way to convince people is to talk to, at, and
around them, drown them if need be, but above all, get the words out
there.

In that, the bedrock of traditional American sexual morality—distasteful silence about distasteful topics—crumbled and was no more.
In brief, Feipel's 1922 librarians would be appalled, for in their
morality, *one does not talk about such things.* Well, today we do, most
of us, and on television to boot. The media is the message, McLuhan
said; we can paraphrase him to encapsulate the powerfully entrenched
1980s consensus that had emerged despite all the apparent clamor.
The debate is the message. It is virtually a minor detail that Pastor A
is saying that homosexuality is all right, while Father B is disagreeing;
the major and all-important fact is that *they are both on television.*
And while Pastor A and Father B busily neutralize each others'
arguments with rhetoric and passion, the message comes across: it is
acceptable and inevitable to talk about homosexuality, abortion, pornography, AIDS, teenage pregnancy, in brief, about all the matters
that Feipel's librarians so eagerly sought to repress and lock up (see,
e.g., Francoeur 1989). Under the glare of 6000-watt lamps and a

television camera, the locked cabinets of the libraries have opened up, and became public property.

Librarians Today

Clearly, it is a complex moral, intellectual, and emotional legacy that today's librarians have inherited from the seven decades that have passed since Feipel's librarians felt so chaotic about sexuality materials. The official stance of the American Library Association is strongly against censorship of any sort, a position it illustrated in practice through its participation in the recent suit against the Librarian of Congress for cancelling production of *Playboy* in braille. (See Chapter 9, "A Case Study of Censorship? The Library of Congress and the Brailling of *Playboy*.") Moreover, at least young adult librarians are reasonably knowledgeable about sexual topics, and, if not strongly liberal, are not particularly conservative (Steinfirst 1989). But even so, it is not obvious that librarianship or librarians in general have achieved their own version of the consensus discussed in the previous section, particularly if implementing a library version of that consensus might mean, for example, starting a nationwide effort to obtain and publicize the existence of collections dealing with AIDS transmission and prevention. Local exceptions notwithstanding, it does not seem that librarians have been overeager to establish The Library—as opposed to uninformed, often uneducated opinion—as the arbiter of what is and is not known, on all sides, in debates on high school sex education courses, abortion, teenage pregnancy, among many other issues. Furthermore, individual librarians on the firing line of purchase and access decision-making must live with a variety of often opposing influences, some based on popular demand for a class of items, others based on community pressure to remove such items (or foreknowledge that such pressure will exist if certain items are bought), still others based on critical or "quality" judgments, and yet still others based on the ideals of the *Intellectual Freedom Manual's* "all points of view on all questions." So it is hardly surprising that the word "chaos" can still be used to describe "our present state of mind in regard to it," to reiterate the comment made by one of Feipel's obviously vexed librarians.

The problem is well illustrated by considering how libraries have and have not provided information about AIDS, certainly one of the most important areas of public concern about sex. SantaVicca (1987c) surveyed public and academic libraries in Ohio about services and opinions regarding AIDS information and observed that

> 12 percent of all responding libraries (including 20 percent of academic libraries) do not own a single monograph on AIDS; 88 percent do not own any audiovisual material; 33 percent do not maintain a vertical file on the subject; 91 percent neither produce

nor distribute any informational materials for patrons; and 70 percent are not sure of the existence of another agency or institution in their geographic area that do [sic] produce or distribute such information. (SantaVicca 1987c, 115)

Moreover, one of SantaVicca's respondents added another comment:

I feel that there is still a reluctance for public libraries to secure important materials [on AIDS] because of the link to homosexuality. (SantaVicca 1987c, 114)

Omitted from SantaVicca's comments, however, is discussion of another problem: even if a library has one, or a few items, on AIDS, how up-to-date, accurate, and objective is the material? A library might possess the October 1988 *Scientific American*, which was devoted entirely to AIDS, but doing so does not qualify a collection as complete or even particularly useful! (SantaVicca himself addresses these issues in several other publications from 1987, including a bibliography on AIDS materials and a useful discussion of how to build files of AIDS-related materials.)[7]

Yet, through fear of seeming pro-homosexual, or for other reasons, it seems that libraries have not *in general* responded to the AIDS crisis in proactive ways. One reason, as one of SantaVicca's respondents points out, may be a library's clientele:

Absence of cases [of AIDS] in the area means absence of threat and absence of demand *or need* for information. Periodicals provide good coverage. (SantaVicca 1987c, 114; italics added)

To be sure, if disease is not currently a problem in one's area, one might be able safely to ignore its spread elsewhere. But it is not clear why this librarian's answer moves from the absence of *demand* to the absence of *need*. If the terms were meant simply as synonyms, then one supposes that the jump is logical, but *demand* and *need* are still not the same. For discussion's sake, if we assume that AIDS might become a general and widespread public health menace, rather than being restricted more or less to certain subpopulations, could this librarian then conclude that because no one asked for AIDS material in 1986, say, there would surely be no need for it in 1990 or 1995? The answer is not in saying that by 1995 (say) anything written in 1985 would be hopelessly out of date; much of the basic material on AIDS prevention already exists and will not be outdated quickly. Accordingly, we can conclude that underneath this respondent's seemingly reasonable comment lies an additional thought: *we* don't have to do anything about it.

But, paradoxically, another respondent would seem to disagree:

As a conservative [religious] institution, we haven't the demand for materials in this area that a university or public library would. (SantaVicca 1987c, 114)

Here speaks the completely reasonable and believable voice of someone who knows his or her library's clientele and function, but who, for that very reason, can equally reasonably see that other, putatively less conservative, libraries could be very different.

Yet it is not clear that they are, at least so far as materials about homosexuality are concerned. Both the Broderick (1962) and Pope (1974) surveys showed that librarians are quite resistant to materials on homosexuality, an impression strengthened when some of SantaVicca's 1987 respondents also seemed explicitly concerned about homosexuality. Today, "safe sex" manuals for gay readers are in fact likely to inspire particular reluctance because of their advocacy point of view and their anatomical and physiological explicitness about alternatives to anal intercourse. (See, for example, Preston & Swann 1986.)

But even if librarians are reluctant, they are trying to deal with the issues posed by sexuality materials (Bob 1986; Buck 1987), certainly not a simple task in a seemingly schizophrenic era that has produced both the antipornography Meese Commission and a small explosion of the "new erotica"—much of it written by women (Bright 1988; Fraser 1990). (See Chapter 15, "An Annotated Bibliography of Quality Erotica.") In fact, lesbian erotica has become a small but noteworthy industry, including among other works the wittily titled *On Our Backs* and the S&M oriented *Outrageous Women* or *OW*,[8] and which has produced in consequence a polemic literature among feminist writers (SAMOIS 1982; Linden, Pagano, Russell & Star 1982).

Furthermore, some of the issues raised by sexually explicit materials in libraries were addressed in a session at the 1987 American Library Association conference in San Francisco. The session description bears witness to librarians' concern:

> *Sex in the Stacks: Providing Access!*
> How are libraries affected by the post-Meese Commission moral panic? Small press author-publishers and librarians discuss access to sex education and erotic publications that flourish despite the times. (American Library Association 1987, 43)

Likewise, in 1987, the Library Association of the City University of New York (LACUNY) focused its annual institute on "Access or Censorship? Libraries and Pornography" (See Chapter 14, "Access or Censorship? Libraries and Pornography: An Annotated Selective Bibliography," which is based on a bibliography created for this LACUNY institute.) Furthermore, a panel session on libraries, erotica, and pornography was held at the 1986 St. Louis meeting of The Society for the Scientific Study of Sex. So it is clear that at least some librarians are actively seeking solutions to the problems posed today by sexually explicit materials. But, still, a great deal remains to be done.

What *Are* Librarians to Do?

Despite—or perhaps because of—a still present "chaotic state of mind," plus pressure from all sides of various public debates, there is need for intellectual and even theoretical reconciliation between traditions that rejected sex in the library and the newer consensus that justifies and fully accepts writing and talking about sex. One resolution to this need, and a course of action as well, is built into librarianship itself. If public debate exists, then a need to know exists, and that is what libraries are for: to provide relevant material to all sides in the debate. However, an older tradition still maintains that libraries are guardians of quality in books. If the librarian him- or herself measures quality by how closely a work adheres to a given moral viewpoint, then the library will not provide materials on both sides, but on only one (or none, if the library chooses the strategy of avoidance discussed previously). So one conundrum of the 1990s is to what extent can libraries represent all sides of the immense public debate about sex or, for that matter, about any topic. Once again, *Whom does the library serve?*

Next, librarians both want and need to know more about acquiring, handling, and making accessible sexuality materials. There remain important questions about quality, for it is as true today as it was in Feipel's 1922 that "books honestly or otherwise offer . . . physiological information" (Feipel 1922, 857). Distinguishing books in the *honest* and *otherwise* categories can pose considerable problems, even for experts. The dearth of medium or full-length book reviews in sexuality, which I (TP) discussed in the Book Review Column of *The Journal of Sex Research* (1987), remains acute. In addition, sexuality collections pose special problems in security and preservation (see Chapter 11, "Providing Access to Materials on Sexuality").

Then too, let us recognize that community needs differ. It is not always a matter of reactionary censorship or Comstockery for a library not to possess a large collection of sexuality works. If no one wonders that a library in a seaport city has a large collection on marine history and trade, no one would wonder that a library in a farming state might not. Likewise, communities differ in their genuine needs to know about different sexual issues, even if certain issues, such as AIDS, seem nationwide in their importance. However, one must clearly distinguish between local differences in needs to know from the influences in some locales, of vocal pressure groups, which can force a library to restrict its purchases or access policies to represent one or a few viewpoints. Libraries are not immune to external politics, and are often pressed into the service of one side—often traditionalist—in the debates about sex. Clearly, new strategies for communicating with different segments of the library's clientele must be developed, for ultimately it is the public that must support the library's efforts to provide quality materials.

And, with that, we come to the final issue. Are library purchase and access policies to be manipulated by one or another community viewpoint or faction, or are librarians themselves to decide how to balance collections between requirements of various needs to know and whatever standards of excellence may exist? Here, the issue comes down to autonomy, and to how libraries can build thorough, reasonably balanced collections about sexuality without becoming the witting or unwitting agents of only one side in any of the debates.

However, doing so does not promise to be easy. Ours is a fragmented society, and the once monolithic view that sex was a distasteful topic best treated with silence has fallen to the wayside. Yet traditionalists, by definition, look back to those times with admiration and a hope of restoring them to bloom, and to preserving such institutions—like libraries!—that seem closest to the ideals of silence. It is no easy task to debate such an individual, especially if he or she has entered librarianship or serves on a library board precisely because it seems to promise an oasis of calm amidst clamor. But let us recall that books and words are about communication, and that a library of course has the responsibility to attend to traditional needs and perhaps even visions of what that house of high culture on Elm Street should be. However, when library purchases and access policies are *dominated* by the traditionalist reverence for silence about sex, the library can all too easily become merely irrelevant to a modern world in which talk and writing about sex are the norm. The Elm Street house might then remain, but it will be only a curiosity, a throwback to times long gone. If the *modern* library is to remain a house of culture, then it has the responsibility to attend to a far more complex spectrum of needs and visions, in which traditionalism is but one voice among many.

So, ultimately, the solution, easy to suggest and hard to implement, is open and genuine communication between the librarian, as custodian of quality and provider of knowledge, and the public*s*, no longer one but many, that ultimately determine if the library is to survive as a vital institution. That is both the hope—and the challenge—to librarians in the 1990s.

AND ABOUT THIS BOOK. . .

This challenge was noted by librarian activist Sanford Berman in 1985 when he first proposed the idea for this book:

> If anything, the question/problem of pornography has grown "hotter" lately. ALA, as well as many local library associations, have publicly opposed Minneapolis-type statutes making porn-trafficking

a "civil rights" violation. SRRT's [ALA's Social Responsibilities Round Table] Feminist Task Force is staging a program, replete with bibliographic handouts, at the Chicago conference [of the ALA] this year: i.e., a pro-and-con discussion. . . . A few library lit. contributors have addressed the matter of "pornography vs. erotica" in collection development. . . . [Yet] to my knowledge, there is no reasonably current book that fully and fairly covers the topic (i.e., what the relationship should be between libraries and either erotica or pornography). But the need is tremendous. . . . And such a work would ideally include lists/bibliographies relating to: a) sex-positive, non-coercive erotica suitable for library collections; and b) the published literature on the "porn" controversy.[9]

Approach and Scope

Berman proposed, and together 14 contributors and the editor have brought *Libraries, Erotica, and Pornography* to fruition. How to design such a work? From the outset, we all felt that there should be a minimum of polemic of the sort, "erotica is good, porn is bad"; or "all libraries should buy *The Joy of Sex*" vs. "keep sex out of the card catalog." Many, many words have already been published on these topics. Instead, our view of the work has been that of a multi-faceted resource—a crystal viewed from some of its many sides, each side revealing a slightly different perspective of the core. And at this core is a Boolean query: sex AND library collections.

In posing this query, we have made an assumption, that the Boolean intersection of these two terms is not a null set. We have assumed that sexuality-related materials are found in every public, academic, and school library, even if only in the *Bible*'s begetting or in the Sears catalog's bra ads. This perspective then renders some of the polemic on the subject moot. *Librarians cannot avoid making decisions about sexuality materials.*

So instead of generating only polemic, and heat, about such decisions, in this book we hope to generate light on the subject—to provide information, and perhaps some answers to the many questions of librarians, both said and unsaid.

About the Contributions

The honor goes to Gershon Legman in opening the following collection of essays, or rather the honor goes to us all that his contribution in Chapter 2 lights up these pages, giving us a too-brief glimpse of "the history, mystery and art of erotica, its creation and collection, even its conservation in great public libraries." Following Legman, in Chapter 3 we tackle the slippery subject of *meaning*. What does it mean to say "pornography in the library"? What is the difference in meaning between *erotica* and *pornography*? Definitions abound, but is there a common core of senses? And how are these meanings changing?

Next, a frankly polemic couplet from two well-known, outspoken, and prolific figures in librarianship: Bill Katz (Chapter 4) and Will Manley (Chapter 5). Katz argues that pornography has much value in the library, whereas Manley asserts that the costs outweigh any benefits. Curiously, their *basic* points of view, however, are not so very different, as each proclaims that excluding pornography from the library *is* indeed censorship, pure and simple.

In Chapter 6, Vern Bullough takes a completely different tack: the value to *researchers* of erotica and pornography in libraries. What are the reasons for preserving such materials, whether deemed "of value" by society or not?

Chapters 7 and 8 focus on feminist views. Christine Jenkins summarizes some of the diverse approaches to erotica/pornography within the women's movement, while Elizabeth McKenzie describes the legal effects some of these approaches have had in drafting the so-called Minneapolis and Indianapolis pornography ordinances. Both stress the implications of this feminist thought for libraries.

Several years ago, the Library of Congress became embroiled in a suit led by the American Library Association and Playboy Enterprises over the exclusion of *Playboy* from LC's program of dissemination of braille magazines. While reported in the library literature, the full import of this "case study of censorship" has never been fully dissected. In Chapter 9, I (MC) review the facts, opinions, and meanings of the case for librarians.

Not only the Library of Congress disseminates *Playboy*, but also many U.S. public and academic libraries. If LC's lending *Playboy* has raised a furor, what of the other libraries? What does happen when libraries subscribe to *Playboy*? In Chapter 10, I (MC) summarize results from my survey of such libraries—and my conclusions only corroborate the "chaotic state of mind" of librarians about sexuality materials in the library.

"That's all very well," the reader may be saying at about this point. "Yes, my library has some materials about sex, and I'm rather intrigued with the idea of buying more. But what do I do with it when I get it? I read about vandalism and community controversy, and I'd like to keep such problems to a minimum. Even more important, how do I find out what to buy? *Library Journal* and *Choice* have only limited coverage of popular and scholarly nonfiction about sex, and little or no coverage of the fiction—the erotica and pornography that all the fuss is about."

What do I do with it when I get it? Chapter 11 is designed to provide guidance for making decisions about processing sexuality materials, from cataloging and classification through coping with vandalism and controversy. I (MC) do not assume that all such materials should categorically be on open shelves, but instead propose that librarians make their own decisions based on local circumstances. In Chapter 12, Gwendolyn Pershing lists and describes a number of established libraries with erotica research collections, and in Chapter 13, Daniel Tsang reviews homosexuality collections, many of which operate on a shoestring outside the mainstream library world. These are all libraries that have faced such processing and access questions on a larger scale than most will ever need to.

How do I find out what to buy? Ah, there's the rub, and even perhaps the excuse for some. "I'd *like* to purchase more sexuality materials, even works of erotica," the reasoning goes, "but I certainly won't buy sleaze. Since there are no reviews of such things, I can't possibly make an intelligent selection." Chapters 14–17 constitute, perhaps, the core of the book, and are designed to wash away such excuses.

Chapter 14, by Evelyn Apterbach, Adam Halicki-Conrad, and Mimi Penchansky, contains a thorough bibliography on the pornography-erotica controversy in the library world and, to some extent, generally, including a section on "Pornography and Behavior." In Chapter 15, David Steinberg provides a list of "quality" erotica, pictorial and written, much of it women-written and women-focused. For libraries that circulate videotapes, Robert Rimmer's Chapter 16 reviews a selection of the best adult films available on video. Finally, my (TP) concluding essay in Chapter 17 recommends a core collection of sex research and education materials for libraries as well as summarizing the role of the library as a haven for ideas as well as books.

So 15 contributors in 17 chapters—17 facets, 17 ways of looking at sexuality materials in libraries. Do the 15 contributors agree? Of course not. However, all are passionately committed to the importance, value, and meaning of books, ideas, *and* libraries.

How to Use This Book

We have said that nearly all libraries (public, academic, school libraries) have materials about sexuality in their collections. Perhaps many should have more, or a wider variety. However, neither we nor this book proposes that all librarians should immediately begin channelling most of their book budgets into LC HQs or Dewey 306s. Each library is its own case study, and each librarian must make his/her own decisions based on budget limitations, patron response (censorious to larcenously enthusiastic), staff level of comfort, and—oh yes!—such professional freedom-to-read ideals as expressed in the *Intellectual Freedom Manual* and the *Library Bill of Rights*.

In making these decisions, consider this book not as dogma from a few "experts" but as a resource—a collection of recipes, a catalog of possibilities, a series of windows on, possibly, new horizons. Some may challenge, some provoke, while others assist or even console the reader. Yet perhaps the main purpose of *Libraries, Erotica, and Pornography* is to assure the Ellensburg Public librarians, and all the other librarians facing their own equivalent of *The Robots of Dawn*, that *you are not alone*, and that *yes, it is worth the effort*—the effort to make decisions about sexuality materials in the library and, the decisions being made, the effort to acquire the materials chosen and to keep them, whether the materials include the *Bible* and the *American Heritage Dictionary;* or *The Journal of Sex Research* and the Kinsey reports; or *The Robots of Dawn,* Judy Blume's *Forever;* or *Playboy* and *The Joy of Sex;* or even X-rated videos.

For sex, see librarian. To one degree or another, this is the case in all public, academic, and school libraries. Yet each library must walk its own tightrope amidst staff, community, and professional priorities. This book is designed to help the librarian to better find a balance on that tightrope.

ENDNOTES

1. We wish to thank Pat Youngman Smith of the Ellensburg Public Library for sending us a copy of the Borrower's Complaint Form from this incident. The library board voted to retain the tape of *The Robots of Dawn* in the collection, despite the complaint. See Coughlin (1988) and Asimov (1989) for further description and commentary.

It is interesting to note that the plot of *The Robots of Dawn* distinctly promotes caring, committed, loving sex—as experienced by two of the characters (and described in one rather unexplicit sex scene), which is deliberately contrasted with the super-casual sex without love that we are told is commonly practiced on the planet Aurora where the novel is set. On this basis, we believe that few would argue the "socially redeeming" quality of Asimov's book!

2. Woods (1978) reports an actual instance of this. "The title of this article ['For SEX: See Librarian'] was found on a catalog card entry in Washington. . . . If you are of the 'old school,' you might interpret the entry correctly to mean that access to materials dealing with sex is restricted" (p. 1561).

3. According to Clifton (In Press), *Fuck You! A Magazine of the Arts* was edited by Ed Sanders of the musical group The Fugs; Sanders is also known to librarians for *The Family,* his 1971 book on mass murderer Charles Manson. *Fuck You!* "lasted from 1959 until 1965, when it became *Intercourse* to help librarians like Dorrance evade censorship. Shortly thereafter, it folded." As a student at Brown University in the 1960s, I (MC) heard of the magazine when a student library aide gleefully described attempting to assign it the call number FU69. His superior, however, decreed that while the FU was acceptable, 69 was not the appropriate number.

4. Fiske's study of California libraries in 1959 revealed that two-thirds of her book-selecting respondents reported such an incident.

5. This transition is described in fascinating detail by Geller (1984).

6. There are some additional factors in the background of Pope's (1974) findings. The 1970s universities were no longer the small Ivy League or private institutions of the 1930s, but had become huge, heavily funded, often state-supported schools with their own diverse student bodies and faculties. Under the rubric of academic freedom, it became easy to urge—or demand—that the library purchase sexuality materials, especially as college-level sex education courses proliferated. Then, too, feminist and gay liberation scholarship were both beginning to make inroads into previously forbidden sexual territories. Underlying it all was the existence of budgets—large, although to the librarians, never large enough!—that could support the policy of buying essentially any book requested for purchase by faculty.

There are of course some conservative university librarians; yet they cannot forbid the purchase of sexuality materials if requested by faculty. Moreover, a purchase requested by a liberal sociologist, say, cannot be countermanded by a conservative member of the Religion Department because academic libraries must serve teaching and research needs of *all* faculty. As a result, a relatively few faculty members—e.g., those teaching human sexuality courses—can fill a university library with a relatively large number of books on sex, both fiction and nonfiction.

But for public and school libraries, funding is not so simply guaranteed. When a public library budget is overseen by a community Board of Trustees, it is easy to enact strategies of denial by refusing to allocate funds to buy books or visual materials on sex. If nothing else, the local politics of public and school library funding may restrict sexuality purchases. In contrast to the university library setting, a conservative local clergyman who serves on the library's board *can* exert considerable influence over purchasing and access policies.

7. SantaVicca, in effect, took it upon himself to ensure that librarians could not use ignorance of available materials on AIDS as an excuse. Most of the Winter 1987 issue of *Reference Services Review* is devoted to several articles by him about how to build AIDS collections (SantaVicca 1987a, 1987b, 1987d). More recently, Lingle and Wood (1988) authored a book devoted solely to finding AIDS information, and Lister (1989) provided an annotated bibliography of serial publications.

8. The title *On Our Backs* is a sardonic twist of *Off Our Backs*, a soberly militant feminist publication. According to Ashley (1982), the first U.S. lesbian magazine, published 1947–1948, was entitled *Vice Versa*.

9. Letter from Sanford Berman to Arthur Stickney, March 7, 1985. Quoted with permission.

REFERENCES

American Library Association. 1987. *106th annual conference; Preliminary conference program.* Chicago: American Library Association.

Ashley, Leonard R.N. 1982. Dyke diction: The language of lesbians. *Maledicta*, 6:123–162.

Asimov, Isaac. 1989. Editorial: Words. *Isaac Asimov's Science Fiction*, March: 4–8.

Avicolli, Tommi. 1986. Gerbil rumors have no basis, say hospitals. *Philadelphia Gay News*, March 14–20: 1, 11, 23.

Baron, Larry. 1990. Pornography and gender equality: An empirical analysis. *The Journal of Sex Research*, August: 363–380.

Berman, Sanford. 1981. "Inside" censorship. *Wilson Library Bulletin*, Spring: 21–24.

Bob, Murray L. 1986. The right questions about obscenity: An alternative to the Meese Commission Report. *Library Journal*, October 15: 39–41.

Bright, Susie. 1988. Introduction. In *Herotica* (pp. 1–5), ed. by Susie Bright. Burlingame, CA: Down There Press.

Bristol, Roger P. 1949. It takes courage to stock "taboos." *Library Journal*, February 15: 261–263.

Broderick, Dorothy. 1962. "Problem" nonfiction. *Library Journal*, October 1: 3373–3378.

Broderick, Frank. 1986. "Gerbil" rumors rampant in Philadelphia area. *Au Courant*, March 24: 3, 8.

Buck, Richard M. 1987. Mae West and you: Are the stacks too sexy? *Urban Academic Librarian*, Fall: 1–7.

Carpenter, Ray L. 1988. Censorship, church, and sex. *Library Journal*, October 15: 27–28.

Clifton, Merritt. In Press. The dirty dozen: 12 magazines that make librarians whisper. *Maledicta*.

Coughlin, Heather A. 1988. Complaints about books carefully handled. *Daily Record* (Ellensburg, WA), June 14: 5.

Donnerstein, Edward, Daniel Linz, and Steven Penrod. 1987. *The question of pornography*. New York: The Free Press.

Estren, Mark James. 1987. *A history of underground comics*. Berkeley, CA: Ronin Publishing.

Feinberg, Joel. 1983. Pornography and the criminal law. In *Pornography and censorship* (pp. 105–137), ed. by David Copp and Susan Wendell. Buffalo, NY: Prometheus.

Feipel, Louis N. 1922a. Questionable books in public libraries—I. *Library Journal*, October 15: 857–862.

Feipel, Louis N. 1922b. Questionable books in public libraries—II. *Library Journal*, November 1: 907–911.

Fiske, Marjorie. 1959. *Book selection and censorship*. Berkeley: University of California Press.

Flanagan, Leo N. 1975. Defending the indefensible: The limits of intellectual freedom. *Library Journal*, October 15: 1887–1891.

Francoeur, Robert I. 1989. *Taking sides: Clashing views on controversial issues in human sexuality*. Guilford, CT: Dushkin.

Fraser, Laura. 1990. Nasty girls. *Mother Jones*, Feb./March: 32–35, 48–50.

Geddes, Donald Porter, and Enid Curie. 1948. *About the Kinsey report*. New York: New American Library.

Gellatly, Peter, ed. 1981. *Sex magazines in the library collection; A scholarly study of sex in serials and periodicals*. New York: Haworth.

Geller, Evelyn. 1984. *Forbidden books in American public libraries, 1876–1939: A study in cultural change*. Westport, CT: Greenwood.

Hawks, Tod H. 1975. Every library needs tall windows. *Canadian Library Journal*, June: 187–189.

Hyde, W. Montgomery. 1966. *A history of pornography*. New York: Dell.

Kabbani, Rana. 1986. *Europe's myths of Orient*. Bloomington: Indiana University Press.

Katz, Bill. 1971. The pornography collection. *Library Journal*, December 5: 4060–4066.

Kendrick, Walter. 1987. *The secret museum: Pornography in modern culture.* New York: Viking.

Kingsley, Sidney. 1949. Detective story. In *Three plays about crime and criminals* (pp. 105–204), ed. by George Freedley. New York: Washington Square Press.

Lacy, Dan. 1965. Censorship and obscenity. *ALA Bulletin*, June: 471–476.

Legman, G. 1964. *The horn book.* New Hyde Park: University Books.

Linden, Robin Ruth, Darlene R. Pagano, Diane E.H. Russell, and Susan Leigh Star. 1982. *Against sadomasochism.* East Palo Alto, CA: Frog in the Well.

Lingle, Virginia A., and M. Sandra Wood. 1988. *How to find information about AIDS.* New York: Haworth.

Lister, Lisa F. 1989. The AIDS dilemma: An annotated bibliography of serial publications. *Serials Review*, Spring: 57–65.

Loth, David. 1962. *The erotic in literature.* New York: Macfadden.

McKenzie, Elizabeth M. 1986. Librarians and the new censorship. *Public Library Quarterly*, Spring/Summer: 23–34.

The Meese Commission exposed. 1987. New York: National Coalition Against Censorship.

Molz, Kathleen. 1966–1967. The public custody of the high pornography. *American Scholar*, Winter: 93–103.

Moon, Eric. 1962. "Problem" fiction. *Library Journal*, February 1: 484–496.

Perper, Timothy. 1985. *Sex signals: The biology of love.* Philadelphia: ISI Press.

Perper, Timothy. 1987. Brief reviews. *The Journal of Sex Research*, February: 133–139.

Photographer removes exhibit in dispute with library. 1990. *American Libraries*, February: 97–98.

Pope, Michael. 1974. *Sex and the undecided librarian.* Metuchen, NJ: Scarecrow.

Preston, John, and Glenn Swann. 1986. *Safe sex; The ultimate erotic guide.* New York: New American Library.

Robinson, Paul. 1977. *The modernization of sex.* New York: Harper & Row.

SAMOIS. 1982. *Coming to power.* Boston: Alyson Publications.

SantaVicca, Edmund F. 1987a. Acquired immune deficiency syndrome (AIDS): An annotated bibliography for librarians. *Reference Services Review*, Winter: 45–67.

SantaVicca, Edmund F. 1987b. AIDS information access: Reference, referral, and education in the library setting. *Reference Services Review*, Winter: 73–78.

SantaVicca, Edmund F. 1987c. AIDS in the minds of librarians: Opinion, perception, and misperception. *Library Journal*, February 15: 113–115.

SantaVicca, Edmund F. 1987d. Building an AIDS resource file: A rationale and a model. *Reference Services Review*, Winter: 69–72.

Shelton, Gilbert. 1971. The Fabulous Furry Freak Brothers go to college. In *The collected adventures of the Fabulous Furry Freak Brothers* (pp. 12–15). San Francisco: Rip Off Press.

Sneyd, Doug. 1982. [Cartoon]. *Playboy*, October: 105.

Steinfirst, Susan, 1989. *The young adult librarian's knowledge of and attitudes about sex.* Metuchen, NJ: Scarecrow.

Stone, Lee Alexander. 1922. *Sex searchlights and sane sex ethics.* Chicago: Science Publishing Co.

Walker, Pamela. 1979. Bibliographic control of sex research materials. In *The new special collection* (pp. 33–39). New York: Bowker. (LJ Special Report #11)

Walton, Alan Hull. 1964. Introduction. In *The perfumed garden of the Shaykh Nefzawi* (pp. 7–55), tr. by Richard Burton. New York: Putnam's Sons.

Wertheimer, Leonard. 1980. Pornography in the public library, are librarians ignoring its role? *Canadian Library Journal*, February: 21–26.

White, Howard D. 1981. Library censorship and the permissive minority. *Library Quarterly*, 51/2: 192–207.

White, Howard D. 1986. Majorities for censorship. *Library Journal*, July: 31–38.

Woods, L.B. 1978. "For SEX: See librarian." *Library Journal*, September 1: 1561–1566.

Woods, L.B., and Claudia Perry-Holmes. 1982. "The flak if we had *The Joy of Sex* here." *Library Journal*, September 15: 1711–1715.

CHAPTER 2
The Lure of the Forbidden

G. Legman

The Lure of the Forbidden is not only both natural and very strong, but also operates in a strangely paradoxical fashion. Only yesterday, I have seen men sitting on the Mediterranean beach at Cagnes-sur-Mer, surrounded by lovely bare-breasted women wearing nothing but a tightly-stretched triangle of cloth over their pubic hair and buttocks, and these men craning their necks trying to look up the flowing skirt of a girl bicycling past on the adjacent highway. How is that to be explained?

In the same way—and that is the subject here—on many a fine spring day for decades now in London, Paris, New York, and other great capitals, dogged searchers after the forbidden leave behind them all the vivid human availabilities and temptations of fashionable avenues, boulevards, and even the grubby little mean streets and corners where prostitutes (of both sexes) stand offering themselves to men for hire, and where graphic pictures of human bodies twined in sexual intercourse or anatomically displaying their genital organs are to be bought for a pittance in 'sex shops'. Instead, these men—seldom women—climb the steps of large, impressively quiet national and university libraries, where they fill out in careful penmanship bits of paper calling for rare and often unique books of bygone centuries and our own, describing in crabbed and often perverted prose and foreign tongues the very same human bodies, organs and acts that they have somehow preferred to encounter here on paper and not in the flesh outside. How is *this* to be explained? We have come a long way since Eve and the 'apple' of Paradise, which I believe the eccentric Dutch author and erotica collector in the early eighteenth century, Adriaan Beverland, was the first to identify openly with woman's genital or-

---

This article is based upon an Introduction prepared for *The Private Case* by P.J. Kearney (London, 1981). Copyright © 1991 by G. Legman.

gans; and likewise Original Sin as simply sexual intercourse, and the serpent of Eden as the penis.

CHRONICLERS OF EROTICA

The history, mystery and art of erotica, its creation and collection, even its conservation in great public libraries after the deaths of creators and collectors alike, is a subject on which whole books could easily be written, and must be written, owing to the secrecy which has always surrounded this subject after centuries of anti-sexual censorship and strict illegality. Several such books have in fact been attempted, of which perhaps the best and certainly the largest are two in German, by Dr. Paul Englisch, his *Geschichte der erotischen Literatur* (1927) and especially his supplementary work, *Irrgarten der Erotik* (The Maze of Erotica, 1931), both of which have been reprinted more recently and are well worth consulting. Mr. Steven Marcus's study of *The Other Victorians* (1966) is also very thoroughgoing for the several English erotic authors it discusses and whose works are described in some detail. The best work in English is Patrick J. Kearney's *A History of Erotic Literature* (London: Macmillan, 1982), with a wealth of documentary illustrations, some of them unexpectedly frank.

There are also, of course, all the main and extremely large published erotic bibliographies in various European languages, compiled over the last century, of which the highlights are: for French, the *Bibliographie des Ouvrages relatifs à l'Amour* by Jules & Jean Gay and others (final edition, 1894–1901) in four volumes; and Louis Perceau's *Bibliographie du roman érotique du 19e siècle* (Paris, 1930) in two volumes; and in particular the recent almost encyclopedic catalogue by Pascal Pia, *Les Livres de l'Enfer* (Paris: Coulet & Faure, 1978), also in two volumes, which offers far more than its delicately ambiguous title—'The Books of Hell!'—seems to promise, and is a complete roundup of French erotic literature during the entire 19th and 20th centuries, seen through its most outstanding works. For German there is the tremendous *opus* in eight volumes, *Bibliotheca Germanorum Erotica et Curiosa* by Hugo Hayn and Alfred N. Gotendorf (1911–1914), with an important supplementary volume by Dr. Paul Englisch (1929); plus the great *Bilder-Lexicon der Erotik* (Vienna: Institut für Kulturforschung, 1928–1931) edited by Leo Schidrowitz in four large and electrifying illustrated volumes, of which volumes II and IV (as well as the final supplementary volumes, not issued until several decades later, edited by Armand Mergen) are largely devoted to bibliographical notes on, and illustrations from the erotic art and literature of many countries.

In the strictly bibliographical line, as to books in English, yet in textual form, certainly the best work we have is Mr. David Foxon's *Libertine Literature in England: 1660–1745* (New York, 1965), a series of closely argued and superlatively documented essays reprinted from *The Book Collector* for 1964. I have also made a start on a similar study myself, but not restricted to England and on a more literary and less bibliographical framework, in my collection of essays, *The Horn Book* (New York, 1964), especially Part I, 'Studies in Erotic Bibliography,' none of which material will be reprinted here. The forthcoming in-depth study of English pornography, 1885–1920, by Mr. Peter Mendes will certainly fill in many missing details.

My own interest in these subjects, from a literary point of view, began at the somewhat late age of fourteen, since I was until then heavily involved in religious studies, and thought of sex more as a practical and poetic matter, as in that most ancient masterpiece of erotic literature, *The Song of Songs*, a typical Levantine epithalamium or marriage-song politely ascribed to King Solomon, though certainly several hundred years more recent than his reign. Until the 1st century A.D., among the Jews, no one under the age of thirty years was permitted to read *The Song of Songs*, as being too erotic for the youthful mind and not entirely respectable. It was given its present frankly erotic prominence in Judaism only by Rabbi Akiba about A.D. 100. The date is not certain for this liberalization, but, implicated in the revolt of the Jews under Bar-Cochba against the Emperor Hadrian, Rabbi Akiba was crucified by the Romans and flayed alive in A.D. 132. Since that time, Akiba's profound dying *pietà* has formed part of the solemn Jewish liturgy, and the complete *Song of Songs* is required to be read, or rather chanted aloud by all religious Jews over thirteen years of age on the afternoon of the Sabbath, as a sort of sex education manual or sacred erotica. Intercourse with one's spouse that afternoon (or on the Sabbath eve preceding) is considered a specially virtuous act, on the basis of *Genesis*, i. 28, *Be fruitful, and multiply*, which we are told were *God's first words to Adam & Eve*, long preceding the fateful prohibition of the 'tree of knowledge of good and evil' in chapter ii.

SEX AND CENSORSHIP

This is not the place to consider in full the very long history of sexual censorship at the speaking, writing and publishing end. It is a subject on which a great mass of printed material exists, both pro and con, usually in connection with religious, political and economic censorships as well, which are far more widespread though perhaps not of the same cruelly intense poignancy as the censorship of sex. Erected into a social and literary system in England in the early eighteenth century, beginning with Alexander Pope's expurgated edition of Shakespeare (1725), and proceeding in similar style in all other European countries since that date, the erotic censorship in England is best studied in two books by Alec Craig, *The Banned Books of England* (1937; and revised, 1962) and *Above All Liberties* (1942); and with full quotations from the incriminated books in Donald Thomas's illustrated *A Long Time Burning* (1969). Wayland Young's *Eros Denied: Sex in Western Society* (1964) also has a good deal to say, and has the courage to say it in plain Anglo-Saxon erotic monosyllables.

The first real cracks in the censorship structure of the West appeared only in the second half of the nineteenth century, especially in France, specifically in the non-political arena, with the avowed pæan to evil of Baudelaire's marvellously written but rigorously anti-moral *Les Fleurs du Mal* (1855-7), exactly echoed within a few years in Swinburne's *Poems and Ballads*; and the courageous naturalism of Victor Hugo in *Les Misérables* (1862) and that of his later greatest emulator, Émile Zola.

One can hardly imagine today the literary sensation created by the famous passage in which Hugo plainly recorded the brave reply, '*Merde!*' flung at the English demanding surrender at the Battle of Waterloo. (But *not* by General Cambronne, to whom this is errone-ously ascribed, as is discussed further in my *Rationale of the Dirty Joke: II. No Laughing Matter*, chap. 15, sect. 7, p. 922.) Hugo's readers were thunderstruck by the spectacle of the greatest literary figure of the nineteenth century not only saying '*Merde!*' spelled out in full, in *Les Misérables*, Vol. II, Bk, I, chaps. 14–15, as the opening gun of the New Freedom, which did not arrive in Britain and America with equal freedom until almost a century later; but also replying to all criticism with several further chapters in disquisition on the subject.

The revolt against the literary and artistic censorship spread seriously to England by the end of the nineteenth century, and to the rest of Europe and America since. Finally Scandinavia, which had never until then absorbed the implications of Henrik Ibsen's drama of revolt just a hundred years ago, now suddenly took the bit between its teeth in the 1950s and '60s, especially in Denmark, and repealed all the anti-sexual censorship laws, though wisely retaining similar prohibitions against the exploitation of sadism in books and mo-tion-pictures.

In Germany and the United States, which then also repealed or allowed to fall into desuetude the laws against *both* sex and sadism in literature and entertainment, the result has been profoundly disturb-ing to many, who seeing a quasi-total liberty for murder and horror, both in print and now in all the much broader electronic media, also see the New Freedom gone putrid. (I am one of these.)

The literature of sexual censorship and the question of the liberation of pornography have now culminated in the last two decades with an astonishing outpouring of second-rate mock-psychological drivel and almost meaningless gloats (various of these graphically illustrated with erotic photos of women spreading open their genitals in 'split beaver' poses, as examples of the New Freedom in action), and even a few laments over the recent end of the anti-sexual censorship in the West. The main problem remains the relative and diminishing liberty for sex in print, combined with the massively increasing liberty for sadism. However, as I have already spent a hundred-page monograph on this dangerous paradox, *Love and Death: A Study in Censorship* (1949 and reprints), it almost does not seem worth pursuing it any further here. I said 'almost' . . .

Our focus here is not on the authors' or purveyors' problems with the anti-sexual laws over the past centuries, but rather on the *other* end of the censorship: that operating on the person wishing to read or consult a forbidden book. This part of the censorship has generally been left to educators and libraries, once the lending-libraries and now the public libraries. The precedent here and format used have been those of the *Index Librorum Prohibitorum* instituted by the Roman Catholic Church in the mid-sixteenth century as part of the Counter Reformation, on the model of the Apostle Paul approving if not inciting the burning of their mystic books by the newly converted Ephesians, as reported in the *Acts of the Apostles*, xix. 19: 'And many that believed came, and confessed, and shewed their deeds. Many of them also which used curious arts brought their books together, and burned them before all men: and they counted the price of them, and found it fifty thousand pieces of silver.'

Now that the church no longer has the power over vast non-Catholic populations of the world to make the strictures of the *Index* stick, various governments—particularly in this present century—have undertaken their own literary police action, and have compiled and published similar expurgatory lists at regular intervals on the basis of governmental actions, prohibitions and seizures. The most extensive lists of this kind have been those issued by the Irish Free State (Eire), France, Germany, and until recently Rhodesia. These lists are, however, so large and heterodox—especially as to politically Marxist heterodoxy—that even the most ardent searcher after the sexually forbidden would seldom care to use them as collecting guides, though there is indeed much of interest to be gleaned from them. Customs seizure lists (which sometimes also gallantly include horror comic-books), such as that of Rhodesia, and the British government's 'Stop Lists,' tend to be much briefer.

In Germany, the censorship which began, as usual, as simply a liberal monarchic and later democratic attempt, recorded in the *Polunbi-Katalog* (1926), to control and prevent the circulation of printed '*Schund und Schmutz*' (trash and filth), intended to be restricted only to 'indecent Pictures, Writings and Advertisements,' ended up within a decade as a wholesale repression and physical destruction not just of books and pictures, but of entire undesired religious and political human minorities and all their works. These dangerous authoritarian levers can be pushed both ways. *Habent sua fata libelli*, they say. People too.

LIBRARIES AND EROTICA

The libraries' censorship, except at the provincial lending-library level, as recently as the 1950's in England, has paradoxically had the opposite effect: that of preserving, in many cases, the very books that would otherwise have been destroyed. That is to say, preserving one or two rare copies, though many—very many—disappear forever, most of their editions having either been enthusiastically read to death, or purposely destroyed by agencies entirely outside the libraries' sphere of influence. It is therefore idle to poke the usual good-natured fun at the odd titles bestowed in some of the older libraries on their special sections in which banned or bannable books, mostly about sex, are locked away. For essentially, the libraries' effort is to protect the books for, and sometimes *against* the readers, and not to protect the readers from the books. This is a point not to be overlooked.

The most famous such collections today are the *Enfer* or Hell of the Bibliothèque Nationale in Paris, of which the complete catalogue has been in print since 1913; also that of the *Private Case* of the British Museum Library in London, first published in very defective style in 1936, and now superseded by *The Private Case: An Annotated Bibliography*, painstakingly compiled by Patrick J. Kearney, with a long introduction by myself (London: Jay Landesman, 1981). The British Library's great collection is now smaller by almost half, it should be mentioned, than in the years before the New Freedom 'de-suppressed' many of the books. There is now also the very extensive library of sexual science of the Kinsey Institute for Sex Research at the University of Indiana, a collection of which I had the difficult honor of being the first bibliographer, and of which both the card-catalogue and books are usually totally available to accredited researchers. A large portion of this catalogue, but *not* including the erotica except as to studies, pp. 162–73, has now been published as *Sex Research: Bibliographies* (Phoenix, Arizona: Oryx Press, 1979), compiled by Joan Scherer Brewer & Rod W. Wright.

Similar but much smaller collections of sexual science and some few forbidden books are the New York Public Library's *** collection in the Reference Division; the cautionary and pleasantly symbolic

'Delta' callmark of the Library of Congress at Washington, of which not all the holdings are as yet catalogued; and the 'Cherry Case' (referring only to the wood it is made of) in another great American library. Such sections or cautionary marks naturally exist in all large public and university libraries, but are now usually more prosaically titled, perhaps with an eye to making them less obtrusive: for example, the New York Academy of Medicine's extensive 'S.102a' section of medical and scientific sexualia. Under the now-advancing reign of library computerization, we can no longer hope for these wayward and amusing appellations to continue—they slide rather poorly into the computers. (As do we!) And there is no hope at all for any such charming jests in the future as the calling of the small relevant collection at the Bodleian Library, Oxford, by the Greek letter ø, punning of course on '*Fie!*' Actually, bawdy books seem rather innocent compared to the current split-beaver magazines, audio-cassette 'sex tapes', and X-rated graphically photographed video-cartridge or cable television: Midnight Blue pornography.

One ghost that has been clanking about for centuries ought certainly to be laid here, as there are still very many people who foolishly believe in it. And that is the wholly erroneous notion that there exists in the Vatican Library at Rome a large—nay, even a 'complete'—collection of all the bawdy books ever published, sent in over the centuries from private seizures from the faithful by confessors and ordinaries all over the world. Alas, but it is not true! Would that it were.

One sees perfectly the mental process involved in the creation and continuation of this legend. The *qualificatores* and consultors of the Congregation of the Index have certainly been reading at least once the books they have for centuries now been banning. And therefore, so the folk-logic runs, they have doubtless been secretly keeping at least one copy of all the banned books (not to mention prints and now motion-pictures, as is made the key subject or punch-line of Terry Southern's black-humor novel, *Blue Movie*, 1970), for later private reading and delectation. The very same sweet, sinful delectation being forbidden to the faithful. In actual fact, such books are seldom kept and are not retained for reading purposes in the Vatican Library, though certain rare editions of older works (usually of the mildest nature) have been openly catalogued and preserved. As to erotic movies, the main real collection seems to be that of *Playboy*, in Chicago.

This legend of the Vatican's secret *Inferno* collection of books, &c. is very tenacious, and is often trotted out with a wealth of irresponsible detail, as when the bumptious and irrepressible Mr. Ralph Ginzburg announced in his massively unresearched *Unhurried* [?] *View of Erotica* (New York, 1958), p. 103, that the Vatican's fabled erotica include '25,000 volumes and some 100,000 prints,' which is exactitude indeed. (See further *The Horn Book*, pp. 94–8.) Mr. Ginzburg similarly reports, at pp. 107–8 of his *Unheard-of View*, that, at the Library of Congress in Washington, erotic works are issued 'to anyone over sixteen years of age, though an armed guard will be assigned to stand over the reader's shoulder, ready to shoot if the book is mutilated.' This is a damned good idea, but is also, unfortunately, untrue.

Despite Mr. Ginzburg's shall-we-say overstatements, he has at least not lost sight of the fact that the librarian's first duty is to protect the books entrusted to the library, from—among other dangers—mutilation or theft by the readers (or staff), both of which are much more common than is generally realized. Responsible librarians also wish to protect their libraries from harmful and usually overcolorful folklore or publicity, as that concerning the Vatican. The librarian is not basically involved in protecting the readers from the books. The books are there to be used, by future researchers, and not to be ripped-off by the current and increasing crop of present-day crooks, cranks, mockers and mutilators.

At its noblest, the librarian's effort is to ensure, as Milton has put it immortally in his *Areopagitica* in 1644—the very same year that the Puritan iconoclasts were pulling down church art in England with ropes and hammers—that the books shall be 'imbalm'd and treasur'd up on purpose to a Life beyond Life.' Of course, 'imbalming' is not always the best fate for books, and surely not all of them are worth it, nor will they have it; but at least it does preserve the books for a few hopeful decades, perhaps even a century or two if the paper they are printed on allows this. And after that, a delusory electronic 'software' immortality?

It is very uncommon today to see, as I have recently been privileged to see, a formal letter from the librarian of a prestigious British university, dated September 1980, and replying to a request from a foreign researcher at the end of five weeks of work at that library, for a microfilm of a rather unsavoury work somewhat on the style of the Marquis de Sade's and his pipsqueak imitator Aleister Crowley's purposely awful outpourings, with angry temporizing and evident obstruction phrased as follows:

'Mr. C. mentioned to me your request for a microfilm of _____
_____. It seems to me to be one of the most obscene (and blasphemous) books I have ever seen, and my experience in this field, after working at the _____ is not small. I feel I ought to protect the Library by asking you for an assurance that the microfilm is for your private study only. This is not a condition of fulfilling the order; I should nevertheless prefer to have it.'

As it happens, I agree completely with this librarian in his hesitation about helping, perhaps, to spread a particularly ugly virus. We have been surrounded for over a century now, since the time of

Baudelaire and Swinburne, with presumably sane and rational persons who nevertheless are urgently searching for evil, and delight in expressions of it. The book in question is one of them. Of course, it is not in books that the ever-present *daimonists* of our time, the publicists, the schlockmeisters, the fake artists, the sociopaths and string-pullers higher up, and the mass-murderers in war & peace, are searching for either inspiration or methods for their evil. Many or most of them never read anything at all, and their anti-human needs are serviced strictly by comic-books, and later television and electronic media industry. Perhaps it is from these they learn their cruelties and crimes. They are not learning them from books.

Beautiful or repellent, normal or perverse, erotic books are not and have never been the school of crime. The customers come readymade, and they know—especially the sadists and other perverts—exactly what they are looking for. As a Soho bookseller once said to me in a moment of candor, when I asked him whether he had any other kind of books and pictures than flagellation: 'You can't sell these rotten buggers any of that *normal perv!*'

This de-fuses, really, the merely literary output of such would-be Devil's Advocates as Sade and Crowley, and their host of imitators and disciples, now pullulating in profitable display of their built-in vices and insanities, in violence motion-pictures, rock & roll electronic disco music, daily crime-&-horror TV, the 'theatre of cruelty,' and all the rest of the Augean stable or madhouse of proudly 'put-on' modern arts. Yet it is unusual today to hear any librarian open his or her heart so unguardedly, and cry out in disgust against what is felt or *known* to be an evil book, which one is nevertheless obliged to protect and preserve, but does not want to see published any further. Of such stuff are heroes made.

CENSORSHIP AND NONSENSORSHIP

When it is a question of the erotica collection, if any, all the logical purposes and operations of sensible library use are generally turned upside down by the library authorities, or have been so in the past. The British Museum Library is not by any means the worst sinner here. At least they have always calmly accepted and preserved the books offered, segregating them as they might in a 'Private Case' (and more recently also in locked 'Cupboards') to protect both the books and library amenities.

The creation of the Private Case probably dates from the receipt in 1866 of the 'phallicism' collection of the antiquarian George Witt. Thereafter, with the Ashbee Bequest in 1900 and many lesser gifts since, ending basically with the main part of the C.R. Dawes library of erotica accessioned in 1964, the Private Case has become not only one of the best but also one of the largest such public collections in the world, along with the *Enfer* of the Bibliothèque Nationale and the Kinsey Institute of Sex Research Library at Indiana. Unfortunately, when anyone has wanted to consult a book in the Private Case—when I came there first in the early 1950s, eager to continue the researches I had already carried on for seventeen years in New York, this was the system and presumably always had been—one was faced theoretically with a blank wall.

The books kept in the Private Case were not then listed alphabetically in the large, old-fashioned pasted-up volumes of the public catalogue at the British Museum Library; and no one was allowed to examine the manuscript 'P.C.' catalogue that did exist, shelved in the office of the Principal Keeper of Printed Books. An even more secret catalogue also existed of books, shelved no one knew where, called the 'S.S.' catalogue, of books that had been banned by court order and supposedly destroyed. As an exceptional kindness to me by the then Keeper, I was allowed to make complete copies of both the 'P.C.' and 'S.S.' catalogues as they then stood, which were much larger than they are today. The same privilege had been offered to Mr. Alfred Rose earlier.

This blank-wall system was not unique to England. It was the same, but much more rigidly enforced, at the Reference Division of the great New York Public Library—and may it flourish forever!—a haven of incredible quiet, and devotion to voluntary private scholarship, set down incongruously, or rather left behind by urban progress and degeneration, at the very busiest and noisiest street intersection of one of the world's largest cities. Here the uncatalogued material included not only the *** collection of about fifteen hundred volumes of sexual science and some few erotica, but also *over thirty thousand further 'reserved' volumes* of milder nature, which had been either the subject of public prosecution or the object of private mutilation in the Library, or were otherwise suspect.

The index-cards for all these books were therefore withdrawn from the public catalogue, their callmarks prefixed with the cautionary number '8-', and they were kept from public access in a special bank of wooden index-card drawers at the librarian's desk in the main Reading Room inside the book-delivery enclosure, and for all I know may still be there. As to the index-cards for the *** collection, these were kept in a drawer in the same locked press as the books themselves! However, a single card for each such book was also filed in the master-catalogue by authors or anonymous titles, on another floor not accessible to the public. The librarians could therefore, on urgent demand and dispensation, determine whether the New York Public Library did possess a desired book. Like the patriarch Jacob blindly courting the wily Laban's daughters, I was required to fight that system almost daily for seventeen years.

At the time of the Ashbee Bequest in 1900, the so-called 'placers' at the British Museum Library did their work with a slapdash insouciance that leaves any booklover reeling. Perhaps they still do. The honorary curator of the Private Case, Dr. Eric Dingwall, once escorted me up through the winding bowels of the stacks of the British Museum to examine Presses 1080–81, 1093–94, and 1102, containing the merely *galante* and not highly erotic books which had come with the Ashbee Bequest, other than his famous collection of editions of *Don Quixote*, and other materials separately shelved in Tables 603–05. Ashbee's semi-erotica—and he had everything, mostly rare eighteenth-century materials—had simply been slung onto the dust-covered shelves of the above-mentioned presses in no order whatsoever, and with no concern as to the books' *sizes*, and therefore their protection from each other especially when unbound, floppy and dust-filled.

It was a disgraceful sight, and not one calculated to inspire any collector to leave the books he has collected lovingly and often at no small expense to the tender mercies of a public library. For all the horror of the usual auction sale after a collector's death, for the benefit usually of the greedy and not needy family, with the collections of a lifetime broken up forever in an hour under the auctioneer's hammer, at least one may hope that the later collectors into whose hands the auctioned-off books may eventually come will treat them a bit better than did the library 'placers' of 1900 with Ashbee's insufficiently erotic books. And today? . . .

Worse also exists, and in a way quite relevant to the original handling of the books in this *Enfer*. This striking testimony, occurring in a great modern country, is completely authentic though it is necessary still to describe it with circumspection. A foreign visitor in a recent year, having shown interest in the 'reserved' books of one of the largest national libraries in the world, the head librarian accompanied him to a small locked room, to which only he had the key, and there showed the visitor, piled high, stacks of fine erotic books and cheap pornography stemming from government seizures. None of these, the librarian stated, had ever been catalogued in all the years the small room was being filled, nor were they likely to be catalogued soon, owing to heavy political pressures acting on the library, a point never to be underestimated.

'What do you think we should do with all these?' the librarian ended frankly. The foreign visitor picked up one book at random. It was a translation of the *Histoire de Dom Bougre, Portier des Chartreux*, by Gervaise de Latouche, an eighteenth-century 'pornographic' classic (recently made into an X-rated motion picture), in a little pocket reprint of the kind tourists have long been buying abroad and bringing home hidden in their luggage. 'I don't want to see any more,' the foreign visitor told the librarian. 'You are doing the right thing.

Keep these books carefully locked up until the day comes when it's safe to catalogue them. *The future will have a lot to learn from them—about us.*'

In France, just a century had passed since Napoleon put away the Marquis de Sade in the madhouse, like Ezra Pound in our time; and the holdings of the *Enfer* of the Bibliothèque Nationale in Paris (which in 1877 had numbered 340 titles, comprising 730 volumes, according to the supplement that year to the *Grand Dictionaire Universel* of Larousse), now came to about 1350 titles, many quite early and rare, and all of them of obvious culture-historical interest. How many came from seizures and how many from gifts is unknown. (See my *The Horn Book*, 1964, pp. 57–60.)

The complete catalogue of the '*Enfer*' or Hell-books collection to about date 1910 was eventually prepared by the erotica specialist Louis Perceau (who also did a typewritten supplement to this later, up to 1935, at the private expense of Mr. Alfred Rose), and was issued openly by the Mercure de France in 1913, crediting the assistance of M. Yves-Plessis, the erudite bibliographer of French *argot* and slang over the centuries since the gallows-poet Villon. The notes on certain of the *Enfer* entries were also collaborated on by two other littérateurs: Fernand Fleuret, who became Perceau's lifelong friend; and Guillaume Apollinaire, an Italian intellectual freebooter and adventurer, of the real name of Dulcigni but privately assuming the surname of his Polish natural father along with an honorary 'particle' of mock nobility, as 'Wilhelm Apollinaire de Kostrowitski,' the Apollinaire being taken from the name of a then-popular carbonated beverage.

A nice example of the scissors-&-paste method whereby this typical *faux-esprit* hacked or whacked together his introductions to the milder erotica being openly published by the brothers Briffaut in Paris all through the 1910s, as advertisement for their real but secret pornographic publications, will be found translated in full in the *Private Case* catalogue by Kearney, at No. 506, in the article on Crébillon's *Tableaux des mœurs du temps*, ghost-written for the millionaire Farmer-General La Popelinière. It will be observed that the entire notice signed by 'Apollinaire,' several pages long, is composed of lengthy extracts from earlier collection-catalogues by other writers, only about twenty lines actually emanating from Apollinaire's own feather-light pen.

According to Jean Texcier, the friend and disciple of Louis Perceau in later years, Apollinaire's introductions were often shamelessly sent to the printer in the form of brown-print rotographs (early photocopies) of the catalogues and other writings he plagiarized, with his brief comments and canny paraphrases sometimes added marginally. Apollinaire particularly cannibalized in this way the painstaking prefaces prepared by the real scholar and defrocked priest, Alcide

Bonneau, for the publisher and bibliophile Isidore Liseux's editions of the same erotic texts, twenty and thirty years before. It is this smooth intellectual fake and *rastaquouère*, Apollinaire, who is now invariably credited with the authorship of Perceau's bibliography of the *Enfer*, owing to the accident of his pseudonym's preceding both of the other collaborators' real names, in the alphabetical order they agreed to use on the titlepage of the published book. That is how literary reputations are created—and not only in France. The *Enfer* catalogue has now finally been brought fully up-to-date and much enlarged in Pascal Pia's *Les Livres de l'Enfer* (Paris: Coulet & Faure, 1978) in two volumes, a remarkably complete and more-than-complete work, filled to the gunwales with divulgations and identifications as to the anonymous and pseudonymous authors of modern French erotica, and their equally secret publishers.

AMERICAN AND BRITISH COLLECTIONS

America remained for a long time *terra incognita* as to erotica, though there were active publishers there throughout the nineteenth century (and even earlier), some publishing quite openly in New Orleans until Anthony Comstock succeeded in having laws passed in the 1870s that drove such publication under cover for almost exactly a century. The Anglo-German scholar Dr. Peter Wagner, under a grant from the Deutsche Forschungs-Gemeinschaft, has now published a study of eighteenth-century erotica in England and America, and one trusts this will later be continued for the nineteenth century as well.

There were notable American collections of erotica from the 1880s on, such as that of the elder J. Pierpont Morgan, whose luxurious erotica were, however, all eventually sent back to France, there to enter among others the Charles Cousin '*Enfer du Grenier*' collection (partial catalogue published in 1890); thus entirely purifying the shelves of the Morgan Library now open to researchers in New York. Even so, erotic poetry and humorous erotic monologues were and remained a tradition in American upper-level clubs until well into the twentieth-century, though currently most bawdy limericks are recited. For example, the Papyrus Club of Boston, before whom Eugene Field delivered some of his most unregenerately bawdy narrative poems; while Mark Twain is himself the authority for the statement that the luxurious secret edition of his erotic burlesque: '*1601*', done at the U.S. Army's Academy Press at West Point by Twain's friend, Charles E.S. Wood, circulated only among kings, millionaires, and on up. (See further my introduction to Twain's *The Mammoth Cod*, first edition, Milwaukee: Maledicta Press, 1976.)

It is quite a puzzle, in fact, to determine where and from whom certain very rare and elegant American erotic publications of the turn of the century stemmed, such as *The Stag Party* (Boston or Chicago? 1888?) containing almost all Eugene Field's erotic compositions; *The Lady and the Flea* (1910?) a very handsomely printed extravaganza on erotic tales; and *The Point of View* (by James C. Harvey, 'International Press,' 1905; my own copy, now in the British Library, not in the Private Case), an elegant collection indeed of private erotic poetry, with overdone *art nouveau* frontispiece and illustrations by Alfons Mucha and others. These problems may wait a long time for solution.

So far as I know, no erotic bibliographies except of homosexual fiction have been published in America, though the private erotic researcher Raymond Thompson prepared material for this purpose during the 1930s, and I believe some preliminary sheets were struck off. The best materials available are the specialist booksellers' catalogues, particularly those recently of Dr. C.J. Scheiner of Brooklyn, New York. I am myself searching desperately for one such tiny volume of erotic poetry and humor, entitled *Select Reading (Profusely Illustrated) for Gay Boys and Naughty Girls* (U.S., ca. 1915? in which 'Gay' does *not* mean homosexual), in any public or private library in the world, as without this anonymous little work I cannot finish or publish my next and final volume on erotic folklore.

With the enormous publicity given to the Kinsey Report on the sexual activities of the 'Human' (American) male in the late 1940s, quite a number of fine existing erotica collections were presented as gifts or eventually sold to Kinsey's Institute for Sex Research at Indiana University; for example, the Havelock Ellis masochism collection, which I catalogued when it was sent *en bloc* to America, and that of film director Josef von Sternberg. (See further *The Horn Book*, pp. 124–8.) During the 1940s, I burned with the ambition to produce a large-scale bibliography of at least the highlights of the world's erotic literature. But having published a 'Minority Report on Kinsey' in my book *The Sexual Conduct of Men & Women* 'by Norman Lockridge' (New York, 1948, pp. 13–32), on what I considered to be Kinsey's substitution of admittedly useful propaganda for honest statistics, and his unavowed purposes, I found the best collection in America closed to me after having had a fair hand in creating it. Coming then to Europe, I suddenly found so much material available both in libraries and for sale—if one had the money—that I realized no single bibliographical world-survey of erotica was any longer feasible, unless it were restricted mainly to a single language (as Hayn/Gotendorf for German, and Gay and later Perceau and Pia for French), or to a single library's holdings, such as the *Enfer* or the Private Case.

European scholars and enthusiasts were still trying for that 'world-survey' until the very eve of World War II. And with the *Erzgründlichkeit* typical of, and often damning Germanic scholarship, something very close to success was achieved by Dr. Paul Englisch, in text form, and even more so in the heavily illustrated *Bilder-Lexikon der Erotik*, a group undertaking. My own small efforts, which were planned to proceed by subject segments, never went further than a hundred-page manuscript introduction, 'Toward an Historical Bibliography of Sex Technique' (New York, 1942), and at the same period a much larger world-bibliography of the scientific and popular literature of homosexuality, kept on index-cards then deposited in the New York Academy of Medicine Library. I believe this was later transferred to the Kinsey Institute Library, and now has been published and edited in part by Professor Vern Bullough of Buffalo. I have never seen the printed copy, as I am too proud to pay cash for my own work, and the more fool I.

In England, at least four researchers have attempted to continue the broad polylingual erotic bibliography approach of H. Spencer Ashbee's three famous volumes published between 1877 and 1885 under the pseudonym of 'Pisanus Fraxi,' and three times reprinted in recent years, one of these reprints with an introduction by myself. (Enlarged in *The Horn Book*, pp. 9–45.) There are also two abridgments of Ashbee, in the alphabetical order of his entries: *A Complete Guide to Forbidden Books*, edited by E.S. Sullivan (North Hollywood, Calif.: Brandon House, 1966), and *Forbidden Books of the Victorians*, edited by Peter Fryer, with excellent biographical materials on Ashbee (London: Odyssey Press, 1970). Aside from an early and disorderly imitation, *Bibliotheca Arcana* by William Laird Clowes (1885, and recently reprinted), none of the later erotico-bibliographical attempts made in England successfully arrived at publication, though one of the last, by Alfred Rose, was published in very defective form after his death, as *Registrum Librorum Eroticorum* under the pseudonym 'Rolf S. Reade,' in 1935, and pirated later by J.R. Brussel in New York. As to the lack of bibliographies, one main reason for this has been the over-ambitious attempt by these compilers to cover 'all' Western languages and literatures, as did Ashbee.

In the end, the unique value of the Rose/Reade *Registrum* has long been as a handlist, otherwise unavailable, of the Private Case and the *Phi* collections as they stood in 1934. Even so, it must be used with caution, owing to the large number of typographical errors. The Private Case's own copy of this work, annotated and corrected in the hand of Dr. Eric Dingwall, honorary curator of the collection, was used by him for years as a handy guide to the Private Case. The piratical offset reprint was issued in New York in 1965 by Jacob R. Brussel, one of the two main American sex-book publishers (the other being Samuel Roth) operating since the 1920s just inside the law, and on occasion outside.

SEX VERSUS VIOLENCE

The prominence, not to say preponderance of sadistic and flagellational books among the holdings of the Private Case of the British Museum Library makes necessary a few remarks about the authors and publishers of erotica in general. Sexual perversion is not funny, not rare, and not to be taken lightly, as anyone who has ever been married to a homosexual or sadist or pervert knows. It is hard for normals even to bear to look at the pitiful lineaments of sexual perversion. Most normal persons who might read an erotic book or watch an erotic motion-picture are in particular disgusted and turned-off by erotic cruelty, whipping, torture, humiliation, bloodshed, and sex-linked murder. They do not find it exciting, but wholly *anti-aphrodisiac.*

In the same way, as is not too well known, many perverts cannot bear the erotic parts of books or motion-pictures, or even the sight of the genital organs, which *they* find anti-aphrodisiac; and publishers and producers serving them are therefore often careful to omit any *'normal perv.'* Homosexual sadism is by far the most viciously cruel, as the whole 'S. & M.' (sado-masochist) propaganda today openly displays, also now among Lesbians! Hardly the 'love of David for Jonathan,' or Ruth and Naomi, that we've been hearing about for centuries, since the Bible. This has long been so, as in duels, initiations, war, etc. See further the repellent *The Undergrowth of Literature* by Gillian Freeman (1968).

Propagandists for wildcat sexual 'liberty' generally always mean liberty for perversion, not normality, and it is by their real and now not-even hidden intentions that they must be judged. There are perhaps millions of *preverts*—as Terry Southern's now-immortal joke in the motion picture *Dr. Strangelove* would have it—and every single one of them is potentially dangerous to himself (or herself, just as often), to sexual partners, and often to society at large. Who will deny that? Those are not the politely so-called odd 'sexual preferences,' or 'alternate life-styles,' of which we are all asked now to be so tolerant.

The Marquis de Sade is the classic case, and his worshipping imitators are seldom far behind. For example, Baudelaire and Swinburne and the other 'poets of evil,' also the entire Futurist-Dadaist-Surréalist movement promulgating anti-human literature, 'music' and art in all countries since the early years of this century. And, as the clown or funny fatboy of the sickie movement, Edward Alexander called Aleister Crowley, also known lovingly to himself as 'the Worst Man in the World', 'The Beast 666,' and other pertinent appellations, of whose four or five openly erotic books the Private Case holds only two (there is another in the *Enfer*), but whose purposeful search for evil, under a particularly cheap & nasty occult screen or soundtrack, is perhaps better seen in his *Diaries*. There have been many other such self-advertising sickies since, in both Europe and America, not just in art & literature but in life. Consider the late Theodore Bundy . . . After all, discounting the cheap Art-for-Art's-Sake twaddle about their poetic art, while carefully overlooking their mentally-diseased message, what else are Baudelaire and Swinburne but De Sade in alliterative rhyme? As, in the same sense, what else is the Atom Bomb but the Marquis de Sade on a government grant? The time for truth has come.

It may be true—it was certainly *not* true of Sade and Crowley—that certain literary perverts can hold their perversion to a paper existence, and are merely letting off aggressive steam. Yet this same blood-tinted steam is being searched for very intensely, and is being read and watched (in motion-pictures and especially on the television screen) by many thousands or perhaps millions of persons who do not even pretend to wish to keep their perversion solely on paper or on the electronic screens. They whip and torture when they can, or they demand others to whip and torture *them*. Some also kill. See your daily newspapers or the six o'clock evening TV news, as to the 'Mr. Goodbars' no sane woman searching even for a *zipless fuck* is waiting for.

When all the normal rules of human deportment are off, and violence and bloodlust are given the go-ahead light, as in jails and during wars and revolution, the perverts who have had to satisfy themselves elsewhere and until then (as on the ever-present blood and horror-laden television screen) with only the paper-thin simulacrum of the horrors that they love, these are now the people who surge forward—who else?—to take the bloody job of torture, mass-murder and human butchery, and never recoil. This is the secret political history of our time.

Under the circumstances, what is the reason then for retaining and allowing sadistic and flagellational literature, and why is it not simply destroyed as evidently undesirable and inimical to the human race, preferably along with the sadists and torturers? The main reason seems to be that *it is really the sadists who are running the show*, owing to the tremendous monetary and power advantage their cold immorality gives them over the majority of normal people who are troubled by a conscience.

Also, the small literary and intellectual fringe or minority, who care about free speech and such social luxuries, is generally composed of normals who are afraid of creating such a precedent of literary *auto-da-fés*, which they understand perfectly well would soon enough be used against themselves and against normally erotic art and literature, as it has been for the past five hundred years at least, and even against literature and drama that are not erotic at all in any conscious way. Otherwise, all sadistic books and films would long since simply have been burned, and of course *should* be burned, as undesirable and inimical to humanity, except that for the above-mentioned reasons it seems impolitic to do so. No one on 'our' side wants to be the first fanatic to light the fires in the style of Savonarola.

Instead, the rare copies of such works that have not been read to bits by their perverted enthusiasts, occasionally are preserved by compulsive (or perverted) book-collectors, and eventually find themselves bequeathed to, and segregated in the various levels of Hells and Infernos in public and university libraries: the Private Cases, Locked Cupboards, and Cherry Cases, the Restricted Collections, Librarian's Desks, and just plain padlocked rooms in the basement as above described. Placed there too are the erotic books that are, by comparison, merely the literary statement of the normal and banal human sexual activities which, being biologically determined, over nine-tenths of all the people in the world continuously engage in and must engage in, and which almost all of them consider to be their dearest pleasure. And to the rest, their worst torment.

Why, over many centuries, sex has been considered a crime on paper, though legal and permissible in fact; and why, *per contra*, sadism and murder which are illegal in fact have always been legal on paper, and are in fact our 'best-sellers,' is not a question that need be considered here. I have noted my hundred-page monograph on this contradiction, *Love & Death* (1949), and I am proud that my question has been heard around the world, and that many or most Western governments, beginning in Scandinavia, are now trying to deal with this question that I was once often told I was an 'unpublishable idiot' for asking.

Yet I was far from the first to ask it. Montaigne makes the same point with great clarity in his essay 'On Some Verses of Virgil' (1588) Bk. 3, chapter 5: '*We bravely say* kill, rob, betray; *but that other we dare pronounce only between clenched teeth?*' More recently, and before I was born, Maurice LeBlond, the son-in-law of Zola, published a truly powerful article in the 1890s, on exactly the same contradiction, under the title *The Pornography of Murder*. To which we must add today our own best-seller and suicidal delight, *The Pornography of Violence*, now ending (one hopes) with horror-TV as prime-time 'entertainment.'

In the face of this almost-total current public acceptance of literary and pictorial murder and torture, in all the media, it seems idle to discuss pontifically the relatively few books on the subject which find themselves locked away because they have offended the reading perverts *by mixing sexuality in with the torture and whipping,* and especially by showing the genital parts. To each his aphrodisiac, and *normal perv.* gets short shrift with your average pervert. The banned books and new midnight television and home-movie *Chain-Saw Massacres* and *Lovers' Lane Mutilations* of this kind are unusual and extreme in their nature, and are therefore perhaps worthy of study by pathologists—but not by me! And, I trust, not for you, either.

Although almost everyone would agree, on reflection, that the authors and certainly the illustrators of sadistic books are evidently perverts, and probably practice their perversions on human flesh and not on paper when they can, it is usual to assume that the publishers of this literature are 'merely' businessmen, and are 'giving the (perverted) customers what they want.' This of course begs the essential question of who made the readers into perverts? I have no way of knowing about publishers in the past, the British, German, and French erotica producers since the 1870s, when this stuff became a visible current in underground publication. Nor do I know anything very private about most of the erotica authors of the past, and have often been puzzled by the mere *volume* of their individual output. For example, the independently wealthy American poet and littérateur, Clement Wood, who wrote scores of volumes of erotica during the 1930s—and obviously not for the money—to supply to a private collector who would accept these in manuscript. Or Alphonse Momas, the *pisse-copie* of French turn-of-the-century erotica and flagellantiana, whose incredible output made necessary the use of nearly a dozen different pseudonyms. However, I have met many recent authors of erotica (including Wood), and I believe almost all the erotica publishers in America during the 1930s and '40s, and of the 1950s to the '80s in France. And I can testify that every single one of them who also or mainly wrote or published sado-masochistic literature was an open, and usually an admitted freak on the subject. And the 'specialty' booksellers too.

This is not something I imagined: it is something they often bragged about and explained in detail to artists and writers they thought might ghost-write for them. As when one undersized Canadian shrimp, who ran a mail-order 'Society of Pain and Pleasure,' told me pathetically, 'I've *got* to have my bondage!' For the real perversion does not lie so much in the action as in the morbid delectation over it. This was made clear to me by another 'Pain and Pleasure' specialist, a woman this time, who pointed out that any man might be moved to strike a woman in anger or passion, or even to beat her severely, but that 'it takes a *real* pervert to want to study the welts!' The literature of sadism and flagellation is the studying of the welts—next morning, ice-cold. Fun for the next Theodore Bundy, who is perhaps not dead, 'but sleepeth . . .'

For further details I can recommend *The Memoirs of an Erotic Bookseller* (London: Luxor Press, Charles Skilton, 1969) by the Dutch bookseller Nicholas Schors under the pseudonym of 'Armand Coppens,' concerning the no-doubt mythical adventures of a bookseller specializing in cheating and on occasion whipping his sado-masochistic clients, by way of pandering honestly to their various needs. At a higher level, but more excruciating because infinitely better written and more sincere, there is the heavily sado-masochistic *Gynecocracy* (1893) by 'Julian Robinson,' which is attributed to a London lawyer, Stanislas de Rhodes, on the authority of the *Enfer* No. 819, but which has been more reliably attributed to the sexologist Havelock Ellis, who also publicly admitted in his memoirs to lifelong undinism, which is almost always a masochistic fetish. I might also add that in cataloguing the Ellis erotic library I was astonished to find it heavily supplied with cheap sado-masochistic semi-pornography of the kind published in Paris in the 'Select Bibliothèque' etc., by such low hacks as Roland Brévannes ('Dr. Brennus') and similar. These items are now mostly in the Kinsey Library, Institute of Sex Research, as is much of the Ellis erotic material, though its provenance is not marked.

'PORNOGRAPHICA NORMALIA'

The authors of the relatively normal erotica are admittedly a less colorful crew. Some of them have even been bibliographers in their spare time (or the reverse?) and I think we must all admit that bibliography is not really a perversion, or perhaps only a larval one when concerned specifically with erotica. Among the bibliographer-pornographers have been James Campbell Reddie, John S. Farmer, more famous as the lexicographer of erotic *slang*, Guillaume Apollinaire, Raymond Thompson, G. Legman; and most remarkable of the lot in every way, Pierre Louÿs. Much of Louÿs' pornographic fiction and poetry has a fantastic and extreme quality about it, and often a purposeful humor that is quite rare in erotica, as in his *Precepts for a Young Lady*, as befits the very sensitive poet he was. His remarkably full and detailed bibliographical and lexicographical index-cards have not, however, been preserved together nor accorded publication, as has almost every other available scrap of his erotica since his death in 1925. (See Pascal Pia, *Les Livres de l'Enfer*, p. 820.)

After about 1900 and until World War I, the field of 'normal erotica' mostly, was dominated for both French and English works by two publishing firms in Paris: Charles Carrington, and the brothers Briffaut, both of whom used on occasion the same imprint of the 'Erotica Biblion Society' to taunt both each other and H.S. Nichols of London, who had by then moved to Paris too. A further publisher, both in English and French, Charles Hirsch, issued only luxurious erotic volumes; and there were also many marginal erotica publishers, then and after World War I, such as Elias Gaucher and Jean Fort. For publishers since that period, see the profuse and very valuable notes and divulgations of Peter Mendes' forthcoming study of turn-of-the-century erotica in England; and *Les Livres de l'Enfer* (1978) by Pascal Pia, who nevertheless, as he warned me, 'could not tell everything he knew,' even though he wrote much of this book on his deathbed. Some people do not care to understand that 'There is a time to be silent, and a time to speak.' That is why there are so few autobiographies that are candid about sex, or about anything else.

All the erotica publishers of course, beginning in the mid-19th century with Dugdale and Hotten in England, and probably before—surely back to Edmund Curll, and Ralph Griffiths, the original publisher of *Fanny Hill* in the early eighteenth century—also issued polite or mildly *galante* works, both to justify and explain their activity to the often curious police (who sometimes black-mailed them), and also to attract customers, who would surely be interested in something a bit stronger too, kept in the back room. One such joyous publishing team, in the early 1950s in Paris, even had *two* secret levels in their bookshop behind the St. Germain church: first the top or open street-level for their surréalist and other mock-revolutionary literary drivel, then the first cellar down for the *galantiana*, and the second cellar or *sous-sol* just for the pure pornography. Two similarly goodhumored erotica dealers in North London about the same period kept their *galantiana* in a 'White Cupboard', and the *stronger stuff*, as one of them phrased it to me, in a 'Black Cupboard' facing. Almost everywhere the official or front-store display was of limited editions, nudism, sporting books, and the like. The modern 'sex shops' (anciently in Japan) have brought it all out into the open.

After Carrington's death in Paris about 1920, two of his clerks, Groves and Michaux, carried on the business till about 1930; one of them later transferring to Tijuana, Mexico, and the other disposing of his stock in Sweden and Portugal for smuggling into the United States. In the 1920s and '30s, erotica publishing in English and French became inextricably combined with a 'front' or cover of avant-garde literature. James Joyce and D.H. Lawrence were published in that way in Paris, and in Florence, Italy. A British subject, Jack Kahane, believed by many to have been a Foreign Office spy in Paris and to have died under peculiar circumstances (having been mysteriously shot dead just on the eve of World War II, as he sat sipping his tea on the terrace of an outdoor café on the Champs-Elysées in Paris) set up an imitation avant-garde firm, the Obelisk Press, about 1930, which published mostly semi-erotic trash—some of it by the publisher himself—and the early great *Tropics* of Henry Miller, in imitation of Céline's powerful *Journey to the End of the Night*. After World War II, Kahane's son carried on the business, under the name of Maurice Girodias, but he never had the luck to find another Henry Miller, and instead published almost entirely pornography, both in Paris throughout the 1950s and later in New York, where he attempted to ally himself with the similar publisher Grove Press.

When the New Freedom came in America in the 1960s, many people were surprised to learn that France under De Gaulle was less liberal now about erotic books, and even about the erotic element in art-novels and motion-pictures, than America and Scandinavia had become. In an article of capital importance, '*Les Livres contraires aux bonnes mœurs*,' by Maître Maurice Garçon, a leading member of the French bar, appearing in the *Mercure de France* for 15 August 1931, a long and invaluable government list was published, principally of erotic works in French and English seized and banned on 11 October 1913, and 21-23 December 1914—the last apparently as a Christmas present for the troops, who were also pretty hard-up for live women. By 1961 the similar bannings, published periodically since 1920 in the *Journal Officiel* and then reprinted in the main French booksellers' publication, were gathered by Daniel Bécourt as *Livres condamnés* (Paris: enlarged 1972). These condemnations continued for another decade at least: my own manual of orasexual technique, *Oragenitalism* (New York: Julian Press, 1969), was prohibited in French translation immediately on publication in 1971.

Meanwhile, in America, the lid blew off with the Supreme Court decisions in the 1960s, permitting reprints of Henry Miller and D.H. Lawrence, and books like *Fanny Hill* to be openly published after two centuries of repression. Small publishers in Los Angeles and San Diego, California, and at least one other in Atlanta, Georgia, suddenly became large and rich, first by publishing piracies of Girodias' uncopyrighted pornography originally issued in Paris, and then branching out to crash-program series of novels of their own by young and usually needy writers, in which incest was a particularly frequent theme, doubtless as the last taboo left to break. There are also numerous homosexual series, and many publicly shown 'blue films' now, on this and other normal and abnormal sexual themes.

This vein had long since been tapped in Restif's *Anti-Justine* in 1800, where the presumed delights of incest are offered to the reader as a sort of cure if not counter-poison for the sadistic delectations of the Marquis de Sade's *Justine*. But nevertheless with the addition by Restif of at least one horrible scene of murder and, I believe, cannibalism as bad as anything anywhere in Sade. Perhaps he was trying to teach Sade a lesson? In the 1940s Samuel Roth published a fake item, purportedly by none less than Friedrich Nietzsche, entitled *My Sister and I*, which I suspect is the real or proximal model of the Hollywood and San Diego incest paperbacks of the more recent period. (See further the excellent article on Roth, 'Nobody Knows My

Names,' by Leo Hamalian, in *Journal of Modern Literature*, 1974, vol. III: pp. 889–927.) Pierre Louÿs' electrifying but gravellous *Trois Filles de leur mère* may also have inspired imitation, but that is about the contrary kind of incest: from the outside in. The key to recent American pornographica is Michael Perkins' over-enthusiastic *The Secret Record* (New York, 1976).

BOOK-CRIMINALS AND EROTICA

In the edges, somehow, of the Christine Keeler/Profumo scandal of the early 1960s, of which the best account I have seen is in Charles Franklin's heavily illustrated *They Walked a Crooked Mile* (New York: Hart, 1972) pp. 121–65, though this obviously leaves a lot untold, a number of erotic books were deposed in the Private Case, coming from the library of George Mountbatten, second Marquess of Milford Haven, and with his armorial bookplate. Also in some way connected with the same scandal is another bequest, of certain modern works and 'Soho typescripts,' which are now preserved in P.C. 14 along with the Milford Haven books, and a group of recent French erotic novels of low calibre in both writing and printing, which I presented to the Private Case in 1963. All these are accession-dated 30 January 1964, since they were processed at the same time, none of these gifts being very large. I am making this distinction precise here, because I never had anything to do with Christine Keeler. I have seen her picture, both naked and clothed in sweat-shirt and blue jeans, in Franklin's *They Walked a Crooked Mile*, pp. 131 and 143, and she is not my type. I am not a lot of people's type, either.

A series of reclassifications or 'de-suppressions' as they are called, allowing Private Case books a less limited circulation among readers, were begun in the British Museum Library at some time after 1964. These have involved mostly the transfer of Private Case books that have in recent years been publicly reprinted, such as Robert Burns' *Merry Muses of Caledonia*, of which Ashbee made a large collection of editions, in the back of one of which (with imprint 'Dublin', about 1826) I had the luck to find Allan Cunningham's copy of Burns' own long-lost manuscript of that important collection of bawdy Scottish folksongs, and have published this (New York: University Press, 1965), with a bibliography of the *Merry Muses*.

Also de-suppressed now are the Earl of Rochester's poems, D.H. Lawrence's stalwartly normal and erotic *Lady Chatterley's Lover*, and other once-banned modern works of literary stature. According to Patrick Kearney, who is in a position to know, at least one-third of the Private Case books listed in Rose/Reade's *Registrum*, as of date 1934, have now been de-suppressed and are at other locations. Many are now preserved in (locked) Cupboards

363 and following, which protects the books still, but with greater availability to readers.

It should be emphasized that the presumable goal of total de-suppression of all the works in any 'Private Case' is neither possible nor desirable. This would merely be playing the game for the psychotic book-mutilators and the professional thieves of rare books. All great libraries suffer a great deal from these dishonest cranks and criminals. At my first visit to the British Museum Library in the spring of 1954, I made friends rapidly with another reader who was interested in modern first editions and bragged that he knew far more about 'future rarities' than did the librarians. Perhaps he did. We took to having lunch together at a little place on Shaftesbury Avenue, near the Museum; me with my little red cardboard accordion packet of 3 × 5″ index cards, and him with his drooping old leather brief-bag, out of which one day he casually took three fine modern first editions and a valuable reference work he had simply walked out of the British Museum with.

'But don't they check briefcases, going in and out?' I asked in astonishment, remembering the brisk but inoffensive frisk readers' books and packages are given at the New York Public Library, both on leaving the reading-room and leaving the building. 'Hell, no!' he replied, with an ugly self-satisfied grin. 'Anybody who uses the British Museum is *a gentleman and a scholar.*'

The Museum had lost so many books over the years to gentlemen and scholars of this stripe that eventually missing books were merely reported as 'Misplaced during the War.' An Australian philologist recently told me he had always believed these reports, until he was given the 'War story' for a book published in 1948! The newly reorganized British Library now examines briefcases, I believe, even of scholars and gentlemen, but that will not bring back the books already stolen, nor repair those already mutilated by insufficiently accredited users under too-casual surveillance. We all believe in freedom, but not in being damn fools. As the old and very apt proverb says: '*God sends rain—but common-sense tells us to wear rubbers.*'

In the years when Dr. Eric Dingwall was honorary curator of the Private Case, he kept a very sharp and suspicious eye on inquirers after Private Case books. One such person, as Dr. Dingwall recounted it, was an American dentist touring Europe. He was rather vague about which books he wanted to see, and exactly what his projected research might be, but finally ventured that he would like to see a copy of *Fanny Hill.* 'But I have to know which edition,' said Dr. Dingwall testily, pulling out his desk copy of the Rose/Reade *Registrum* giving all the callmarks. The dentist craned to look over Dr. Dingwall's shoulder at the bibliographical listings. 'Say,' he said interestedly, 'what does it mean there where it says all the time "eight-voe" and "twelve-moe"?' Dr. Dingwall slammed the book shut, and ushered the dentist politely out.*

Sometimes all this works in the opposite direction. The effort is not made to take things out of the library, or even to misuse its services, but to improve its collections—with stolen books. Books stolen, that is to say, from other libraries, thus making a vicious circle of loss and theft. Most large libraries all over the world will no longer buy rare books from individuals for this reason, though they do accept gifts. On one of my trips to London, a well-respected bookseller tried to get me to offer (for sale) to the Private Case of the British Museum Library two copies of the famous homosexual work, anonymously by Antonio Rocco, the very rare *Alcibiade fanciullo a scola,* in rare seventeenth-century editions, one of which had the library stamp of an Italian public library scraped off but still legible on its final page; while the other had the page pared down and remounted, on which the library stamp had evidently been present in the margin. I declined both copies with thanks.

Another honest bookdealer, this time in Holland, sent me a large multivolume set of books on erotic folklore, in which the original public library stamps were not even scratched off the backs of the ti-tle-pages. When I sent him back these books he refused to refund my money, *explaining* that 'ever since the War many former library books are floating around Europe.' I'll bet. Those gentlemen and scholars again, liberating literature. The bookseller was extremely shocked by my poor sportsmanship when I wrote again to tell him that I would be pleased to receive my money by return of post, or he would shortly be receiving a visit from the Interpol services dealing with thefts and 'fencing' of gems, books, and other art-valuables. I guess that proves I am no gentleman.

---

*Editor's Note: For readers—not librarians, of course!—who, like this unfortunate dentist, do not know (or have forgotten) what '8vo' and '12mo' mean, these terms refer to the way sheets of paper for printed books are folded after printing. The largest size is the 'folio' (abbreviated 'fol'.), where the printed sheet is folded once, to produce two 'leaves,' or four pages (numbers 1 and 2 for the first leaf, and 3 and 4 for the second). Next down in size is the 'quarto' ('4to'), where the sheet is folded twice, to give four leaves and therefore eight pages. Then the 'octavo'—the '8vo' of Legman's story—where the sheet is folded four times, giving eight leaves and 16 pages. A 'duodecimo' ('12mo') book is made from a sheet folded to produce twelve leaves and 24 pages. The results are books that differ in their dimensions, with folio the largest, and the others proportionately smaller. After the printed sheets are folded, they are sewn and glued into the binding as 'signatures,' giving the final book, the pages of which are then cut to separate the leaves. (Students of foreign languages and literatures will remember coping with books with uncut signatures. Our copy of Legman's anonymously edited *The Limerick,* published in 1953 by Les Hautes Études of Paris, was issued and arrived uncut.) The terms are useful though, for identifying a given printing of a book and—as librarians know well—for assigning shelf-height for any book, as below.

AN AUTOBIOGRAPHY OF INNOCENCE

In years gone by, I was not solely interested in these matters from a bibliographical point of view. About 1938 a rather peculiar bookscout known as 'Slapsie Maxie' approached me in New York, on the recommendation of the erotica publisher Samuel Roth, and as I later learned on the account of a bookdealer and agent called Rudolph Bernays, and asked me if I had read a recent erotic mimeographed work called *An Oxford Thesis on Love*, attributed to a Hollywood writer, Lupton Wilkinson. He wanted me to write some continuations of this for a private customer, in the same style, at $50 for each one-hundred page erotic manuscript; and finally agreed I could write in any style I liked. I wrote a number of these manuscripts, but eventually found it impossible to continue, as it was making me just as impotent sexually as it was presumably making the

---

The author adds: It should be observed that, like improper fractions—the only erotica of mathematics, as the Conjunction of Mars and Venus is the only such allowed to astronomers—the Latin names of book sizes swell all the larger and longer as the books get shorter and more exiguous, if we make ourselves clear? Thus, next smaller after 'duodecimo' ('12*mo*': from 17.5 to 20 cm. high) stands 'sextodecimo' ('16*mo*': 15 to 17.5 cm. high), followed downward toward total bibliographical non-entity, by 'vicegesimo-quarto' ('24*to*': 12.5 to 15 cm.) and—if you can bear to subdivide the belovèd little books that far, and won't 'forget' this time—'tricegesimo-secundo' ('32*do*': 10 to 12.5 cm.) Beyond that, most librarians throw in the sponge and just say 'Miniature Books' or even 'Toy Books'!

Some wild-eyed French radicals have also attempted to slip some kind of an '18*mo*' into the already sufficiently complicated matter, one would think; but as no one knows exactly what size it is, nor how in the Hell ('*Enfer*') you fold paper to get it to make eighteen pages, nor even how to *pronounce* it in Latin, it has been put out at second thought as a wild throw. What is important in all this, as that snobbish mock-foreigner Legman has made us all see now, is not to mix up the 'moes' and 'voes' (as in duodecimo and octavo), with the 'toes' and 'does' (as in '24*to*' and '32*do*': or maybe that's *vice versa*. Otherwise we too will be disgraced, like that unfortunate dentist from Baltimore, if we ever get to the British Museum, now British Library.

All of this is, in any case, becoming only a bit of baroque antiquarianism, since modern book-cataloguing descriptions make no use of all this complicated Latinity at-all, but use simple height-measurements in centimeters (as above), or even translated into vulgar inches, to indicate the shelving height needed. (Just add two centimeters to each, to get your finger in, to pull the book out.) Again, as we all know, computerization has already pushed the old Napoleonic would-be scientificism of the centimetric system into the discard. European and Oriental book-publishers now buy and print upon only *one* standardized large sheet-size of printing paper, of which the folded height stands to the width in classic Pythagorean proportions, for just that artistically archaic touch that 'humanizes' the machine-crushing of everything that once was charming. All book-sizes are now to be referred to coldly as A2, A3 and so forth, for easier computerization for librarians of the New School who prefer never to have to count any higher than from zero to binary one.

customer super-virile. I felt I was being cannibalized, and turned the job over to a friend of mine named Robert Sewall, very talented at pastiche. A similar imitation of *My Secret Life* had been commissioned about 1932 as the 'Lord Roxboro' series.

Sewall continued in this vein for quite a while, and then branched out into parodies of Henry Miller's *Tropic of Cancer*, taking off from the opening scene where Miller announces, in what I suppose is intended as dithyrambic prose in his usual imitation of Louis-Ferdinand Céline and James Joyce, that he is going to 'bite off a woman's clitoris and spit out two-franc pieces.' Sewall then went on to a parody of the style of Dashiell Hammett's 'tough' murder-mysteries, and himself privately reissued this series later in mimeographed form as *The Devil's Advocate* by 'Wood C. Lamont,' about 1942, with certain sadistic scenes expurgated by me. This was also reprinted twice in the 1960s, once under the title of *The Sign of the Scorpion* by 'Bruce Abbott' (Grove Press, 1970) with the sadistic scenes put back in. Sewall had finally been removed from the project at the request of the customer for the manuscripts, who also did not care for the excessive amount of sadism in the *Devil's Advocate* scripts, nor for the climax where naked women are branded on the lower belly with the Sign of the Scorpion. Like most normals, the customer could accept uneasily a very small or incidental amount of sadism, but not much.

Meanwhile, I had been in contact with this customer, to whom I was directed by the erotic artist, Clara Tice, who had extra-illustrated books for him, and, in particular, a full set of the then-rare *My Secret Life*, which I was anxious to find and read. This secret customer was an oil millionaire, Mr. Roy Melisander Johnson of Ardmore, Oklahoma, an old man who had 'all' the printed erotica in English, but who found—like the readers of murder-mysteries—that each story excited his imagination and his jaded virility only once. He therefore continually needed a harem of fresh manuscripts written for him, two a week, one being supplied to him by an agent in California, and others from Chicago or New York, solidly bound and by airmail. The cost of each manuscript was $200 apiece, of which the agent was to give the writer $100, but—as I had found—paid only $50. The erotica business is not filled with scrupulously honest dealers.

I never learned who the West Coast agent was, though I was told that many Hollywood writers had written for this combine, including Gene Fowler, who wrote for it in the early 1930s his strange *The Demi-Wang* by 'Peter Long,' and *Nirvana* by 'Dr. Desernet', both later published in printed form probably from carbon-copies retained by the author. A California bookseller, Mr. Mel Royer, who supplied the collector with sporting books and had seen his collection, told me that the erotic books and manuscripts were kept in vertical steel filing-cabinets painted olive-drab, in his business office, as his wife would not allow them in their home! Like 'Granny' Ashbee, perhaps she too had had a few literary surprises she could not stomach. He himself was a strict Seventh Day Adventist, and never ate *meat* since he was seven years old.

Mr. Johnson wrote guardedly that he was willing to lend me the set of *My Secret Life*, and would send it for my use to his agent in New York, a bookseller whom we referred to as Rudolph Bernays, though that was not his name. Bernays refused to assist, and was furious that Johnson had led me to him. He asked me, however, through my contact-man Slapsie Maxie, whether the manuscripts coming to him as being by Henry Miller, were authentic. I told him they were only parodies, but that I knew Miller and was just then reading the proofs for the 'Medusa' edition of his *Tropic of Cancer* about to be published secretly for the first time in America, by Brussel in New York in 1940. The agent explained that if I could get Miller really to write erotica for the customer in Oklahoma, I would receive $25 per manuscript myself as agent. I let this pass, but sent word on to the always-impecunious Miller, with whom I was no longer in contact as we did not like each other personally, through his close friend the American surréalist poet, Kenneth Patchen, whom Brussel was also planning to publish openly.

Miller did not come to our appointment, at Frances Steloff's famous intellectual bookshop, the Gotham Book Mart in midtown Manhattan. Instead, he sent an elegant and exotic Spanish woman, whom I presumed, perhaps wrongly, to be his mistress, named Anaïs Nin, who had written or perhaps only signed a splendid preface for the original Paris edition of *Tropic of Cancer* (omitted for reasons of space from the New York reprint, for which she never forgave me!) I explained matters to her, giving all the figures and names except that of the eventual customer. I also told her that the agent would pay $100 per hundred-page manuscript if pushed—especially to Miller—as that was what the customer was offering.

I added that she ought to write a few of the manuscripts herself, since she said they both needed money, having just arrived in New York as refugees from the War. No woman that I knew of had ever authentically written erotica, and I thought it would be marvellously valuable to men to know *what women really think* about sexual intercourse, in a totally frank way. The erotic books famously signed with women's names have almost always been fabrications by men, like John Cleland's *Fanny Hill*, Pierre Louÿs' *Chansons de Bilitis*, and most recently the delightful *Memoirs of Josefine Mutzenbacher* by Felix Salten (author also of the children's book, *Bambi*), one of the few erotic books written with intentional humor. I cited these to Miss Nin, and especially *Die Weisheiten der Aspasia* (1923), the finest modern sex-technique manual, also actually by a man, Fritz Foregger von Greiffen-Thurn. 'What do men want to know most?' Miss Nin asked. I looked down at her high-heeled suede wraparound shoes—she was dressed like a real *poule de luxe*—and I answered: 'We want to know if women really have orgasms, or if you're just faking it half the time.' And we left it at that . . .

Finally, I cautioned Miss Nin to retain carbon-copies of Miller's manuscripts for the customer, and of her own if she wrote any as I urged her to do. The customer was already quite old, and when he would eventually die the manuscripts could be revised and published under their authors' names—perhaps in Paris, which was still the only possible place—when the War would be over. Miss Nin thanked me and we parted. She said she had the feeling she was taking my job away from me, but I assured her I didn't want it. 'I did it for two years,' I told her, 'and I'm ready to scream. You'll scream too. . .' Another chapter, following on here, as to our subsequent relationship, will appear in my 'Autobiography of Innocence,' *Peregrine Penis* (in progress), of which one springtime chapter has already been published as 'Trio Amoroso,' in *Libido: The Journal of Sex and Sensibility* (Chicago, Summer 1989, Nos. 5 and 6).

I never saw either Miller or Anaïs Nin again after that, and did not know till decades later whether they had gone on with the project. Meanwhile, to make sure that Miller would not be cheated out of his royalties on the American edition of *Tropic of Cancer*, as James Joyce and D.H. Lawrence had been cheated before him, by Samuel Roth and others, we arranged that half the edition of one thousand copies would be supplied to Miss Steloff for sale at $10 a copy, and that on delivery she would pay $500 to Miller, or to Miss Nin for him. The other half of the edition would go to the erotica bookseller-publisher Ben Abramson in Chicago, who would be required to pay on delivery in the same way, and who also did so—with a little shoving and pushing, as I will one day describe in my own Memoirs as above, if I live to complete them.

The manuscripts Henry Miller wrote for the Oklahoma collector, Roy M. Johnson, were later revised and enlarged, and were published by Maurice Girodias in Paris under the title of *Sexus* and others similar. Miss Nin also kept carbon copies of her erotica, as I had suggested, and the best of these were also finally openly published, as *Delta of Venus* and *Little Birds* (New York, 1977–79), with great success. She gives the full story of how they came to be written, in her published *Diary, Vol. III: 1939–1944* (New York: Harcourt, Brace, Jovanovich, 1969), especially at pages 147, 157, and 177–8, and other locations indexed under 'erotica' and 'collector.' Some of these striking passages are gathered as the preface to her *Delta of Venus*, the mistresspiece of her erotic art, though very different from the ferocious sexual honesty of the Shere Hite *Reports* (1976 *ff.*), and the violent, let-it-all-hang-out realistic style of Erica Jong's *How to Save Your Own Life*. These are closer to Henry Miller's 'wild, barbaric yawp' method, and so are the new erotic autobiographies of whorehouse madams and pornographic movie-stars, of which outstandingly the best is *Superstar* (1970) by 'Viva,' who is also a fine, no-nonsense writer.

Anaïs Nin certainly does not have the genius and power of Henry Miller in his early *Tropics*—his *Sexus* and other late erotic items are mostly incompetent swill, apparently intended as a work of revenge, to cover his first wife with filth. But Nin is an elegant artist of exquisite sensibility, and it is almost a miracle that by accident such a woman was led to write erotic books. Although I feel that Miller's late erotica such as *Sexus* would have been better left unwritten, I am proud of the small part I played in bringing Anaïs Nin to the writing of beautiful erotic fantasies, something that I certainly had never been able to do.

Her cold, but passionate and pointed judgments on erotic writing and its readers are the best conclusion for the present introduction. Anaïs Nin never knew who the client was that she was writing for, and perhaps that is just as well. No one ever really writes for money: the words don't come. And I doubt that she would have been inspired to write beautifully and passionately, of her sexual fantasies and inner erotic temperament, if she knew her words were going to be masturbated over once, and then filed in olive-drab steel cabinets in an oil company's office. In her *Diary* she tells how shabbily she and Miller were treated by the agent, Rudolph Bernays, who even wangled valuable signed copies of Miller's earlier books on the pretext of getting them for the 'old man,' who did not want any poetry—just pornography. And she fought the job and client continuously in her mind, just as many of us did; and stopped writing for him, apparently, after less than two years, turning instead to printing her own poetic books on a platen-press in a loft in Greenwich Village, with her next lover.

She then got other writers to take the job on, just as I had, and mockingly referred to herself (*Diary: III*, page 151) as 'the madam of this literary, snobbish house of prostitution-writing, from which vulgarity was excluded.' She adds: 'Laughing, I said: "I supply paper and carbon, I deliver the manuscripts anonymously, I protect everyone's anonymity".' She succeeded, too, and when the 'old man' died and the mass of original manuscripts appeared on the erotica market, they were snapped up for open publication by the new erotica publishers of the 1960s in San Diego, California; Atlanta, Georgia; and other centers of culture. They then were published as by one 'A. de Granamour,' etc., vaguely supposed to be a mysterious Paul Little of Chicago, but actually the collective pseudonyms Anaïs Nin used in turning over her repatriated writing-group's manuscripts to the inquisitive Bernays, who then had them bound up and airmailed out to the old client. But no one will ever be able to match up the real authors' names.

Her real associates Anaïs Nin identifies frankly in her *Diaries*, two of them also being women: the painter Virginia Admiral, and Caresse Crosby, the young widow of an avant-garde Paris-American publisher who had just committed suicide. Both these women wrote manuscript erotica under Henry Miller's faked name, when he broke down on the job. These fakes, along with several by Robert Sewall and myself, were recently published by Grove Press under the idiotic title of *Opus Pistorum* as authentic! Aside from Henry Miller, among the men who worked in Anaïs Nin's 'snobbish house of prostitution-writing' were Harvey Breit, James Cooney, Robert Duncan, and the English poet George Barker, who drank away the money he earned in this way. This is not to suggest that the money carried a curse. I spent mine mostly on books. Not all of us have the advantage of Casanova, in his erotic *Memoirs* first published completely from the manuscript in 1961 by Brockhaus, a century and a half after being written in 1797, that no one can suspect us of hoping to trade our erotic fantasies for money. Says Miss Nin (*Diary: III*, page 157):

'I gather poets around me and we all write beautiful erotica. As we have to suppress poetry, lyrical flights, and are condemned to focus only on sensuality, we have violent explosions of poetry. Writing erotica becomes a road to sainthood rather than to debauchery . . . The homosexuals write as if they were women, satisfying their desire to be women. The timid ones write about orgies. The frigid ones about frenzied fulfillments. The most poetic ones indulge in pure bestiality and the purest ones in perversions. We have to cut out the poetry, and are haunted by the marvelous tales we cannot tell. We have sat around, imagined this old man, talked of how much we hate him, because he will not allow us to make a fusion of sexuality and feeling, sensuality and emotion, and lyrical flights which intensify eroticism.'

Finally she cannot go on any longer, and writes a farewell letter to poor old Johnson, which of course she has no way of sending to him; and also notes on the same page that she continues, for a while anyhow, to 'write ten or fifteen pages of erotica a day.' She tells him candidly (*Diary: III*, pp. 177–78):

'Dear Collector: We hate you. Sex loses all its power and magic when it becomes explicit, mechanical, overdone, when it becomes a mechanistic obsession. It becomes a bore. You have taught us more than anyone else I know how wrong it is not to mix it with emotion, hunger, desire, lust, whims, caprices, personal ties, deeper relationships which change its color, flavor, rhythms, intensities.

'You do not know what you are missing by your microscopic examination of sexual activity to the exclusion of others, which are the fuel that ignites it. Intellectual, imaginative, romantic, emotional.

This is what gives sex its surprising textures, its subtle transformations, its aphrodisiac elements. You are shrinking your world of sensations. You are withering it, starving it, draining its blood.

'If you nourished your sexual life with all the excitements and adventures which love injects into sensuality, you would be the most potent man in the world. The source of sexual power is curiosity, passion. You are watching its little flame die of asphyxiation . . . Sex does not thrive on monotony . . . How much do you lose by this periscope at the tip of your sex, when you could enjoy a harem of distinct and never-repeated wonders? Not two hairs alike, but you will not let us waste words on a description of hair; not two odors, but if we expand on this, you cry "Cut the poetry" . . .'

One hears in every line the accents of the wisely encouraging French psychoanalyst Miss Nin had become professionally during the 1930s. And what a pity it was she did not stay in that dedicated profession, instead of allowing herself to become the temporary darling of the expatriate intellectual snob crowd, on the basis of her hand-printed books, like a new and equally misapprehended William Blake. I have permitted myself this long quotation, as it is in a way a letter to me too, though certainly it was not I who ever told her to 'Cut out the poetry!' On another page (*Diary: III*, page 147), Anaïs Nin applies to the literary and not emotional problem of erotica another of her coldly passionate private assessments: 'The joke on me,' she says, concerning her own writing of erotica, 'is that France had a tradition of literary erotic writing, in fine elegant style, written by the best writers. When I first began to write for the collector I thought there was a similar tradition here, but found none at all. All I have seen is badly written, shoddy, and by second-rate writers. No fine writer seems ever to have tried his hand at erotica.'

Of course, she is omitting herself here, among writers in English, and perhaps overlooking D.H. Lawrence's *Lady Chatterley's Lover*, and Joyce's final soliloquy of Molly Bloom in *Ulysses*. That she does not make an exception for Miller is significant. There is also all the elegant traditional erotica of the last four centuries, in prose and verse, that Miss Nin is alluding to, some of which, like Chorier's *Dialogues of Luisa Sigea* (France, about 1650, also pretendedly written by a woman), are little more than well-written apologies for wife-swapping, etc., or their authors' abnormalities and letches. Viewed, however, from the literary side, these are indeed the books that the Private Cases of the world's great libraries have been instituted to preserve and protect 'to a Life beyond Life.' The crude pornography of these last centuries and the catchpenny sex-fodder of recent open publication, not to mention the hideous and repulsive sadistic works that are kept side by side on the same shelves, are really there only on sufferance. Many of them—many of the books in any such catalogue—are no more than the monstruosities of human literature, kept for historical study by calmer minds at some hypothetical later date, like abortions bottled in formaldehyde in a social pathologist's cupboard.

At their presumably opposite ends of the spectrum of eroticism, Sade's *120 Journées de Sodome* (1789) and the anonymous *My Secret Life* (1894) are both equally the cruel and explicit records of one man's ugly and mad anti-erotic imaginings, as of another's ugly, exploitative sexual obsessions. Both authors are essentially woman-haters, revolving like mechanical killing-devices in their endless permutations of would-be eroticism and would-be anti-eroticism, in which the human dimension is not ever once achieved. Anaïs Nin's beautifully styled erotic fantasies are something else again, and offer us a forlorn hope. They are the only possible pattern for the erotica of the future.

CHAPTER 3
Words, Libraries, and Meaning

Martha Cornog and Timothy Perper

What does it mean to say, "pornography in the library"?

> "When *I* use a word," Humpty Dumpty said, in a rather scornful tone, "it means just what I choose it to mean—neither more nor less."
> "The question is," said Alice, "whether you *can* make words mean so many different things."
> "The question is," said Humpty Dumpty, "which is to be master—that's all." (Carroll 1963, 269)

Many words have been applied to writings about sex: *pornography, erotica, erotic realism, erotic art, obscenity, sex education, sex research*, and—still in *Sears List of Subject Headings—sexual hygiene*. And for some years, feminists, censors, anticensors, legislators, liberals, conservatives—and librarians—have attempted to be master of these words. The "erotica/pornography" controversy alone is certainly up to Humpty Dumpty's best efforts at prescriptive lexicography.

DIFFERENT DEFINITIONS

A precise definition of *pornography* has proven frustratingly elusive for many years. As Bravard points out,

> [P]ornography is impossible to define in any useful fashion. . . . All efforts at achieving a definition move in a circle from pornography to obscenity to prurient to licentious to indecent to lascivious to lewd and back again. (1989, 34)

We can readily observe this tangled circularity in that most august and traditional of references, the *Oxford English Dictionary*, published in the mid-1930s. Its authors essayed the following attempts at defining *pornography*—and related terms:

> **Pornography:** . . . the expression or suggestion of obscene or unchaste subjects in literature or art.
> **Obscene:** Offensive to modesty or decency; expressing or suggesting unchaste or lustful ideas; impure, indecent, lewd.
> **Unchaste:** . . . impure, lascivious.
> **Lascivious:** Inclined to lust, lewd, wanton.
> **Lewd:** Lascivious, unchaste.
> **Impure:** Not pure morally; defiled by sin; unclean, unchaste; filthy.
> **Indecent:** Offending against the recognized standards of propriety and delicacy; highly indelicate, immodest; suggesting or tending to obscenity.
> **Wanton:** Lascivious, unchaste, lewd.
> **Immodest:** Wanting a due sense of decorum or decency; improper, indelicate, indecent, lewd, unchaste.
> **Indelicate:** Wanting in, or offensive to, a sense of delicacy or propriety; coarse, unrefined; bordering upon what is immodest or indecent.

It is only when we at last fight our way through this lexicographic thicket to *lust* and *chaste* that we get a sense of the heart of the matter:

> **Lust:** Sexual appetite or desire. Chiefly and now exclusively implying intense moral reprobation.
> **Chaste:** Pure from unlawful sexual intercourse; continent, virtuous.

Thus, by indirect and elaborate reduction, the *OED*'s authors defined *pornography* as the expression or suggestion in literature or art of sexual appetites or acts, particularly those considered immoral, unlawful, or offensive.

The *OED* has no definition for *erotica* but defined *erotic* as "Of or pertaining to the passion of love." By 1971, however, *erotica* had entered the lexicon. Consider, now, this cycle of definitions from the *American Heritage Dictionary* (*AHD*):

> **Erotica:** Literature or art concerning or intending to arouse sexual desire.
> **Pornography:** Written, graphic, or other forms of communication intended to excite lascivious feelings.

Do we perhaps detect a trace of circularity here as well? Let us follow this one out also.

Lascivious: 1. Of or characterized by lust; lewd; lecherous. 2. Exciting sexual desires.
Lewd: Licentious; lustful.
Licentious: Lacking moral discipline or sexual restraint.
Lust: Sexual craving, especially excessive or unrestrained.
Lechery: Excessive indulgence in sexual activity.

Thus, according to the *AHD*—somewhat more direct than the *OED*—both erotica and pornography are intended to excite sexual desire, or in colloquial English, to turn on the consumer. From the *AHD*'s definitions, we infer three distinctions between the two terms: 1. **Erotica** is literature or art, presumably implying a distinction of quality, whereas **pornography** can be any form of communication; 2. **Pornography**, being *lascivious*, may be intended to arouse lust, that is, *excessive* sexual feelings and, via *lewd* through *licentious, morally undisciplined* sexual craving, whereas the sexual desire associated with *erotica* has no such negative qualifiers attached; and 3. **Erotica** may *concern* sexual desire rather than (or in addition to) arousing it.

Although phrases like *moral discipline* or *sexual restraint* may themselves be unclear, we nonetheless see that for pornography, *AHD* has preserved the sense of *immoral*, added *excessive*, but dropped *unlawful* and *offensive*. Equally important, the definition has changed from exclusive emphasis upon sexual content to emphasis upon both sexual content *and* intent to cause sexual arousal.

More recent definitions add other senses and impose other distinctions.

Perhaps one could simply say that erotica is about sexuality, but pornography is about power and sex-as-weapon. . . . (Steinem 1980, 38)

Erotica means any visual matter a dominant characteristic of which is the depiction, in a sexual context, or for the purpose of sexual stimulation of the viewer, of a human sexual organ, a female breast or the human anal region. . . .
Pornography briefly means any visual matter that shows

    1 (a)   i -   sexual conduct in any of sub paragraphs ii-iv and involves a minor
              ii - impairment of the body/bodily functions in a sexual context
              iii - sexual violent conduct
              iv - a degrading act in a sexual context
              v - bestiality, incest or necrophilia
              vi - masturbation, ejaculation, vaginal, anal or oral intercourse
    (b) any matter or commercial communication that entices, promotes, encourages or advocates any of the conduct i-vi. (Jarvis 1987, 1–2)

The feminist proposal is that *pornography* should not be used for all sexually explicit arousing material but only that which has a particularly objectionable content, and *erotica* should be reserved for sexual material with a different content. . . .If [as some feminists restrict the term] *erotica* means sexual material containing depictions of love, then erotica is quite distinct from pornography. . . .(Soble 1986, 178, 180)

Between, say, *Ulysses* at one end and *Snuff* at the other, erotica/pornography conveys all sorts of mixed messages that elicit complicated and private responses. In practice, attempts to sort out good erotica from bad porn inevitably come down to "What turns me on is erotic; what turns you on is pornographic." (Willis 1983, 463)

When asked to distinguish between pornography and eroticism, Alain Robbe-Grillet, the leading practitioner of the French New Novel, is reported to have said: 'Pornography is the eroticism of others' (*'La pornographie, c'est l'éroticisme des autres'*). (Charney 1981, 1)

In pornography (hard core obscenity) *the main purpose is to stimulate erotic response* in the reader. And that is all. *In erotic realism, truthful description of the basic realities of life, as the individual experiences it, is of the essence*, even if such portrayals (whether by reason of humor, or revulsion, or any other cause) have a decidedly anti-erotic effect. (Kronhausen & Kronhausen 1959, 18, italics original)

While at this point we may feel more confused than enlightened, these definitions do have one point in agreement. We may not be quite sure exactly what pornography and erotica may be, but somehow, by cultural consensus, erotica is "higher" than pornography; it connotes better quality, more complexity, nonviolence, being not "objectionable," the depiction of more socially acceptable sexual acts, a portrayal of life and love, or a reflection of sexual equality. Erotica is literature or art, as opposed to mere "communication." Susie Bright sums up these points of agreement in reference to women's writings:

There's still a lot of confusion about what the label "women's erotica" means. At its worst, it's a commercial term for vapid femininity, a Harlequin romance with a G-string. The very word "erotic" implies superior value, fine art, an aesthetic which elevates the mind and incidentally stimulates the body. "Women's pornography," on the other hand, is a contradiction in terms for many people, so convinced are they that pornography represents the darker, gutter side of lust. (Bright, 1988, p. 3)

Erotica, perhaps, is pornography that went to college.

DIFFERENT VALUE JUDGMENTS

If erotica is somehow "better" than pornography, then we may infer that to term something *erotica* is often to pay a compliment or impute respectability. Erotica is humorous or loving or exciting or passionate or beautiful or uplifting or true-to-life. Indeed, erotica is becoming part of the sacred and pure side of Western sexuality (Perper 1985, ch. 8). Some recent works of, or about, sexual fiction doubtless were so titled to evoke such positive connotations for the reader: *Ladies Home Erotica, Herotica, Erotic by Nature, How to Write Erotica.*

By contrast, *pornographic* is an insult and—regardless of the *AHD*—is frequently used to mean *obscene*, that is, personally offensive as well as sexually exciting. (Note the *OED* definition of *pornography*.) *Pornography* is part of the *impure* side of Western sexuality (Perper 1985, ch. 8). If we call something *pornographic*, we usually mean that it offends us, and that we expect it will offend, or should offend, most people; thus the use of the term generally reflects the speaker's attribution of an inherent or intrinsic offensiveness to that which is labelled *pornographic*. In a sense, then, calling something *pornographic* externalizes the individual's own internal sense of having been offended. So, the statement, "It is pornographic"—made about an object of some kind, a book, say—replaces the statement "I am offended by that book because it might incite lust in someone."

The word *pornography* allows a second attribution as well. Whereas the formal definition (such as the *AHD*'s) may refer to the *intent* to produce sexual excitement, actual use of the term frequently revolves more around its attributed *effect*. When we call something pornographic, we state our belief that it *will* excite in (other) people excessive, immoral, or inappropriate sexual feelings. Thus, the intent of the writer/artist/filmmaker may be often judged irrelevant. We may also use *pornography* to refer to any material we believe will encourage the consumer to actually engage in sexual behavior (i.e., sexual advocacy) if we believe that engaging in such behavior is undesirable.[1]

THE TROUBLE WITH WORDS

Since people often use the term *pornography* according to their beliefs about the effects of the material—as well as their beliefs about whether such effects are good or bad—literally any treatment of sexuality, fiction or nonfiction, may potentially be labelled "pornography" by someone.

> In some people's eyes, libraries *do* distribute porn. I refer doubters to the bibliographies in the kits for each year's Banned Books Week and to the *Newsletter on Intellectual Freedom*, which reports on censorship attempts. Among the titles cited as being "pornographic," "sexually offensive," or "obscene," are *The Diary of Anne Frank; The Chocolate War* by Robert Cormier; *Are You There, God? It's Me, Margaret, Deenie,* and other titles by Judy Blume; *Show Me,*

Our Bodies, Our Selves, and other books on sexuality for young people; and Alice Walker's *The Color Purple*. (Kamm 1987, 117).

Moreover, if a title is viewed as promoting sex in any way, it
may be termed "pornographic" by someone who does not believe that
sex should be promoted, particularly for certain types of sex or for
certain readers, such as:

- Books for homosexuals on how to prevent AIDS, because they
  encourage tolerance of and permission for homosexual activities, which are seen as immoral.[2]
- Sex research books and journals such as the Kinsey reports
  because they report large numbers of people having extramarital affairs and thus make infidelity seem commonplace and
  permissible.
- Pictures of women in attitudes construable as suggesting sexual
  receptivity because male viewers may be led to believe that all
  women are receptive to men indiscriminately, and therefore
  these male viewers may then try inappropriately and even
  illegally to induce women to have sex with them.
- Sex education books, because they do not always contain the
  values and warnings that some believe should surround such
  matters as masturbation.
- Novels for teenagers containing episodes of premarital sex,
  because young readers may be led to imitate such behavior.
- Books for children that describe sexual intercourse, because
  then they may try it with each other.
- Novels for women describing sex with handsome strange men
  as ecstatic and wonderful, because these women may then
  become dissatisfied with their husbands and marriages.

In this way, *pornography* may be applied to any material seen as
promoting an undesirable, immoral, or dangerous sexual anarchy (see
Kendrick 1987, 219–220).

However, sexual anarchy is often a matter of individual perspective:

- A man may reject all depictions of sex ("pornographic" or
  "erotic"), believing that one's turn-on should come only from
  one's spouse.
- A woman may feel profoundly repelled by X-rated movies but
  enjoy sexually explicit romance novels.[3]
- Another woman happily watches X-rated videotapes but rejects
  any with S&M or violence themes.
- Still a third woman, insecure with men about feeling over-
  weight, derives reassurance from pictures in *Playboy* of erotically posed plump models.

One person's erotica may be another's porn; one person's porn may be another's sex education. Says Charney (1981) in his book, *Sexual Fiction*:

> I have avoided fine distinctions between terms such as 'pornographic,' 'obscene,' 'sexual' and 'erotic', because all these words are more or less synonymous, depending on the value judgments and class orientation of individual users. (p. 2)

DEFINITIONS OF THE LIBRARY

Charney (1981) renounced all definitions of *pornography* and *erotica*, preferring to title his book simply *Sexual Fiction*. Do these definitions have any meaning for librarians, or are they merely the harmless drudgery of lexicographers, lawyers, and culture watchers?

These definitions *do* have meaning for librarians, because of the definition of the library itself. Yet to understand *that* definition, it must be understood that a library is far more than a repository of books: it is also a social institution, subject to social rules and expectations.

By that phrase, we do not mean that certain "social events" occur in libraries, such as story hours for children, although they occur, nor that young men and women meet and hold hands in libraries, although that too happens. Instead, the concept refers to the sociological notion of an *institution*, a group of people organized for a socially recognized purpose. Such institutions do not simply or merely reflect their staff's or patrons' personal opinions or feelings but react to a collective sense of definitions and meanings as to what the institution should do and should be.

Let us approach a definition of the library with the following example. Consider a "book disbursement center," existing in some other social system than ours, and therefore obeying different social rules.

> We enter a large building, a warehouse, dimly lit, with a wooden counter. Surrounding us on the walls are old calendars, xerocopies of "The Rules and Regulations of the Middletown Book Disbursement Center," and behind the counter is a man wearing a greenish shirt, reading a newspaper. He does not look at us.
>
> "Excuse me," we say, "I'd like to borrow a book."
>
> "Hmmm?" he says without looking up. "Let's see your description slip."
>
> We hand him a small card, containing the book's title and author, followed by three lines of symbols and numbers. He stares at it, and finally decides to do something.
>
> "Hey, Harry," he bawls out, "got somebody here who wants an HGT-1107-frg2. Whatcha got back there like that?"
>
> Harry mumbles something, and the man in the greenish shirt puts down the slip. "It'll be a while," he says. "In the meantime, lemme see your authorization."

We hand him a purple, embossed leatherette folder, stamped "Authorization to Obtain Books and Written Materials from the Middletown Book Disbursement Center." It has our photograph in it.

The man in the greenish shirt shifts his weight as he stares at the picture and then at us. "This don't look like you. Got some other ID?"

"My driver's license," we say, hesitating.

"Gimme." He thumbs through it, and at last puts it down indifferently. "Take a seat," he says, picking up his newspaper again. "It'll take a while."

If the reader's reaction is amusement, a point has been missed. We know, with complete conviction, that this "book disbursement center" is not what we mean by a "real library." Yet a complete analysis of why we feel that way is not easy to attain.

It is not the man's bureaucratic suspicion about a false ID card that makes us say that this is not a library. How many youngsters have had their identity challenged by a suspicious librarian? Nor is it the building itself, for many libraries may seem dim and dismal, although architects have in recent years tried very hard to create light and airy ambiances for library buildings. Nor is it the man's total indifference to our presence, although few if any librarians are indifferent! These are all mannerisms or style, matters of secondary importance.

Yet our sense of what defines a library somehow does not include a place like the Middletown Book Disbursement Center, and the reason is this. The major difference between this "Book Disbursement Center" and a library is *respect*, not for the client, but for the book itself and the *value of its contents for society*. For all anyone knows, the man in the green shirt and Harry might be functionaries whose job it is to hand out widgets in a not-particularly-pleasant industrial environment. We expect that in a "real library" the staff hold books, as books, in respect and treat them as objects of value. They are not merely items to be disbursed upon proper presentation of authorizations and identification cards.

Accordingly, we see why Harry and the man in the green shirt are not librarians and the warehouse is not a library. They do not care that we want a *book*; for them our request is merely a number, not Milton, not Joyce, not Kinsey, not gardening. But librarians *do* care about books and what they mean, to individuals and to society.

CONFLICT AMONG DEFINITIONS

We argue that such concern for the social importance of books has always been part of the definition of libraries in the U.S. Yet *how* that concern is expressed and what form it takes have undergone considerable change in recent years, as Evelyn Geller (1984) describes.

For much of our history, libraries have traditionally been defined as special places containing matter that is socially valuable. In brief, as an institution, a library was to contain good words written for our edification and moral instruction. Thus librarians for many years have acted—and have been expected by the public to act—as guardians of both literary quality and literary purity. When a library added a book to its collection, it put an institutional stamp of approval upon it. The librarian was not expected—indeed, this definition precludes it—to provide, as the Introduction to the *Intellectual Freedom Manual* specifies, "all points of view on all questions."

If this view represents the traditional meaning of an American library, then it is easy to see how this vision has collided with two phenomena. First, are recent changes in public acceptance of material once deemed as having no (or marginal) social value or function. As a result, at least some members of the public expect to find in the library much of what one would expect to find in an average bookstore: advertised and reviewed books by known authors and published by mainstream presses, regardless of subject or viewpoint.[4] The second phenomenon is the change in the library profession and among librarians as to what is socially valuable. In this newer, modern view, greater "social value" lies in providing "all points of view on all questions" (or an approximation, limited by availability, space, and budget) than lies in culling for release to the public only the highest quality and most acceptable works.

So, given shifting definitions of *pornography* and *erotica*, increased public acceptance of sexually explicit materials, and changing definitions as to how a library can best serve the public good, controversy and confusion are inevitable among librarians and the public. By no means do all segments of either group subscribe to newer definitions, either of erotica or of libraries as social institutions. To those who believe that libraries should hold only materials of accepted and obvious "social value," the library is by definition no place for lewd, lascivious, unchaste, indecent, or impure works, i.e., *pornography*. For it is precisely these books that are still deemed by some to have no socially redeeming value. Such individuals may then readily perceive a library that lends sexually explicit material on demand as far closer to our mythical "Middletown Book Disbursement Center" than to their ideal of what a library should be. And they may be equally ready to join together with likeminded citizens to demand that the library return to that traditional ideal by ridding its shelves of all that is socially unredeemable, especially titles that deal with sexuality. For them, there is no contradiction between the ideal of the library and a "clean out the smut" campaign; the campaign is seen as furthering and promoting the ideal of socially valuable librarianship.

When librarians are trying to cope with such a citizen's group, they want to defend their own ideals and their purchasing decisions, but they are in a cleft stick. On the one hand, the practice of librarianship in the U.S. has historically accepted the notion that libraries contain primarily, if not solely, works of redeeming social value, not "lewd" or "unchaste" sexual ephemera like a risqué best seller. Yet, simultaneously, librarians may feel—and feel strongly—that this sort of traditional valuation of books excludes modern and minority opinions on an immense variety of topics and, specifically, has excluded much of considerable importance concerning human sexuality. In their effort to include such works—for they believe it needful for a library's holdings to represent many points of view about what is socially valuable—they must, first, deny that they are merely a sleeker, architecturally fancier version of the Middletown Book Disbursement Center, and, second, build a new ethos and ethic of librarianship, in which *all* books are respected, regardless of how traditional tastes and values might assess them. In brief, this newer movement in librarianship asserts that the social value of the library is *precisely* in its wide-ranging coverage of topics and viewpoints, and not in its limitation to topics and books that are, and always have been, accepted by those adhering to traditional values.

What remains is a conflict not of policies, but of meanings. What does it *mean* for a library to consider buying a sexually explicit book? One answer is no longer practical, if it ever was: "Oh, it doesn't mean anything. The library just bought the book, that's all." One set of voices—call them *traditional*, if you like—replies, "But you should not buy such smut! It has no social value!" The other set of voices—call them *modern*, perhaps—replies differently: "But *of course* the library should buy such works! The topic is of immense social significance today!"

Both traditional and modern viewpoints exist within the library community, and each has its vocal and ardent spokespeople. Yet, even if the viewpoints clash, their adherents each feel strongly that in their ideal library, books are deeply and profoundly respected. Neither wants the library as a social institution to become the grim "Book Disbursement Center" of our little parable. It is just that these viewpoints hold to different ideals of social value and the meaning of the library itself, either as guardian and repository of social traditions *or* as haven and repository for all ideas, traditionally acceptable or not, sexually explicit or not.

And the conflict is much broader than that between individual patrons or librarians over a certain book; it is a conflict of definitions, of meanings as surely as the conflict over *erotica* and *pornography*. If the library has *Return to the Valley of the S&M Dolls* or perhaps even *Tropic of Cancer*, then, in one view, it is not a library any more than is our hypothetical Middletown Book Disbursement Center.

MEANING AND VALUE

So, what *does* it mean to say "*pornography* in the library"? It means what the speaker chooses it to mean—neither more nor less. Today's librarian is caught in a crush of Humpty Dumpties, few of them recognizing that other meanings exist for other people. Humpty Dumpty may very well say that by *glory*, "I meant 'there's a nice knock-down argument for you!'" Nonetheless, Alice objects: "But 'glory' doesn't mean 'a nice knock-down argument'" (Carroll 1963, 269).

We all agree that a library is not a "book disbursement center." And we all—patrons and librarians alike, traditional and modern alike—agree that libraries should embody respect for ideas, and for books and the value of their contents for society. Where we disagree is in the meaning of *value*. Does value lie in making available only books reflecting someone's ideas of literary quality, accuracy, morality, or "good taste"? Or does value also (or instead) lie in embodying respect for all books and also for the *patron*, making available a broad offering of ideas and texts? And are there situations when one type of *value* is more appropriate than the other?

"There's a sense," wrote Susan Sontag, "in which *all* knowledge is dangerous . . . [and] we must ask what justifies the reckless unlimited confidence we have in the present mass availability of *other* [i.e., other than pornography] kinds of knowledge . . ." (1967, 211–212, italics added). Perhaps even the "value" provided by the highly traditional library, offering the most carefully screened works, is as dangerous as the "value" provided by the newer, all-points-of-view approach.

Now in considering this, we do not mean to advise the reader categorically that "since all knowledge may be as dangerous as 'pornography,' therefore there is nothing the library should not buy, and all scale of value and meaning for books are worthless." That is, in effect, saying, "The hell with it"; we might as well close the library and direct our patrons to that new book disbursement center. . .

We do wish to suggest, however, that times change, notions of *value* change, meanings change. Musical compositions that once evoked riots in concert halls—like Stravinsky's *Rite of Spring* and Ravel's *Bolero*—are now considered classical "warhorses," even suitable as movie music. Likewise, many books that were considered "questionable" or "objectionable" in 1922 (Feipel 1922) and even "problem" or "controversial" fiction and nonfiction in 1962 (Moon 1962; Broderick 1962) would barely raise an eyebrow in most libraries today. (Feipel mentioned, for example, Boccaccio's tales and *The Arabian Nights*; Moon, Lawrence's *Lady Chatterley's Lover* and Broderick, Mead's *Male and Female*.)

Moreover, the adherents of both traditional and modern librarianship find meanings shifting *within* each viewpoint. For example, certain types of sexually explicit films are specifically created by and for medical professionals today to aid in sex education and sex therapy, which is certainly promoting "social value" in quite a traditional sense. On the other hand, the modern librarian attempting to provide many points of view is still faced with the problem of selecting the "best" or "most valuable" for the library; as a near infinity of schools of thought multiply on nearly every issue, no one library could expect to represent all of them.

However, *pornography, erotica*, and *libraries* will always have meaning and social value, although these will be different for different individuals and groups. Erotica may evoke "glory" or it may evoke "a nice knock-down argument." Librarians must realize that neither they nor anyone else can be master of these words; yet the librarians are the watchers, the stewards, the custodians of the words, the ideas, the meanings. Fortunately, both traditional and modern librarians have recognized this trust and have held it sacred, and that is a shared meaning and value indeed.

ENDNOTES

1. Culturally assigned meanings become very important in these definitions. For example, lingerie and swimwear catalogs designed to be perused by women are not generally considered pornographic or even erotic; the assigned meaning or purpose is to stimulate desire for the clothing, not for the model. Equally, of increasing social respectability is the aptly nicknamed "fuckerwear party," in which a group of (typically) married women get together to model and purchase sexy underwear and nightclothes from one of their friends. Here, the purpose is to "spice up one's marriage"—certainly considered a desirable end.

2. In an effort to promote "safe sex" in positive and desirable terms, some authors have written AIDS prevention manuals in the style of erotica/pornography. See, for example, Preston & Swann (1986). Here indeed is a dilemma for the librarian who wishes to purchase AIDS educational materials but fears accusations of collecting "gay porn"!

3. Romance novels have been described as "female porn" and have become increasingly sexually explicit in the last few decades. See Thurston (1987), Ramsdell (1987), and Radway (1984). Moretto & Weidenburner (1984) note rather dryly that "Romance readers with 'high moral standards' present a real challenge to the staff" in their library, which has a large

collection of romance fiction (p. 1728). They mean, of course, that most romance novels today feature episodes of sex described more or less explicitly, and frequently involving partners who are not married—at least to each other.

4. Far from being concentrated in the output of a few publishers, as once was the case—one remembers Olympia Press, Grove Press, and Lyle Stuart—today, books about sex pop up from nearly all mainstream presses. To take only one but noteworthy example, the heavily illustrated *Skin to Skin: Eroticism in Dress* (by Prudence Glynn, surely the most proper-sounding name imaginable) was published in 1982 by Oxford University Press. Yet apologia still remain: "This is not a book about 'dirty clothes,' nor is it a 'dirty' book about clothes," it begins (p. 15).

REFERENCES

Bravard, Robert S. 1989. Actualities of regulating pornography. *Collection Building*, 9/2:33–35.

Bright, Susie. 1988. Introduction. In *Herotica* (pp. 1–5), ed. by Susie Bright. Burlingame, CA: Down There Press.

Broderick, Dorothy. 1962. "Problem" nonfiction. *Library Journal*, October 1: 3373–3378.

Carroll, Lewis. 1963. *The annotated Alice: Alice's adventures in Wonderland & Through the looking glass.* Introduction and notes by Martin Gardner. Cleveland, OH: World Publishing.

Charney, Maurice. 1981. *Sexual fiction.* New York: Methuen.

Feipel, Louis N. 1922. Questionable books in public libraries—I. *Library Journal*, October 15: 857–862.

Geller, Evelyn. 1984. *Forbidden books in American public libraries, 1876–1939; A study in cultural change.* Westport, CT: Greenwood.

Jarvis, Nancy. 1987. *Bill C-54, an act to amend the criminal code; Synopsis for OAAG members.* Toronto: Ontario Association of Art Galleries.

Kamm, Sue. 1987. The censor's next target. *American Libraries*, February: 117.

Kendrick, Walter. 1987. *The secret museum: Pornography in modern culture.* New York: Viking.

Kronhausen, Eberhard, and Phyllis Kronhausen. 1959. *Pornography and the law.* New York: Ballantine.

Moon, Eric. 1962. "Problem" fiction. *Library Journal*, February 1: 484–496.

Moretto, Shirley, and Kathleen Weidenburner. 1984. "We'll take romance!" *Library Journal*, September 15: 1727–1728.

Perper, Timothy. 1985. *Sex signals: The biology of love.* Philadelphia: ISI Press.

Preston, John, and Glenn Swann. 1986. *Safe sex: The ultimate erotic guide.* New York: New American Library.

Radway, Janice. 1984. *Reading the romance.* Chapel Hill, NC: University of North Carolina Press.

Ramsdell, Kristen. 1987. *Happily ever after: A guide to reading interests in romance fiction.* Englewood, CO: Libraries Unlimited.

Soble, Alan. 1986. *Pornography: Marxism, feminism, and the future of sexuality.* New Haven, CT: Yale University Press.

Sontag, Susan. 1967. The pornographic imagination. *Partisan Review*, Spring: 181–212.

Steinem, Gloria. 1980. Erotica and pornography: A clear and present difference. In *Take back the night* (pp. 35–39), ed. by Laura Lederer. New York: Morrow.

Thurston, Carol. 1987. *The romance revolution*. Urbana, IL: University of Illinois Press.

Willis, Ellen. 1983. Feminism, moralism, and pornography. In *Powers of desire: The politics of sexuality* (pp. 460–467), ed. by Ann Snitow, Christine Stansell, and Sharon Thompson. New York: Monthly Review Press.

CHAPTER 4

Pornography in the Library? Yes!

Bill Katz

Despite all the verbal noise, I find it difficult to take the fuss about pornography, obscenity, and erotica seriously. Anyone with a sex drive and a grain of common sense can persuade themselves that *their* version of sexual intercourse is pure, not a delightful sin. Conversely, others will argue that the only good sex is dirty sex. The definition of pornography is as relative as good and bad sex and just as personal.

WHAT MOTIVATES CENSORSHIP?

It seems to me that censors of pornography, contrary to common folklore, are rarely sexually repressed. But they often *are* downright silly. For example, the failure of Congress to appropriate money for the braille edition of *Playboy*, even without pictures, was something out of the Monty Python show.

Certainly, censorship of pornography is a class consideration. The censors tend to recruit those who not only lack a sense of humor, but also have restrictive views of freedom and individual rights, are less than well educated, and often are disaffected, "born again" types. There are exceptions. Former Attorney General Meese is well educated but a friend of censorship. Still, it's a class issue, and what it comes down to eventually is who has the power to define the concepts involved in "pornography" and "obscenity."

WHAT IS PORNOGRAPHY?

The Supreme Court chooses to link pornography and obscenity with an embarrassing term, "prurient." It is a less than tolerable description of what is supposed to be bad in that, by definition, it means "marked by restless cravings." Pornography is also equated with "lascivious thoughts or desires." There is nothing inherently disagreeable about either turn of phrase unless you lack craving and desire and cannot understand them in others.

Granted, pornography takes many shapes, including religious, racial, and political intolerance. Its true conspiratorial significance is that it poses a threat to the authority of fairness and good taste. This, however, is to view pornography as something greater than itself. The conclusion is more symbolic than real. One may pause at the point where pornography is equated with violent behavior, yet this connection appears tenuous. Neither the liberal nor conservative minded have proven that pornography has various declensions in terms of behavior, for good or ill.

Aside from the natural problems of definitions of terms, one can't help but be puzzled at both the fierce opposition to and determined support for pornography among thoughtful and morally reflective people. Feminists, for example, may take strong exception to the image of pornography while going to jail to defend the right to argue. Part of the answer is that all of us deplore evil and all of us seek the good, but we have a different notion of their patterns. What is good to one is evil to another.

PORNOGRAPHY AND THE LIBRARIAN

Nevertheless, it seems to me we have reached that point where the librarian must now come to grips with that dark center of literature called pornography. It is not depravity to admit it exists, if only in a mild form, in all libraries. Its demoniac power is wed to almost any new novel and certainly to many popular periodicals. The very causes we are trying to serve—i.e., entertainment, culture, and information—are frustrated when we categorically deny pornography a place in the library.

Let us say for the purposes of this discussion that "pornography" is anything that hints at prurience (i.e., promotes sexual arousal) and is legal within the interpretation of the courts—that is, as the Supreme Court has said over and over again, has some "serious literary, artistic, political, or scientific value." (Anything legally judged obscene and prohibited must remain outside the scope of this essay.)[1] Further evaluation must then be made by the librarian in terms of what a reasonable person in that community considers accept-able—the final Supreme Court criterion for legality.

The harrowing and depressing problem lies in defining "reason-able person." The assumption is that the library lies within a community with such people about. Furthermore, the librarian must be a reasonable person. This supposes an ideal world that, if it existed, would not be much bothered with pornography anyway but concerned with why such a large percentage of adults are illiterate, underfed, and living in squalor. Given proper perspective, the whole notion of dirty books and films is nothing. Compared to findings that few kids or adults can tell Beowulf from Chaucer, or for that matter can locate Japan or Brazil on a map, the discussion of what is acceptable in a library is less than exciting. Still, one must get on with the ancient and, one suspects, enduring debate.

So what should be included in our modified pornography, or, if you will, dirty book section?

SELECTION CONSIDERATIONS

First, if cataloged by the Library of Congress or found in the records of OCLC, RLIN, etc., it is worth consideration. This is to stay within the field of earthly nature as recognized by acquisitions sections in every part of the globe.

Next, and more within the bounds of specific library interests, one should consider for acquisition: (1) Any book on the best seller list, whether or not the content or style is considered pornographic by the librarian or a few community members. (2) Any popular maga-zine with a readership of over one million. If that many people purchase a magazine, it surely has some redeeming social qualities, if only prurient ones. The one million circulation, by the way, will not include *The New Yorker* but will include most comic books and almost all of the "skin" magazines. (3) Any titles requested by more than one or two people. (4) Finally, all books that any group wishes removed from the shelves. If the books are not there now, use the ubiquitous lists (e.g., in the *Newsletter on Intellectual Freedom*) as buying guides.

The rationale for all of this is threefold: (1) Such a buying policy is in the tradition of meeting the demands of the community, both expressed and unexpressed. (2) Given a broad definition of pornogra-phy, almost anything falls within the net, and simply to exclude this or that title because it is overly involved with sex is to admit to personal bias that has little to do with the real demands of the public. (3) One may subscribe to quality rather than demand, but there are such things as *quality* comic books, men's magazines, and X-rated films.

HYPOCRISY, ELITISM, AND COMMUNITY STANDARDS

Duplicity entices us all. It's perfectly natural that Americans who overwhelmingly support an estimated $2 billion to $10 billion pornography industry strenuously object to X-rated videos in the public library. These can be the same individuals who have made "Deep Throat" more than $50 million in profits. Some of the pornography industry output is pretty crass stuff, but don't think consumers are limited only to men. According to *The New York Times*, "A recent survey of 500 retailers found that women rented 32% of all X-rated videos, while men rented 37%; heterosexual couples rented the balance" ("Recession in X Rated Industry" 1986).

At another time, I considered the "pornographic imagination" and libraries (Katz 1971) and quoted what still seems the best definition of the elusive term:

> Pornography is writing that seeks primarily, even exclusively, to bring about sexual stimulation. This can be done crudely or delicately. In the former case it would be bad literature; in the latter good. I would certainly support the presentation of good pornography. (Tynan 1969)

The definition, however, poses a problem. Its author, Kenneth Tynan, wants his pornography with literary style. This automatically cuts out Harlequin "temptation" romances (standard popular fare in many libraries), not to mention various issues of *Cosmopolitan* as well as selected numbers of *Elle*. Their only crime is that they serve up life in what they believe to be a "natural" way but often without much consideration of intellectual dressing. The catch is that millions consider all of this material as quality, at least of a sort.

Still, one may accept a good deal of pornography as defined by Tynan. This will range from the cousins and uncles of the Kinsey report (which number in the thousands) to Anaïs Nin, Terry Southern, as well as such current authors as Patrick Suskind and, if you consider them acceptable as examples of bad taste raised to an art, Jackie Collins and Karleen Koen. Similar examples may be dredged up in film, recordings, and lessons on diet and physical development.

Certainly many Americans who tune into family sitcoms and violence every night on television can't stand what Freud and *Cosmopolitan* term natural. According to a recent poll, 51% believe it is necessary to censor obscene books to protect the community from itself. Another 48% believe novels that explicitly describe the sex act should be banned (*Chronicle of Higher Education* 1984). But take heart, at least if you are fairly young and relatively well educated. According to Howard White, whereas the majority are for censorship, this falls away rapidly if one does not live in the South, is not "aged," and is well educated. In fact, this is the very group which since the beginning of libraries has used them and are as a whole against any form of censorship (White 1986).[2] The Supreme Court defined obscene (i.e., illegal material) by "applying contemporary community standards." If we grant that the "community" using a library is *opposed* to censorship of sexual material, let's get on with giving them what they want.[3] One can draw the line at "hard core" because it is not cataloged on OCLC or elsewhere.

STANDARD COMMUNITY FARE?

In any case, print pornography may be turning into something of a moot issue. According to *The New York Times* (1987), dirty books are victims of the videocassette recorder. Why read when you can look at an X-rated film? A combination of the sexual revolution and modern technology has induced numbness when it comes to considering the various forms of today's pornography—with or without literary style.

Playboy is now middle aged, if not merely the dirty old man's touchstone with the days when the centerfold was the ultimate in pornographic thrills. Other widely distributed magazines, from *Hustler* to *Penthouse*, are fighting a lost battle for subscribers. Interest in such sexual fantasy magazines comes largely from men who fail to realize the potential of video or, more likely, who hope to keep their secret viewing disguised between the innocuous pages of sport, fast living, and the joys of grooming. Still, just because Bacchus is getting older is no reason to exercise methodical age bias in the library. Most of these titles should be where the old boys can find them.

Switch on the television or pop into a movie, and the invasion of the nude is overwhelming. If Hedy Lamarr once shocked with a long distance view of her behind, now the only joy left is the couple who go to bed without showing the viewer every pimple on their bodies. Saturation, boredom, and VCRs conspire to make the old battles about pornography as academic as whether Eve should have taken a bite out of the apple.

COPING WITH CENSORSHIP

So, granted, if you will, the ubiquity of sexual images all around us. And also granted, at least in theory, an appreciation of the difference between pornography as sexual material with serious literary, artistic, political, or social value (see definition of pornography at the beginning of this chapter), and obscenity as material banned in a specific court case. Then why all the fuss about *pornography*? The answer is that the concept of pornography generalizes and becomes a spear carrier for a much more dangerous type of censorship, in which the target is not set by a court decision but by something much broader. If former Attorney General Meese can say that the librarians and publishers "failed to provide us with evidence to support claims of excess suppression in the name of obscenity laws," this is to read the record from the point of view of the general who launches the warriors. True, there may be no specific "record of any prosecution of a librarian on obscenity charges," (Attorney General's Commission on Pornography 1986) but what is one to make of the report from the American Library Association:

> The rate of reports of book banning nationwide sent into the ALA's Chicago headquarters had held steady at about 300 per year until an explosion five years ago, when librarians and writers saw a need to establish Banned Books Week. Now, the number of yearly reports has topped 1,000. But because the vast majority of incidents go unreported, [Judith] Krug believes that figure in reality is closer to 5,000 a year. (*The Albany Times Union* 1987)[4]

What does *Back Door Housewife* have in common with *Silas Marner*? Both are considered dirty books. The former is included on the list of paperbacks worth banning by the Attorney General's Commission on Pornography (*Final Report*, p. 1549). George Eliot's classic is labelled "immoral" by a fun loving group in California, as is, incidentally, A.E. Hotchner's Doris Day biography by a group in Alabama (*The Albany Times Union* 1987).

The librarian is in an odd position. One can be opposed to the "housewife at the back door" and still have an understandable love for Doris Day. No matter. If either book is on the shelves, the librarian is fond of pornography. Ridiculous? Anti-intellectual? Shocking? All of this, but welcome to the double-speak world of the censor.

You challenge this type of nut with a firm sense of your professional duty—and that duty should be to defend what is in the library, harmless, pornographic, sophisticated, or not. Assuming the selection is carefully considered, once the material is on the shelves, there it stays until dated, worn, or exhausted. But under no circumstances must it fall victim to the censor's debilitating notion about sex or anything else.

Vagueness is the classic tool of oppressive censorship, particularly from the religious and political right. Right-wing censors may not be quite sure what the film *Last Tango in Paris* is really about, but it's dirty. Ditto for *La Cage aux Folles*. (See the report on objections to both films at the Miami-Dade Public Library, *Library Journal*, September 15, 1987, p. 18.) The librarian, on the other hand, can fight this type of uncertainty only with the conviction that both films are not only "acceptable" in the library, but necessary as examples of much favored "hits" in the eyes of the public.

When evangelists such as Pat Robertson object to textbooks that promote "godless views" (including notions about sex), they can only be checked by equally firm stands by librarians. Eventually, the courts come around to common sense: e.g., an Atlanta judge recently ruled against the banning of 33 textbooks in Alabama. Meanwhile, it's up to the librarian to stand and be counted.

Applause, then, for everyone from the Librarian of Congress, who objected to discontinuing the brailling of *Playboy*, to Glenna Nowell, director of a Maine library, who fought a battle against Maine's so-called pornographic referendum, and, incidentally, won the Hugh M. Hefner First Amendment Award for Education in 1987.

All of this is easy to discuss, but as Gerald Shields points out, fights against the censor can be costly in terms of energy and just plain emotion. "Most of those librarians he interviewed (for an upcoming book) quit the profession out of disillusionment following a book banning battle." (*The Albany Times Union* 1987)

Numerous librarians take another stand and freely admit to being themselves censors. They do not acquire books that they consider "pornographic." As Will Manley puts it, "The public library has to draw the line of censorship. The public demands it. Too often when librarians get on their soapbox and preach a message of intellectual freedom extremism they forget about some basic practical considerations" (Manley 1987).[5] Manley is on the line. I am about a million miles removed. I don't agree with him or others with his point of view, but respect is in order.

More to the point, though, is the conviction of not a few working librarians that they know "reality." Speculation about the meaning of that word is as confusing as the definition of pornography. Those with their feet in the cement of "reality" may regard the rest of us with cynical amusement, including the aforementioned victims of censorship listed by Mr. Shields. Yet, who is to say who has a more positive definition of reality?

THE REAL THREAT OF PORNOGRAPHY

A much stronger argument than community feeling may be made against pornography. It is pernicious, threatening to undermine our culture by encouraging bigotry, sexism, violence, and intolerance. There is a tension between the delights of pornography and the harm it may cause, but still, this seems wildly overdone, and, moreover, the problem is not unique to pornography. A much worse danger is the resurrection of another Anthony Comstock, the nineteenth-century censor who terrorized the publishing world for many years. Attempts by those who hope to reclaim his role are chronicled regularly in *The Newsletter on Intellectual Freedom*.

In his *The Secret Museum* (1987), Walter Kendrick points out time and time again that pornography is a synonym in many people's minds for anarchy. Censorship often is a form of social and political control, with pornography as a created and convenient scapegoat. If one accepts this idea, then it seems much worse to ban pornography under the mistaken notion that this in itself will control unacceptable behavior.

I don't wish to brush aside the feminist concern. Pornography usually degrades women; there's no question that this is true. It's also true in your average romantic novel and countless issues of popular women's magazines. It's more vicious in pornography, but the end result is no different. However, it seems to me that the evolution of women's rights can't include repressive censorship, or the distinctive character of its battle will be lost.

PORNOGRAPHY IN THE LIBRARY

In conclusion, the library should have its share of good pornography, certainly the stuff that surfaces in everything from modern advertising and Erica Jong's delightful novels to buttock films and the steamy sex suggested by rock music. The object of this improbable and, to a few, degenerate argument is that the vast majority of elements in pornography, no matter what name it carries, are of popular origin and are now part of our society; to ignore this is to cripple the capabilities of serving a literate, discriminating, and rational audience.

Like anyone else, I have a blacklist of unfavorite books, magazines, and films. I consider it bad taste to shout about them, but at least I'm not trying to keep, for example, *The Reader's Digest* out of the library. Let's hope readers of this chapter can say the same about their biases, including their definition and ideas of pornography.

ENDNOTES

1. **Editor's Note:** This definition is the crux of Katz' argument. He is *not* using the term *pornography* as a casual or colloquial synonym for *obscenity*, an equation often made in common discourse. Instead, he is retaining the concept of "obscene" for material that has been banned by a court and is using "pornographic" for material that has *not* been so banned, i.e., is legal to possess, distribute, and show. From this, it follows that pornography is not "obscene," no matter how easy it is to use the terms as synonyms in contexts other than this essay.

2. *The Chronicle of Higher Education*, January 18, 1984, reported the same discovery, i.e., that only about one quarter of the "better educated" favor any type of censorship.

3. In *Pope v. Illinois*, 1987, the court ruled that the social value of material must be evaluated from the standpoint of a "reasonable person." It seems safe to say that most people who regularly use libraries are not only a minority (no more than 30% of the public), but also "reasonable."

4. See any issue of *Newsletter on Intellectual Freedom* for reports on these cases. For example, the July 1987 issue shows among "targets for the censors" such titles as *The Confessions of Nat Turner* and *Oedipus the King*.

5. For another equally thoughtful argument for censorship, see Carol Hole, "Who, Me, Censor?" *Top of the News*, Winter, 1984: 147–153; as well as a follow-up article by Hole in the Spring 1985 issue, pp. 236–247.

REFERENCES

The Albany Times Union, September 20, 1987: G1, 2.

Attorney General's Commission on Pornography. 1986. *Final report*, July: 270.

Chronicle of Higher Education, January 18, 1984: 5, 8.

Katz, Bill. 1971. The pornography collection. *Library Journal*, December 15: 4060–4066.

Kendrick, Walter. 1987. *The secret museum: Pornography in modern culture.* New York: Viking.

Manley, Will. 1987. Facing the public. *Wilson Library Bulletin*, February: 33.

The New York Times, August 31, 1987: B1.

Recession in X rated industry. 1986. *The New York Times*, October 5: 6.

Tynan, Kenneth. 1969. Pornography? And is it that bad? *The New York Times*, July 15: Sec. 2, p. 3.

White, Howard D. 1986. Majorities for censorship. *Library Journal*, July: 31–38.

CHAPTER 5

Pornography in the Library? No!

Will Manley

Getting pornography into libraries is a lot like having sex in the 1990s. Our motives always look fine; our intentions always appear pure. The person we're having sex with is always someone we care about, someone with whom we want to express our affection in a most intimate way. We tell ourselves that having sex with another person is a particularly effective way of saying "I'm attracted to you, I care about you, and I want to explore a deeper relationship with you." At least that's what we say in our more sanctimonious moments. What we tend to forget about are the tragic results that can occur.

Likewise, when we talk about getting pornography into libraries, we talk in the most idealistic terms. We talk about intellectual freedom, creative expression, and Constitutional rights. But in all this idealism we blissfully ignore the obvious downside—pornography in the library can create the impression that we are merely sophisticated smut peddlers. And in today's "safe sex" environment, can we afford to have that image? That is the bottom line. That is what this issue is all about.

A LITTLE HISTORY

Pornography probably gained whatever legitimacy it now enjoys during the 1960s. Beginning in that decade, sex became freed from the chains of monogamous obligation and was no longer a sacred right or duty reserved to spouses. It became something free, common, and democratic. In the post-pill paradise of the 1960s, social norms changed, and it became socially acceptable for anybody to have sex

with anybody else. Certain taboos—adultery, miscegenation, homosexuality, bondage, etc.—became not only tolerable but desirable.
Swingers' clubs, topless restaurants, and gay bath houses grew up and
propagated at a rapid rate. The big bestseller of the 1960s was John
Updike's *Couples*, an ode to suburban adultery. Sexual freedom had
moved from the red light district of the big city to Main Street
U.S.A., and Hugh Hefner moved from being called a smut peddler to
a social philosopher. Sex became a big banquet, and everyone was
encouraged to feast.

And then came the morning after—the skyrocketing divorce rate,
the alarming number of abortions, the explosion of teenage pregnancies, and the spread of an eclectic array of troublesome, new venereal
diseases: such as herpes, vaginal warts, cervical cancer, and Chlamy-
dia. But the real awakening was AIDS; the party was over and the bill
had arrived.

Suddenly, it was the 1950s all over again. Condoms, with a new
upscale image, once again became a growth industry. Monogamy was
now trendy, and books were being written on the joys of celibacy.
This new attitude of "Puritan chic" now alive in the land was
dramatically manifested in the public flogging Gary Hart received for
committing an indiscretion that in the 1960s probably would have
been condoned.

The sexual revolution had come full circle. Culturally, the movie
"Fatal Attraction" was the flip-side to Updike's *Couples*. Adultery was
now seen as a dangerous and deadly act. In her role as the crazed,
spurned lover, Glenn Close seemed to represent not only the dark
side of random promiscuity (a kind of personification of AIDS), but
also the unwillingness of the 1980s woman to be exploited sexually.

Women were now no longer eager to be used. They had had it
with men who, intentionally or not, spread pregnancy and venereal
diseases as if they were tools of social regimentation. By 1987,
women seemed to be saying that the sexual revolution of the 1960s
had been a male revolution after all. It was time to change the rules.

Ironically, in the sexual ethics of the 1980s a most unusual and
uncomfortable alliance had evolved. The Liberty Bible Church had
been mated with Women Against Pornography. The women's libbers
were now in the same bed with the fundamentalists. These partners
may not have been having group sex together, but they were certainly
in the same bed. Both wanted an end to pornography—the fundamentalists for religious reasons, and the feminists for holistic reasons.

It is within this new frame of reference that the issue of pornography in libraries must now be examined. The old arguments are no
longer sufficient. And in this context it must be freely admitted that
librarianship is largely a profession of women. Although women may
not dominate the positions of leadership and power within the profession, there can be no argument that they dominate the day-to-day

operation of libraries. It is the women of the profession, by and large, who select, catalog, process and check out the books. Solely on the basis of gender, therefore, it would appear that libraries would not be fertile grounds in which to sow the wild oats of pornography and erotica.

IDEALS AND REALITY

But this does not take into consideration the strong commitment that most librarians, male or female, have to an extreme form of intellectual freedom. Trained by library school professors who acknowledge no legitimate limits to collection development and guided by a Library Bill of Rights that boldly says, "Librarians should challenge censorship," most librarians would prefer being charged with homicide to being accused by their professional peers of practicing censorship.

This professional ideal has been not only reinforced but strengthened by the euphoria created by the recent Bicentennial celebrations for the U.S. Constitution. Inebriated with a renewed sense of purpose, librarians now more than ever pose as fervent defenders of the First Amendment. So at a time when pornography is coming under greater and greater criticism, librarians are ironically giving renewed thought to including pornography and erotic materials in their collections as an exercise of what they see as their First Amendment rights. Thus we are presented with the anomaly of a female-dominated profession defending the right of Hugh Hefner and Bob Guccione to have their publications line up cheek to cheek with the likes of *People, McCall's,* and *Ceramics Monthly* on library periodical display racks.

Certainly there is a kind of nobility in defending something that one considers deplorable. It takes courage to say, "I don't agree with what you are saying, but I agree with your right to say it." That argument, while valid when applied to the First Amendment in general, does not necessarily apply to library acquisitions policies. In fact, there is a built-in tension between the First Amendment and the process of library book selection. On the one hand, the First Amendment is almost unlimited in its openness; on the other hand, library book selection is by its very nature a limiting task.

Any responsible library book selection policy spells out those limitations. "We will not buy textbooks." "We will not buy technical, legal, and medical books." "We will not acquire light romances or love stories." All these limitations have appeared in the book selection policies of various libraries. Why do these limitations exist? For one very practical reason: The given library does not feel, for one reason or another, that it has either the responsibility or the resources to provide its users with these materials. The reason may be lack of money, or it may be lack of purpose. The important question to ask is, how often is the accusation of censorship leveled at the librarian who intentionally disqualifies textbooks from the collection?

CENSORSHIP AND PORNOGRAPHY

The obvious answer is that since no library can be all things to all people, it is inappropriate to confuse censorship with the necessity of making choices based on economic constraints. But this begs a further question: When does a librarian commit the sin of censorship? By and large library censorship occurs in two situations: 1) when a librarian sets overly restrictive limitations on the collection (for example, a public library decides not to collect any materials on Islam), and 2) when a librarian intentionally fails to provide balanced or comprehensive coverage for a subject that legitimately falls within the scope of the library's collection (for example, the librarian decides to develop a collection on communism but intentionally excludes the works of Lenin).

On the basis of the first censorship situation, do librarians perpetrate acts of censorship if they purposefully exclude pornographic works from their collections? On what grounds can pornography legitimately be excluded from a library collection? Take your pick. Librarians have self-righteously banned what they have deemed to be pornography on any number of grounds: religious, moral, ethical, social, or feminist.

Each of these grounds can, however, be easily refuted and are therefore intellectually dishonest rationalizations. Take, for example, the argument that pornography violates mainstream religious or ethical norms. The same thing can be said of any number of other subjects such as communism, abortion, or euthanasia. Does that mean that we should not provide coverage of these issues? To exclude pornography from a collection on the basis of morals is to walk on the quicksand of relativity. Whose moral norms are you going to use—Billy Graham's or Hugh Hefner's? Have fun explaining that one to your patrons. How about the feminist argument that pornography should be suppressed because it promotes the subjugation of women? If we hang our hat on that hook, then we must be prepared to suppress any number of other books that define the role of the woman strictly in terms of the traditional housewife, homemaker, and mother. How about the argument that pornography encourages violence? On those lines are we prepared to suppress every sophisticated British murder mystery that might incite its reticent, pipe-smoking reader to acts of homicide? The problem with justifying the suppression of pornography is that it opens so many doors that lead to the censorship of other types of materials.

If we accept the premise that there are no logically consistent reasons for not collecting pornography, then we move on to censorship situation two. Here is where the intellectual freedom extremists eventually lose their nerve. The U.S. publishing industry offers a rather lavish and delectable banquet of pornographic soups and salads, meat and potatoes, sauces and syrups. Unfortunately, the First Amendment enthusiasts of our profession seem to be under the illusion that the state of the art of contemporary American pornography is solely defined by Hugh Hefner and his winsome daughter, Christie. *Playboy* magazine, however, is no more representative of mainstream American pornography than the Harlequin romance is representative of contemporary American literature. *Playboy* is the Winnie-the-Pooh of eroticism and not nearly so warm and fuzzy. If librarians think that *Playboy* is what the connoisseur of today's upbeat raunch really desires, they really haven't done their homework.

But this is understandable. Pornographic and erotic materials are neither intensively nor extensively reviewed in our profession's standard book reviewing journals. Therefore, a visit to the local adult bookstore is a necessity to the librarian whose commitment to intellectual freedom is more than just tokenistic lip service. Just as the dedicated collection developer should beat the bushes to collect propaganda from all the nickel-and-dime churches in the community to give a sense of balance to the religion section, he or she should also check out the scene at the local porn shop.

I am confident that such a trip will deflower the intellectual virginity of even the most ardent intellectual freedom extremist. Here in all of its unexpurgated oozings and interlockings is what pornography is all about—not exactly stuff that you'd want to take home to Gramps unless, of course, Gramps happens to be into bondage, bestiality, and bisexuality. But once you decide to put your big toe into the shallow waters of soft core porn, how are you possibly going to justify staying out of the depths of the hard core stuff? There's no way you can begin and end your pornography collection with *Playboy*. That's like calling it quits after foreplay. It's not only intellectually indefensible, it's also discriminatory. *Playboy* is obviously oriented around servicing the tastes of the heterosexual American male. But there is a vast cornucopia of materials intended for women and gays. They too have needs to be serviced. The librarian who buys *Playboy* and chooses not to give patrons a taste of the other types of pornographic pickles and sauces is just as much a censor as the one who refuses to buy *Playboy* in the first place. When it comes to intellectual freedom and pornography in libraries, no one's a virgin.

Keeping pornography out of libraries or limiting the scope of pornography is censorship, pure and simple. There is no way to have our cake and eat it too on this subject. If we keep pornography out of our libraries we are, as much as we hate to admit it, censors pure and simple. We are violating the sacred Library Bill of Rights.

A PRACTICAL PROPOSAL

But to say that is not to say that we are acting irresponsibly if we do not collect pornography. We have violated no laws and committed no sins. We have made our decision on very sound management grounds, namely, a concern for good public relations. Unfortunately many librarians consider the term *public relations* to represent something less than honorable. Making a stand based on PR appears cowardly, and we don't want to appear cowardly. We want to appear as though we make our tough decisions on the basis of firm professional principles.

What we librarians as a profession have never understood, however, is that *public relations* is not a dirty word and that creating a favorable image for ourselves is not a "sell-out." The fact of the matter is that if librarians were more public relations oriented and more image conscious, the field of librarianship would not be the occupational doormat that it now is.

Pornography and eroticism are sensationalist materials that draw far more attention to themselves than they could possibly merit. I can think of about 999 other things that are of greater danger to Western civilization than pornography. But, unfortunately, pornography rates right up there with cruise missiles and AIDS as a national issue. This has something to do with America's residual puritanism. Nathaniel Hawthorne got it right. Deep down inside, many Americans think that sex is sinful. It is for this reason and this reason alone that libraries should exclude pornography. From a public relations standpoint, there is nothing to gain and everything to lose by getting into the skin trade. We do not need to give the growing hordes of fundamentalist Christians and women's libbers further moralistic ammunition for monkeying around with library acquisitions policies. We do not need to raise a red flag for our taxpayers to charge at. We do not need to give our governing bodies nice, moralistic reasons to vote down library budgets. With all the other negative image baggage we carry around, we do not need to be seen in public with Hugh Hefner or Larry Flynt. It is wishful thinking to hope that some of their insouciance might give to librarians just enough tarnish to make our own up-tight, virginal image seem almost normal. It would be like Richard Nixon hanging around Hulk Hogan to absorb some of his blue collar macho—not only hopeless but bogus.

It's time for librarians to cease all the preaching about the moralistic reasons compelling them to exclude pornography from their collections and face the truth. The truth is that today keeping pornography out of the library is good public relations. Who wants to fly in the face of a strong alliance of parents, right-wing fanatics, and left-wing feminists? Only a fool.

To say this is not to be so naive as to deny that there are millions of normal, well-adjusted people who enjoy pornography and who consume it by the truckful. And, if the truth be known, many of the parents, right-wing fanatics, and left-wing feminists alluded to in the previous paragraph are among those who regularly sample its delicacies. But, by and large, Americans prefer to experience the enjoyments of pornography in the privacy of their own homes and they prefer to pay for these enjoyments with their own money. They do not expect libraries to satisfy their erotic needs.

However, by excluding pornography from libraries, librarians are not excluding pornography from society. We may be censors, but we're not violating anyone's First Amendment rights and we're not ruining anyone's sex life.

CHAPTER 6

Research and Archival Value of Erotica/Pornography

Vern L. Bullough

Some of the most valuable research tools in any library are found in those sections of special collections where erotic/pornographic materials are kept. Such collections not only give us insights into the mindsets of past librarians, but they are also one of the major sources of information about sexual practices in the past. Moreover, they give data about certain kinds of social problems—data that cannot be found anywhere else.

PAST LIBRARIANS

Granted that most libraries keep any significant amount of material dealing with sexuality in some kind of special collection if only to avoid theft and mutilation, there still are many items in special collections that are there only because someone in the past regarded them as either too erotic or too pornographic to leave on the open shelves. I have found in special collections, for example, many of the writings of Pierre Louÿs (1870–1925), best known for his *Chansons de Bilitis,* prose poems about lesbian love in ancient Greece, and his *Aphrodite,* a novel about a courtesan in ancient Alexandria. Many of the Louÿs works found in the special collections of some libraries are part of the Lotus Library series published by Liveright in the 1920s. This series included the works of such other French writers as Gustav Flaubert (1821–1880), the advocate of realism in fiction, and the more macabre Theophile Gautier (1811–1872), best remembered for his *Mlle. de Maupin* (1835). Also found in special collections in these same libraries are the writings of Pierre de Bourdeilles, Seigneur de Brantôme (1535?–1614), whose writings are full of gossip about his contemporaries (1933); the lesbian novel, *The Well of Loneliness* (1929) by Radclyffe Hall; and the classic study by Henry Reed Stiles (1934) on bundling. Probably no librarian today would consent to having such works put in special collections unless they were first editions; but the fact that such books were once put there and in some cases still remain is an effective reminder about past attitudes toward sexuality.

It is also interesting to find out what works are *rarely* included in special collections even though they are major sources of data about sexual practices. Included in this category are legal, medical, and theological works that, in today's terminology, include sexually explicit materials. Undoubtedly, the library patrons who protested some of the more sexually explicit aspects of literary works apparently either never consulted such specialized books or perhaps believed that because many of the authors put a few of the sexually explicit terms in Latin or Greek no one would understand them. They may have also believed that professionals for whom such books were written would never read just to satisfy any prurient interest.

PAST SEXUAL PRACTICES—AND EFFECTS

Though gathering data about what constituted erotic or pornographic material in the past is important, the most valuable function that such collections serve in the library is to provide data usually not available elsewhere. This is particularly true in the case of sexual practices that were and to some extent still are stigmatized. It is from classical pornographic works, for example, that we find that it is possible to document that the Greeks were accustomed to use different positions in intercourse than the Romans (Marks 1978). It is from such works as the "pornographic" *Aristotle's Masterpiece* (n.d.) that we get detailed information about erotic arousal or foreplay (Bullough 1973), whereas the writings of Casanova (1932) give us data about the early use of contraceptives. Similarly "pornographic" works give information that is difficult if not impossible to find elsewhere about such stigmatized sexual activities as homosexuality, bondage, and masochism.

Sometimes the data gathered from such works emphasize the existence of possible institutional problems and practices in the past that require the historian to reassess popular assumptions. A good example is the underground writing about flagellation in the Victorian period in England.

The pseudonymous Pisanus Fraxi (actually Henry Spencer Ashbee) (reprinted 1962) wrote about spanking and birching:

> Books innumerable in the English language are devoted to this
> subject alone; no English bawdy book is free from descriptions of

flagellation, and numerous separate plates exist, depicting whipping scenes. . . . [In the nineteenth century] very sumptuously fitted up establishments, exclusively devoted to the administration of the birch, were not uncommon in London, and women of the town [prostitutes] served, as it were, an apprenticeship in order to acquire the art of gracefully and effectively administering the rod. (pp. xl–xli)

The validity of this statement is effectively demonstrated by the pornography of the time. In such books as *The Merry Order of St. Bridget* (1857), *Sublime of Flagellation* (n.d.), *The Romance of Chastisement* (1866), and *Venus School Mistress* (c. 1830) and similar works, boys or young men are spanked or birched, usually by older women. There are even semi-scholarly pornographic studies of spanking (Cooper 1896).

Since few of the pornographic works detail spanking by parents but rather emphasize spanking by nonfamily members, it would seem that spanking acquired erotic connotations outside the family, most probably in the English schools—particularly the English public schools—where birching was a standard practice. Without attempting to apply modern psychoanalytic techniques, which would demand a much longer discussion, it would seem that this common practice was leaving scars upon the psyche of students. This pornography certainly gives a different view of the effects of English schools than the one available from standard sources, and it reinforces the efforts of modern experts in child development to use caution in spanking as a punishment.

Similar questions are raised about "petticoat punishment," which apparently was often used in the home. The surviving fictional accounts of this practice recount how recalcitrant and unmanageable boys underwent some form of petticoat punishment to make them docile and feminine. An adult female, sometimes the mother, other times a female relative or governess, is the dominant figure.

Two such works are *Miss High Heels* (reprinted 1969) and *Gynecocracy* (reprinted 1971). In the first, Dennis Evelyn Eryls is transformed under the direction of his step-sister, Helen, into a very proper young woman. This was achieved by putting him in corsets and sending him to a girl's school where each infraction of his discipline led him to be put in ever more restrictive corsets. He becomes almost totally subject to the whims of Helen and her female friends.

In the second, Julian Robinson, Viscount Ladywood, like Dennis, had demonstrated too much energy as a boy, and so his parents had shipped him away to be disciplined. The novel concluded:

The petticoat, as administered by Mademoiselle and then by Beatrice, after all is said and done, I considered extremely beneficial. . . A woman can make a man. In the first place she has the monopoly of the making, for she alone can conceive and give birth to him, and in the next place she can make him by discipline, by instilling her common sense into him and by keeping him rigidly under thumb. . . I confess. . . that I love my bondage and I love my tyrant. . . . There is a wonderful luxuriousness and sensuality in being made to bow down before a woman, and to perform her behests. . . . My lady's stockings and drawers upon me give me, whenever I am reminded that I want them, an electrifying thrill through and through. And as for the management of affairs, well they are much better managed by my wife than they could be by me. . . . This world is woman's earth, and it is petticoated all over. Theirs is the dominion, turn and twist the matter as you will. (pp. 405–406)

Perhaps it was through reading such "pornographic classics" that specialists in child development came to urge parents not to engage in petticoat punishment. Certainly if such books have any validity, the sequellae of such punishment continued long after the child became an adult.

By far the most numerous of underground books and submerged or repressed verses are those dealing with homosexuality, particularly male homosexuality. Anthologies published in the last two or three decades, and derived from previously restricted collections of erotica and pornography, emphasize just how widespread writing on such themes was in the past (Smith 1970; Reade 1970). It is the resurrection and republication of this previously restricted material that has helped gay men and lesbian women come to terms with themselves.

PRACTICES AND ATTITUDES, PAST AND PRESENT

Erotic and pornographic writings also serve to emphasize that standards change and that some of the burning issues of today existed in the past but were not regarded in quite the same light. This is an important corrective in such areas as child abuse, which some conservative critics seem to imply is a result of the decline of the family and the absence of the mother into the work force. Instead, what the current emphasis on child abuse represents is a changing attitude towards children and towards adult-child sexual interactions.

Many respectable individuals in the past formed attachments to either prepubescent children or adolescents. George Gordon, Lord Byron (1788–1824), was attracted to a young French-Greek lad, Nicolo Giraud, who had been a painter's model before Byron found him. Later, Byron was involved with Loukas Chalandritsanos, a 15-year-old who was with Byron when Byron was killed (Crompton 1985).

Charles Dodgeson ("Lewis Carroll") and J.M. Barrie, well-known authors of popular classics, would have been charged with child molestation if they were still alive. Carroll was attracted to prepubescent girls, whom he enjoyed photographing in the nude (Bullough 1983). Barrie's classic *Peter Pan* seems to have reflected his own ideal sexual partner more than is generally realized (Birkin 1979).

Both young girls and young boys were commonly prostituted in the not-too-distant past (Bullough & Bullough 1987); and though the prostitution and exploitation of children can be documented from a variety of sources, it is only in the so-called pornographic works that detailed descriptions appear. Through these descriptions it becomes possible to understand the mindset of a time in England when a child at the age of 12 could consent to his or her own seduction, an attitude that most Americans find difficult to understand.

A good example comes from the anonymously authored memoirs, *My Secret Life* (1902, reprinted 1966). The author wrote the following about having sex with young girls:

> Verily a gentleman had better fuck them for money, than a butcher boy [fuck them] for nothing. It is the fate of such girls to be fucked young, neither laws social nor legal can prevent it. Given opportunities—who has them like the children of the poor—and they will copulate. It is the law of nature which nothing can thwart. A man need have no "compunctions of conscience"—as it is termed—about having such girls first, for assuredly he will have done no harm, and has only been an agent in the inevitable. The consequences to the female being the same, whosoever she may have first been fucked by. (*My Secret Life*, II, 206)

He reported that the youngest girl with whom he had sex was 10-years-old and for which act he had paid her "aunt" 10 English pounds. He added, however, that she "was the youngest I ever yet have had, or have wished to have" and complained that she could not give the pleasures "that fully developed women could." Nonetheless, he reported having had several orgasms with her (*My Secret Life*, II, 206).

Obviously, the great value of erotic and pornographic collections of the past is in giving us the kind of insights into their period that today might be derived from a psychiatrist's or clinical psychologist's notebook. Such insights also serve to put us on guard by emphasizing the necessity of looking beneath the seemingly calm surface of past institutional history for the existence of many of the same problems that we face today. In sum, a significant number of doctoral dissertations might be written from the data found in the erotic and pornographic collections in major (and even some minor) libraries. These collections give the researcher the kind of historical data that society has deemed important to repress; but it is just such data that can prove to be most helpful in understanding both ourselves and our ancestors.

REFERENCES

Aristotle's masterpiece or the complete works of Aristotle. 1711–1900?. Various publishers.

Birkin, Andrew. 1979. *J.M. Barrie and the lost boys.* New York: Charles N. Potter.

Brantôme, Pierre de Bourdeilles, Seigneur de. 1933. *Lives of fair and gallant ladies.* Translated by A.R. Allison. New York: Liveright.

Bullough, Vern L. 1973. An early American sex manual, or Aristotle who? *Early American Literature,* 7: 236–246.

Bullough, Vern L. 1983. Lewis Carroll. *Medical Aspects of Human Sexuality* 15, October: 134–140.

Bullough, Vern L. 1976. *Sexual variance in society and history.* Chicago: University of Chicago Press.

Bullough, Vern L., and Bonnie Bullough. 1987. *Women and prostitution.* Buffalo, NY: Prometheus Books.

Casanova, Jacques. 1932. *The memoirs of Jacques Casanova de Seingalt.* Translated by Arthur Machen. New York: A. and C. Boni.

Cooper, William H. 1896. *A history of the rod in all countries.* Revised. London: William Reeves.

Crompton, Louis. 1985. *Byron and Greek love.* Berkeley: University of California Press.

Fraxi, Pisanus [Henry Spencer Ashbee]. 1962. *Bibliography of prohibited books.* Introduction by G. Legman. Reprinted. New York: Jack Brussel.

Gautier, Theophile. 1835. *Mlle. de Maupin.* Many editions, including one in Modern Library.

Gynecocracy: A narrative of the adventures and psychological experiences of Julian Robinson (afterwards Viscount Ladywood) under petticoat rule. 1971. Reprinted. New York: Grove Press.

Hall, Radclyffe. 1929. *The well of loneliness.* New York: Covici Friede.

Louÿs, Pierre. 1913. *Women and puppet.* Translated by G.F. Motherhead. New York: Brentano's.

Louÿs, Pierre. 1926. *Collected works.* New York: Liveright.

Marks, Margaret Carole. 1978. Heterosexual coital positions as a reflection of ancient and modern cultural attitudes. Ph.D. Dissertation, State University of New York, Buffalo.

The merry order of St. Bridget: Personal recollections of the use of the rod. 1857. York, England: Printed for the Author's Friends.

Miss high heels. 1969. Reprinted. New York: Grove Press.

My secret life. 1966. Introduction by G. Legman. Reprinted in 11 vols. New York: Grove Press.

Reade, Briane, ed. 1970. *Sexual heretics: Male homosexuality in English literature from 1850 to 1900.* New York: Coward McCann.

The romance of chastisement: Or the revelations of D'Arcy. 1866. London: n.p.

Smith, Timothy D'Arch. 1970. *Love in earnest: Some notes on the lives and writings of English Uranian poets from 1889–1930.* London: Routledge and Kegan Paul.

Stiles, Henry Reed. 1934. *Bundling: Its origins, progress and decline in America.* Reprinted. New York: Book Collectors Association.

Sublime of flagellation: In letters from Lady Termagent Flaybum of Birch Grove to Lady Harriet Tickletail of Bumfiddle Hall. n.d. London: George Peacock.

Venus school mistress; Or birch sports. c. 1830. n.p.

CHAPTER 7

Feminism, Pornography, and Libraries

Christine Jenkins

Pornography, like rape, is a male invention, designed to dehumanize women, to reduce the female to an object of sexual access, not to free sensuality from moralistic or parental inhibition. The staple of porn will always be the naked female body . . . . Pornography is the undiluted essence of anti-female propaganda. (Brownmiller 1980)

In itself, pornography—which, my dictionary and I agree, means any image or description intended or used to arouse sexual desire—does not strike me as the proper object of a political crusade. As the most cursory observation suggests, there are many varieties of porn, some pernicious, some more or less benign. About the only generalization one can make is that pornography is the return of the repressed, of feelings and fantasies driven underground by a culture that atomizes sexuality, defining love as a noble affair of the heart and mind, lust as a base animal urge centered in unmentionable organs. (Willis 1983, 462)

The woman's sex is appropriated, her body is possessed, she is used and she is despised: the pornography does it and the pornography proves it. (Dworkin 1981)

Perhaps one could simply say that erotica is about sexuality, but pornography is about power and sex-as-weapon—in the same way we have come to understand that rape is about violence, and not really about sexuality at all. (Steinem 1980)

Copyright © 1991 by Christine Jenkins. The author wishes to thank the feminist librarians who participated in the discussion on feminist librarians' responses to pornography and the feminist anti-pornography movement, chaired by the author at the 1985 ALA annual conference, as well as friends and colleagues who lent ideas, insights, questions, and support to the writing of this chapter.

Between, say, *Ulysses* at one end and *Snuff* at the other, erotica/por-
nography conveys all sorts of mixed messages that elicit complicated
and private responses. In practice, attempts to sort out good erotica
from bad porn inevitably come down to "What turns me on is erotic; what turns you on is pornography." (Willis 1983, 463)

Not all pornography is violent, but even the most banal pornography objectifies women's bodies. An essential ingredient of much
rape and other forms of violence to women is the "objectification"
of the woman. This is not just rhetoric. It means that women are
not seen as human beings but as things. Men are reared to view
females in this way, pornography thrives off this and feeds it, and
rape is one of the consequences. (Russell 1980)

While all feminists deplore violence against women, there is a broad
range of opinion among feminists on the interrelationship of sexuality, violence, and pornography. Some feminists do not believe that
pornography causes violence in any simple and direct way. Many
feminists, even those who are critical of pornography, are as dis-
turbed by the idea of putting limitations on First Amendment
protection of free speech as they are by the presentation of unsatis-
factory images of women in pornography. (FACT 1985)

FEMINISTS CONSIDER PORNOGRAPHY

There is no single feminist position on the issue of pornography.
As the above quotes illustrate, feminists have found themselves divided, even splintered, on this issue. There is a wide range of opinions and theories, and few lend themselves to easy summarization.

For some, feminism's response to pornography conjures up
images of picketers outside convenience stores that sell *Playboy* and
Penthouse. This is one aspect, but by no means the only one. Again,
there is no monolithic feminist position on pornography. In reality,
feminists have a long history of supporting the publication, sale, and
distribution of materials that many people have (and do) consider
"pornography." Women's health information, including birth control
information, has been controversial since the 1800s, and feminists
like Margaret Sanger have been prosecuted under obscenity statutes
for distributing "family-planning" publications. More recently, *Our
Bodies, Ourselves*, a popular feminist health and sex education book
for women, has faced repeated challenges in libraries (and appeared
on the Eagle Forum's "hit list") because it contains information about
a range of options regarding women's sexuality and because it does
not predicate a woman's sex life on marriage and family.

Some groups have labelled this material "pornographic," particularly when it is aimed—as it often is—at young people. Feminists do
not make this equation. Although some may not care for a particular
book's approach or tone, the majority of feminists want the discus-

sion of sexual matters to occur in a free and open manner. Books and audiovisual materials containing explicit information about human reproduction and sexual behavior and health (including AIDS information) are *not* considered pornography by feminists.

The precise definition of "pornography" has been debated ever since the word entered the English language in the mid-1800s (Kendrick 1987, 1-11). In twentieth-century Western society, "pornography" generally refers to material that is considered sexually explicit, potentially arousing, and unsuitable for display to the "general public." The feminist pornography debate, or as some have come to call it, the Porn Wars, is over the magazines, books, and videos produced by the "sex industry" and available from newsstands, adult bookstores, and mail-order houses. The images in this material are created expressly to arouse the viewer sexually. The industry that produces much of this material is large and profitable. Estimates of yearly sales within the U.S. run into billions of dollars.

Traditionally, men may view pornography, but it has been considered off-limits for women and children. "Adults only" bookstores and display racks are male territory in our culture. Just as sexual slang is called "locker room talk," sexually explicit magazines are "men's magazines," and sexually explicit films are "stag movies." Nearly all of this "pornography" is created by and for men. Although there is male-only porn aimed at the gay male audience, most pornography depicts women.

THE DOUBLENESS OF SEX FOR WOMEN

Feminists are aware (as Joanna Russ put it) of "the doubleness of sex for women." Men get one predominant message about sexual activity and its place in their lives: sex is positive. Women get several conflicting messages.

> Sex is ecstatic, autonomous, and lovely for women. Sex is violent, dangerous, and unpleasant for women. I don't mean a dichotomy (i.e. two kinds of women or even two kinds of sex) but rather a continuum in which no one's experience is wholly positive or negative, and to which different women will give very different weightings. (Russ 1985, 101–107)

Given this background, it is hardly surprising that men and women have different perceptions of pornography's content and meaning. In the public's eye, feminists (as women's advocates) should be intolerant of pornography (that is, sexually explicit materials written to arouse) and are therefore allies of the forces of censorship. This view is not shared by all women and/or feminists, but there are several reasons for the assumption.

First, there are societal stereotypes about the sexes. Women must serve as the guardians of the family, the hearth, finer feelings, commitment, and sex within marriage. Men are lusty, anything-goes, adult-bookstore customers who wish (or believe) that all women are as available and willing as the models in commercial porn magazines. According to these stereotypes, men produce, sell, and consume commercial pornography, and women abhor it. Therefore, feminists, taking the woman's point of view, would seek to abolish pornography.

Another similar, but not identical, view exists. Feminists are concerned with the exploitation of women. Commercial pornography presents a false image of women as sex objects. In this medium women are constantly available and willing to display themselves to the (male) viewer. They possess all the "ideal" aspects of air-brushed feminine beauty—smooth skin, long hair, big breasts, small waists. Most women do not fit this narrow mold and find themselves wanting, inferior, not good enough. Thus, pornography creates problems for women by leading men to expect this appearance and behavior from actual women and to feel disappointed, even cheated, when they don't get it.

The production of pornography in photographic form may also oppress the women who model for it. Women are generally paid for posing in "adult" magazines and videos, but if the photos become public (as in the case of Vanessa Williams, the Miss America who was disqualified when nude photos of her were published in *Penthouse*) the woman's reputation is tarnished. And those who condemn the women involved often justify their ostracism/punishment with the same "she asked for it" rationale applied to many raped or battered women. Thus, the sex industry provides more opportunities for women to be injured and exploited.

As feminists, we do not want women to be victims. However, we see women's bodies used to sell everything from liquor, to cars, to carpeting. Our sex is turned against us in countless assaultive ways, from sexual harrassment at the workplace to unwanted attention on the street. We are raped by men who know us as well as by strangers. As Ellen Willis states, "If rape warns that without the protection of one man we are fair game for all, the hard-core pornographic image suggests that the alternative to being a wife is being a whore" (Willis 1983, 461). And what do we do when we *do* want sex? Does that make us more like the "real women" pictured in pornography? Or does it make us less like "real women" because we have stepped out of our roles as the guardians of social purity?

FEMINIST RESPONSES TO PORNOGRAPHY

Much has been written on the intersection of the issues of feminism and pornography. *Feminists, Pornography, & the Law: An Annotated Bibliography of Conflict, 1970–1986*, by Betty-Carol Sellen and Patricia Young, contains over 500 annotated citations of books, magazine and news articles, and other works about these issues. Perusing the book's 204 informative pages gives the reader an idea of the depth and breadth of opinion within and without the feminist community. An additional feature of the book is a chronology of major mainstream newspaper articles on the intersection of pornography and feminism, which grows from one article in 1976 to 42 articles in 1984.

There is also a news chronology within the feminist community that began in the late 1970s with the reaction to the now-infamous billboard for the Rolling Stones' "Black and Blue" album. The billboard pictured a disheveled and bruised woman with the words "I'm 'Black and Blue' from the Rolling Stones and I love it." The resulting protest and boycott against Warner Bros., organized by Women Against Violence Against Women, brought the issue of commercial depictions of sexual violence into focus within the feminist movement.

In 1978 the first feminist conference on pornography was held, and in 1979 the group Women Against Pornography (WAP) was organized. The feminist antipornography anthology *Take Back the Night: Women on Pornography* was published in 1980. During this period, however, feminists were by no means in agreement on this issue. As traced by Alice Echols in "The Taming of the Id" (Snitow et al. 1983, 439–459; Vance 1984, 50–72), there have been critics of this antipornography position within the women's movement right from the beginning. However, these voices were not being published in the feminist press at the beginning of the feminist porn wars. Then in 1982, the Feminist and the Scholar Conference at Barnard University served as a watershed event, as the split between the "antis" and the "pros" became irrevocably public (Snitow et al. 1983, 38; Vance 1984).[1] The Feminist Anti-Censorship Taskforce (FACT) arose from this struggle.

THE ANTI-PORN ORDINANCES: A TACTICAL SHIFT

In 1983, feminists Catharine MacKinnon and Andrea Dworkin drafted an antipornography ordinance for the Minneapolis City Council, which refocused the pornography debate onto legal remedies. This proposed model law defined pornography as:

[T]he graphic sexually explicit subordination of women through pictures and/or words that also includes one or more of the following:

1) women are presented dehumanized as sexual objects, things, or commodities;
2) women are presented as sexual objects who enjoy pain or humiliation;
3) women are presented as sexual objects who experience sexual pleasure in being raped;
4) women are presented as sexual objects tied up or cut up or mutilated or bruised or physically hurt;
5) women are presented in postures or positions of sexual submission, servility, or display;
6) women's body parts—including but not limited to vaginas, breasts, or buttocks—are exhibited such that women are reduced to those parts;
7) women are presented as whores by nature;
8) women are presented being penetrated by objects or animals;
9) women are presented in scenarios of degradation, injury, torture, shown as filthy or inferior, bleeding, bruised, or hurt in a context that makes these conditions sexual. (MacKinnon & Dworkin 1985)

According to this view, pornography is a form of sex discrimination against women and legally actionable as such. Since first drafted, this civil rights approach to pornography has been debated extensively. A version of the law passed in Indianapolis, but was ruled unconstitutional when the U.S. Supreme Court let a lower appeals court ruling stand. However, the Meese Commission's 1986 report on pornography suggested that the wording be reworked to comply with the Constitution. It could then be used as a model law to combat sexually explicit material on local and national levels. While the Commission took much of the law's language for its own, the Commission's agenda is, for the most part, quite different from that of feminists.

THE PROBLEMS PERSIST

For some feminists, the battle lines are still sharply drawn on this issue. For others, the struggle is no longer a frequent topic of conversation, and we no longer open the latest issue of a feminist magazine or newspaper to read what fresh controversy has erupted. Many feminists have picked their way through the various stands to arrive at their own personal viewpoint, reconciling diverse views in their own minds.

Some protest antipornography legislation, feminist or not, but also protest a sexist billboard. Some are irritated when R or X movie ratings restrict a show with explicit sex, while explicit violence rates

only a PG-13. Some might want to view a sexually explicit film but
avoid going to a movie theatre filled with men who greet women's
bodies with whistles and howls of . . . what? glee? lust? derision? jeal-
ousy? arousal? The milieu of the sexually explicit is generally not a
friendly one to women

On the one hand, feminists want both women and men to have
free access to information about human sexuality and its possibilities.
On the other hand, much of what appears in sex magazines is clearly
men's ideas of what women want. However, women-created sexually
explicit materials are not necessarily the answer either. As Carole
Vance explains, "I call it Vance's One-Third Rule: You put forward
any personally-favored erotic image, and one-third finds it disgusting,
one-third finds it ridiculous, and one-third finds it hot" (Vance 1985).
The question of definitions for sexually explicit material and human
response(s) to it persist. The answers are informed by our own
experiences and will be subjective. But we must all come up with
something better than "Erotica is what *I* like, and pornography is
what *you* like."

THE DILEMMA OF THE FEMINIST LIBRARIAN

Societal stereotypes of feminists and librarians (both male and female) hold us to be people who would keep sexually explicit material
away from the innocent minds of women and children and the
vulnerable minds of men. Actually, we work at selecting material for
our libraries to create a balanced collection that reflects a diversity of
viewpoints. We have come a long way from the restrictive views of
earlier generations of librarians (and community members) who saw
the selection of materials as placing the community's stamp of approval on the contents, and who consequently kept all potentially
controversial (and often sexual) material in locked cases. We are no
longer the *de facto* guardians of public morality, though this does not
mean that we find our task as selectors less challenging. We all have
our private biases, but we also have a public responsibility to acquire
materials that represent various viewpoints in many controversial
areas.

Perhaps this question would not be so troubling to librarians if
librarianship were not a female-intensive profession. As such, librarians, particularly women librarians, come face to face with important
feminist issues such as childcare, career ladders for women, com-
parable worth in salaries, and sex discrimination. Thus, the concerns
of librarianship are often synonymous with the concerns of women.
As librarians, we support the Library Bill of Rights, which affirms the
rights of access to material and information for all. As feminists, we
are aware of the sex discrimination involved in much commercially

available pornography. As one librarian put it, "As a librarian, I abhor censorship. As a feminist, I abhor pornography. Where do I stand?" Where do feminist librarians stand? Right in the middle.

Our selection policies generally preclude acquiring *Slinky Sex Slaves* or *Latex Love*, except in specialized research collections. However, we do try to select what the public wants to read and view. What about women's swimwear and lingerie magazines (*Swimwear International* or *Sheer Fashion: The Magazine of Sensual Attire*), or body-builder magazines (like *Muscle and Beauty* and *Women's Physique World*), or wrestling magazines (like *GLOW: Gorgeous Ladies of Wrestling*)? All of these popular publications contain women in positions and attitudes of bodily display, although they do not have the amount of nudity contained in commercial pornography. What about books like *Golden Dreams, Thorn of Love, Beloved Betrayal, Untamed, What Wild Ecstacy, Passion's Peak*, and *The Savage Marquess*, all popular titles at local bookstores? These "bodice-rippers" are not shelved on the "adults only" rack but are available in the romance section, and their audience is almost exclusively female. So far, the feminist debate on pornography has not specifically concerned these materials, although any legislative "solution" may affect all of them.

When we begin to think about pornography in our role as librarians and as feminists, we must look at both the personal and the political. We must consider the issues from our vantage points as feminists in a woman-intensive profession and as policy makers and selectors, as well as potential censors and potential defenders of intellectual freedom. We all have our public faces and private biases. How do we reconcile the two? Or three? Or many?

We *are* in a position of power with regard to what other people (adults and children) may read and have access to. We have responsibility for selection within our own institutions, and we are professionals who are listened to and respected by many in our communities. First Amendment issues are seen as our area of expertise. If they are not, they should be, because others will expect it of us.

We may make policy or selection decisions in harmony with our personal experiences or at odds with our own beliefs (e.g., we may not wish to purchase *Playboy* ourselves, but might order a subscription for our library).

STEPS TOWARD A SOLUTION

We must first recognize and acknowledge our own views; only *then* can we go on to make professional decisions that avoid unconscious subjectivity. We can begin by reading and listening to a variety of writers and speakers who address this issue. We must begin by thinking about our own experiences and feelings on the subject, and by thinking and talking about this thorny issue/problem/challenge with friends, colleagues, and co-workers. This is not an issue that will go away.[2]

It is easy to locate a vast amount of writing on various facets of the pornography debate. Conservative and liberal forces alike all have something to say about this. Phyllis Schlafley's Eagle Forum, Jerry Falwell's Liberty Lobby (formerly the Moral Majority), and the American Civil Liberties Union, among many others, all have written articles and positions on the subject. The intent here is to familiarize yourself with the specifically feminist strands of the debate.

To acquire a background of information about this complex and ongoing feminist pornography debate, seek the following:

1. Information by and about the feminist antipornography movement. This includes books and articles supporting groups like Women Against Pornography (WAP) and various allied local organizations throughout the country. Important authors include Susan Brownmiller, Andrea Dworkin, Susan Griffin, Susanne Kappeler, Dorchen Leidholdt, Catharine MacKinnon, Robin Morgan, and Gloria Steinem. (For these and the authors listed below, see the bibliography to this chapter.)
2. Information by and about the feminist anti-antipornography movement. This group is also called anti-censorship, or pro-sex. It includes organizations like the Feminist Anti-Censorship Taskforce (FACT) and authors such as Hannah Alderfer, Laurie Bell, Varda Burstyn, Lisa Duggan, Kate Ellis, Carole Vance, and Ellen Willis.
3. Information about the MacKinnon-Dworkin model law, also known in various forms as the Minneapolis or Indianapolis ordinance, which embodies the civil rights approach to antipornography legislation. Most coverage of the Meese Commission's report includes information about this model law.
4. Information providing a feminist analysis and/or overview of the "porn wars." Authors include Mary Kay Blakely, Judith Levine, B. Ruby Rich, Joanna Russ, Anne Snitow, Carole Vance, and special issues of *Off Our Backs* and *Changing Men.*

As librarians, we need to identify our own thoughts, feelings, and experiences about and with pornography/erotica. If we do not examine our own prejudices, we risk making "objective" selection and policy decisions that are actually quite subjective. After we have thought out and discussed these issues, we can approach selection decisions with an informed mind, and be ready to discuss and defend our decisions with our patrons.

It is probably impossible to make a Final Decision on all sexual material, given the complexity of the topic and the multiple meanings of the material under consideration. But we can make informed decisions while acknowledging our personal biases, reservations, enthusiasms, and blind spots and, hopefully, become wiser in the process.

ENDNOTES

1. For coverage of this conference see also *Off Our Backs*, June 1982 and following issues.

2. At ALA's 1985 Midwinter Meeting in Washington, DC, the American Library Association's Feminist Task Force first began talking about including a program on the feminist antipornography movement and librarians' responses to it. At first it was thought that a panel discussion would best familiarize conference participants with the issues involved in the intersection of feminism, pornography, and librarianship. As we talked, it became evident that this was already an emotionally charged issue for many members, and not one on which we could easily produce a statement or resolution that would reflect an official feminist librarian's position on the subject.

A committee was formed to plan and facilitate a discussion meeting at that summer's Annual Conference. Our goal was to have a discussion in which to state and talk over our various points of view in a non-divisive manner. The issues surrounding pornography have at times polarized the feminist community to an alarming degree, and we had no desire to replicate that split within our own group. Indeed, part of the problem with the then-current debate was the very *lack* of discussion involved and the resulting willingness of some to become arbiters on who was indeed a feminist, based solely on one's position on some aspect of the porn debate. We wanted to avoid the attitude of "If you are not for us, you are against us." Instead, we sought to learn from each other's thoughts and experiences pertaining to this issue.

We spent most of the meeting in small groups and proceeded to discuss the issue. Our directive was to generate a list of our concerns, problems, questions, and solutions about and for the issues of pornography and the feminist antipornography movement. Questions we asked ourselves included:

- How does this issue/information affect me personally?
- What have been my experiences with pornography/sexually explicit material? As a child? As an adolescent? As an adult? In my personal life? In my surroundings? In my relationships?
- What are the negative messages I have received from this material?
- What are the positive messages I have received from this material?
- What are our concerns: as feminists? as librarians? as citizens? as parents? as educators? as advocates of intellectual freedom? as women/as men?

Our efforts resulted in a heightened awareness of the diversity of opinions within ourselves and our colleagues. We do not have an official stand as a group, but we do recognize (again, as a group) the complexities of the issues involved. We have this experience and information to build on for future programs, activities, writing, and so forth.

REFERENCES

Brownmiller, Susan. 1980. *Against our will: Men, women and rape.* New York: William Morrow. 394. (Excerpted in Laura Lederer, ed., *Take back the night: Women on pornography,* 32)

Dworkin, Andrea. 1981. *Pornography: Men possessing women.* New York: Perigree. 223.

FACT (Feminist Anti-Censorship Taskforce). 1985. Feminism and censorship: Strange bedfellows? *Changing Men,* 15, Fall: 12.

Kendrick, Walter. 1987. *The secret museum: Pornography in modern culture.* New York: Penguin.

MacKinnon, Catharine, and Andrea Dworkin. 1985. Model anti-pornography law. *Changing Men: Issues in Gender, Sex and Politics,* 15, Fall: 23.

Russ, Joanna. 1985. *Magic mommas, trembling sisters, puritans & perverts.* Trumansburg, NY: Crossing Press.

Russell, Diana E.H., with Laura Lederer. 1980. Questions we get asked most often. In *Take back the night: Women on pornography* (p. 24), ed. by Laura Lederer. New York: William Morrow.

Snitow, Ann, Christine Stansell, and Sharon Thompson, eds. 1983. *Powers of desire: The politics of sexuality.* New York: Monthly Review Press; and Vance, Carole S., ed. 1984. *Pleasure and danger: Exploring female sexuality.* Boston: Routledge & Kegan Paul.

Steinem, Gloria. 1980. Erotica and pornography: A clear and present difference. In *Take back the night: Women on pornography* (p. 38), ed. by Laura Lederer. New York: William Morrow.

Vance, Carole S. 1985. Porn, politics, and pleasure. *Gay Community News,* February 23: 9.

Willis, Ellen. 1983. Feminism, moralism, and pornography. In *Powers of desire: The politics of sexuality,* ed. by Ann Snitow, Christine Stansell, and Sharon Thompson. New York: Monthly Review Press.

BIBLIOGRAPHY

Articles

Blakely, Mary Kay. "Is One Woman's Sexuality Another Woman's Pornography?" *Ms.* April 1985, 37–47+, (plus response in "Letters," July 1985).

Coward, Rosalind. "What's in It for Women?" *New Statesman.* June 12, 1986, 23–25.

Duggan, Lisa. "Forbidden Fantasies: Censorship in the Name of Feminism." *Village Voice.* October 16, 1984, 11–12+, (plus Dworkin's response, below).

Dworkin, Andrea. "Dear Editor." *Village Voice*, November 6, 1984, 5, (response to Duggan's article, above).

Ehrenreich, Barbara. "Pornography as Paradox." *New York Times Book Review*, September 29, 1985, 50, (plus response in "Letters," November 10, 1985, 53).

Herlihy, Sean. "Anti-Censorship Forum." *Gay Community News*, April 13, 1985, 10–11.

Levine, Judith. "Perils of Desire." *Village Voice/Voice Literary Supplement.* March 12, 1985, 12–15.

Press, Aric et al. "The War Against Pornography." *Newsweek*, March 18, 1985, 58–66.

Rich, B. Ruby. "Anti-Porn: Soft Issue, Hard World." *Village Voice*, July 20, 1982, 11+, (plus response in "Letters," August 17, 1982, 3+).

Robson, Ruthann. "Pornography, Power, and the First Amendment," in Berman, Sanford, and Danky, James, eds. *Alternative Library Literature, 1982/83*. Phoenix, AZ: Oryx Press, 1984, 68–75.

Russ, Joanna. "Pornography and the Doubleness of Sex for Women," in *Magic Mommas, Trembling Sisters, Puritans & Perverts: Feminist Essays.* Trumansburg, NY: Crossing Press, 1985, 101–119.

Steinem, Gloria. "Erotica and Pornography: A Clear and Present Difference," *Ms.* November 1978, 53+, (also appears as a chapter in the author's *Outrageous Acts and Everyday Rebellions.* New York: Holt, 1983).

Van Gelder, Lindsy. "Pornography Goes to Washington." *Ms.* June 1986, 52–54+.

Magazines (Special Theme Issues)

"Coming Apart: Feminists and the Conflict Over Pornography." Special issue of *Off Our Backs*, vol. 15, no. 6, (June 1985). Articles in this special issue include:

> Colker, Ruth. "Moving Toward Common Ground on the Pornography Issue."
> Douglas, Carol Anne. "A House Divided."
> "Feminists Against Pornography: Support for a Civil Rights Approach."
> Henry, Alice. "History of Debate."
> Hunter, Nan and MacKinnon, Catharine. "Debate."
> "Indianapolis Ordinance."
> Wallsgrove, Ruth. "Feminist Anti-Censorship Taskforce: The Case Against Indianapolis."

"Men Confronting Pornography." Special issue of *Changing Men: Issues in Gender, Sex and Politics* (301 N. Brooks, Madison, WI 53715), no. 15, (Fall 1985). Articles in this special issue include:

> Citizens for Media Responsibility without Law. "Sex Is Not Obscene!"
> Ellis, Kate. "No Sexuality without Representation: A Feminist View."
> Guerrieri, Dexter. "Pornography and Silent Men."
> MacKinnon, Catharine and Dworkin, Andrea. "Model Anti-Pornography Law."
> Small, Fred. "Pornography and Censorship."
> Stoltenberg, John. "Pornography and Freedom."
> Wagner, Sally Roesch. "Suffrage in the 1870's and Anti-Pornography in the 1980's."

Books

Alderfer, Hannah et al. *Caught Looking: Feminism, Pornography and Censorship.* Seattle, WA (3131 Western Avenue, #410, 98121-1028): Real Comet, 1987.

Bell, Laurie, ed. *Good Girls/Bad Girls: Feminists and Sex Trade Workers Face to Face.* Seattle, WA (P.O. Box 13, 98111): Seal Press, 1987.

Burstyn, Varda, ed. *Women Against Censorship.* Vancouver BC: Douglas and McIntyre, 1985.

Cole, Susan G. *Pornography and the Sex Crisis.* Toronto, ON: Amanita Enterprises, 1989.

Downs, Donald Alexander. *The New Politics of Pornography.* Chicago: University of Chicago Press, 1989.

Dworkin, Andrea. *Pornography: Men Possessing Women.* New York: Perigree, 1981.

Griffin, Susan. *Pornography and Silence: Culture's Revenge Against Nature.* New York: Harper and Row, 1981.

Gubar, Susan, and Hoff, Joan, eds. *For Adult Users Only: The Dilemma of Violent Pornography.* Bloomington, IN: Indiana University Press, 1989.

Kappeler, Susanne. *The Pornography of Representation.* Minneapolis: University of Minnesota Press, 1986.

Kendrick, Walter. *The Secret Museum: Pornography in Modern Culture.* New York: Penguin Books, 1987.

Kimmel, Michael S., ed. *Men Confronting Pornography.* New York: Crown, 1990.

Lederer, Laura, ed. *Take Back the Night: Women on Pornography.* New York: William Morrow, 1980.

Malamuth, Neil M., and Donnerstein, Edward, eds. *Pornography and Sexual Aggression.* Orlando, FL: Academic Press, 1984.

Russ, Joanna. *Magic Mommas, Trembling Sisters, Puritans & Perverts: Feminist Essays.* Trumansburg, NY: Crossing Press, 1985.

Sellen, Betty-Carol and Young, Patricia A. *Feminists, Pornography, & the Law: An Annotated Bibliography of Conflict, 1970–1986.* Hamden, CT: Library Professional Publications/Shoestring Press, 1987.

Snitow, Ann, Christine Stansell, and Thompson, Sharon, eds. *Powers of Desire: The Politics of Sexuality.* New York: Monthly Review Press, 1983.

Vance, Carole S., ed. *Pleasure and Danger: Exploring Female Sexuality.* Boston: Routledge & Kegan Paul, 1984.

CHAPTER 8

The Feminist Attack on Pornography: The Minneapolis and Indianapolis Porn Ordinances

Elizabeth M. McKenzie

Most American librarians have, at least since the McCarthy era, taken a strong stance against censorship. The ALA's Library Bill of Rights embodies the profession's statement of principle on the issue, challenging censorship even of the most offensive publications. Having such a strong free speech position, many librarians were startled when feminists joined the fight of conservatives to censor pornography. The feminist attack on pornography had the potential to expose libraries and librarians to lawsuits by individuals claiming they had been harmed by their own or another's exposure to materials available in many libraries. The ordinances inspired by this attack have been struck down as infringing on First Amendment free speech rights, but the arguments raised by the feminist thinkers should continue to spark arguments among thoughtful, socially conscious librarians for years to come.

In the early 1980s, feminist theorists began redefining the problem of pornography as one of violence towards and repression of women, not one of morals. These thinkers typically distinguish pornography, which they seek to suppress, from erotica, which they would protect.[1] They define pornography in various terms but generally end by arguing that, as redefined, pornography is no longer protected by the First Amendment of the Constitution. Their most

The author gratefully acknowledges the assistance of Mead Data Central, Inc., and of Kim Kossman for providing research assistance through the NEXIS news research and information retrieval service.

successful arguments have characterized pornography as an incitement to violence against women. These feminists tend to see pornography as the premier women's issue of the decade,[2] and they have had remarkable success in putting their attack on pornography before the public.[3]

THE MINNEAPOLIS ORDINANCE

On December 30, 1983, the Minneapolis City Council voted to pass a historic amendment to the city's basic civil rights ordinance, including pornography as a violation of women's civil rights. Until then, the only legal controls on the pornography industry were criminal sanctions for obscenity and for violation of local zoning laws. The celebrated "Minneapolis Porn Ordinance" began when a neighborhood group trying to zone pornography out of their neighborhood requested testimony from feminist writer-activist Andrea Dworkin and law professor Catharine MacKinnon, who together were teaching a course on pornography at the University of Minnesota. When the two testified at the City Council's Zoning and Planning Committee public hearing, they attacked the use of zoning laws that allow pornography but seek to limit it. Dworkin argued that since pornography is central in creating and maintaining an inferior status for women, pornography is a violation of women's civil rights. MacKinnon then outlined the legal steps the city would have to take to create an ordinance defining pornography as a civil rights violation.

The five-member Government Operations Committee unanimously approved a motion directing the City Attorney to pursue that approach. Dworkin and MacKinnon were contracted to draft the ordinance and to organize public hearings on the effects of pornography. The Government Operations Committee heard testimony from national experts and celebrities, local experts, and local citizens at the very heavily attended hearings. Women told of the tragic effects pornography had had in their lives. The entire City Council then voted 7–6 to approve the amendment drafted by Dworkin and MacKinnon. The vote did not follow either party or sexual lines.[4] The Council's vote was based on its finding that pornography promotes civil inequality between the sexes and is a systematic practice of exploitation and subordination based on sex. The Council further found that pornography fosters acts of aggression, bigotry, and contempt (*Washington Post* 1983).

The primary purpose of the amendment was to allow women a civil cause of action against pornography, rather than solely criminal avenues. The ordinance would allow individuals to file a complaint with the Civil Rights Commission, seeking damages for injury or an injunction to prevent the production, sale, distribution, or showing of pornography. The statute provided legal recourse for those coerced into performance, those physically hurt as a direct result of pornography, and those who have pornography forced upon them in public places or at home.

Under the Minneapolis ordinance, women could sue the producers of pornography that led directly to an attack, as well as husbands or friends who forced pornography upon them. The terms of the ordinance appear to include libraries if they are distributing materials that fall within the ordinance's definition of pornography.

The Minneapolis ordinance was vetoed by the mayor, who feared it would be struck down in a constitutional challenge for vagueness. The Council failed to override the mayor's veto, and that ordinance never became law. In July 1984, the Council passed a similar ordinance, but voted to delay implementation until a legal challenge to a similar ordinance passed in the meantime in Indianapolis was resolved. The mayor also vetoed the later ordinance ("Clash Over Smut Leads to Arrests" 1984).

Interest in this type of attack on pornography was spreading. The authors of the Minneapolis ordinance appeared on such nationally viewed television shows as "Sixty Minutes," "The Phil Donahue Show," and even "Late Night with David Letterman." Part of their presentation was an illustration of the extremely violent pornography of which most women have been completely unaware. The issue was featured in such news magazines as *Newsweek*, which quoted one civil liberties attorney as stating that "MacKinnon has already won. She's changed the way people think about the problem" (Press et al. 1985).

THE INDIANAPOLIS ORDINANCE

In April 1984, the Indianapolis City-County Council voted 24–5 to pass an ordinance somewhat different from the original Minneapolis law.[5] The ordinance, also drafted by Professor MacKinnon, referred pornography complaints for investigation to the city equal opportunities board, which governs sex discrimination complaints. If it deemed the complaint warranted, the board would seek a court injunction against distribution of the material. If the court order was ignored, the distributor would be subject to court-imposed penalties. Civil damages were also available from producers and distributors of pornography to anyone who had been injured by a consumer of pornography.

The ordinance prohibited "trafficking" in pornography, coercing others into performing in pornographic works, or forcing pornography upon another. Trafficking was defined as the "production, sale, exhibition, or distribution of pornography." The ordinance excluded exhibition in a public or educational library, but a "special display" in a library could be sex discrimination. It was not a defense that the trafficker did not know or intend that the materials were pornography. As in the Minneapolis ordinance, civil damages were made available to anyone injured by someone who had seen or read pornography. However, damages were not available in trafficking cases unless the complainant proved the defendant knew or had reason to know that the materials were pornographic. It was also a complete defense to a charge of trafficking that the materials in question were pornography only by virtue of section (6) in the definition.[6]

Indianapolis mayor William Hudnut III signed the ordinance into law on May 1, 1984. An hour later, a lawsuit was filed, and the federal district judge enjoined the city from enforcing the law (Shipp 1984).

On November 19, 1984, the federal district court for Indianapolis ruled that the ordinance was unconstitutional. The judge ruled that "pornography" as defined in the ordinance was speech, not conduct, as the law's proponents had argued. (Conduct is less strongly protected than speech by First Amendment decisions.) Because the ordinance prohibited speech that would be legal under the current rules governing obscenity, the ordinance suppressed protected speech. Furthermore, the state's interest in prohibiting sex discrimination did not outweigh the individual's interest in free speech. The ordinance was also found to be unconstitutionally vague; it failed to give fair notice as to what speech or conduct was prohibited and was open to arbitrary and discriminatory interpretation by police, judges, and juries. The court also found that certain provisions of the ordinance imposed unconstitutional prior restraint on First Amendment expression (*American Booksellers Assoc. v. Hudnut* 1985a).[7]

An appeal was immediately filed to the U.S. Court of Appeals, Seventh Circuit. While these legal matters were pending, the Los Angeles City Council considered a similar ordinance. The ordinance provided a civil cause of action for those coerced into taking part in making pornographic material, those who had it forced upon them, or those who were harmed by someone incited to violence by such material. This version of the ordinance was drawn up by an assistant city attorney, not by Professor MacKinnon. The original Los Angeles ordinance apparently was very similar to those from Minneapolis and Indianapolis. However, after the district court decision on the Indianapolis ordinance, the Los Angeles ordinance was redrafted to broaden the class of people entitled to sue. The alterations caused the women's groups that had been catalysts for the measure to withdraw support. The City Council voted 8–4 to defeat the law (Clifford 1985).

At this point, the tide began to turn. At one point, at least 10 city governments other than Indianapolis and Minneapolis were said to be considering implementation of similar legislation (Hamm

1984–1985). When a similar ordinance was put on a ballot in Cambridge, Massachusetts, in the fall of 1985, voters "decisively" rejected it ("The Nation" 1985)

Meanwhile, the Indianapolis case had been decided on appeal. The district court's ruling was affirmed on August 27, 1985. Requests for rehearings were denied in September. The Court of Appeals, Seventh Circuit, specifically held that the new definition of "pornography" as a practice that discriminates against women (without reference to the "obscenity standard" of appealing to prurient interest, offensiveness, or standards of the community) is unconstitutional.

> The ordinance discriminates on the ground of the content of the speech. Speech treating women in the approved way—in sexual encounters "premised on equality" (MacKinnon, *supra*, at 22)—is lawful no matter how sexually explicit. Speech treating women in the disapproved way—as submissive in matters sexual or as enjoying humiliation—is unlawful no matter how significant the literary, artistic, or political qualities of the work taken as a whole. The state may not ordain preferred viewpoints in this way. The Constitution forbids the state to declare one perspective right and silence opponents. (*American Booksellers Assoc. v. Hudnut* 1985b)

While holding the ordinance unconstitutional, the judges nevertheless accepted the premises underlying the ordinance.

> Pornography is an aspect of domination. . . . In this view, pornography is not an idea; pornography is the injury. There is much to this perspective. . . . Depictions of subordination tend to perpetuate subordination. The subordinate status of women in turn leads to affront and lower pay at work, insult and injury at home, battery and rape on the streets. In the language of the legislature, "[p]ornography is central in creating and maintaining sex as a basis of discrimination. . . ." (*American Booksellers Assoc. v. Hudnut* 1985b, 328–329)

However much pornography may influence people's worldview, thus affecting society's treatment of women, the judges held that pornography was nevertheless speech, protected by the First Amendment unless found obscene under current standards. "Any other answer leaves the government in control of all of the institutions of culture, the great censor and director of which thoughts are good for us" (*American Booksellers Assoc. v. Hudnut* 1985b, 330). Thus, the Court of Appeals disposed of the Indianapolis ordinance. The judgment was summarily affirmed by the Supreme Court on February 24, 1986 (*Hudnut v. American Booksellers Assoc.* 1986). There was no discussion of the case.

IMPLICATIONS FOR LIBRARIANS

In the aftermath of *Hudnut*, it is unlikely that any further ordinances will appear attempting to redefine and thus restrict pornography.[8] However, the feminists' arguments remain. As librarians, we must attempt to deal with the issues they have raised. Even if we do not face local laws allowing libraries to be sued for "distributing" pornography, we need to reexamine our role in society in light of the feminists' arguments.

The feminist redefinition of pornography raises the question of whether pornography is most appropriately addressed as a free speech issue or as a civil rights issue. By supporting pornographers' free speech rights, are we perpetuating a form of propaganda for the oppression and abuse of women?

Anyone who has read Andrea Dworkin's writing on this subject has been sensitized to the misogynistic qualities in pornography. After reading these theorists, one sees everywhere images depicting violence against or oppression of women.[9] At the same time, the difficult question arises: How far will the censor's hand reach? If any production depicting the degradation of women as sexually arousing can be defined as pornography, will not many classics and much contemporary literature be implicated? In fact, in the absence of a statutorily defined set of guidelines, one suspects antipornography activists will move against a much larger set of works than they could with these ordinances.

If we accept the argument that reading affects one's worldview and, therefore, one's actions, we must take the feminists' rally against pornography seriously. But let us be consistent. Should we not rethink our free speech stance on *all* writing that oppresses racial groups, age groups, nationalities, and religions? If women's civil rights are violated by pornography, doesn't *Mein Kampf* violate Jews' civil rights? Doesn't Klan literature violate the civil rights of blacks? If we are willing to stop stocking our shelves with pornography on the basis of this argument, we must apply the same treatment to all literature. Where will the censorship (or boycott) end?

Librarians must also address the larger question of what political statements we make by our book selection. In light of Dworkin's analysis of pornography,[10] is it possible to think ourselves politically neutral in selecting our books? Even if we attempt to present "equal time" for every side of an argument, some theorists have argued that such book selection is not thereby neutral. Marxist thinkers as well as feminists have assailed this approach to the marketplace of ideas. They argue that whatever ideas currently are the standard ones in a society have so much more power and access to the public that the only fair counter to them is to stress nonmainstream concepts to the detriment of mainstream thinking (Marcuse 1970).[11] By presenting a neutral selection displaying all sides of an argument, we do nothing to correct an injustice and thus perpetuate it. Should we therefore engage in an "affirmative action campaign" to redress the imbalance of power in favor of all oppressed groups?

Even if we try to counter adult prejudices by offering "antidotes" to the propaganda of pornography, research on the effects of reading seems to say our patrons will not get our message. In a 1976 survey of research on the impact of reading on behavior, the authors cite studies showing that neither prejudiced nor open-minded people tend to read materials that do not support their own views. In addition, the "Mr. Bigot" studies showed that racially prejudiced individuals, when presented cartoons satirizing bigotry, distorted the message to support their own biases. Other studies showed that, over the long term, individuals tended to retain best any information that supported their own position (Voigt & Harris 1976, 181–185). There are many more studies covered in the survey and many done since then. The main message is that the impact of reading on individuals is complex and subtle, not easily predicted or measured. There seems to be no solid research as yet to guide socially responsible librarians in book selection. More research is underway, and more is needed.

If we cannot present "neutral" collections, should we then consider removing offending publications from library collections? Do the concerns raised by the feminists outweigh librarians' traditional free speech concerns? Yet, from another perspective, are we not engaging in "historical revisionism" when we remove from libraries the evidence of misogyny contained in pornography?

But part of the basis of our previous stand for free speech has been that we as librarians believe books are important, that they have an effect. How, then, can we say the pornography we make available has no effect at all? There must be alternatives to selecting materials that advocate oppression. Is it necessarily tantamount to endorsing censorship to oppose oppression? Librarians must rise to the challenge of the issue of pornography. There are no easy answers, but we must at least undertake an informed consideration of the questions.

ENDNOTES

1. The problem of distinguishing pornography from eroticism is one of the keys to writing a constitutionally sound antipornography law, as will be seen in later discussion of the so-called "Indianapolis Porn Ordinance." The feminists' distinction between pornography and eroticism serves in part to distance them from the conservative ideologues who seek to censor pornography and all erotica on grounds of morality.

2. Two of the leaders in the feminist assault on pornography, Catharine MacKinnon and Andrea Dworkin, told a *New York Times* reporter in 1984 that "their campaign has resulted in the 'breakthrough' needed to unite women of all persuasions behind issues usually identified with the feminist

movement." See E.R. Shipp, *New York Times*, Late City Final Edition, June 10, 1984, Sec. 4, p. 2.

3. These women are sincere in their belief that pornography is one of the strongest tools in the oppression of women. This struggle against pornography often calls forth powerful, emotional demonstrations of outrage. Andrea Dworkin "crashed" the 1985 annual convention of the National Organization of Women and wrestled an organizer for the microphone. She spoke in tears to the delegates, saying, "We are living at the beginning of a holocaust against women." See Ellen Debenport, "Dworkin to lead Bourbon Street march," United Press International wire, July 20, 1985, AM cycle.

In Minneapolis, while the City Council was considering a radical amendment to its civil rights ordinance that would include pornography as a violation of women's civil rights, a 23-year-old woman doused herself with gasoline and set herself afire. She was carrying a backpack filled with "Stop Porn Now" leaflets and had just written a Council member a four-page letter about how sexism had shattered her life. See "Around the nation," *New York Times*, Late City Final Edition, July 12, 1984, Sec. A, p. 12.

4. The amendment's key section defines pornography as

> . . . the sexually explicit subordination of women, graphically depicted, whether in pictures or in words that also includes one or more of the following:
>
> (A) women are presented dehumanized as sexual objects, things, or commodities, or
> (B) women are presented as sexual objects who experience sexual pleasure in being raped;
> (C) women are presented as sexual objects who enjoy pain or humiliation;
> (D) women are presented as sexual objects tied up or cut up or mutilated or bruised or physically hurt;
> (E) women are presented in postures of sexual submission or sexual servility, including inviting penetration;
> (F) women's body parts—including but not limited to vaginas, breasts, and buttocks—are exhibited, such that women are reduced to those parts;
> (G) women are presented as whores by nature;
> (H) women are presented being penetrated by objects or animals;
> (I) women are presented in scenarios of degradation, injury, torture, shown as filthy or inferior, bleeding, bruised, or bruised [sic], or hurt in a context that makes the condition sexual.
>
> The use of men, children, or transsexuals in the place of women is pornography for the purposes of this statute.

See Jeanne Barkey, "Minneapolis porn ordinance," *Off Our Backs*, XIV (February, 1984); 1–2. In the mainstream press, see Aric Press et al., "The war against pornography," *Newsweek*, March 18, 1985: 66.

The careful reader of the above definition of pornography will see how the drafters attempted to avoid suppression of "erotica," which does not depict women as degraded or depraved. At the same time, one can apply the definition to any number of favorite books, short stories, movies, or even advertisements and find that the selection falls within the ordinance's definition of pornography. Critics of the ordinance posit the example of the film, *Swept Away*. A wealthy woman yacht owner is shown as cruelly rude to her young male deck-hand. After they are stranded on an island, the man takes revenge by raping and assaulting his former boss. The woman first resists, then falls in love with the man, and he with her. The film, which was well-received by critics (even by a reviewer for *Ms.* magazine), would be pornography within the definition of the ordinance above. The woman character is depicted as coming to enjoy sexual humiliation and domination by the man. Clearly, the film fits within a number of the categories set out in the definition.

5. The Indianapolis City-County Council specifically found that

Pornography is a discriminatory practice based on sex which denies women equal opportunities in society. Pornography is central in creating and maintaining sex as a basis for discrimination. Pornography is a systematic practice of exploitation and subordination based on sex which differentially harms women. The bigotry and contempt it promotes, with the acts of aggression it fosters, harm women's opportunities for equality of rights in employment, education, access to and use of public accommodations, and acquisition of real property; promote rape, battery, child abuse, kidnapping and prostitution and inhibit just enforcement of laws against such acts; and contribute significantly to restricting women in particular from full exercise of citizenship and participation in public life, including in neighborhoods.

See Indianapolis Code Section 16–1(a)(2), "Findings, policies and purposes." Quoted in *American Booksellers Association, Inc., et al. v. Hudnut, et al.*, 598 F.Supp. 1316 (U.S. District Court, Southern District of Indiana, November 19, 1984), at 1320.

6. The definition reads:

. . . the graphic sexually explicit subordination of women, whether in pictures or in words that also includes one or more of the following:

(1) women are presented as sexual objects who enjoy pain or humiliation; or

(2) women are presented as sexual objects who experience sexual pleasure in being raped; or

(3) women are presented as sexual objects tied up or cut up or mutilated or bruised or physically hurt, or as dismembered or truncated or fragmented or severed into body parts; or

(4) women are presented as being penetrated by objects or animals; or

(5) women are presented in scenarios of degradation, injury, abasement, torture, shown as filthy or inferior, bleeding, bruised, or hurt in a context that makes these conditions sexual; or

(6) women are presented as sexual objects for domination, conquest, violation, exploitation, possession, or use, or through postures or positions of servility or submission or display.

The use of men, children, or transexuals in the place of women in paragraphs (1) through (6) above shall also constitute pornography under this section.

See Indianapolis Code Section 16–3(q). Quoted in *American Booksellers Association, Inc., et al. v. Hudnut, et al.*, 771 F.2d 323 (U.S. Court of Appeals, Seventh Circuit, August 27, 1985), at 324–26.

This definition appears to encompass even more material than the definition used in the Minneapolis ordinance, above. One example of such a production is Michael Jackson's mega-hit rock music video, "Thriller." This musical short depicts Jackson walking his girlfriend home past a cemetery after a horror movie. Monsters and ghouls climb out of the graveyard and begin to chase the pair while Jackson sings the pounding background music. At the end, however, Jackson himself turns into one of the monsters and pursues the girl at the head of the pack. Another example of nonobscenity that might be pornography under the above definition is a billboard advertising the Rolling Stones rock group which appeared in California several years ago. A bruised woman was depicted in a posture suggesting sexual bondage with the statement, "I'm black and blue for the Rolling Stones."

7. An interesting note is that the judge in this case was a woman, Sarah Evans Barker, Judge of the United States District Court for the Southern District of Indiana.

8. In November 1988, Bellingham, Washington, passed a similar ordinance. It, however, was struck down by a court in February 1989. See Claudia McCain, "Bellingham civil rights law against pornography," *ALKI: The Washington Library Association Journal*, March 1989: 16–18.

9. For example, Andrea Dworkin, *Pornography: Men possessing women*, New York: Putnam, 1981. A good introduction to a variety of feminist writers on this topic is Laura Lederer (ed.), *Take Back the Night: Women on Pornography*, New York: Morrow, 1980.

10. Dworkin, generally. For a summary of her arguments, see my article "Librarians and the new censorship," in *Public Library Quarterly*, 7, Spring/Summer 1986: 26–27. For another very interesting treatment, see Rosemarie Tong, "Women, pornography, and the law," in *Academe, Bulletin of the American Association of University Professors*, September–October, 1987: 14–22.

11. A very short explanation of Marcuse's reasoning is that the "institutionalized inequality" of our society so suffuses our thinking that it limits and defines the thoughts we think and thus restricts the effect of "equal access" in the marketplace of ideas before it begins to operate. Marcuse says that "The antagonistic structure of society rigs the rules of the game. Those who stand against the established system are *a priori* at a disadvantage, which is not removed by the toleration of their ideas, speeches, and newspapers." See Herbert Marcuse, "Repressive tolerance," in Robert Paul Wolff, Barrington Moore, Jr., & Herbert Marcuse, *A Critique of Pure Tolerance*, Boston: Beacon Press, 1970: footnote, p. 92.

He further argues that presenting all sides of an issue does not redress the imbalance of power, following John Stuart Mill, ". . . free and equal discussion can fulfill the function attributed to it only if it is rational expression and development of independent thinking, free from indoctrination, manipulation, extraneous authority." (Marcuse, "Repressive tolerance," p. 93). This, Marcuse concludes, is not possible in our society since the mass media and the educational establishment limit our thinking to a narrow range of possible realities. Although other ideas can be expressed, they are automatically understood in terms of this established worldview, which is that of the conservative majority. Alternatives are *a priori* precluded from consideration by this system, which has predetermined the direction in which the thought process moves.

Marcuse thus concludes that censorship is justified when it is directed against this hidden censorship permeating the "free" media. Tolerance of propaganda for inhumanity (which Marcuse and these feminist thinkers consider to reflect the majority worldview) reinforces the mass media's already powerful impediment against change for the "better." To tolerate such propaganda is to assist in the repression it advocates.

REFERENCES

American Booksellers Association, Inc., et al. v. Hudnut, et al. 1985a. 598 F.Supp. 1316.

American Booksellers Association, Inc., et al. v. Hudnut. 1985b. 771 F.2d 323 (C.A.7 1985), at 325.

Clash over smut leads to arrests. 1984. *The New York Times*, July 14: Sec. 1, p. 46.

Clifford, Frank. 1985. Council rejects anti-pornography law. *Los Angeles Times*, June 22: Metro Sec., p. 1.

Hamm, Valerie J. 1984–1985. The civil rights pornography ordinances—An examination under the First Amendment. *Kentucky Law Journal*, 73: 1082, referring to ABC News Transcript Nightline Show Number 867, "Women and Pornography," at 3.

Hudnut v. American Booksellers Association, Inc., et al. 1986. 106 S.Ct. 1172, 89 L.Ed.2d 291.

Marcuse, Herbert. 1970. Repressive tolerance. In *A critique of pure tolerance* (pp. 80–95), by Robert Paul Wolff, Barrington Moore, Jr., and Herbert Marcuse. Boston: Beacon Press.

The nation. 1985. *Los Angeles Times*, November 12: Part 1, p. 2.

Press, Aric et al. 1985. The war against pornography. *Newsweek*, March 18: 60.

Shipp, E.R. 1984. A feminist offensive against exploitation. *The New York Times*, June 10: Sec. 4, p. 2.

Voigt, Melvin J., and Michael H. Harris, eds. 1976. *Advances in librarianship.* Vol. 6. New York: Academic Press.

Washington Post, December 31, 1983: A3.

CHAPTER 9

A Case Study of Censorship? The Library of Congress and the Brailling of *Playboy*

Martha Cornog

It certainly seemed like a case of strange bedfellows. In 1986 a major item of discussion throughout the library community was Congress' budget cut of Library of Congress funds for brailling *Playboy* magazine, and the resulting joint suit against LC by Playboy Enterprises, the American Council of the Blind, the Blinded Veterans Association, three blind individuals, and the American Library Association to ensure the continuation of *Playboy* in braille, funds or no. Commented columnist Will Manley sardonically, "And while many of us might consider such a resolution of Congress to be an act of mercy on behalf of blind people, the stalwarts at ALA considered it to be censorious" (Manley 1986, 55).

Many librarians supported ALA's action in joining the suit. Some did not. Wrote Rosalee McReynolds to the editor of *American Libraries*:

> ALA has treated [Congressman] Wylie's proposal as attempted censorship, even though he apparently never suggested that the publication of *Playboy* in braille be forbidden or that the blind be denied access to the magazine's contents through other means. . . . By making the loss of *Playboy* in braille a cause célèbre, ALA has trivialized the very meaning of censorship and has publicly embarrassed our profession. (McReynolds 1986, 237)

What were the facts of this "cause célèbre," and what are the implications of the incident—and its outcome—for libraries?

BACKGROUND: THE NLS AND *PLAYBOY*

The National Library Service for the Blind and Physically Handicapped, Library of Congress (NLS), produces braille and recorded ("talking book") versions of selected books and magazines and circulates them free of charge to qualified blind and physically handicapped individuals through a nationwide network of participating regional library centers. In rendering publications, including magazines, into braille, the entire text is included except for advertising, pictorial materials and captions, and cartoons.

The program was established by an act of Congress in 1931 and has been expanded several times subsequently. Much of its funding comes from congressional appropriations, and for federal fiscal year 1985 these amounted to $36,592,000—about 61%—out of a total NLS expenditure budget of about $60,000,000. The remaining 39% were contributed by state, local, and other sources (*American Council of the Blind, Complaint*, 1985, 9). Circulation of 20,230,400 items to 657,060 individuals was reported for 1985 (Ruth Nussbaum, NLS, Personal communication, 3/9/89).

Daniel J. Boorstin, the librarian of Congress in 1985, was known to favor strongly the NLS program. Under Boorstin's tenure as librarian, which ran from 1975 to 1987, the number of individuals participating in the program more than doubled—from 318,300 in 1974 to 682,500 in 1986. Moreover, circulation of books and magazines increased over 75% within that period ("NLS Services Expand" 1987). In 1987, Boorstin commented:

> The National Library Service for the Blind and Physically Handicapped continues to be one of our nation's most popular reading programs. In this area the Library of Congress provides a uniquely extensive and effective program, essential to provide equal access for blind and physically handicapped citizens. ("NLS Services Expand" 1987, 2)

In 1985, *Playboy* was one of 36 magazines produced in braille and circulated through the NLS network. Others included *Good Housekeeping, Ladies Home Journal, Psychology Today*, and *National Geographic*. Magazines are selected through suggestions and recommendations from an advisory committee, individual readers, and LC staff. Every three months, a braille edition is produced of at least one new magazine, which is offered to readers on a trial basis. The readers complete a questionnaire that LC uses to determine which magazines will be brailled regularly. The advisory committee of 12 consists of four blind or physically handicapped people, one from each of four U.S. regions as defined by LC; four professional librarians, one from each of the same four regions; and one representative from each of four advocacy organizations: the American Council of the Blind, the Blinded Veterans Association, the National Federation of the Blind, and the National Council for the Physically Handicapped (*American Council of the Blind, Complaint,* 1985, 10–11).

Playboy was selected for inclusion in the program in 1970, at which time its publishers granted LC a free license to reproduce the magazine. From 1970 to 1985, *Playboy* was consistently one of the six or seven most requested magazines, with an annual circulation of over 1,000 out of some 17,000 readers of the program's braille magazines. In 1980, its circulation surpassed that of *Good Housekeeping* and *Ladies Home Journal* (*American Council of the Blind, Complaint,* 1985, 10–11).

ENTER CONGRESSMAN WYLIE

Chalmers P. Wylie, Republican Congressman from Ohio, first attempted to stop the brailling of *Playboy* in early 1981, when a "blind constituent complained" ("Ignoring Boorstin" 1985, 534). In March, Wylie requested information from the Library of Congress about its selection policy for brailled books and magazines. He then wrote Librarian Boorstin: "I ask that you, as the Librarian of Congress, discontinue the policy of reproducing in braille and distributing free copies of *Playboy* magazine" ("Statement of the Librarian of Congress" 1986, 334).

Boorstin responded to Wylie about two weeks later: "It is our judgment after reviewing your request that we do not have any substantial reason to discontinue issuing *Playboy* in braille" ("Statement of the Librarian of Congress" 1986, 334). Wylie, however, persisted, triggering a second internal review concerning "the appropriateness of continuing to offer *Playboy* in braille to eligible blind persons" (*American Council of the Blind, Complaint,* 1985, 12).

In July, Wylie sent a "Dear Colleague" letter to members of the House of Representatives, announcing his intention to introduce an amendment to an upcoming bill for LC appropriations that would "provide that none of the monies appropriated for the braille services may be used for this purpose" (i.e., reproduction of *Playboy* in braille). Such an amendment was proposed by Senator Mack Mattingly at a September conference on the bill, but the amendment was not adopted ("Statement of the Librarian of Congress" 1986, 334).

Meanwhile, after a "rigorous internal review, using established standards and criteria" that were part of longstanding and approved procedure, the LC staff determined in December 1981 that *Playboy* remained "top notched . . . in terms of the quality of the writing, which is a prime consideration for selecting periodicals for this program." Thus the publication of *Playboy* in braille was continued, based on its good circulation and the professional judgment of LC *staff,* rather than on the opinion of Boorstin alone (*American Council of the Blind, Complaint,* 1985, 12).

CONGRESSMAN WYLIE, ROUND TWO

In July 1985, Wylie renewed his efforts to stop LC from producing *Playboy* in braille. He introduced in the House an amendment to an appropriations bill, HR 2942, reducing funds to LC by $103,000, the precise amount needed for one year's brailling of *Playboy*. After discussion, the amendment was defeated by a voice vote. Wylie, however, insisted on a recorded vote. After a five-minute recess to obtain a quorum, a recorded vote was taken, and the amendment passed, 216 to 193. "There is no indication in the legislative history that there was any further debate after a quorum was present, or that any of the Congressmen who voted in favor of the amendment who had not been present during the initial floor debate were aware of that debate or of Rep. Wylie's reasons for the amendment" (*American Council of the Blind, Complaint,* 1985, 16). Later in July, the Senate passed the bill as amended, and it was signed into law by President Reagan in November as P.L. 99-151.

The legislation as written merely reduced funding for the NLS program by $103,000 and made no mention of *Playboy*. However, on the House floor, Wylie explicitly stated his intention in introducing the amendment:

> I do not think the public should be left with the impression that the Federal Government sanctions the promotion of sex-oriented magazines such as *Playboy*. I have asked the Library of Congress to stop using the money to reproduce *Playboy* in braille. They have not stopped using the money for this purpose, and so I am offering this amendment today; . . . it would reduce the amount of money . . . [by] the amount I was given as being the cost to reproduce and distribute *Playboy* last year. . . . It seems to me that reproducing *Playboy* in braille does not have literary merit, and it is not a good use of taxpayers' money. . . . Some [of the articles] talk about wanton idleness, of wanton and illicit sex, and so forth. ("Books for the Blind" 1985, H5932–5934)

When Rep. David Dreier (R-CA) asked Wylie "what assurance he has that the $103,000 reduction will not see the elimination of some other publication," Wylie responded, "I think the debate here on the floor will clearly indicate my intent" ("Books for the Blind" 1985, H5933).

LC RESPONDS

On the day the House passed HR 2942 with the Wylie amendment, Librarian Boorstin issued a statement in response, affirming his recognition of Wylie's intent:

> I feel profound regret at the action of the House of Representatives to reduce the appropriations of the Library of Congress as its way of censoring material made available to the blind community through our Library of Congress service. The next step might be to deny funds to the Library of Congress for purchase of books which the House deemed inappropriate, subversive, or unacceptable to the majority of the House. Censorship has no place in a free society. . . . Action by the U.S. House of Representatives to deny funds for the production of a braille edition of *Playboy* is regrettable and sets a precedent for the program which has for over 50 years brought reading pleasure to our blind and physically handicapped citizens. (*American Council of the Blind, Complaint,* 1985, App. A)

Shortly after, Boorstin wrote a letter to the chair of the Senate subcommittee considering the bill, asking that the $103,000 be restored by the Senate. When the Senate passed HR 2942 in late July, however, the funds were not restored.

In late September, Boorstin issued another statement, which concluded:

> Debate on the [Wylie] amendment indicated that the House of Representatives was voting on whether to allow or disallow funds for the Library of Congress to continue to produce *Playboy* in braille. The intent of the House of Representatives to deny funds in fiscal 1986 for the reproduction of *Playboy* in braille is clear. When the Senate considered H.R. 2942, they. . . did not increase the appropriation. I have directed that no contract for the reproduction of *Playboy* in braille be awarded for the calendar year 1986. (*American Council of the Blind, Complaint,* 1985, App. B)

And, in fact, the Library of Congress announced in an October letter to NLS subscribers that "[i]n accordance with the intent of the U.S. House of Representatives," the Library of Congress "will cease publishing *Playboy* in braille with the December 1985 issue" (*American Council of the Blind, Complaint,* 1985, 19).

THE JOINT APPEAL

Meanwhile, plans were being made by a number of parties to combat Congressman Wylie's "intent." In July, on the day the Senate passed HR 2942, Rep. Vic Fazio (D-CA) met with Boorstin and lawyers representing Playboy Enterprises and the American Council of the Blind. Fazio was the chair of the Subcommittee on the Legislative Branch, House Committee on Appropriations, and he had spoken against the Wylie amendment on the House floor:

> I rise in opposition to the amendment . . . because the people who determine which publications are going to be translated into braille at the Library, in their Books for the Blind Program, are the blind themselves . . . and I think we ought not to intrude; I do not think we ought to become the censor; I do not think we ought to make the decision that should be best left to the people who utilize the service, who [from] among other publications decide they would like access to *Playboy*. ("Books for the Blind" 1985, H5933)

At this meeting, "Dr. Boorstin and Representative Fazio urged Playboy Enterprises, Inc., to sue. . . . In order . . . to secure the clear judicial affirmation of the rights of the blind to equal access to knowledge, The Librarian has become technically the defendant . . ." ("Statement of the Librarian of Congress" 1986, 333).

His token position as censor was surely repugnant on principle to Boorstin, and LC's later description of the affair suggests this:

> If there had been any other approach, consistent with his responsibilities as Librarian of Congress, The Librarian would have taken it. The full record . . . [in retrospect] confirms the determination of The Librarian to preserve the Library of Congress as, in the words of former Librarian Archibald MacLeish, "a fortress of freedom." ("Statement of the Librarian of Congress" 1986, 333)

By December, when the "Complaint for Declaratory and Injunctive Relief" was filed in the U.S. District Court of the District of Columbia, the Blinded Veterans Association, three blind individuals, and the American Library Association had joined as plaintiffs with Playboy Enterprises and the American Council of the Blind. The ALA Executive Board had made the decision to lend support to the suit in a "four hour closed session" at the end of October ("ALA Authorized to Join Suit" 1985, 813). The defendant, of course, was Daniel Boorstin, Librarian of Congress. It was surely ironic that Boorstin, who had openly condemned what he called Congress'—actually Wylie's—attempt at censorship, should be sued himself as the censor. However, his precise actions and role in this regard were almost certainly critical in determining the outcome of the case, as we shall see later.

The 30-page complaint (*American Council of the Blind, Complaint*, 1985) is a fascinating document, summarizing the history of the Wylie amendment and HR 2942, describing the NLS and its braille magazine program, and giving background and intentions of the seven plaintiffs. The heart of the complaint, however, revolves around four major points.

> 1. In its [then] 31 years of publication, not one issue of *Playboy* has ever been held obscene by any state or federal court. In fact, courts have held that *Playboy* does not meet even one of the

three tests a publication must meet before it can be found obscene. (p. 5)

This paragraph means that possession or distribution of *Playboy* has never been found illegal on grounds of obscenity.[1]

> 2. The Wylie amendment . . . can be given full force and effect without requiring defendant Boorstin and the Library of Congress to delete *Playboy* from the regular list of braille edition magazines, or otherwise to deviate with respect to *Playboy* from their established selection procedures and criteria. . . . [O]rdinary canons of statutory interpretation preclude reference to the ambiguous floor debate preceding passage of that amendment to change or restrict the otherwise plain meaning of that amendment, particularly . . . when the enabling statute, §135a, expressly vests in the Librarian (*not* the Congress) control over expenditure of sums appropriated . . . . (p. 17)

Here, the complaint maintains that Boorstin was under no legal obligation to follow Wylie's "intent" for his amendment. In other words, Congress can only give Boorstin the money; the law has given *him* the power to spend it.

> 3. Nevertheless, defendant Boorstin believes that the Wylie amendment does prohibit him and the Library of Congress from producing braille and/or recorded editions of *Playboy*, and therefore requires him to disregard the Library's viewpoint-neutral selection criteria, procedures, and historical practices with respect to selection of program materials. Defendant Boorstin's decision to delete *Playboy* Magazine from the program without regard to the Library's established selection criteria and procedures is without support in the Wylie amendment [as described above], conflicts with the procedures and viewpoint-neutral standards mandated by U.S.C. §135a, and violates the First and Fifth Amendment rights of the plaintiffs. (pp. 17–18)

> 4. If the Wylie amendment is interpreted to require defendant Boorstin and the Library of Congress to delete *Playboy* from the regular list of braille edition magazines, the amendment constitutes discriminatory suppression and government censorship of a lawful [see 1, above] magazine because of the content of the magazine and the ideas and viewpoints expressed therein, and denies the blind and physically handicapped access to that information in violation of the First and Fifth Amendments to the United States Constitution. (pp. 19–20)

The essence of the fourth point is that the amendment may be unconstitutional on its face. And, indeed, on the House floor, Wylie made it quite clear that he was objecting to the content of *Playboy*. Yet, the complaint continued:

> In several decisions, the United States Supreme Court has made it clear that . . . the government may not discriminatorily subsidize or permit some lawful speech and refuse to subsidize or permit some

other lawful speech when the basis for the distinction is the government's agreement or disagreement with the *content* of the speech or with the ideas or views of the speaker. (p. 20, emphasis added)

Thus, the complaint argues, if Boorstin was under no obligation to follow Wylie's intent but did so anyway, he was acting illegally (point 3). If he *were* under obligation to follow Wylie's intent, maintains the complaint, then the amendment itself was unconstitutional and illegal.

The complaint raises an additional and interesting point of constitutional law. The Wylie amendment, its intent included,

constitutes a civil Bill of Attainder which punishes, penalizes and prohibits the future speech of *Playboy* because Congress has determined, retroactively, that portions of *Playboy*'s past speech were, in the view of Congress, unacceptable. (p. 22)

A bill of attainder is a legislative act that, without trial, convicts and punishes, or removes the civil rights from, a named person or persons. Article I, Section 9 of the U.S. Constitution expressly forbids Congress to pass bills of attainder, which had been used in England as a way for leaders of Parliament to punish political rivals without what we now term "due process." Stated Supreme Court Justice John Paul Stevens, in reference to *Nixon v. Administrator of General Services, et al.*:

By special legislative acts, Parliament deprived one statesman after another of his reputation, his property, and his potential for future leadership. The motivation for such bills was as much political as it was punitive—and often the victims were those who had been the most relentless in attacking their political enemies at the height of their own power. In light of this history, legislation like that before us must be scrutinized with great care. (Murphy and Pritchett, 1979, p. 476)

The complaint concludes by requesting that the court either

1. Declare Wylie's intent not binding and direct Boorstin to consider *Playboy* for inclusion in the NLS program, using the same procedures and standards as are applied to all other magazines, *or*
2. Declare the Wylie amendment unconstitutional and direct Boorstin to consider *Playboy* for inclusion in the NLS program, as above.

The complaint was filed on December 4, 1985, and was heralded with a press conference and considerable media coverage. In June 1986, Rep. Vic Fazio and 42 other sympathetic House members filed a 60-page amicus curiae brief on behalf of the plaintiffs. The library world and the braille *Playboy* subscribers settled in to await a decision.

THE MEMORANDUM OF OPINION AND ORDER

A hearing on the complaint was held on August 28, 1986, before U.S. District Court Judge Thomas F. Hogan. Afterwards, Hogan announced an oral decision from the bench: the Librarian of Congress "violated the First Amendment when he made a viewpoint-based decision to discontinue the production and distribution of braille editions of *Playboy* magazine" (*American Council of the Blind, Memorandum Opinion,* 1986, 1).

Hogan's written opinion was filed on September 23. The first part, *Memorandum Opinion,* summarizes the findings of fact in the case as presented by the plaintiffs and the defendant, and then gives conclusions of law. After declaring that, in this case, the doctrine of sovereign immunity does not bar the plaintiffs' action against Boorstin as a federal official, Hogan declares that:

> The Supreme Court emphasizes that "above all else, the First Amendment means that government has no power to restrict expression because of its message, its ideas, its subject matter or its content."
>
> . . . All parties agree that the statute appropriating funds to the National Program for the Blind and Physically Handicapped is constitutional on its face. No reference to *Playboy* or to any magazine is made. It is in the defendant's application of the budgetary cut that the constitutional claim arises.
>
> . . . The Librarian was faced with a budgetary cutback which he could have enforced for any content-neutral reason rationally related to the braille program. . . . Instead, Boorstin based his decision solely on his interpretation of the House floor debate to the extent that he understood and adopted the view that *Playboy* was to be eliminated because of its sexual orientation. This Court finds that defendant's action in overruling his staff and eliminating *Playboy* from the program was viewpoint-based discrimination impinging on freedom of expression.
>
> Defendant used a backdoor approach to a formalistic game that Congressmen were playing to eliminate future editions of *Playboy* . . . . Censorship whether by Congress or by the Librarian of Congress is equally abhorrent to a society built on tenets of freedom of speech and expression.
>
> Therefore, in following his sense of Congress the defendant made his own non-content neutral decision in violation of the First Amendment. (pp. 7, 9–10)

The second part, *Order,* directs Boorstin to resume production and distribution of *Playboy* in braille as of January 1987, produce recorded versions of 1986 issues, and notify all appropriate persons and libraries that such steps are being taken.

WHAT WERE THE ISSUES?

Had ALA, in supporting *Playboy*, "trivialized the very meaning of censorship" as McReynolds (1986) maintained? Or was ALA's intervention appropriate? Did the issues in the case, in fact, concern censorship at all?

Censorship and Selection Policy

Yes, censorship was the major issue, in this case, content-based censorship implemented by means of a budget cut. Wylie's amendment was, as noted previously, not censorious on its face because it made no mention of eliminating a particular magazine to correspond with the $103,000. However, Wylie's *personal* intent seems quite clear, regardless of legal issues arising when congressional intent is interpreted judicially.

Why conclude that Wylie's intent was censorious? Because his floor comments clearly attacked the magazine's content, his efforts encountered the First Amendment, which guarantees freedom of speech and the press regardless of subject matter or content. However, Wylie's intent could be attacked for nonconstitutional reasons also. In specifying a particular magazine for exclusion, *for whatever reason*, he would have acted contrary to law because responsibility for selection of particular magazines for the NLS braille program has been vested *in LC and its established procedures*, not in Congress. If Wylie had proposed elimination of a different magazine, say, because it was available in braille elsewhere, his proposal could have no force because the law places selection in hands other than his.

An *appropriate* political way for Wylie to have influenced magazine selection would have been to write to the advisory committee and appropriate staff at LC, recommending that selection criteria be revised so as to include additional standards or criteria. One could, for example, suggest a criterion that brailled magazines should appeal equally to both sexes. Of course, this might eliminate *Good Housekeeping, Ladies Home Journal,* and *Boys' Life* as well as *Playboy*.

The Special Case of Obscenity

It is important to note that no issue of *Playboy* had ever been found legally obscene. (See reference to *Miller v. California* and other cases, cited in *Memorandum Opinion,* p. 7.) Some might call *Playboy*—or any material treating sex—"pornographic." *Pornography,* however, is not a legal concept; *obscenity* is. By law, obscenity inheres in a specific document, not in a class of documents or in a periodical in general. A particular work, such as a specific issue of a periodical, may be found obscene by a particular court at a particular time. But only a court using due process can make this determination, not Congress. Only then does that particular issue become illegal to possess or distribute. If this has not happened for a work, or if the work has been found by a court to be *not* obscene, it cannot be banned just because someone is offended by its sexual content.

Expediency

However, the nagging question remains: Why did Boorstin seemingly collaborate with Wylie when (as the judge stated) he could have cut the $103,000 using LC-based, content-neutral criteria? Why, in particular, did he attribute *Wylie's* intent to the House of Representatives and to Congress as a whole? His action, if not deliberately censorious, could be interpreted as a cowardly giving-in and retreating in what Hogan called the "formalistic game that Congressmen were playing to eliminate future editions of *Playboy*" (*American Council of the Blind, Memorandum Opinion,* 1986, 10). Why did Boorstin collaborate with this rather shifty maneuver rather than fight against it in the best tradition of librarians upholding the freedom to read?

While Boorstin has not to my knowledge clearly explained this in the library press, I believe that the key lies in the statement quoted earlier:

> In order ... to secure the *clear judicial affirmation* of the rights of the blind to equal access of knowledge, The Librarian has become technically the defendant.... ("Statement of the Librarian of Congress," 1986, 333, italics added)

Wylie had been attempting to eliminate *Playboy* from NLS since 1981. If Boorstin had passed over this intent through literal interpretation of the amendment, Wylie might have harassed LC in ways based on firmer legal precedent. He could have recommended other budget cuts, promoted investigations, or called the activities of particular personnel into question. In plain English, he could have gone on to become even more of a pain in the neck, to LC, the plaintiffs, and others, and he might have enlisted others in his cause.

Thus I believe that Boorstin purposely took the courageous path, risking opprobrium for his "cowardice," but for a reason. Neither he nor any of the plaintiffs could have sued Wylie directly or applied other legal sanctions to him because Wylie's intent was not reflected in the wording of the bill. But by acting *as if it were,* Boorstin and those working with him stated the case so that a *court* would find Wylie's efforts unconstitutional, even though exemplified by Boorstin rather than Wylie himself. The ultimate purpose was to force Wylie (and any potential allies) to get off LC's back and to avert similar congressional efforts in the future. Even if Judge Hogan's order was directed to Boorstin, its message was also to Congress. And, as we have seen, this tactic was successful. By specifically requiring LC to continue to braille *Playboy*, the court has very likely forestalled any continuation of such efforts by Wylie or anyone else.

WHAT DOES IT MEAN FOR LIBRARIES?

Librarians embroiled in their own local censorship battles may take some reassurance that even the largest and most powerful library in the land has similar troubles. There are other things we can learn from this case, however.

- **An appreciation for the complexity and power of the law against censorship.** No less than three points of constitutional law were brought to bear upon Wylie's "intent" by the astute and legally knowledgeable plaintiffs: the First Amendment, guaranteeing freedom of speech; the Fifth Amendment, guaranteeing due process under law; and Article 1, Section 9 of the U.S. Constitution, prohibiting bills of attainder. Only the First Amendment was needed.[2]
- **Recognition (again) that a (good) selection policy is the best defense against censorship.** ALA and the library press have said this many times. (See Johnson 1989)
- **A coalition is a friend indeed—and in deed.** Two coalitions assisted the positive outcome of the case. First, NLS' magazine selection policy specifically incorporates opinion from members of the user group. It is more difficult to justify eliminating library materials when the community that the library is serving has itself participated in selecting them. (Incidentally, this approach is axiomatic with other sexual issues. In instigating school-based sex education programs, the rule of thumb is "involve the parents.") Second, the plaintiffs themselves represented a coalition; and it did not hurt that *Playboy* was joined by organizations whose reputations would be difficult to impugn. It just does not look good in the United States to attack blind people, veterans, and libraries.
- **Sometimes you can win by seeming to give in.** Boorstin's "collaboration" with Wylie set the stage for a successful suit, throughout which others carried the ball against censorship.[3]

But the best thing, perhaps, is the lesson this case teaches us about the courts, the law, and how censorship can be found unconstitutional. Yet more than the Constitution is involved. Censorship, a focussed suppression of knowledge, must be met by knowledge itself.

And with increased knowledge of the law comes respect for its power against censorship.

Yet we cannot dismiss too readily those forces behind censorship. With increased knowledge of history, psychology, and sociology come respect, also—respect and even fascination, if not approval—for those social impedimenta with which society sometimes burdens sexuality and other controversial areas. These impedimenta may not lightly or eternally be set aside.

ENDNOTES

1. Hogan is referring to the so-called "Miller test" for obscenity:

The basic guidelines for the trier of fact must be: (a) whether "the average person, applying contemporary community standards" would find that the work, taken as a whole, appeals to the prurient interest, (b) whether the work depicts or describes, in a patently offensive way, sexual conduct specifically defined by the applicable state law, and (c) whether the work, taken as a whole, lacks serious literary, artistic, political, or scientific value. (*Miller v. California*, 413 U.S. at 24, 93 S.Ct. at 2615)

2. Schneider (1988), herself blind, makes the following point about censorship and blind people:

Why, you may ask, is a feminist like me defending the existence of Playboy in Braille? It's a lousy magazine that exploits women. . . . Even though there is much that is wrong with Playboy's presentation of sexuality, it is the only one of the 36 magazines in Braille offered through the NLS that regularly talks about sex. . . .
  Passage of this [Wylie's] amendment has ramifications far beyond the publication of Playboy in Braille. Withholding information from us, especially information about sex and sexuality, will never enable us to begin to make knowledgeable judgements about what does actually occur in this society. I believe that some people, if they could, would legislate away all access to anything about sex that anyone might want to read. And they would do that whether or not we agree that what is presented is, for example, pornographic, or enjoyable, or useful. Blind and disabled people are more vulnerable to having what we read censored through legislation because a good deal of the literature we can get is produced through government funds. (p. 19)

3. For a fascinating historical discussion on library attitudes towards controversial materials, see Evelyn Geller's *Forbidden Books in American Public Libraries, 1876–1939: A Study in Cultural Change*, New York: Greenwood, 1984. In essence, Geller's work is a history of the Library Bill of Rights, first adopted by ALA in 1939. For bibliographies of recent materials on censorship and what to do about it, contact ALA's Intellectual Freedom Committee and the American Society of Journalists and Authors. The American Civil Liberties Union is another valuable resource.

REFERENCES

ALA authorized to join suit against Librarian of Congress. 1985. *American Libraries*, December: 813.

American Council of the Blind, et al. vs. Boorstin. 1985. *Complaint for declaratory and injunctive relief.* (Civil Action 85–3836, filed 12/4/85 in the U.S. District Court for the District of Columbia).

American Council of the Blind, et al. vs. Boorstin. 1986. *Memorandum opinion.* (Civil Action 85–3836, filed 9/23/86 in the U.S. District Court for the District of Columbia).

American Council of the Blind, et al. vs. Boorstin. 1986. *Order.* (Civil Action 85–3836, filed 9/23/86 in the U.S. District Court for the District of Columbia).

Books for the blind and physically handicapped. 1985. *Congressional Record*, July 18: H5932–5935.

Ignoring Boorstin, Senate cuts funds for braille *Playboy*. 1985. *American Libraries*, September: 534.

Johnson, Cameron. 1989. Are videos different? *ALKI: The Washington Library Association Journal*, March: 9–11.

Manley, Will. 1986. Facing the public. *Wilson Library Bulletin*, September: 55–56.

McReynolds, Rosalee. 1986. Right action, wrong reason [letter to the editor]. *American Libraries*, April: 237.

Murphy, Walter F., and C. Herman Pritchett. 1979. *Courts, judges, and politics: An introduction to the judicial process.* 3rd ed. New York: Random House.

NLS Services expand and improve during Boorstin years. 1987. *News*, April–June: 1–2. (Published by the National Library Service for the Blind and Physically Handicapped, Library of Congress).

Schneider, Marj. 1988. House moves to stop *Playboy* in Braille: How did it happen and what does it mean? In *Throw away your stereotypes: Articles from the Womyn's Braille Press Newsletter* (pp. 17–19). Minneapolis: Womyn's Braille Press.

Statement of the Librarian of Congress on freedom of access to library materials and related statements. 1986. *Library of Congress Information Bulletin*, September 29: 333–335.

CHAPTER 10

What Happens When Libraries Subscribe to *Playboy*?

Martha Cornog

Although *Playboy* magazine—with its *Playboy* philosophy, bunnies, and centerfolds—may not generally be considered "standard" library fare by either patrons or librarians, at least 300 libraries in the U.S. are (or recently have been) subscribers.[1] Its centerfolds and philosophy make *Playboy* a good case study for speculation and investigation about the treatment of sexual materials by librarians. On one hand, it is a quality publication. Its fiction and nonfiction regularly win awards and feature well-known, respected authors. It is widely quoted and is generally considered to comment sagely on many current issues. It is even indexed.[2] On these bases, librarians should surely wish to make *Playboy* widely accessible.

On the other hand, there are all those naked women. While the cover is comparatively tame these days and the magazine contains little that is kinky or even remotely violent,[3] *Playboy* deals unabashedly with sex, complete with advocacy, how-tos, and graphics that could promote sexual arousal. And, as described in Chapter 1, sex has long been considered an "objectionable" subject heading in libraries.

In her 1984 book, Evelyn Geller describes two library "ideologies" that I will refer to as "The Guardianship of Society" and "The Freedom to Read." The first proclaims the librarian's right and duty to provide patrons with only the highest quality reading matter, thereby promoting wisdom and society's good. Books judged to be of poor quality or as likely to "corrupt" or "deprave" readers should not be made freely accessible, particularly to "susceptible" readers such as the young and less intelligent. Although some librarians might acquire and keep such items—for, say, research or archival purposes—this ideology mandates keeping them carefully secluded and imposing restrictions upon access.

The second ideology maintains that unrestricted and uncensored access to books and "the right to read" are the library patron's fundamental right. While librarians might sometimes deliberately select "better quality" materials, any possible "bad" influence of books or topics upon the reader is not relevant. This second ideology charges the librarian to collect and make available publications representing many points of view rather than solely those presently deemed by the librarian, patron, or even, perhaps, "outside experts" as most "acceptable" or "healthy" or "beneficial to society."

Geller argues that the first ideology dominated public librarianship in the nineteenth and early twentieth centuries. Thereafter, she suggests, a transition occurred towards the second ideology, which has become the official stance of nearly all library organizations and most librarians.

Even so, the Guardianship of Society ideology is still alive and well among librarians (see Chapters 1 and 3), and is often in real conflict with the Freedom to Read ideology. How might this conflict be reflected in librarian attitudes towards, and treatment of, sexual subject matter in general, and *Playboy* in particular?

Furthermore, library patrons and concerned citizens have their own ideologies, which may or may not coincide with the library's official stance. Treatment of *Playboy* may readily reflect these factors as well, so that librarians' decisions about *Playboy* are likely to represent the interaction of a variety of factors.

Accordingly, we may ask the following questions:

1. Do librarians, with respect to *Playboy*, hold primarily to the Guardianship of Society or to the Freedom to Read ideology?
2. Do patrons' reactions to *Playboy*, in terms of their own ideologies, exceed in number and strength any librarian reactions? *Or . . .*
3. Is *Playboy* considered so tame today by everyone (in comparison with other publications and videos) that it seems to evoke no particular ideology at all, but is treated no differently than, say, *Newsweek*?

More specifically, some further interesting questions are:

1. What selection decisions are given for subscribing to *Playboy*, and who makes those decisions? Is *Playboy* chosen in spite of—or because of—its treatment of sex?
2. What is the relative proportion of complaints about *Playboy* (if any) originating with patrons versus those coming from

staff? Are there any differences by type of library? Do complaints have any effect, e.g., subscription cancellation?
3. Is access to *Playboy* usually controlled or restricted and, if so, how and in which types of libraries?
4. How heavily is *Playboy* used? Is amount of usage related to access restrictions?
5. How much vandalism (theft and mutilation) is visited upon *Playboy*? Is vandalism related to the amount of use or to the degree of access restrictions? Do librarians react any differently to vandalism of *Playboy* versus vandalism of non-sexual materials?

THE SURVEY

By way of turning speculation into investigation, in 1987 I sent a questionnaire to 309 libraries listed by OCLC as having holdings of *Playboy*. I also placed a notice in *Library Journal* and *American Libraries* asking for experiences from libraries subscribing to *Playboy*. In addition, several colleagues handed out the questionnaire at the 1987 American Library Association meeting in San Francisco.

The Questionnaire

The questionnaire asked for the titles of "popular sex magazines" to which the library subscribed, whether in print or microform; how the selection decisions were made; and whether the subscriptions were gifts or purchases. It also asked about access policies and restrictions, degree of patron use, degree of vandalism, reactions from patrons and staff, and how reactions were handled. Respondents were assured anonymity.

The Responses

I received 108 useable questionnaires (response rate: 34.9% or 108/309). Of these, about ¾ were academic (college or community college), and about ¼ public (73.1% or 79/108 vs. 26.9% or 29/108). This ratio was quite similar to that of the full group of 309 libraries to which the questionnaire was sent; respondent bias, at least by type of library, did not seem to have occurred.[4]

Three letters were received that could be analyzed in lieu of questionnaires, giving 111 useable responses. The final breakdown was 73.9% academic and 26.1% public (82/111 and 29/111).

Of the 111 libraries, about ⅓ subscribed to *Playboy* in print only, over half had or were planning to have both print and microform subscriptions, either simultaneously or in succession, and the remaining 10% subscribed to microform only (32.4% or 36/111; 57.7% or 64/111; 9.9% or 11/111). Few libraries subscribed to any "sex magazines" other than *Playboy*.[5,6]

RESULTS

Selection Decisions

Why did these libraries subscribe to *Playboy*? Respondents mentioned most often the quality of content—interviews, fiction, articles, or "socially significant journalism"—together with the fact that *Playboy* was indexed (34.2% or 38/111; 20.7% or 23/111). Curiously, not all seemed to know exactly which indexes actually cover *Playboy*.[7]

Balanced access was mentioned by two respondents:

> They [issues of *Playboy*] seem to represent an open-mindedness, freedom to read symbol in the library (#110)

> Our task, as I understand it is to attempt, within our administrative structures, to provide access to all types of materials and all viewpoints so our patrons may make up their own minds. (#107)

Only one respondent alluded to choosing *Playboy* because of its sexual content: "High calibre of models" (#3).

Nearly half the time the library staff decided to acquire *Playboy*, and sometimes the director was mentioned. Library users (patrons/faculty) constituted the impetus for acquisition for about ⅓ of the respondents, while around 10% cited some mix of staff and users (44.1% or 49/111; 30.6% or 34/111; 9.0% or 10/111; nonrespondents = 18).

Users had greater influence over selection decisions in academic than in public libraries. When "users" plus the mixed "users and staff" categories are combined, about 40% of academic library decisions regarding *Playboy* arose from staff influence alone and the same proportion from users plus the "mix" group combined (41.5% or 34/82 for both categories). Public libraries, however, attributed over 50% of the decisions to staff but only about ⅓ to users (51.7% or 15/29 vs. 34.5% or 10/29).

Nearly all subscriptions were purchased; a few were gifts, or both, during the lifetime of the subscription (88.3% or 98/111; 5.4% or 6/111; 5.4% or 6/111; nonrespondents = 1).

> [T]he library staff recommended dropping Playboy, National Lampoon, and four or five others that the [university] Student Government Organization [then] decided to fund (They now fund 14 subscriptions). (#113)

Complaints and Other Reactions

While one might imagine that *Playboy* in the library could excite numerous reactions from patrons and staff, nearly half the libraries reported "none" or "none that I know of." About ¼, however, reported an occasional complaint from patrons, and half as many reported staff complaints, usually recurrent (42.3% or 47/111; 25.2% or 28/111; 12.6% or 14/111). Four libraries mentioned both patron and staff complaints, and are counted twice above, so that a total of ⅓ of the libraries reported a complaint (34.2% or 38/111).

Over 15% said that the only reaction took the form of (sometimes jocular) requests from women patrons or staff to add *Playgirl* magazine to the collection "for balance." A few reported a positive reaction from patrons: "pleasant surprise," and "students want more—so do male librarians" (16.2% or 18/111; 6.3% or 7/111). Altogether, queries about *Playgirl* (considered a neutral response) and positive responses totalled over 20% (21.6% or 24/111). Five libraries reported both complaints and neutral/positive responses, and are counted twice above (nonrespondents = 7).

Patron Complaints. For all patron complaints described, the individual complained to a librarian, who defended *Playboy* (on the grounds of quality writing, indexing, selection policy, and/or anticensorship and freedom of access factors), and the complainant did not pursue it further.

> One negative response to Advocate [a gay newspaper] from patron; director cited freedom from censorship, freedom of press, freedom of speech; patron departed abashed. (#29)

> For 20 years we have had no problems until this year when a patron—a young adult student—took a copy of Playboy and took it to his church counselor and complained. The church counselor called the library to complain. We pointed out that the young lad was in possession of stolen property (Playboy does not circulate) and we haven't heard anything since. (#57)

> The title *Playboy* caught the eye of the Dean of the campus, who called me in for a discussion. He did not feel that the title was appropriate, and felt that it might cause offense . . . . When he requested that I have the subscription cancelled immediately, I told him we were conducting an evaluation, and if low usage was shown, it would be dropped, . . . and I refused, pointing out that removal of materials from the Library at the request of an individual, for reasons not related to our academic mission, sounded like censorship. The discussion became heated, and I reminded the Dean of the memo announcing the addition the previous year, which he did not recall. Following additional discussion on censorship, the Dean withdrew his request, saying he relied on my judgement [sic], and that I should do as I thought best . . . . No further problem has arisen. (#39)

Staff Complaints. Of the libraries reporting staff complaints, a majority linked complaints with disapproval of, or extra work connected with, vandalism of *Playboy*; a few mentioned disapproval of content; and a few gave no reason (8/14; 4/14; 3/14). Some libraries gave more than one reason. Below are a few typical comments.

> Staff is not thrilled with the title because of the problems it poses. Very little reaction from public. (#90)

> [Negative reactions] from women staff members having to retrieve material. (#25)

> Negative reaction from staff led to cancellation of paper copy, summer 1987. Fresh semen found more than once in pages. Admin. decision to cancel paper copy after second incident. (#76)

The last comment was unique: no other library reported explicit sexual utilization of the magazine.

Reactions by Type of Library. More than twice as many responding academic libraries reported patron complaints as responding public libraries (29.3% or 24/82 academic; 13.8% or 4/29 public). However, a slightly lesser percentage of academic as compared to public libraries reported staff complaints (12.2% or 10/82 academic; 13.8% or 4/29 public).

Reporting neutral/positive responses were, again, twice as many responding academic as public libraries (25.6% or 21/82 academic; 10.3% or 3/29 public).

When the responses are divided into *no response* and *any reaction* (positive or negative) categories, nearly twice as many academic as public libraries reported reactions of *any* kind (58.5% or 48/82 academic; 31.0% or 9/29 public).

Controlled Access to *Playboy*

A majority of nearly ⅔ restricted *Playboy* behind the reserve or circulation desk; a patron would need to request it from a librarian and would sometimes be required to show or leave identification (62.2% or 69/111). Sometimes only the current issue or year was restricted. A small number of these libraries also specifically mentioned permitting access to *Playboy* only to those over 18 years old or with an adult library card; no other type of patron was specifically denied or permitted access (5 out of 69). Another group, some 12% of the libraries, reported controlling access to all periodicals, *Playboy* included, through closed stacks (12.6% or 14/111).

However, about ¼ of the libraries reported not restricting access to *Playboy* at all (24.3% or 27/111). Two of these had removed previous restrictions because patrons complained (nonrespondents = 1).

When the libraries restricting *Playboy* are counted together with the closed-stack libraries, about ¾ controlled access to *Playboy* in some way (74.8% or 83/111).

Controlled Access by Type of Library. A larger majority of academic versus public libraries restricted *Playboy* (65.8% or 54/111 academic; 51.7% or 15/29 public). This was reversed with closed stacks, with only half as many academic as public libraries reporting this type of control (9.7% or 8/82 academic; 20.7% or 6/29 public).

Combining restricting libraries with closed-stack libraries, a slightly *higher* proportion of academic than public libraries controlled access to *Playboy* (75.6% or 62/82 academic; 72.4% or 21/29 public). Correspondingly, a slightly *lower* proportion of academic as public libraries reported not controlling access at all (23.2% or 19/82 academic; 27.6% or 8/29 public).

Usage

Playboy proved a popular item among patrons, although not uniformly so. Over ⅓ of the libraries reported high usage, somewhat fewer medium usage, still fewer low usage, and several reported usage dropping considerably when access became restricted (38.7% or 43/111; 26.1% or 29/111; 19.8% or 22/111; 1.8% or 2/111; nonrespondents = 15). One of the libraries reporting medium usage commented: "No doubt use would be heavy if they were on open shelves" (#35). Altogether, nearly ⅔ reported high to medium usage (64.9% or 72/111).

Playboy was reported more popular in public libraries than in academic. About 60% of academic libraries reported high to medium usage, about ⅕ reported low usage, and a few reported usage dropping (61.0% or 50/82; 20.7% or 17/82; 2.4% or 2/82). Among public libraries, however, about ¾ reported high to medium usage and less than ⅕ low usage (75.9% or 22/29; 17.2% or 5/29).

A few libraries reported cancelling or planning to cancel *Playboy* because of low usage (see below; 4/111).

Vandalism

Together with usage, vandalism was also high, with nearly ⅔ of the libraries reporting current theft or mutilation—and sometimes a good deal of it. Almost 15% in addition reported that vandalism had occurred in the past until access was controlled or until the print subscription was replaced by microform (64.9% or 72/111; 13.5% or 15/111). Thus over ¾ reported past or current experience with vandalism (78.4% or 87/111). However, nearly 20% reported little or no vandalism (18.9% or 21/111; nonrespondents = 3).

Vandalism and Patrons vs. Staff. While not all of the libraries reporting vandalism described the source of the problem, a few (5 academic, 1 public) did explicitly trace at least some of the vandalism to *staff*, e.g.:

> Theft is our primary problem; students aren't responsible generally but staff members who have access to library when it is closed. (#62)

> Gave up collecting physical copies because of staff and public theft and mutilation. (#55)

> An occasional theft of a paper issue has occurred, usually at some point during the transition from check-in at Periodicals to processing at Reserve. (#114)

> Microfilm [of *Playboy*] disappeared into the Humanities-Social Sciences librarian's office. Hmmmmmm! (#88)

Vandalism and Type of Library. More academic than public libraries reported current or past vandalism: over 80% compared to not quite 70% (81.7% or 67/82 academic; 69.0% or 20/29 public).

Vandalism and Use. Cross-tabulation of vandalism and use shows that more vandalism was reported where usage was higher. Of the libraries reporting high use of *Playboy*, nearly 90% reported experience with vandalism; for medium use, about ¾; but for low use, around 60% (88.4% or 38/42; 75.9% or 22/29; 63.6% or 14/22).

Controlled Access, Medium, and Vandalism. Was vandalism less where access was controlled, or where copies were in microform? Current and/or past vandalism was reported for restricted, closed stacks, and unrestricted subscriptions and for both print and microform. More of the libraries having uncontrolled access, however, reported current vandalism than did libraries with either restrictions or closed stacks (74.1% or 20/27 uncontrolled; 61.4% or 51/83 restricted *or* closed stacks). For closed stacks alone, a much lesser proportion reported current vandalism (28.6% or 4/14).

Of the few libraries reporting neither controlled access nor vandalism, most held only microform subscriptions, suggesting that microform may discourage vandals (80.0% or 4/5). However, over ¼ of the libraries reporting current vandalism specifically described theft or mutilation of microform in their comments (29.2% or 21/72).

Librarian Reactions to Vandalism. Most of the libraries reporting past or current vandalism of *Playboy* reported taking some type of action in response (70.1% or 61/87). These included instituting or tightening controlled access (37 libraries); cancelling all *Playboy* subscriptions (10); voicing staff complaints (8); cancelling print copy while retaining or instituting a microform subscription (7); instituting microform subscriptions in addition to or instead of print (4); switching from color to black-and-white film (2); circulating photocopies of key articles instead of the magazine (1); buying extra subscriptions

(1); replacing copies or film after they were vandalized (1); or using interlibrary loan for requests of material from missing or mutilated issues (1). A number of libraries reported more than one type of action.

Substantially more academic libraries reported taking action than did public libraries (59.7% or 49/82 academic; 41.3% or 12/29 public).

Of the libraries reporting little or no vandalism, nearly ¼ described having taken prophylactic measures against vandalism, such as instituting restrictions from the beginning or choosing to buy microform (23.8% or 5/21).

Vandalism of *Playboy* and Other Items. It is not clear to what extent librarians reacted similarly to vandalism of items other than *Playboy*. On one hand, six libraries explicitly reported also controlling access to other high use/high vandalism items without sexual content, such as *Time, Variety, Jerusalem Post, Rolling Stone, Consumer Reports*, and the "investment tools." As the question was not asked directly, doubtless more than six do so. Three additional respondents opined that *Playboy* is not *that* different from other popular items:

> Since I do not consider Play. sexually explicit, there is no comparison to X rated material which we do not purchase. (#47)

> *Playboy* is hardly *Debbie Does Dallas* [an X-rated film] . . . . *Playboy* and the other publications, like *Esquire* of yore, have aged to genteel sexuality. (#73)

> Quite frankly, the erotic appeal of any paper media [sic] pales before that freely available in any corner video store. (#107)

Still another respondent added:

> Library staff do not regard this title as a sex magazine, sexist perhaps . . . . I have never discussed this title with any patron using the library. [But] I have received requests for *Playgirl* and I have received negative comments concerning *Off Our Backs* and *Ms* [*Off Our Backs* is a feminist publication]. (#109)

On the other hand, two respondents commented:

> It would certainly be hard to distinguish between censorship and fear of mutilation or theft in our not placing [sexually] explicit material on the open shelves. For example, we already face heavy theft and mutilation in our sections on Marilyn Monroe, gays, and Nazism [presumably on open shelves]. (#102)

> We recently decided to drop [*Playboy*] because of difficulties in managing it . . . . In considering dropping the subscription, the main Library said they didn't want to deal with it anymore [sic] and no branch library would agree to take it.
>
> [But] we put up with theft of all kinds of materials and never consider not purchasing anymore—in fact, if patrons steal Fortune, or People, we simply add another copy.

> Much as I hate the sexist rag, it is censorship to not renew, no matter what reason our librarians give. (#38)

Cancellations and Other Factors

All of the libraries reported having acquired *Playboy* at one time. However, about 20% had cancelled a subscription—print, microform, or both. Several more were considering cancelling a subscription, totalling about 25% (21.6% or 24/111 + 3.6% or 4/111 = 25.2% or 28/111). More of these were academic than public libraries (26.8% or 22/82 academic; 20.7% or 6/29 public).

Some of these libraries cancelled only a print subscription, but retained or instituted a microform subscription. Nearly all gave "vandalism" as the reason. Most were academic libraries also (7 out of 28 libraries; 6 mentioned vandalism; academic = 5, public = 2).

Eliminating the libraries that retained microform, we have nearly 20% that cancelled (or planned to cancel) *all* their *Playboy* subscriptions (18.9% or 21/111). Reasons given were vandalism (10 libraries), budget cuts (8), low usage (4), lack of indexing "at that time" (1), declining quality (1), and "not appropriate" (1). Some gave more than one reason. Here, too, academic libraries outnumbered, proportionately, public libraries (20.7% or 17/82 academic; 13.8% or 4/29 public).

Because cancellation appears to be a particularly interesting phenomenon vis-à-vis sexual material in the library, these occurrences of total cancellation were cross-tabulated against usage, vandalism, controlled access, and complaints.

Cancellations vs. Usage. Of libraries cancelling all subscriptions to *Playboy*, less than 40% reported high-to-medium usage; whereas of libraries not cancelling, or shifting from print to microform, over 70% reported high-to-medium usage (38.1% or 8/21 cancelling; 71.1% or 64/90 others). Thus, cancellations appear associated with lower use. However, as I discuss below, there is probably *not* a direct cause-and-effect relationship here.

However, libraries cancelling because of vandalism reported a greater proportion of high-to-medium usage than those cancelling for other reasons (60.0% or 6/10 vandalism; 18.2% or 2/11 other reasons). Too few libraries gave budget cuts or low usage as the reason for cancellation to permit any meaningful cross-tabulations for these factors.

Cancellations vs. Vandalism. Libraries cancelling all subscriptions reported slightly less vandalism than the other libraries (76.2% or 16/21 cancelling libraries; 77.8% or 70/90 others). However, all libraries cancelling because of vandalism explicitly described vandalism, as did all of the libraries cancelling a print subscription but retaining microform.

Cancellations vs. Controlled Access. Libraries cancelling all subscriptions to *Playboy* reported a much lower rate of controlled access (restricted access or closed stacks) than other libraries (52.4% or 11/21 cancelling all; 71.4% or 5/7 cancelling print; 80.7% or 67/83 no cancellations). Libraries cancelling all subscriptions because of vandalism reported an even lower rate of controlled access (50.0% or 5/10).

Cancellations vs. Complaints. Libraries cancelling all subscriptions to *Playboy* reported nearly double the rate of both patron and staff complaints than the other libraries (patrons: 38.1% or 8/21 cancelling all, 22.2% or 20/90 other; staff: 19.0% or 4/21 cancelling all, 11.1% or 10/90 other). Below are the responses for the libraries reporting both cancellations of all subscriptions and *staff* complaints.

> Playboy was indexed . . . so we received numerous requests for articles from it. They [the issues] were heavily used. We did keep the paper copy behind the periodicals desk, holding the patron's i.d. while it was out. [But] Playboy [was] cancelled [in] 1985 after several years—not because of content, but because the hardcopy and microform editions were mutilated beyond use.
>
> Some staff and faculty felt that the money could be better spent elsewhere. (#41)

> They were always in disarray on the shelf. Very high rate of theft & mutilation. I don't remember negative reactions except exasperation at mutilation and theft. Because of high theft & mutilation and lack of indexing (at the time), when cuts were made several years back, these subscriptions were among the first to go. (#42)

> Staff hate it, they object to the content, they resent the loss rate, etc. We recently decided to drop it because of difficulties in managing it. (#38)

> When I first came to the _____ library in 1972, we subscribed to the hard copy of *Playboy*. Along with our other popular periodicals we kept it in back of the circulation desk and signed it out on demand. Some of the young women who worked at the desk objected to handing this material out all the time. As we also found that the back copies were being stolen we cancelled our subscription.
>
> We then had complaints from some users (all male) about no longer having *Playboy* available. We then started getting it in microfilm only. Like most compromises this didn't really satisfy either faction, but at least the material was available, and workers did not have to handle it on a daily basis.
>
> However, we then found that our reels of microfilm were being stolen despite the fact that they were not even in color. We finally gave up on subscribing to this publication . . . . [T]he main problem for us was protecting the material from theft, and it didn't seem worth the monumental effort it would have taken. (#108)

Libraries cancelling all subscriptions reported a much lower rate of neutral/positive reactions than other libraries (9.5% or 2/21 cancelling all; 24.4% or 22/90 others).

DISCUSSION

What may we deduce from this admittedly small survey about libraries and sexual materials? One finding is especially noticeable but perhaps easily accounted for.

Academic vs. Public Libraries

The astute reader will have remarked differences between academic and public libraries on nearly all the questionnaire items. Specifically, academic libraries, as compared to public libraries, reported:

- Greater patron influence in acquisitions (41.5% vs. 34.5%)
- More patron complaints (29.3% vs. 13.8%)
- More requests for *Playgirl* and more positive reactions (25.6% total vs. 10.3%)
- More reactions of all types (58.5% vs. 31.0%)
- More restrictions upon access to *Playboy* (65.8% vs. 51.7%)
- More vandalism (81.7% vs. 69.0%)
- More librarian reactions to vandalism (59.7% vs. 41.3%)
- More cancellations of *all Playboy* subscriptions (20.7% vs. 13.8%)
- More total cancellations of *Playboy* (26.8% vs. 20.7%)

But academic libraries also reported, as compared to public libraries:

- Lower usage (61.0% high-to-medium vs. 75.9%)
- Fewer with closed stacks (9.7% vs. 20.7%)
- Slightly fewer staff complaints (12.2% vs. 13.8%)

The total pattern here appears to point *not* to greater conservatism among academic patrons and librarians as seemingly indicated by the higher rates of complaints, restrictions, and cancellations, but to a higher involvement level in the library among different groups of individuals within the academic community. Academic libraries report more reactions of *all* types to *Playboy*, especially positive ones, and greater user involvement in acquisitions. The academic community as a whole may be presumed more educated, more outspoken, more inclined to take matters seriously, and more activist than the community comprising a public library, even though in a large city the differences may be less.[8] Moreover, academic libraries may place more emphasis upon preserving the valuable research collection and thus might react more strongly to vandalism by instituting restrictions and cancellations. By contrast, the patrons—and, to some degree, the staff—of public libraries appear more passive.

Passive or blasé? We may also conjecture that the public library community, anchored in the "real world" of the corner newsstand and video store, is more likely to simply consider *Playboy* and its vandalism "no big deal" than are the inhabitants of a, theoretically at least, somewhat idealistic community.

Why the lower use of *Playboy* in academic libraries? The difference is not great—about 10%—and I propose to attribute it to the "study" vs. "leisure" orientation of the two environments. Most academic patrons come to the library for research first and leisure reading second, while the reverse is true for public libraries. So the lower usage of *Playboy* in academic libraries is likely due both to its comparatively lesser value as a research tool in that setting (in comparison to academic journals and books) and the lesser impulse of academic patrons toward *Playboy*'s entertainment value. Also, academic libraries usually have other nonfiction materials about sex, making the academic library patron less likely to use *Playboy* for sex education purposes.

By contrast, in the public library setting, *Playboy*'s value for research increases, as public libraries in general have fewer research resources than do academic libraries. Furthermore, public library patrons likely seek leisure reading at the library in larger numbers, and are also drawn to *Playboy* for recreation.

The two groups of libraries are most alike in the total number controlling access to *Playboy*: more academic libraries through restrictions; more public libraries through closed stacks. Here again, greater use of restricted access for *Playboy* in academic libraries does not necessarily imply a conservative approach to sexual materials. Academic libraries have a pre-existing institution tailor-made for high use, high vandalism items—the reserve room. Academic reserve rooms typically house a variety of fare, from local city guides, to investment tools, to reprints required for courses, to software directories for the local campus computer system, to the newsweeklies. Adding *Playboy* to a reserve room of this type is a logical and nondiscriminatory action. However, closed stacks in public libraries are somewhat unusual, and I suggest that this finding has nothing to do with *Playboy*, but with the fact that only the larger public libraries tend to be OCLC members, and those are just the libraries most likely to have periodical collections of such value and size that closed stacks are instituted to protect them.

Differences between academic and public libraries aside, let us turn to a quite striking finding that was perhaps less noticeable among the wealth of data in the previous section.

Complaints and Other Reactions to *Playboy*

Combining categories of complaints versus other (neutral or positive) reactions plus no reactions, about ⅓ of all the libraries reported patron and/or staff complaints, while *nearly ⅔ reported requests for Playgirl, positive reactions, or no reactions.* Moreover, isolating patron—as opposed to staff—reactions, nearly as many libraries reported neutral/positive reactions as complaints (21.6% vs. 25.2%). In other words, for most of the libraries, *Playboy* was perceived neutrally or positively by patrons, perhaps as not that different from other library materials. So the library has *Playboy*. Neat. Or, why not? Or, ho-hum. Certainly the number of requests for *Playgirl* is an indication that more of the same in the library, prurient interest or no, might be seen as a good thing.

This sample of OCLC libraries subscribing to *Playboy* is probably not typical of U.S. academic and public libraries as a group. Libraries on the OCLC network (particularly public libraries) tend to be larger, located in more sophisticated cosmopolitan areas, have better educated clientele, and be better funded. (Howard White [1986] reported that censorship of controversial materials such as sex-related items tended to be more favored by, among other groups, the *less* educated and, by implication, more rural—i.e., South and Midwest—populations.) Moreover, this survey by its nature excluded libraries that had subscribed to *Playboy* before the recent past, but had cancelled their subscription, perhaps because of complaints, and been removed from the OCLC listing of *Playboy* subscribers.

Still, the low patron complaint rate is striking. Moreover, the 25% that reported patron complaints all described them as "one" or "occasional" and relatively easily handled through the library's taking a firm stance behind its acquisition decision and the *Intellectual Freedom Manual*.

This seems to imply that our libraries *do* uphold the Freedom to Read ideology and, in fact, find it relatively easy to do so. After all, nearly ⅔ of the libraries report no complaints, and the additional 25% or so reporting patron complaints dismiss them as easily handled. So, no problem, right?

The catch is the nearly 20% cancelling or planning to cancel all subscriptions to *Playboy*. For these libraries, required analysis is rather more complex, as we shall see.

The Public vs. Private Face of Librarians

En masse, librarians say that they refuse to cancel *Playboy* because of patron complaints. But nearly 20% actually cancelled or are planning to cancel all subscriptions. For what reasons? And can we deduce reasons admitted publicly and reasons perhaps held privately that enter into the decisions?

Public Reasons. The major "public" reasons for cancellations were vandalism, budget cuts, and low usage. While budget cuts and low usage have been time-honored, if regretted, reasons for periodical subscription cancellation, vandalism, when one thinks about it, is an odd reason indeed. Almost by definition, vandalized material is *popular* material, so much in demand that patrons will transgress the usual rules of the library and society to possess it. Theoretically, at least, librarians should be delighted to possess such items because they draw people to the library. And, from that viewpoint, reasonable responses to vandalism are buying more copies (print and/or fiche), making photocopies of popular selections, and restricting the rate or duration or privacy of use through limited circulation or a reserve room system. Many libraries do these things, but some do not or do not continue to do them for *Playboy*.

We might ask, in this regard, whether vandalism is used as a reason for cancellation of other items besides *Playboy*. We have no evidence that it is. In fact, one respondent, as quoted above, remarked, " . . . if patrons steal *Fortune* or *People*, we simply add another copy." It could be argued that *Fortune* is an essential, serious periodical, worth replacing. But the same could not be argued for *People*.

Why, then, is vandalism given as a "reason" for cancelling *Playboy*? Perhaps there are private reasons *behind* the publicly stated reasons of budget cuts, low use, and vandalism.

Private Reasons. I propose that, for some librarians, vandalism of *Playboy* provokes a particular sense of outrage, which vandalism of other magazines does not. And this outrage seems linked to the recreational use—specifically, use of *Playboy* for sexual arousal—rather than research use, say, of the *Playboy* interview. Out of 10 libraries describing specific parts of the magazine that were torn out and stolen, 8 mentioned the centerfold, pictures, or photos. The following quotes are typical, and suggest a level of exasperation beyond mere annoyance at the "normal" effects of heavy use:

> Staff wonders why we bother getting it since so few issues remain on shelf! (#36)

> They were always in disarray on the shelf. Very high rate of theft and mutilation. I don't remember negative reactions, except exasperation at mutilation & theft. (#42) [Cancelled.]

> Theft—so much, that we finally cancelled subscription on grounds that we should not support the one or two stealing. (#60) [Cancelled.]

Paper copies lost much weight in the form of photos of nubile young women. They even mutilated the microfilm . . . . Why? They weren't even in color! (#88) [Cancelled.]

Negative reaction from staff led to cancellation of paper copy, summer 1987. Fresh semen found more than once in pages. Admin. decision to cancel paper copy after second incident. (#76)

It is difficult to see, in terms of principle, how semen on the pages of *Playboy* is any different from peanut butter on the pages of *Jack and Jill* in the children's room. For one thing, not all children apply sticky fingers to their reading matter, and few librarians would deprive the majority of youngsters access to spite the minority. Similarly, respondent #76 reported subscribing to *Playboy* since 1953, with "heavy use" of the paper copy; presumably, these two incidents were unique and probably the work of only one or two individuals. Why deny the magazine to the vast majority of other readers?

The remedy for peanut butter in the children's room is friendly vigilance over young readers. The remedy for masturbatory use of *Playboy* in the library is placing the magazine on reserve or restricting its use to public areas so that copies cannot be transported to the men's room or other private nook. Neither eating nor masturbation need be considered offensive *per se*, but their manifestations in the library are certainly inappropriate, particularly in preventing other readers from using the materials. But somehow the actuality that anyone—even one or two people among a large university library clientele—should use *Playboy* for sexual purposes is judged particularly offensive, viewed with rather the same mixture of horror and scorn with which exhibitionists and voyeurs are regarded, and cancellation is viewed as the only option.

And who is offended? The librarians. Recall that libraries cancelling all subscriptions to *Playboy* reported nearly double the rate of staff complaints. And, despite stated refusals to cancel because of patron complaints, these libraries reported nearly double the rate of patron complaints as well, plus less than half the rate of neutral/positive reactions. These librarians do appear to be reacting to patron offense as well as to their own.

But perhaps, we say, it is really that the staff, with their complaints and cancellations, are reacting to an extreme of vandalism that no amount of controlled access will allay. Perhaps the librarians really *are* at their wits' end, as some of the comments suggest. We might imagine, then, that the following pattern would be typical for our libraries that cancelled all subscriptions: high use, heavily controlled access, but with near universal vandalism despite controls. However, the data do not substantiate this picture.

First, these libraries report lower use of *Playboy* than the other libraries, even that subset of libraries cancelling because of vandalism. Second, they experienced slightly *less* vandalism, on the average.

True, those cancelling because of vandalism reported 100% actual vandalism, but so did the libraries that cancelled a print subscription *but* maintained one in microform. Third and most interesting, libraries cancelling all subscriptions to *Playboy* reported a much lower rate of controlled access than the other libraries, and the lowest rate of controlled access was reported by libraries cancelling because of vandalism. It appears that these libraries were not trying very hard to prevent the vandalism that they decried.

We can now see the pattern that occurs in perhaps 20% of the libraries. *Playboy* receives moderate to low use, but average vandalism. Staff and isolated patrons voice complaints about content, suitability, or the vandalism. The reaction at this point could be to restrict access, replace copies, or maintain microform subscriptions. But these libraries do not take these actions. In particular, many do not restrict access, even though a majority are academic libraries and presumably have a reserve room or similar institution. We can only conclude that they do not believe *Playboy* is *worth* restricting. Yet in these libraries, other vandalized periodicals, even such as *People*, *are* restricted and replaced.

In *these* libraries, *Playboy* is viewed as different from other periodicals such as *People*, and the patrons who vandalize it are viewed as different from the patrons who vandalize *People*. Thus cancelling *Playboy* is seen almost as a way to frustrate once and for all those oversexed, misbehaving patrons. No librarian would cancel *Fortune* on the grounds that a few patrons were stealing it to get rich off the advice, to the expense of other patrons' use. But one library did cancel *Playboy* "on the grounds that we should not support the one or two stealing."

I have said that 20% of libraries react to *Playboy* in this way. Why do the other 80% not do so?

Sex—And Other Factors

Again, this is not simple either. Many of the 80% or so that do not cancel *Playboy* experience vandalism and some (a lesser amount, proportionately) receive patron or staff complaints. But this is not because the Freedom to Read ideology has permeated these libraries to the extent that sexual content, particularly sexually stimulating recreational reading, is welcomed or tolerated in the library, at least as an "opposing viewpoint."

To the contrary, four respondents, all quoted earlier, testified explicitly that to them, *Playboy* does not "mean" sex:

I do not consider Play. sexually explicit . . . . (#47)

Playboy . . . [has] aged to genteel sexuality. (#73)

> The erotic appeal of any paper media pales before . . . video . . . (#107)

> Library staff do not regard this title as a sex magazine . . . (#109)

So it is not that these libraries find open sexuality acceptable but that they deny that *Playboy* depicts sexuality.

Other libraries use a different rationale. For them, *Playboy's* intellectual content justifies—and might even be said to *redeem*—the sexually explicit and possibly stimulating content. Recall that the quality of the writing was overwhelmingly cited by respondents as the major reason both for acquisition and for retention, in the face of budget cuts *and* patron or staff complaints:

> At the beginning we had some criticisms, but we were able to show the quality of articles & interviews. (#15)

> My feminist leanings are bothered by Playboy, but there are enough serious articles I wouldn't drop it after all these years . . . (#19)

This rationale was also given in connection with *Playgirl* for both retention *and* cancellation:

> [*Playgirl*] appeals to the prurient interests like Playboy, but also occasionally carries useful articles on topical subjects. (#19)

> *Playgirl* was discontinued during the year of the big periodical subscription purge due to funding problems. I have never reinstated it because, in my opinion, the quality of *Playgirl* leaves something to be desired (compared to *Playboy*). (#26)

This stance is but an echo of the third criterion of the so-called Miller definition of pornography:

> (c) whether the work, taken as a whole, lacks serious literary, artistic, political, or scientific value. (*Miller v. California*, 413 U.S. at 24, 93 S.Ct. at 2615)

Thus, for these libraries, *Playboy* has sexual content, even appeal to prurient interests; but it is acceptable in the library because it has "serious value" that outweighs the sex. On the other hand, the librarians who cancel *Playboy* imply—by their actions—that its redeeming "serious" value is not, for them at least, sufficiently redeeming. For them, *Playboy is* "about sex"—at least as they perceive the patrons' usage of the magazine. These librarians perceive a conflict between their own intent in buying *Playboy* and the patron's intent in using it. Librarians buy it for literary and intellectual content, but the patrons read it for sexual stimulation. And somehow, the contrast is more obvious, disillusioning, and objectionable for these libraries than for the others.

CONCLUSION

For all of our libraries, the Freedom to Read ideology is followed in letter and, for most, also to a large extent in spirit. While some librarians are offended by *Playboy* and cancel it, most librarians just cope, buying microfilm or extra copies, or keeping it in the reserve reading room with other popular titles.

Yet for nearly all our libraries, sex is still a questionable heading in the card catalog. Many librarians who did not cancel categorically swept aside the sexual content of *Playboy*, either by denial or by asserting redeeming "serious" value. Only two implied through comments any acceptance of the sex in *Playboy*:

> [Reason for purchase:] High calibre of models & requests from patrons. (#3)

> [Positive or negative reactions from staff:] Staff who pick them up in odd corners & men's room stalls—handled with a sense of humor. (#58)

Sadly, no librarian acknowledged any possible positive contribution from *Playboy* as an information or reference source on sexual topics, although advice and descriptions given in the magazine are generally quite accurate and quote respected scientific and medical experts. Ironically, it was a blind feminist, Marj Schneider (1988), who wrote about the prospective cessation of *Playboy* in braille (see Chapter 9):

> Why, you might ask, is a feminist like me defending the existence of Playboy in Braille? It's a lousy magazine that exploits women . . . . Even though there is much that is wrong with Playboy's presentation of sexuality, it is the only one of the 36 magazines in Braille offered through NLS [National Library Service for the Blind and Physically Handicapped] that regularly talks about sex . . . . Withholding information from us [blind people], especially information about sex and sexuality, will never enable us to begin to make knowledgeable judgements about what does actually occur in this society. I believe that some people, if they could, would legislate away all access to anything about sex that anyone might want to read. And they would do that whether or not we agree that what is presented is, for example, pornographic, enjoyable, or useful. (p. 19)

To be sure, librarians—at least most of them and at least publicly—do not wish to legislate the freedom to read away from their patrons. Yet *privately*, for at least some, "research indicated that librarians give strong support to the concepts of intellectual freedom and open access to information but do not necessarily implement these concepts in their libraries" (Pope 1974, 183–184). Consider the following comment from a library that reported very little vandalism, but was still planning to cancel:

There is a growing feeling that this [periodical] is not appropriate for our collection, and as periodicals librarian I have been pushing to get rid of it. We are also concerned with issues of censorship and hesitate to set a precedent which could backfire on us (e.g. right-wing faculty demanding the removal of radical literature). The case which we are preparing to make in the near future will probably rely on the fact that as we have improved our new fiction collection both in books and periodicals it is no longer necessary to keep this subscription for that reason and we do not see any other justification for it. (#80)

We can only conclude that "not appropriate" here means that the subject or *content* is not appropriate, for why else would this library be afraid of setting a censorship precedent? Here is a clearly two-faced position where the library is drumming up another reason to cancel, simply to "look good" to the public and probably also to the library community. The only question is why "low use," reported elsewhere in the questionnaire, was not chosen as the official reason to cancel.

With *Playboy*, librarians find themselves on the horns of a dilemma, even for those most truly committed to the Freedom to Read position. While they seem to have little difficulty justifying its purchase to patrons (quality articles, indexing), they do have difficulty justifying it to themselves. "As I have repeatedly said," sex researcher William Masters (1983) once commented, "the basic principle upon which all the work [at the Masters and Johnson Institute] has been based is that sex is a natural function . . . [but] none of us ever treat it that way—the culture won't allow it."

And even so for librarians. Despite an official and often genuine "freedom to read" stance, librarians—as was conjectured in Chapter 1—are still undecided about sex. While other magazines are stolen and mutilated, *Playboy* remains somehow different for most librarians than *Rolling Stone* and *The Jerusalem Post*.

ENDNOTES

1. Search conducted July 22, 1987, on OCLC of libraries on the OCLC network holding *Playboy*.

2. According to *Ulrich's* (1988, 2409), *Playboy* is indexed in whole or in part by *Access: The Supplementary Index to Periodicals, Film Literature Index, Magazine Index* and InfoTrac, *Media Review Digest,* and *Popular Magazine Review* (now *Magazine Article Summaries*).

3. Recently, researchers analyzed portrayals of violence themes in *Playboy* pictorials and cartoons, 1954–1983. Overall, less than one page per 3,000 pages and less than four out of every 1,000 pictorials has depicted violence themes (Scott & Cuvelier 1987).

4. Interestingly enough, this approximately 3-to-1 ratio is almost exactly the ratio of academic to public libraries on the OCLC network: 36.2%

academic (including community and junior colleges) to 13.4% public. (Statistics obtained from Diana Bitting of PALINET, 11/13/89.)

5. Seven libraries listed *Playgirl*, 4 each *Penthouse* and *Advocate*, 3 *Christopher Street*, 2 *Cosmopolitan*, and 1 each *Yellow Silk, Drummer, James White Review, Ms.,* and *Redbook.*

6. Formal tests of statistical significance have not been conducted on the data for the following reason. As I am drawing conclusions from interrelationships among numerical variables on one hand and narrative comments on the other, statistical significance testing can be misleading rather than illuminating. For example, there appeared to be a "statistical" association between low usage of *Playboy* and high rates of cancellations. In fact, the association is probably real, but—a point obscured if one then merely appends "$p < .05$"—the association likely exists because librarians wishing to cancel for various reasons of sexual morality and purity find it convenient and easy to then "notice" that the magazine has low usage. However, one can draw this new—and rather less optimistic—conclusion only by examining the numbers in the context of the *written* comments. Thus, verification of effects reported in this study can be done only by recourse to the great confirming methods of investigation: replication of the findings by others, using such techniques as in-depth ethnographic studies of *Playboy* usage as well as sociological analysis of the conditions under which libraries subscribe to *Playboy* and then either do or do not retain the subscription.

In such research, we must ask further *why Playboy* is so problematic. Of course, the librarian who wrote that *Playboy* is tame compared to sex videos is totally correct. So why do librarians feel that sexuality, even of the mild and (generally) quite acceptable form represented in *Playboy* is nonetheless not the proper stuff of library holdings? There are a number of possible conjectures, including the rejoinder that the society as a whole is similarly schizophrenic. Even though *Playboy* is widely available and sells millions of copies, groups of irate citizens can still shut down a publicly funded and highly acclaimed art show on the grounds of pornography (Vance 1989). *Playboy* in braille was cancelled in one breath by congressional action and restored in the next breath by the court (see Chapter 9). Is it any wonder that librarians remain undecided?

7. *Playboy* was listed *by respondents* as being indexed in *Access, Readers' Guide to Periodical Literature, Magazine Index* and InfoTrac, *Popular Periodicals Index,* and *Alternative Periodicals Index* (which does not exist: the correct title is *Alternative Press Index*). See endnote 2 for the correct list of indexes covering *Playboy.* The misperception of *Readers' Guide* covering *Playboy* is curious; according to an editor at The H.W. Wilson Company, the publisher of *Readers' Guide, Playboy* is not now covered by that index and has not been for at least the past 10 years. (Personal communication with Jean Marra, 11/17/88.)

8. In the great cartoonist Gilbert Shelton's parody of campus activism, revolutionary students invade the library and remove the books from the shelves to the floor as a "disruptive tactic." The more hedonistic Fat Freddy, however, vows as his part to "liberate [i.e., steal] the fuck books in the name of the revolution." See page 6.

REFERENCES

Geller, Evelyn. 1984. *Forbidden books in American public libraries, 1876–1939; A study in cultural change.* Westport, CT: Greenwood.

Masters, William H. 1983. A three-decade retrospective of the Masters and Johnson Institute. Presented at the 26th Annual Meeting of the Society for the Scientific Study of Sex, November 18–20, Chicago, IL.

Pope, Michael. 1974. *Sex and the undecided librarian.* Metuchen, NJ: Scarecrow.

Schneider, Marj. 1988. House moves to stop *Playboy* in Braille: How did it happen and what does it mean? In *Throw away your Stereotypes* (pp. 17–19). Minneapolis, MN: Womyn's Braille Press. (First published in *WBP Newsletter*, 5/1, Summer 1985.)

Scott, Joseph E., and Steven J. Cuvelier. 1987. Sexual violence in *Playboy* magazine: A longitudinal content analysis. *The Journal of Sex Research*, November: 534–539.

Ulrich's international periodicals directory. 1988. 27th ed. New York: Bowker.

Vance, Carole S. 1989. The war on culture. *Art in America*, September: 39–45.

White, Howard D. 1986. Majorities for censorship. *Library Journal*, July: 31–38.

CHAPTER 11

Providing Access to Materials on Sexuality

Martha Cornog

Relatively few libraries collect erotica *per se*. Yet most libraries have a fair amount of material about sexuality dispersed throughout the general collection. Such materials may include clinical or scholarly books, such as a history of prostitution, the Kinsey reports, or textbooks. Also present in most libraries are literary or artistic treatments: a popular romance novel with steamy passages, *Lady Chatterley's Lover*, art photography and paintings of the nude. Other categories include sex education (from Victorian marriage manuals to Dr. Ruth) and a variety of popular works about sex and morality (from *Playboy* on one hand to the Meese report on the other). The dispersal of sex-related material throughout the collection, as well as its diversity and the diversity of attitudes surrounding it, raises the question: How do we provide access?

At the outset, let me say that except for particular special collections,[1] these materials should remain dispersed throughout the library collection rather than being sequestered together physically simply because they all happen to deal with sexuality in one form or another. "Sex is a natural function," said William Masters (1983). Thus, sex should be considered a natural part of life, of letters, and of library collections. Moreover, it seems totally impractical to sort through an entire modern collection merely to find and reclassify everything that deals with sex. So, except for specialty collections, in all likelihood sexual materials probably will—and should—remain dispersed throughout a library's holdings.

Thus, to provide access means answering two seemingly opposed questions:

- How should we integrate sexuality materials appropriately into the general collection?
- Simultaneously, how can we address the issues of sometimes obscure or inconsistent cataloging/classification, patron embarrassment, high demand and use, high rates of vandalism, and community and staff controversy or hostility about "pornography" or "erotica"?

In short, we need to treat sex like any other library subject, while also sometimes treating it *differently*. How can we do both?

Let us explore access issues and alternatives in two stages. First, how can the library patron, or the librarian acting for the patron, discover what sex-related materials are in the collection, especially when there is an urgent need-to-know, for example, following a local TV special about the community's adult bookstore zoning controversy? Second, what kinds of physical storage and access are most appropriate for sexuality materials? While the discussion below deals specifically with sexuality-related matter, the suggestions also address broader questions of access to the entire collection.

FINDING OUT WHAT IS IN THE COLLECTION

Discovering what the library holds involves asking about how books are arranged on the shelves (classification); the quality and accuracy of subject indexing and bibliographic entries in card, COM, or online catalogs; and the availability in the library of bibliographies and flyers on special topics (e.g., AIDS) and more general reference tools such as periodical holdings lists. In short, the first stage of access involves determining if that library has anything appropriate to a reader's request, whether the request be for a specific book (such as Mark Twain's *The Mammoth Cod* or Foucault's *The History of Sexuality*), for an answer to a question (What is the average length of the penis?), or for information on a particular topic (Do you have anything on bundling?).

Shelf Order and Classification

Many patrons *and* librarians browse the stacks when looking for books, remembering, sometimes vaguely, that works about sex seem clustered "on the middle shelf of the bookcase by the far window." Moreover, users seeking a specific book will, upon finding it, often inspect its neighbors on the shelf to evaluate their potential relevance. Therefore, the classification system used by the library for sexuality will frequently determine success in finding desired materials both directly and indirectly: directly, through retrieval by the specific call number; indirectly, through association of similar materials through the sequence of call numbers.

Most libraries use either the Dewey Decimal Classification (DDC), typically public libraries, or the Library of Congress Classification (LCC), typically academic libraries. Both systems have codes assigned at the Library of Congress (although by different individuals for each system), and both systems now tend to class sexual *non*fiction in either psychology (BF or 155) or sociology (usually HQ or 306). Beyond that, their treatments vary somewhat. Following, I discuss how sex is classified within the sociology division of each system.

DDC differs in general from LCC in its shorter length and less detail about all subjects. More specifically, in DDC sexual topics may be classed within sociology as either "institutions pertaining to relations of the sexes" (306.7) or as "problems and controversies related to public morals and customs (363.4). Thus, at first glance, the 306 series seems to contain the "good sex" and the 363 series the "bad sex"—raising all sorts of nasty questions of how the cataloger, or anyone else!—is expected to determine just what subjects were, are, or should be considered "problems of public morals" at any given time, what to do when the times change, or whether catalogers (or librarians in general) should make such assessments in the first place.

However, it is not even *that* simple, nor is it a case of either/or. Provision is made for some topics to be classed in *both* sequences: *homosexuality* as either 306.76 or 363.49; *prostitution* as 306.74 or 363.44; and *pornography* as 306.77 or 363.47. How is the cataloger supposed to handle that one? *Are* there books about homosexuality, prostitution, or pornography that treat these topics solely as "institutions" and other books that treat them solely as "problems or controversies"? How do the folk at LC match up the books with these codes?

A check of my and my husband's personal library suggests that, at least recently, DDC classifiers appear to place most works on homosexuality and prostitution in 306.7. However, of nine books about pornography, three are classed in 306.7 and six in 363.47. The curious question remains: If some works on these three topics are classed as "problems and controversies" in 363, why are not *all* works on these topics classed there? All three are controversial and—for some people and communities—problematical. Certainly, the idea of just what is represented as "problems and controversies related to public morals and customs" changes with history and with the individual cataloger. If catalogers make different and contradictory moral and classificatory decisions, their shifting viewpoints can only confuse and mislead patrons and librarians.

LCC seems to pose fewer problems with its HQ class in sociology (a bit euphemistically called "The Family. Marriage. Woman"), which is quite detailed and contains no preconceptions about "public morals." For example, *homosexuality, prostitution*, and *erotica* (including pornography) each have their own comprehensive series of numbers. It is interesting to note that *homosexuality*, with its lesser range of numbers HQ75–76, appears originally to have been accorded less importance than either *prostitution* or *erotica*, with their wider ranges of HQ101–285 and HQ450–471, respectively.

There are some areas to watch out for, however, *erotica/pornography* being one of them. The *erotica* range of HQ450–471 includes a series of numbers for "Erotica, History" and "Erotica, General works" (HQ458–460), a series for the actual literature (HQ461–470), *and* a number for "Pornography. Obscene literature" (HQ471). Here the cataloger is faced with two types of choices. First, books *about* erotica/pornography may be classed as either erotica (HQ458–460) or as pornography (HQ471). How does the cataloger, we muse, decide which book is an HQ460 and which is an HQ471? As we recall from Chapter 3, differences between *erotica* and *pornography* have been largely subjective as well as under gradual shift. Secondly, books *of* erotica/pornography may be classed in either HQ461–470 or with other literature, in the Ps.

Consulting our own book collection once more, I find that nonfiction books with *pornography* in the title are classed in HQ471, whereas Valerie Kelly's *How to Write Erotica* is classed in HQ460 (erotica). Logical? *Only* from the title, for Kelly's book is a (very funny) manual for writing explicit male-directed sexually arousing material, what many people would call "just plain porn"—no soft focus, no heaving ecstasies usually associated with the more socially acceptable term, *erotica*, no "art." It looks as though LC has used the title as the major criterion of distinction.

As for erotic works themselves, both LCC and DDC seem to place sexual fiction consistently in literature—the Ps or the 800s. *Pleasures*, however, a collection of erotic nonfiction anecdotes edited by Lonnie Barbach, is classed in HQ462/306.7. It could also have been classed in literature, with collections of nonfiction essays, which would have been consistent with LCC's treatment of sexual fiction. Yet it was not.

The point is that with sexual topics, whether classed in DDC or LCC, similar material can be dispersed in different parts of the stacks depending upon the classification system and who happened to catalog that particular book. True, books about prostitution, homosexuality, or pornography *as crimes* should be classed elsewhere, in criminology or law; religious views about them classed under religion; and so on. But what are we to make of *Tales from Time Square*? Although its chapters deal with such topics as stripteasers, prostitutes, and peep shows—in short, the sex industry—LC classed it as 974.71, a "New York" notation appropriate for history and civilization books.

Cataloger Sanford Berman of the Hennepin County Public Library (HCL) in Minnesota reported the error, which he deftly described as "bibliocide by cataloging." HCL promptly reclassed the book in the 300s (Berman 1985).

Furthermore, DDC and LCC viewpoints for particular books are not always consistent. *Sexual Loving*, a sex manual by Joseph and Lois Bird, was classed in DDC as psychology and in LCC as sociology. *Sexuality Today*, a textbook by Nass and Fisher, was classed in HQ (sociology) for LCC, but in the 600s (medicine) for DDC.[2]

How can the poor librarian cope with such inconsistent and sometimes downright erroneous classifications? There are several possibilities. One is to say, in effect, the devil with it so far as classification is concerned and come to depend more on the catalog than on shelf-browsing. This retrieval technique generally imposes no great burden upon library staff, nor even on many patrons of academic libraries, who learn to sink or swim in the catalog during freshman year. However, public library patrons depend more upon shelf-browsing to "find something interesting" *now*. They do not need to know (through the catalog) what the library has on a topic, but what it has on the shelves for check-out this evening.

Another possibility is library-produced finding aids (see "Bibliographies and Flyers," below) listing various call numbers for popular subjects. These benefit only those who pick them up, and only those whose queries fall into these subject areas. Signs in the stacks listing classification ranges and coverage can be of help also, but are not detailed enough to be really effective and would not provide cross-references among class numbers.

There is really no help for it except for the librarian to keep an eye on incoming books about sex and reclassify them selectively, particularly in public libraries. For nonfiction, the librarian should ask: Which areas are heavily in demand? Are the titles scattered inappropriately throughout various sequences? Should some be reclassed so that the overall effect is more consistent and useable? Do patrons and librarians rely heavily on the older class numbers (e.g., DDC's early use of 612.6 for sex manuals) so that new material could more usefully be placed with the old, contrary to more recent DDC or LCC policies? Or does most of the material currently in greatest demand constitute new material, so that *older* items may be more simply reclassed?

For sexual fiction and other erotica/pornography, the librarian must consider whether to choose the more esoteric option of classing examples in HQ (sociology), as LC classed *Pleasures*, or to take the more usual route of integrating them consistently into general fiction and literature. Some librarians might wish to take a third option, that of considering sexual fiction as a type of genre fiction. Many libraries have separate ranges and/or spine labels for genre fiction, such as gothic, romance, mystery, science fiction. Thus a separate range and/or spine label for sexual fiction could be completely consistent and perhaps desirable in these libraries.[3]

The librarian's overview and evaluation of the collection should then lead to a set of formal or informal policies regarding classing sexual materials. Since most libraries make their own rules concerning, for instance, local authors or where to class biographies or bibliographies (as separate sequences or with the subjects), policies about classing sexual materials become an expansion of care already exercised. At the very least, however, new acquisitions about sex *must* be checked to pick out those obviously out-of-place, such as books about the sex industry classed as history and civilization.

Libraries that do not want to use either DDC or LCC for sexual materials may want to consult some of the libraries described in Chapter 12, "Erotica Research Collections," for suggestions and advice.

Subject Access and Subject Headings

Even in the ideally useful classification for sexual materials, relevant items on most topics are *still* likely to be found in more than one place, particularly in larger collections. Thus a systematic searcher can gain a comprehensive view of the library's resources only by consulting the subject headings in the catalog. Therefore, we shall next examine how the major subject heading lists influence access to sexual information.

Most libraries use either *Sears List of Subject Headings* (Sears)—typically smaller public libraries—or the *Library of Congress Subject Headings* (LCSH)—typically larger public libraries and academic libraries. In both, subject headings are assigned to books at the Library of Congress. And, as with the two classification systems, Sears and LCSH treat sex topics a bit differently.

LCSH is extremely detailed; the "sex-to-sexuality" headings alone run to nearly six pages, three columns to the page (less two columns for the "sextet" headings, which interrupt the sequence). The "erotic" headings are ample as well, over three columns. From the viewpoint of the cataloger or indexer, books discussing erotica/pornography can be assigned the headings "Erotica," "Erotic literature," "Pornography," "Sex in literature," "Love in literature," "Sex oriented businesses," or even "Literature, Immoral" and "Literature and morals." Also, we find "Erotic songs," "Music and erotica," and "Bawdy songs," as well as "Erotic poetry," "Love poetry," and "Bawdy poetry." Truly, a heading for everyone!

With such diversity, it is inevitable that similar material be assigned different subject headings—placing the onus upon the searcher to read the cataloger's mind—unless LC were to assign four to six headings to every work, which is rarely done. In our own collection, all the books with *pornography* in the title have an LCSH heading beginning with "Pornography—." Yet the sole subject heading of Kelly's *How to Write Erotica* is "Erotica—Authorship"! Anyone looking under "Pornography" alone would miss it completely. This seems to be another case of cataloging by key-word-in-title. If the book had been dubbed *How to Write Pornography* (against all advice from the publisher's marketing department, no doubt), would the LCSH heading have been any different? Who knows.

In Sears, the "sex-to-sexuality" headings occupy less than two pages, with only one column per page. For material about erotica/pornography, the cataloger or indexer has the choice only of "Erotica," "Erotic literature," and "Pornography." With such a lesser number of headings, dispersion of materials is obviously less of a problem, although the erotica/pornography dichotomy would still create difficulties unless both terms were assigned together much of the time. To the contrary, the major problem may be not enough headings to choose from. For example, Sears does not provide for *sex therapy, sexual disorders,* or *sex-oriented businesses,* all fairly broad concepts.

So whether the library uses LCSH or Sears, a book about sex may be supplied with misleading headings or simply undersupplied. *Tales from Times Square,* the book about the New York City sex industry described earlier, had been assigned LCSH headings beginning only with "Times Square—" and "New York—." As well as assigning a new class number, the Hennepin County Public Library also assigned six new subject headings: "Sex industry," "Sex shops," "Stripteasers," "Peep shows," "Prostitutes," and "Sex customs," all subheaded with "Times Square, New York City."

So, for incoming books in sexuality, the librarian should check the subject headings as well as the call numbers, with an eye to adding ones more appropriate and useable where necessary. For *How to Write Erotica,* for example, "Pornography—Authorship" and "Sex oriented businesses" should have been added. Certainly, some problems with fragmented nonfiction headings can be alleviated with appropriate and copious *see also* references as, for example, within the "erotica/pornography," "erotic songs," and "erotic poetry" families of LCSH headings.

Subject access to sexual *fiction* would also greatly improve access to sexual information. (In fact, subject cataloging of *all* fiction would be a great benefit for library patrons; see Berman 1988, 9–17.) Current LC cataloging policy limits assigning form/genre and topical headings only to literary *collections.* The result is that most fiction, poetry, or drama about AIDS, say, is just not retrievable as such. Or, if the library did possess the English translation of *Chin P'ing Mei,* a marvellously convoluted soap opera of the licit and illicit bedhoppings of a sixteenth-century Chinese merchant and his six wives, no interested reader could find it unless that reader or a librarian remembered the exact Chinese title. *Chin P'ing Mei* loosely translates as "plum blossom in metal vase," but this bit of information is not included on the title page, being buried in an introduction by Arthur Waley. Thus, the logical remedy is to assign the subject heading "Erotic literature, Chinese." (The English translation, which is not particularly explicit by current standards, would doubtless compete favorably with "Dallas" if adapted to video; Washington-Beijing relations, however, might not be thereby improved.)[4]

While it may take some time for LC to expand its policies about cataloging fiction, individual libraries can certainly begin assigning subject headings at the grass roots level. Even one heading assigned per novel, play, or book of poetry could vastly improve access.

However, additional or different subject headings can improve access only if the wording of the headings—and their cross-references—are user-friendly. Berman (e.g., 1981, 1984, 1988) has written widely on LCSH outdated terms in headings, such as "Sex instruction" instead of "Sex education." Other problems noted by Berman include a dearth of colloquial cross-references, such as "Balls (generative organs) see Testis" and a maddening slowness to incorporate terms and concepts widely used by the media and the public, such as "sex manuals" or "telephone sex." So librarians should seriously consider supplementing LCSH or Sears with carefully chosen terms and cross-references from additional sources.[5]

The following sources are suggested for sexual terms and cross-references:

Hennepin County Public Library Authority File
About 500,000 entries in one alphabet: subject headings with cross-references (mixture of LCSH and HCL terms); plus personal and corporate authors; name, author, and title added entries; uniform title headings; and series forms. Recumulated quarterly. Available on 42x microfiche for $7.50/quarter, $30.00/year (4 cumulations), from:
Hennepin County Public Library
Technical Services Division
12601 Ridgedale Road
Minnetonka, MN 55343

Whereas certainly not all libraries may want to adopt HCL's detailed subject heading list or even their approach, the list nonetheless serves as a fruitful source for ideas for headings and represents quite faithfully a detailed attention to current distinctions among topics. Examination of the HCL lists is a must for any library seriously engaged in classification.

Sexual Nomenclature: A Thesaurus
Compiled by JoAnn Brooks and Helen C. Hoffer of the Kinsey Institute, Indiana University. 1977. About 2,000 descriptors and their hierarchies, plus 250 cross-references. Available for $100 from:

G.K. Hall
70 Lincoln Street
Boston, MA 02111

Gay Studies Thesaurus
Compiled by Dee Michel. 1985. About 1,000 descriptors. Available
for $12 from the author (prepayment only). Also available for $16
in a combined package with a *Cataloging Manual* and the
Michel/Moore Classification Scheme, both for use with lesbian and
gay materials.

Dee Michel
11070 Mississippi Avenue
Los Angeles, CA 90025

Lesbian Periodicals Index
Compiled and edited by Clare Potter. 1986. An author and subject
index to 42 lesbian periodicals, some dating back to 1947. Available
for $29.95 from:

Naiad Press
P.O. Box 10543
Tallahassee, FL 32302

The Bibliographic Record

We have considered some ways to improve the subject cataloging
of sexuality materials. Let us say that our patron or librarian has
found—*mirabile dictu!*—a series of entries in the catalog under a
likely sounding heading. It now must be decided which of these
entries might be most fruitful to locate.

Now, in the case of four or five entries, one merely jots down the
call numbers and proceeds to the appropriate library locations. But
suppose the entries fill a drawer and a half—as I actually found, in a
university library that shall remain nameless, under the (legitimate)
LCSH heading "Sex."

The patron or librarian may perform the necessary triage fairly
easily if the titles are indicative, the authors familiar, or accurate and
appropriate subject tracings indicated. But if not, the only hope is a
"contents" or "partial contents" note on the records. Added retrospec-
tively, such contents notes can partially compensate for too broad or
misleading initial cataloging. Take, for example, Charney's *Sexual
Fiction*. You'd find it under "Sex in literature," but that alone does
not tell you much. Charney could have been writing about the prev-
alence or absence of sex scenes in popular novels. The table of
contents, however, provides a superb summary:

Sexuality and the life force: *Lady Chatterley's Lover* and *Tropic of
Cancer*

Sexuality and self-fulfillment: *Portnoy's Complaint* and *Fear of Flying*

Sexual Fiction is thus revealed quite clearly as "about" classic erotica/pornography.

A contents note thus can serve as a sort of abstract for books. And why not provide searchers among books with some of the conveniences accorded to searchers among journal articles? While any cataloging "enrichment" takes time, notes based on the table of contents at least need no intellectual effort but can simply be transcribed onto the main entry card or online record.

Bibliographies and Flyers

Libraries can also improve subject access in sexuality by making available flyer-bibliographies on selected topics, which patrons may select discreetly from a larger display. Such handouts allow libraries to respond to high popular interest while preserving patron privacy. Not all patrons are willing to march up to the reference desk and ask for help finding materials about rape, AIDS, child sexual abuse, or birth control. And for many, the catalog is intimidating as well. Who knows what all those little drawers are, or how to operate a computer terminal?

A flyer on AIDS, for example, would list the major books held in the library with brief contents notes and call numbers; describe any vertical file holdings; suggest appropriate print or online indexes such as (in an academic library) *Index Medicus*/MEDLINE and (in academic and public libraries) *Magazine Index, Readers' Guide to Periodical Literature, Alternative Press Index*, and newspaper indexes; and mention such related topics as sexually transmitted diseases, epidemiology, viruses, immunology, and public health.

Other obviously valuable topics for such flyers might include homosexuality, bisexuality, sexual dysfunction, birth control, rape, and child sexual abuse. The "Sources" page of *Library Journal* often lists these kinds of short bibliographies. See also the Appendix to Chapter 17, "For Sex, See Librarian? Reprise."

The children's room should also have a display of simpler, colorful flyers. Amid "mysteries" and "dinosaurs" might also be found references to the basics of reproduction ("Where did I come from?"), AIDS, and child sexual abuse ("unwanted touching").

Vertical File Topics

The library may—and generally should—have sexual topics in the vertical file. But do the patrons know what a vertical file is? The very name sounds peculiar; "clipping file" is the usual, nonlibrary usage.

Signage about the file, plus a list of topics covered, should be placed near the reference and circulation desks and near the indexes. In addition, "see also vertical file" cards can be inserted into the catalog at appropriate headings.

Special Collections Announcements and Catalog

Some libraries have a special collection relating to sexuality, e.g., underground periodicals reflecting the sexual revolution of the 1960s, Victorian marriage manuals, or figure photography (including studies of the nude). Access to such collections can be vastly improved in several ways:

- Flyers about the collection describing holdings and access/use policies
- Description in "about the library" brochures
- Good signage and directional indicators
- Mention in the catalog under appropriate subject headings

A separate catalog for the special collection is generally necessary even if items are fully integrated into the main catalog, and is essential, of course, if the holdings are arranged in specific or unique ways. The separate catalog may need only accession number, author, and title; but subject access might also be useful and annotations are often desirable. The catalog, in multiple copies, should be readily available where patrons may browse through it without having to ask the librarian, preserving patron privacy as well as saving staff time.

List of Periodicals Received

Patrons usually have no trouble learning if the library subscribes to a particular periodical. The record of titles received is available, as a list, cards, printout, or online. But supposing the question is about periodicals on a *topic*: Do you have any magazines on weightlifting? Do you have any gay newspapers? In a small library, a quick scan through the list or through the librarian's memory usually provides the answer. However, in a large library a subject or keyword index to the periodical collection is much more useful. Furthermore, when such a list is available, the patron need not ask the librarian about it.

So large libraries should consider producing a keyword subject index to their periodical titles. A relatively simple and inexpensive technique would be to "enrich" the titles with a few keywords (e.g., for *Playboy*: men, sexuality, popular culture; for *Christopher Street*: gay, homosexuality, sexuality), then run the enriched titles through a KWIC (Key Word In Context) or KWOC (Key Word Out of Context) indexing program. The result would be a second list, looking something like this:

Sex	*Journal of Sex Research*
	Sex Roles
Sexual	*Archives of Sexual Behavior*
Sexuality	*Journal of Homosexuality*
	Medical Aspects of Human Sexuality
	Playboy
	Playgirl

Because new periodicals are acquired less frequently than new books, the list need be updated only once a year or so.

Such a list also answers a different patron question: a request for a specific periodical when the exact title cannot be recalled. For example, *Archives of Sexual Behavior* might be misrecalled as *Journal of Sexual Behavior* (which does not exist) or as *Journal of Sex Research* (which does exist), or as "something with *sex* in the title."

PHYSICAL ACCESS TO SEXUALITY MATERIALS

Intellectual access to sexual topics is only a portion of the picture. Physical access to the books and periodicals is also crucial. Whereas poor cataloging/classification and patron embarrassment are best addressed by improved topic access, the issues of high use, vandalism, and controversy are central to physical access. (Physical access affects patron embarrassment as well.)

For some libraries, books and periodicals with sexual content cause little if any problem. (As noted in Chapter 10, "What Happens When Libraries Subscribe to *Playboy*," *Playboy* is nearly invisible in some libraries.) However, other libraries report mutilation or theft of such items, or fear of mutilation or theft. Some libraries report extraordinarily high use; still others, complaints from patrons or staff. Such libraries, then, need solutions to physical access that minimize these problems.

However, I wish to stress at this point that librarians must be frank with themselves as to what their real problems and priorities are. It is one thing to affirm commitment to improved *intellectual* access to library materials about sex; it may be quite another to—publicly—commit the library to better *physical* access. In the remainder of this chapter, I have assumed that the library is actually interested in such a commitment, within time and budget constraints. It may not be.

And here's where the honesty comes in. If a reluctance to make sexuality materials accessible genuinely arises from concerns about vandalism, controversy, etc., then my suggestions below will help. If, however, such reluctance arises from *a priori* antipathy to sexual materials in the library, then no amount of "solutions" will satisfy those who see that sex = problem.

For example, how many librarian readers would consider putting together a lobby case display on sex education, or sex in popular culture, or sexuality in different cultures? All would make highly interesting visual displays, especially when coupled with appropriate objects or illustrations. (Such a display, incidentally, need not have any sexually explicit visuals.) A locked case would be advisable, but this would also contribute to the message: *Of course the library has books on sexuality, which we treasure, preserve, and display proudly. Sex is real, it is important, and it is fascinating. And these books are only part of the great riches of this library.*

For those who could not even consider such a display for concerns about public outcry, rest assured that people eventually lose interest in sex, as in anything else, when information is presented openly and in quantity. First-time visitors to our home are initially drawn to the 1,000+ collection of "sex books," but after paging through several, they invariably turn their conversation to the latest movie they have seen, or to their new car.

So beware of *too*-great concern over public outcry, high use, or vandalism as regards sexual materials in the library. No amount of care, caution, or compromise will answer such concern. But for libraries for which sex information is first and foremost *information*—requiring special treatment, sometimes, but all the same, information to be offered freely—then the approaches outlined in the remainder of this chapter may be useful.

From the librarian's point of view, high use and vandalism are similar in that they both reduce access, one temporarily, the other permanently. In either case, patrons cannot consult materials if other patrons are using them or if they are mutilated or stolen. Accordingly, high use and vandalism can both be handled by increasing the number of copies and/or controlling access. However, controversy and complaints about library materials are more complex. As these are discussed elsewhere in the library literature from the viewpoint of censorship, the freedom to read, and enforcing good selection policies, I will not duplicate this approach here but instead suggest how judicious use of controlled access may be helpful.

Increasing the Number of Copies

High use and vandalism are similar also in both being bell-wethers of high interest. And so both mean that the library is doing something *right*, that part of its collection, at least, is relevant, important, necessary. And while controlled access may prove necessary in one form or another, the first response of the librarian to high use *or* vandalism should be to add *more*: more items on the topic and more copies of the item, in one form or another. There are several ways of doing this.

1. Purchase additional copies of books, additional subscriptions to periodicals, and additional books on the topic, either popular or scholarly, depending on what is needed. Although the obvious remedy, this is not often possible because of shrinking budgets, although additional purchases can sometimes be managed when items are available in paperback.

2. Investigate used bookstores and back-date magazine dealers for additional copies and new items. Philadelphia has one particularly good used book store, where reside two full book stacks of popular and scholarly sex books, all at half-price or less. There is also, of course, the Universal Serials and Book Exchange, in Washington, DC.

3. Arrange for gift copies/subscriptions. On campus, student groups are sometimes willing to donate popular subscriptions (see "Adopt-A-Magazine" 1985). Homosexuality advocacy/support groups may be willing to donate subscriptions to gay periodicals. Gifts of particular items might be encouraged by disseminating a want-list and offering something in return: a percent of the retail price, dollars-off coupons on surplus books-for-sale, small premiums, tickets to a raffle of some desirable item, or forgiveness of fines. Sometimes patrons who have personal subscriptions to periodicals can be induced to donate their back issues to the library.

4. Arrange for back-up photocopies of popular items. This is best done by anticipating demand. If an instructor assigns the *Playboy* interview regularly, the librarian should have a number of extra copies available for checkout.

5. Purchase microfilm or fiche copies. Microform materials are less often vandalized than paper, but also less often used. Hence reliance on microform is a support rather than a front-line strategy. Convenient and easy-to-use readers and reader-printers can help, however.

6. Interlibrary loan. Likewise, this is a support rather than a front-line strategy, more suitable for scholarly research than for recreational use, since the process takes too long to help many patrons—and is anything but private.

Controlling Access

Controlling access is a second approach to dealing with high use and vandalism, and traditionally often chosen for sexuality materials.

Ideally, controlled access can *increase* use, by rationing it, while providing a level of monitoring and protection designed to discourage vandalism. In practice, however, controlled access—particularly the more restrictive types—often reduces use, which may sometimes be the covert purpose all along, although not often admitted. However, it is a valuable technique against overuse or misuse of materials by a few patrons at the expense of others. And sometimes controlled access is designed to protect certain patrons from the collection, as we shall see.

Types of controlled access range from the quite mild to the highly restrictive, as we will explore next.

Considering types of controlled access. In a library with completely open access, patrons may wander through the stacks, pick out books and periodicals personally, and peruse them in reading areas anywhere in the library or check them out to take home. Departing from this, many different options for controlling access may be used singly or in combination:

1. Items have shorter circulation period, sometimes as little as overnight or even measured in hours.
2. Items do not circulate.
3. Items are shelved in circumscribed area and must be used in that area.
4. Patrons must show ID to enter circumscribed area.
5. Stacks are closed to patrons; items must be requested from a library staff member.
6. Patrons must show ID to request items.
7. Patrons must sign for items to use them in the library (or leave ID).
8. Patrons' bags may be searched when leaving circumscribed area.
9. Reading tables within circumscribed area are set up in full view of desk attendant.
10. Items are tagged as part of an electronic security system.

A "circumscribed area" may range from a separate, locked room to a series of stacks surrounding an open area, to which entrance is possible only through a turnstile.

Thus, the most restrictive form of controlled access might be conceived of as follows:

> Items are shelved behind a counter in a circumscribed area. Patrons must show ID to enter area, request items from staff at counter, sign for them, and read them in full view of the staff member. Items may not be removed from the area, and patron's bags are searched at the exit.

This type of controlled access is most commonly found in valuable special collections or small research libraries.

Various lesser combinations of these control options exist routinely. In fact, few libraries, if any, have completely open access for the entire collection. Many have electronic security systems. Reference collections do not circulate. Reserve room items must be requested at a counter and used nearby. Best sellers circulate for shorter periods. And, as I will discuss below, controls are sometimes held in force for only certain groups or relaxed for others, as when children may use but not check out items from the adult collection or when faculty may check out bound journals overnight.

Implementing controlled access. While increasing the number of copies of items may be done *ad hoc*—as many copies as necessary for a particular book, say—controlled access is usually applied to classes of items according to certain policies, whether official or unofficial. The following are policies commonly found in many libraries, together with their usual rationales:

1. Control access to the entire collection (generally a research collection or special library with confidential or valuable holdings).
2. Control access to a segment of the collection by "appropriateness" for age or educational level or status of patron (e.g., dividing a public library into "adult" and "children's" collections, or earmarking sections of a university library as "undergraduate," "graduate," or "faculty").
3. Control access to a segment of the collection by medium (e.g., all reference books or all periodicals, generally because of high use and financial/archival value).
4. Control access to a specific special collection (because of its financial or archival value or irreplaceability).
5. Control access to a segment of the collection that is heavily used (the "reserve room" concept, so that all might have equal, but not unfair, access).
6. Control access to a particular set of items or topics that have been vandalized in the past (e.g., *Playboy*, looseleaf investment services, *Consumer Reports Buyers Guide*, *Sports Illustrated* annual swimsuit issue).
7. Control access to a particular set of items or topics that are judged controversial or which someone has complained about (e.g., erotica, Black power, anti-holocaust, creationism, birth control).

While this list covers much of what libraries actually do, is this what they *should* do? Let me comment on these policies and their rationales.

Types 1 and 3–5, I believe, raise few ideological problems for either librarians or patrons. None discriminates against any patron group, and none uses content or subject *per se* as a basis for being singled out. Whereas, for example, a reserve room may be an inconvenience, no one feels stigmatized using it if it has a varied assortment, and patrons know that the materials they need are going to be there.

Type 2 is tricky and, I think, basically unfair. Fortunately, many control systems of this type have an override, i.e., the child may use the adult collection if the parent's signature is obtained, or the undergraduate may use graduate or faculty materials if a faculty member gives the OK. Depending on the purpose of the control, however, it is possible to modify such a system to make it less unfair.

If the primary purpose is to ensure priority use for the one group, the other group(s) may be given access, but lesser privileges. The child may browse the adult stacks, but may not check out items. Or the undergraduate may check out graduate materials but may be required to return them upon request from graduate students or faculty. Such policies are already in place in many academic libraries, where faculty (but only faculty) are permitted, say, to check out back journals on overnight loan.

If, however, the primary purpose is to protect the secondary group from exposure to the materials—often the case when children's library privileges are restricted—then we have a very different situation. One must ask who judged the children in need of protection. If it is first and foremost the library staff, than I shall not argue but urge that access be broadened as far as possible and that the library build overrides into the system and liberally apply them. But if the impetus comes from parents' groups, then one may broaden access through a different tack—inverting the override. In other words, children may be given full or limited access to the adult collection *unless* the parent specifically designates on the application form that the child may only use the children's room. Parents are still being given control over their children's reading (if they wish it), but access to adult materials is presented more as a normal option rather than an exceptional case-by-case privilege.

Types 6 and 7, restricting only vandalized or controversial items, border on content-based censorship and cannot help but convey to the patrons that a stigma is attached to these materials and that anyone interested in consulting them is either deviant or a thief.

How does one modify restrictions of the type 6 or 7 so that they become less off-putting and less censorious? Broadly speaking, vandalism and controversy are both related to high interest and high use. Therefore, I suggest that items that have been restricted because of these reasons be grouped together with other items requiring controlled access because of high use. In practical terms, this means putting them "on reserve" in some sense, creating a reserve room if one does not already exist. Thus public libraries not having a reserve room might adopt the concept from academic libraries and incorporate into it all materials needing controlled access. Thus "high use" and "fair access to all" can be the rationale for all protected materials.

A final note on controlling access, with respect to patron embarrassment: generally, the greater the control, the greater the potential for embarrassment. If individuals can choose their own books from the shelves, however, rather than having to ask staff, embarrassment is minimized. From this viewpoint, it might be preferable to try a "reserve room" design with open stacks, but with patrons signing a log at the door or turnstile and with visible tables rather than carrels.

Providing the Most Appropriate Physical Access

We have discussed two approaches for physical access to sexuality materials: providing additional copies and controlling access. Both may involve a variety of options, which may be used singly or together.

So how may we choose the best, the most appropriate approach for a given situation out of the large menu presented above? Consider some examples.

Four patrons have determined that the library *does* have what they are looking for. The first consulted *Magazine Index* and wants a particular issue of *Playboy*. The second picked up a bibliography-flyer about AIDS and wants a book described therein. The third perused the catalog for the special collection of "localiana" and picked out a Victorian marriage manual by a once-local author. The fourth—aged 10—looked under "sex" in the children's catalog and found a book that seems like it might tell her "how the baby got *in* there."

In the Best-of-All-Possible-Libraries, all four patrons need only note the call number or location, find the item, and check it out. And in many libraries, all four of these items might be on the open shelves for circulation. However, let us take each of these four examples and discuss the options more broadly.

The issue of *Playboy*. Should *Playboy* be shelved with the other popular periodicals like *Esquire, National Geographic, Newsweek*? One must first observe the type of use, level and use, and amount of vandalism.

In one public library, *Playboy* might have high use and high vandalism, with use primarily recreational in nature rather than research related. For this library, an optimal strategy might be as follows: Keep the current issue on reserve, so that use may be rationed and vandalism reduced during the period of peak relevance. When the next issue arrives, the old issue then goes out on the open stacks.

Those that survive the vandalism after a year or two may be discarded. The relatively few research requests for articles out of back issues or mutilated issues may be handled through interlibrary loan, photocopying key articles in advance, or possibly a microform subscription kept on reserve.

An academic library, in which *Playboy* has more archival and research value, might take another tack. A microform subscription alone could be adequate, with the reels on reserve if vandalism is a problem. A print subscription in addition, not on reserve, would of course improve access and raise use. This print subscription could perhaps be solicited as a gift or acquired as donated copies.

What about a third library, where staff or community controversy is a major problem? A few librarians do not want to hand out and reshelve issues, or patrons maintain that the selection is unsuitable, particularly for children wandering about in the collection. While librarians should do their best to set collection policies and stick to their guns, resolving internal dissent and putting up a firm front against outside interference, sometimes compromise is necessary in such matters.

Here, a subscription on black-and-white microfilm is a good approach. This could be supplemented by photocopies of significant articles and fiction, available in the vertical file.

The book about AIDS. No two ways about it and no excuses. Every academic and public library *must* have books on AIDS, both in reference or on reserve *and* on open shelves, available for checkout in sufficient quantities—paperback, if necessary. (See the SantaVicca entries in the bibliography to Chapter 1, "For Sex, See Librarian: An Introduction.") If use of these books is exceptionally high, circulation periods should be shortened rather than risk having nothing on the shelves.

The Victorian marriage manual by a once-local author (first edition). This special collection of "localiana" probably deserves special treatment, depending upon financial and archival value. Such treatment could range from simple "does not circulate" to fairly restrictive controlled access, including shelving in circumscribed area where patron must request, sign for, and use the item. The circumscribed area should include a photocopier.

The "where-did-I-come-from" book. As with the case of the AIDS book, all public libraries with children's rooms should have age-appropriate sex education books on the open shelves for check-out as well as in reference, and in sufficient copies so that high use and "sticky fingers" (in both senses) do not constitute major problems. Controversy in the form of parental objections, however, is another matter. Librarians can sometimes defuse such controversies in the children's room by facilitating access to the materials by *parents*, in advance or simultaneously with access by children. This can be done, for example, by:

- having a "new books" table, where all new items are put out in highly visible display prior to circulation for parents to peruse.
- posting a list of new children's books in a conspicuous place.
- establishing a Children's Room Parents Committee, which would have input to (but not decision making over) new book evaluations and purchases.

In the last instance, the committee should represent the entire community and not an exclusively right-wing or liberal focus. The chair of such a committee could also sit on the Library Board.

A DELICATE BALANCE

Because of the physical access problems discussed in the second half of this chapter, the intellectual access issues discussed in the first half become especially critical. We may have to protect or restrict access to certain materials by holding them on microform or keeping them on reserve; the least we can do is make sure that the patron knows that they are there. And this is especially important in relation to sexuality materials for two reasons.

First, many patrons cannot or will not use outside sources to obtain such materials;[6] the library is their only source. In the library, the President of the Student Council may avidly consult *Treat Yourself to a Better Sex Life*, or the town's most senior citizen can read *Love, Sex, and Aging*, and both can leave the books to be reshelved without anyone knowing who read them. Secondly, many patrons equally cannot or will not be open and vocal in their need for materials. If the catalog or shelf order stumps them, they will not ask staff for help. For sex, the *last* source they will seek is the librarian, no matter what the catalog says.

So providing access to sexuality materials in the library means continually resolving contradictions. The librarian must integrate the materials appropriately into the collection and promote their use while at the same time dealing successfully with a constellation of potential problems often unique to the subject. To repeat, sex needs to be treated both the same and yet also sometimes differently from other library materials.

And there are no right answers, no perfect solutions. High use should be the librarian's goal, whether for Homer or *The Joy of Sex*, but heavily used items are not available on the shelves for remaining patrons and are sometimes vandalized in addition. And like the classic relevance/recall relationship of information science familiar to online searchers,[7] frequency of use is often inversely related to degree of restriction.

It is a delicate balance, but one not new to librarianship. What *is* new is the particular constellation of sensitivity, embarrassment, and controversy that all too often surrounds sexuality. Yet information on sexuality is still information and—for those who do not delude themselves into seeing only problems and outcries—can be treated as information. Writing of archivists, Mason (1975) puts the matter succinctly:

> A properly administered archive is involved in a working compromise between the maximum availability of the records and the maximum protection for those records—at the minimum inconvenience to the researcher. All three of these elements are important, none can be neglected. The challenge to the archivist is to make the compromise work. (p. 497)

ENDNOTES

1. Sex-related special collections come in a wide variety of forms. At the New Jersey Library Association conference in 1972, which I attended, a perplexed librarian from Alan Ginsburg's hometown described receiving a donation of his collection of "underground" periodicals from the 1960s. What, she wondered, should be *done* with them? "Microfilm them!" came the urgent voice from a wiser head in the back of the room.

2. According to Berman (personal communication, 6/6/88), DDC editions prior to edition 19 consistently classed sex manuals and texts in 612.6; DDC 19, however, switched such items to the 300s.

3. Such spine labels frequently use a symbol as well as the category name: spaceship for science fiction, hearts for romance, sixshooter for Western, etc. What should the spine symbol be for sexual fiction? I suggest the biological symbols for male and female in the appropriate combination: ♂ ♀ for heterosexual, ♀ ♀ and ♂ ♂ for gay. (One could develop this system to baroque and amusing extremes, e.g., ♀ ♂ ♂ ♂ ♀ ♂ for group sex; ♀ or ♂ for male or female nudes or masturbation; ♂ ☿ = for *soixante neuf*, etc.)

4. According to Gershon Legman (personal communication, 1/4/90), there are two English translations of the *Chin P'ing Mei*, the first by Egerton, published in London—possibly by Routledge—in the 1920s and "quite expurgated . . . The *good* translation in English was published by the Bodley Head, London, 1939, as *The Mandarin and His Six Wives*, translated by Bernard Miall from the German version (itself abridged but not expurgated) by Franz Kuhn." I believe the English edition in my library is the Routledge one, although no publisher is listed anywhere within the volume. It certainly does not appear to be abridged, consisting of 852 crumbling pages divided into 49 chapters. As few Chinese could read in the sixteenth century, it may have been meant to be read aloud in episodes. The detailed descriptions of food, wine, luxurious feminine clothing, ornaments, and jewelry all suggest that women were expected to be included in the audience—as with "Dallas."

5. Recommendations have recently been made—and given a "high priority" ranking—that LC enrich new catalog records with "free text" subject terms from tables of contents and other readily available sources (*Report*

1988, 141). This would be a step in bridging the current gap between LCSH terms and current usage.

6. The Sexuality Library is a mail-order service, recently designed by a woman sex therapist with such folk in mind. It offers about 150 carefully selected sexual self-help and erotic titles, and the catalog contains descriptions of each item. Public libraries in particular should keep the catalog on hand to help staff select, evaluate, and acquire sexuality materials. For information, write The Sexuality Library, 1210 Valencia Street, San Francisco, CA 94110.

7. This principle states that, in searching, relevance is inversely related to recall. Relevance is expressed as the ratio of relevant items retrieved out of total items retrieved ("hits" versus "hits" plus "false drops"); recall is expressed as the ratio of relevant items retrieved out of total relevant items in the database. In plain English, this means that if you use very precise search terms to ensure that you retrieve *only* documents relevant to your request (high relevance), you will miss many other pearls buried in the garbage that you excluded (low recall). Similarly, if you try to retrieve these pearls as well by using broader search terms (high recall), you will retrieve a lot of garbage as well (low relevance).

REFERENCES

Adopt-A-Magazine program buys Idaho library's mags. 1985. *Library Journal*, March 1: 26.

Berman, Sanford, 1981. *Joy of cataloging: Essays, letters, reviews, and other explosions.* Phoenix, AZ: Oryx.

Berman, Sanford, ed. 1984. *Subject cataloging: Critiques and innovations.* New York: Haworth.

Berman, Sanford. 1985. Consumer, BEWARE! *Technicalities*, April: 11–12.

Berman, Sanford. 1988. *Worth noting: Editorials, letters, essays, an interview, and bibliography.* Jefferson, NC: McFarland.

Mason, Philip B. 1975. Archival security: New solutions to an old problem. *American Archivist*, October: 477–498.

Masters, William H. 1983. A three-decade retrospective of the Masters and Johnson Institute. Presented at the 26th Annual Meeting of the Society for the Scientific Study of Sex, November 18–20, Chicago, IL.

The Report of the Management and Planning Committee to the Librarian of Congress. 1988. Washington, DC: Library of Congress.

CHAPTER 12
Erotica Research Collections

Gwendolyn L. Pershing

The Kinsey Institute for Research in Sex, Gender, and Reproduction is one of the few libraries actively collecting and archiving erotica. In this chapter, I describe the Kinsey Institute's erotica collection and provide some historical comments on the history of erotica. Then I briefly discuss other libraries that also undertake this unusual responsibility.

THE KINSEY INSTITUTE

The Kinsey Institute for Research in Sex, Gender, and Reproduction
313 Morrison Hall
Indiana University
Bloomington, Indiana 47405
(812) 335-7686

Dr. Alfred C. Kinsey began to collect erotica and research materials pertaining to sexuality in 1938 to support his pioneering research in human sexual behavior. From Kinsey's early efforts, the Institute's collection has grown to include a library of over 70,000 print items (of which approximately 25,000 volumes are considered to be erotic), 28,500 pieces of erotic art, 100,000 photographs, 6,500 films, and 600 videocassettes.

The 25,000 erotic works appear in a variety of formats, such as books, magazines, comic books, and pamphlets. The Institute purchases some of the erotic materials with private funds and relies heavily on donations from individuals. Whereas many libraries are reluctant to accept donations of erotica, the Kinsey Institute actively seeks donations of such materials by contacting potential donors and responding to advertisements in many sources.

The Kinsey Institute has acquired many unique and rare items. More commonplace items, such as paperback novels and men's magazines, are also collected since they provide important documentation of societal attitudes and trends. These popular items are unlikely to be retained in most other research archives.

Among the treasures in the Kinsey Institute's erotic literature collection is an 11-volume set of the privately printed *My Secret Life.* This work was authored and privately printed by a rich Englishman; *My Secret Life* is a detailed account of the author's secret sexual adventures and has been described as "a book of pure, unmitigated lust" (Carrington 1902, 36). It is not known how many copies of *My Secret Life* were published. While the owner of the original manuscript requested that only six copies be printed, Charles Carrington claimed to have seen several sets and thought that at least 25 copies had been produced (Carrington 1902, 35). Gershon Legman states that Carrington, by admitting knowledge of at least 25 copies, indicated a low printing figure in order to maintain a high price. In any case, Legman says that only four sets have been traced to the United States (Legman 1964, 34).

In addition to the 11-volume set of *My Secret Life*, the Kinsey Institute possesses a set of the first three volumes of *My Secret Life* reprinted in a limited edition and a reprint of volume five retitled *Marital Frolics.*

The erotic literature collection also contains copies of such rare works as *Whippingham Papers* by A.C. Swinburne, *The Double Life of Cuthbert Cockerton, Esq. Attorney-at-Law of the City of London*, and *Suburban Souls. The Double Life of Cuthbert Cockerton* is an adaptation of a French work by Restif de la Bretone, *L'Anti Justine*, and was printed from an original manuscript dated 1798 (Carrington 1902, 221). *Suburban Souls*, published in 1901, is an erotic memoir by an English scholar, John Stephen Farmer (Kearney 1981, 43).

Some of the works contained in the collections may be categorized as erotic folklore. For example, *Some Yarns* is a collection of jokes from the World War I period, which was issued by Carrington in 1918. The Kinsey Institute's copy is the only one known to exist (Legman 1964, 485).

The "vulgar" songs collected along with other folksongs from the Ozarks by Vance Rudolph were excluded from a four-volume set of *Ozark Folksongs* published by The State Historical Society of Missouri. In order to preserve the bawdy songs he thought were critical to the understanding of American folklore, Randolph transcribed them and presented manuscripts of "'Unprintable' Songs from the Ozarks" to approximately 20 libraries, including the Kinsey Institute (Randolph 1954, 1).

Bawdy songbooks, such as the *Frisky Songster* and *A Collection of Sea Songs and Ditties*, are included among rare items housed at the

Institute. Only two copies of the *Frisky Songster* are known to exist (Legman 1964, 375), and the Institute has the only known copy of *Sea Songs and Ditties.*

The collection of men's (girlie) magazines at the Institute numbers over 1,300 titles and 15,000 individual issues. The holdings include titles published in the United States from the 1920s to the present as well as selected examples from other countries. The Institute has complete holdings of *Playboy* and *Screw* and many others in the mainstream of this genre, but some of the nonmainstream titles are incomplete and may be represented by only a single issue. In many cases, only one issue was ever published. This collection of men's magazines has been developed almost exclusively from donations.

Captain Billy's Whiz Bang from the 1920s and *Ballyhoo* from the 1930s are examples of early men's magazines that include bawdy humor and suggestive cartoons with only an occasional photograph of a scantily-clad woman. *Captain Billy's Whiz Bang* originated by accident, as a result of the publisher's practice of distributing copies of jokes to World War I servicemen. The mimeographed sheets became so popular that the publisher decided to produce them in magazine format and make them available to the public. *Captain Billy's Whiz Bang* reached its peak in 1923 and ceased publication in 1932 (Gabor 1972, 76). Art, photography, and Hollywood fan magazines were among the earliest form of pictoral erotic entertainment for men.

Illustrations of the pin-up girl with an emphasis on leg shots were representative of men's magazines in the 1940s. The 1940s publications held by the Institute include *Titter, Click, Flirt,* and *Giggles.*

Playboy and an emphasis on the bosom were a phenomenon of the 1950s. *Playboy* continues to be the premiere men's magazine despite numerous imitations that have been published over the years. *Cabaret, Dude,* and *Jem* are just a few of the many *Playboy* imitators available at the Kinsey Institute.

Men's magazines from foreign countries are also represented in the Kinsey Institute collection. These include *Club* and *Mayfair* from England, *C'est Paris* from France, and *Gala* from Denmark. Japan, Spain, Mexico, Canada, and Sweden are also represented.

Men's magazines also appeared in the form of nudist magazines in the 1940s. Publishers may have viewed this genre as an opportunity to market full nudity under the protection of the First Amendment (Gabor 1984, 70). Some early titles emphasize healthy living, as illustrated by the Institute's holdings of *Sunshine and Health, Modern Sunbathing and Hygiene,* and *Sunbathing and Health Magazine.*

In addition to the men's and nudist magazines, the Kinsey Institute owns a large collection of paraphilia (or fetish) magazines. This collection is comprised primarily of materials acquired by donation instead of purchase. A December 1987 donation has increased these holdings significantly, and the collection now contains fetish materials currently available on the market in addition to a broad span of historical publications. Magazines representing body part fetishes (*Foot Worship*) and inanimate fetishes (*Rubber Life*) are included as well as magazines illustrating bondage, sadomasochism, and other interests.

The Kinsey Institute collection contains over 1,000 erotic comic books, also called eight-pagers, Tijuana Bibles, or bluesies. This form of popular erotica was first produced during the late 1920s or early 1930s and essentially disappeared in the late 1950s. Most of the behavior illustrated in the eight-pagers is heterosexual intercourse, but a few illustrated such sexual variations as zoophilia. Interestingly, sadomasochistic behavior was not represented (Raymond 1972, 26).

The origin of the erotic comics remains a mystery. Otis Raymond, author of *Sex Comic Classics*, believes they originated in either the Los Angeles, San Francisco, or San Diego areas (Raymond 1972, 15); whereas Maurice Horn, author of *Sex in the Comics*, states that most were produced in Cuba (Horn 1985, 84).

There is also some disagreement as to which type of characters were first used in erotic comics. Raymond states that the sexual antics of comic strip characters such as Popeye, Dick Tracy, and Dagwood and Blondie appeared first, to be followed by public figures (Raymond 1972, 25). However, Horn says that illustrations of public figures appeared first and were later followed by the comic strip characters (Horn 1985, 84–85).

The Kinsey Institute also collects paperback novels and pamphlets. These materials are not always copyrighted and therefore are not submitted to or held by the Library of Congress. The Kinsey Institute collection has not been entirely cataloged, but approximately 3,000–4,000 novels published by Greenleaf Classics, Eros Publications, and others are included. An estimated 500 erotic pamphlets also appear in the library collection bearing such titles as *Hot Tears* and *Lady of Pleasure*.

The art collection of the Kinsey Institute contains approximately 25,000 two-dimensional and 3,500 three-dimensional works from many cultures and historical periods, in both original form and in reproduction. The reproductions are collected because they are documents indicative of the erotic works produced in a particular country at a particular period in history and are, therefore, valuable to scholars in a variety of disciplines. This collection has been partially cataloged; however, scholars using the collections often find it easier to browse through works themselves rather than to use the incomplete catalog.

Many of the works are originals and are unique to the Institute. For example, approximately 100 works by Pavel Tchelitchew, a twentieth-century Russian artist, were donated to the Institute in the

1970s. Most of the Tchelitchew works are sexually explicit ink and sepia drawings. Original works by Pierre Auguste Renoir, Aubrey Beardsley, Jean Genet, and Howard Chandler Christy are also represented in the Institute's collections. Such works can provide important insights into the lives and times of particular artists.

In addition to the original works of art, the Institute holds many reproductions, such as prints, photographs, and journal illustrations of erotica. For instance, the erotic work of Belgian artist Felicien Rops is included in the collections, with holdings of approximately 13 etchings and numerous other reproductions.

The Institute holds a large collection of erotica produced by individuals institutionalized in prisons and mental hospitals. Many of the works are pencil sketches on notebook paper or produced in booklet format in imitation of erotic comics.

The three-dimensional artifacts are shelved in locked cabinets and arranged according to geographical origin. Objects held include ceramics, ivory carvings, aphrodisiacs, altered coins, condoms, and sadomasochistic devices; the range is from fine works of pottery and sculpture to popular novelties. Stone fertility objects dating from approximately 4,000 B.C. and Roman oil lamp bases dating from 300 B.C. to 300 A.D. are among the oldest items in the three-dimensional collection.

Over 100 Oriental erotic scrolls dating from the sixteenth to the twentieth centuries are contained in the collections. Many of the scrolls are fragile and may not be safely handled. In order to make them available for use by scholars, the Institute has produced photographic slides of each scene of the most fragile scrolls.

In 1954, Dr. Kinsey and his staff visited Peru to study the Peruvian pre-Columbian erotic ceramics in the Peruvian National Museum and a privately owned collection. The examples of ceramics gathered on this visit by Dr. Kinsey and his staff, as well as hundreds of photographs, enable scholars to analyse the sexual attitudes and practices of an extinct culture.

Dr. Kinsey had numerous contacts world-wide who have been willing to donate their collections to the Institute for archival purposes. American law enforcement agencies as well as professional and amateur photographers have donated the majority of the 100,000 photographs housed at the Institute. For example, a donor in Germany agreed to make copies of the erotic daguerrotypes included in his own collection for the Institute. In this way the collection of daguerrotype copies was greatly expanded and permits research in photographic images dating back to 1855.

Since most of the producers of the Institute's erotic photographs are either anonymous or wish to remain anonymous, the collection is arranged alphabetically by the sexual behavior illustrated, with a few exceptions. Photographs by such well known artists as George Platt

Lynes and Wilhelm von Gloeden are shelved together in order to facilitate access.

The films in the Institute may be considered an historical record of erotic films; the oldest is *El Satario* dating from 1911. The collection includes approximately 6,500 films in 8mm, 16mm, and 35mm format. As an ongoing preservation project, a videotape copy of each film is being made to be used as the projection copy.

It is the Institute's policy to restrict the use of the commercial films to Indiana University. Commercial films may be viewed by scholars at the Institute or may be shown as an educational aid to students by an Indiana University faculty member. Films produced by the Institute, such as *Mammalian Sex Behavior*, may be lent to scholars for research and instructional purposes. The restriction on access to the commercial films results from an agreement made between the Institute and the film distributors when the films were donated.

The Institute has recently contacted several distributors of commercial erotic videocassettes in an effort to develop a contemporary collection of this popular modern genre. As of this writing, the holdings number about 600, and the collection is growing on a weekly basis.

Use of the Kinsey Institute's collection is limited by law to scholars and professionals with demonstrable research needs. This policy on access is based on the 1957 decision of the United States District Court, Southern District of New York in the landmark customs case of *United States vs 31 Photographs*. In this case the court recognized the legitimate rights of scholars to have access to erotic materials for research purposes.

Individuals wishing to use the collections on site must submit a letter indicating their research needs and citing their academic and professional credentials. Access fees are charged for all collections, and fees are charged for staff time for use of the art, film, and photograph collections.

The library materials are not available through interlibrary loan, but the Kinsey Institute Information Service provides photocopies by mail for a fee. The Institute reserves the right to deny the photocopying of fragile materials that may be physically damaged as a result of copying.

OTHER EROTICA COLLECTIONS

In addition to the Kinsey Institute, a few other libraries collect erotica. None of these collections are as historically rich, nor do they contain the volume of materials housed at the Kinsey Institute. These libraries nonetheless are potentially important for researchers and often contain valuable works.

British Library
2 Sheraton Street
London, England W1V 4BH

The British Library has a large collection of erotic literature more commonly known as the "Private Case." This collection was not purchased, but rather exists due to private donations and posthumous bequests (Kearney 1981, 63). A complete bibliographic listing of the materials contained in the Private Case has been compiled by P.J. Kearney in the *Private Case*, which includes an introduction by Gershon Legman.

The Private Case materials are available to the general public. In order to gain access to this collection, a special form must be completed in addition to the application slip used to obtain library materials (Kearney 1981, 62).

Cornell University
Cornell University Libraries
Collection on Human Sexuality
Ithaca, New York 14853-5301
(607) 255-4144

Cornell University has recently received a collection of homosexual erotica assembled by the Mariposa Education and Research Foundation. The materials, which appear in a variety of formats such as films, books, journals, and artifacts, were donated to Cornell University to support the multi-disciplinary center for the study of human sexuality (Mariposa Education and Research Foundation, Inc. 1988).

The collection is available for use, although the processing of materials is not yet completed. The materials are available to scholars and the general public for use at the library and will have the same photocopy restrictions as other materials in the Cornell University Libraries Manuscript Department (Tom Hickerson, telephone conversation with the author, April 6, 1988).

Institute for Advanced Study of Human Sexuality
1523 Franklin Street
San Francisco, California 94109
(415) 928-1133

Elaini Gardner, a librarian at the Institute, has described the library at the Institute for Advanced Study of Human Sexuality as having a large collection of erotica in the areas of literature and audiovisual materials. The library relies heavily on donations and purchases very little. Many of the materials donated to the collection are stored in warehouses throughout the country due to space limitations at the Institute. The literature collection contains over 250,000 items, including books, magazines, newspapers, pamphlets, film catalogs, art reproductions, and posters.

The oldest book in the collection is Italian and was written during the fifteenth century. Included in the book collection are works by Marquis De Sade, *My Secret Life*, art books, and pulp paperback books.

The magazine and newspaper collection is comprised of historical and current men's magazines, including *Playboy*, fetishism works such as *Fetish Times*, and magazines for special interests such as spanking and sadomasochism.

The audiovisual collection is quite extensive and contains approximately 107,000 items, including feature films, film loops, and video and audio cassettes as well as 300,000 slides and photos.

The feature films are available on 35mm and 16mm and the loops on 16mm and 8mm. The earliest film in the collection is a 16mm cartoon from the early 1920s titled *Ever Ready Hardon*. The feature film collection includes popular films such as *Behind the Green Door*. Many of the historical feature films have been converted to ¾" and ½" videotape.

The library is open to students and faculty of the Institute for Advanced Study of Human Sexuality. Others working on specific research projects may apply to use the collections. The materials from the Institute are not available on interlibrary loan, but an effort is made to provide photocopies of materials if the materials are not available elsewhere (Elaini Gardner, telephone conversation with author, January 1988).

Library of Congress
Washington, D.C. 20540
(202) 287-5000

The Rare Books and Special Collections Division of the Library of Congress holds erotica in its collections but, according to Peter Van Wingen, the Head of the Reference and Reader Services Section, they do not purposefully seek to acquire erotic materials. Many of the items classified as erotica are sent to the Library by the Copyright Office. In other instances staff or individuals may identify materials as being erotic and needing the protection and security offered by the Rare Books and Special Collections Division.

LC's erotica was once designated as the Delta Collection. It was dismantled and integrated into the Rare Books and Special Collections Division in 1964. Although the Delta books have been integrated into the collection, most of them fall into the Library of Congress classification HQ (the family, marriage, and women). This segment of the classification contains approximately 2,000 items, including erotic works as well as scholarly journals and texts. The bound periodical collection in the Rare Books and Special Collections Division includes titles such as *Playboy, Penthouse, Oui,* and *Playgirl.*

The Rare Books and Special Collections Division also houses hundreds of erotic paperback books published by Greenleaf Classics, Beeline Classics, and Beeline Double Novels. These paperbacks arrive on a weekly basis through copyright deposit (Peter VanWingen, letter to the author, June 17, 1987).

The Library of Congress collection includes approximately 200 volumes of erotic photography books that were once a part of the Delta Collection. These volumes are now shelved in the TR Locked Cage located on Deck 10 of the Adams Building, a Library of Congress annex (Selth 1985, 85).

Materials in the Rare Books and Special Collections are available to persons 18 years of age and older. The materials are not available through interlibrary loan but may be photocopied through the Library's Photoduplication Service if the physical condition of the original permits (Library of Congress 1987).

New York Public Library
5th Avenue and 42nd Street
New York, New York 10018
(212) 930-0800

The New York Public Library's collection development policy states that the library collects works of literature, whatever their controversial nature, and that the library collects in all languages and historical periods. This may include materials that seem erotic or pornographic to some but are judged nevertheless to have literary value.

Juanita S. Doares and her staff described the erotica collections of the New York Public Library (letter to the author, July 23, 1987). The General Research Division has microfilms of comics, pictorial magazines, pamphlets, and pulp novels. These items are purchased in an annual buying trip to bookstores in the New York area that specialize in pornography. These purchases are then microfilmed for use by library patrons.

Once the items are microfilmed, representative samples are sent to the Ephemera Collection of the Rare Books Room. This collection is contained in seven manuscript boxes and ranges from nudist magazines to X-rated illustrated magazines. The collection exemplifies various interests, such as fetishisms and bondage, and is maintained in order to preserve the material in its original format.

The New York Public Library General Research Division is open to the general public, and the Rare Books Room is open to persons with a card of admissions. Applications for a card of admissions are available in Room 316. Applicants must show valid identification and be able to demonstrate their research needs.

Providence Athenaeum
251 Benefit Street
Providence, Rhode Island 02903
(401) 421-6970

The Providence Athenaeum has approximately 175 uncataloged German imprints and French titles with an emphasis on the early twentieth century. The Athenaeum recently acquired a collection of foreign erotica that includes books in German, Russian folklore, French limericks, and accounts of the mating practices of the American Indian (Ash & Miller 1985, 647).

This collection is available to members of the general public even though it is still unprocessed.

University of North Carolina
J. Murrey Atkins Library
UNCC Station
Charlotte, North Carolina 28223
(704) 547-2211

The University of North Carolina in Charlotte has a collection of 100 cataloged erotica and scholarly works. Many of the books are classics by writers such as Frank Harris, D.H. Lawrence, and Norman Douglas (Ash & Miller 1985, 647).

The library collections are open to the general public for on-site use. Residents of North Carolina not affiliated with the university must purchase a community borrowers card to gain borrowing privileges.

Homosexual Archives

Several of the homosexual archives in the United States collect erotica. Alan V. Miller, in the *Directory of the International Association of Lesbian and Gay Archives and Libraries* (1987) notes 12 such libraries, which are located in Georgia, Illinois, California, New York, Kentucky, Florida, Texas, Pennsylvania, and Minnesota.

The archives' primary responsibilities are to archive gay and lesbian association documents and erotica. In most cases the archives' collections are small. The largest contains 18,000 volumes, and the smallest consists of three shelves. Miller's work may be consulted for a complete list of the archives and a description of their holdings.

Erotic materials are clearly valuable historical documents for scholars in a variety of disciplines, such as history, literature, film studies, and fine arts. Traditionally, erotica has been collected by individuals for their private libraries but was often destroyed or dispersed upon the death of the owner. Academic and public libraries have been reluctant to archive erotic materials. Fortunately, this reluctance is disappearing as societal attitudes about sex change, and scholars are now able to gain access to resources denied to them in the past.

REFERENCES

Editor's Note: A number of collections dealing with other aspects of sexuality, such as sex research and sex education, are listed in the works of Ash and Miller (1985) and Selth (1985), below. In addition, Vern Bullough (author of Chapter 6, "Research and Archival Value of Erotica/Pornography") informs me that the collection that he established at California State University, Northridge, contains a good deal of material on transvestism, homosexuality, and prostitution, including German sexological journals and some Chinese material.

Ash, Lee, and William Miller, comps. 1985. *Subject collections: A guide to special book collections and subject emphases as reported by university, college, public, and special libraries and museums in the United States and Canada.* 6th ed. New York: Bowker.

[Carrington, Charles?]. 1902. *Forbidden books: Notes and gossip on tabooed literature.* Paris.

Gabor, Mark. 1972. *The pin-up: A modest history.* New York: Universe Books.

Gabor, Mark. 1984. *The illustrated history of girlie magazines from National Police Gazette to the present.* New York: Harmony Books.

Horn, Maurice. 1985. *Sex in the comics.* New York: Chelsea House Publishers.

Kearney, Patrick J., comp. 1981. *The Private Case: An annotated bibliography of the Private Case Erotica Collection in the British (Museum) Library.* Introduction by G. Legman. London: Jay Landesman Limited.

Legman, G. 1964. *The horn book: Studies in erotic folklore and bibliography.* New Hyde Park, NY: University Books.

Library of Congress. [1987?]. *Rare books and special collections in the Library of Congress.* Pamphlet. Washington, DC: Library of Congress.

Mariposa Education and Research Foundation, Inc. [1988]. *The Mariposa Education and Research Foundation.* Pamphlet. Los Angeles, CA: Mariposa Education and Research Foundation, Inc.

Miller, Alan V., comp. 1987. *Directory of the International Association of Lesbian and Gay Archives and Libraries.* Toronto, Ontario: International Association of Lesbian and Gay Archives and Libraries.

Randolph, Vance, comp. 1954. "Unprintable" songs from the Ozarks. Typescript. Eureka Springs, AR, August 10.

Raymond, Otis. 1972. *An illustrated history of sex comic classics.* Vol. 1. New York: Comic Classics.

Selth, Jefferson P. 1985. *Alternative lifestyles: A guide to research collections on intentional communities, nudism, and sexual freedom.* Bibliographies and Indexes in Sociology, no. 6. Westport, CT: Greenwood Press.

CHAPTER 13

Homosexuality Research Collections

Daniel C. Tsang

While archives or special collections on homosexuality have proliferated in the last two decades since the Stonewall Rebellion of 1969,
much of the evidence of their existence remains hidden from the
professional literature of librarianship. Knowlton (1987) found only
one reference to homosexuality in seven years of indexes to *The
American Archivist*, and it was a citation to a letter. Standard directories of special collections, such as *Directory of Special Libraries and
Information Centers* (1989), *Subject Directory of Special Libraries and
Information Centers* (1989), and *Subject Collections* (Ash & Miller
1985), do, by now, index several dozen unique lesbian or gay collections. However, references to such collections are still more likely to
be located in the lesbian and gay press, as well as, of course, in the
publications published by the lesbian and gay archives themselves.
(See, for example, the numerous entries under LIBRARIES AND
ARCHIVES and under LESBIAN HERSTORY ARCHIVES in *The
Lesbian Periodicals Index*, Potter 1986.) Indeed, some 100 such archives are listed on the mailing list of the International Association of
Lesbian and Gay Archives and Libraries (Miller 1987).

Copyright © 1991 by Daniel C. Tsang. Earlier versions of this chapter were
presented at the annual conference of the Society for the Scientific Study of
Sex, St. Louis, November 14, 1986, and at the annual conference of the
American Library Association, Dallas, June 26, 1989.

HISTORY AND HERSTORY

In fact, the existence of specific collections on homosexuality predates Stonewall. The first such major collection (if we ignore the one reputedly at the Vatican) was the library and archive at the Institute for Sexual Science in Berlin, founded by Magnus Hirschfeld. Created in 1919, it met an early and untimely death at the hands of Nazi stormtroopers and Hitler youth. In May 1933, the Institute was raided, and its books and manuscripts burned in public (Anonymous 1933; Haeberle 1981; Wolff 1986, 175. 377–379; see also Steakley 1985).

Only through the diligent efforts of Hirschfeld's one-time lover and curator Karl Giese were portions of this collection spirited to safety in unoccupied Europe (Wolff 1986, 376–377), parts of it to end up eventually at the Kinsey Institute in Bloomington, Indiana. In Berlin, a Magnus Hirschfeld Society exists to commemorate and promote his work and to re-establish an institute of sexology ("The Magnus Hirschfeld Society, Inc.," in Steakley 1985, inside back cover.)

For years and even today, libraries around the world have restricted access to erotic materials, with the excuse that these materials need special protection from theft or mutilation. Various names were devised to describe such collections; at the British Museum, then Library, erotica (and for many years, gay literature such as Edward Carpenter's *The Intermediate Sex*) were kept in a "Private Case" and omitted from the public catalog (Loth 1962, 185–186; Fryer 1966, 52–54; Kearney 1981). At the Library of Congress, erotica has been shelved in the "Delta Collection" (Loth 1962, 184–185; Kearney 1981, 17); and at the Bibliothèque Nationale in Paris, there is "*L'Enfer*"—the "Hell" collection (Loth 1962, 186; Kearney 1981, 16). At New York Public Library, erotic books are cataloged with five stars (*****) (Kearney 1981, 17); and even at a relatively new library, such as at the University of California, Irvine, the tiny erotica collection is kept with other materials deemed subject to mutilation in an "X-Collection."

Today, any seeker of contemporary lesbian or gay erotica collections will find a few "straight" libraries that actively collect such materials; but much of it is preserved in independent, community-based lesbian and gay archives around the world. In addition, lesbian erotica can often also be found in the many feminist and women's archives located the world over. (For a recent essay on women's archives, see Marston 1988.)

ACADEMIC AND RESEARCH COLLECTIONS

The most accessible collection in academia currently is located in Ann Arbor at the University of Michigan. The sexual freedom materials that form part of the University's Labadie Collection contain a veritable range of erotica, including 1950s pornography as well as more recent magazines from Europe, now banned in the U.S. Known primarily as a major collection of materials on anarchism under its long-time curator, Edward C. Weber, the Labadie Collection now can boast the best U.S. collection on a university campus covering the modern lesbian and gay movement. Its holdings are now searchable online by those with access to the university's computer. (See Tsang 1980, for an early listing of periodical titles received.)

A smaller collection is included in the Contemporary Culture Collection at Temple University Libraries in Philadelphia (Tsang 1979). The best collection on homosexuality in literature is located at the Harry Ransom Humanities Research Center at the University of Texas, Austin, to which many authors have donated their papers (Conner 1983).

A bequest from the estate of the late *Advocate* publisher, David B. Goodstein, recently established the History of Human Sexuality Collection at Cornell University in Ithaca, New York (Anonymous 1988; Baumann 1988; Cornell University 1989; Mitgang 1988). In 1989, its first curator, Brenda Marston, began working with core material from the Mariposa Foundation library and other collections forthcoming in the pipeline. Its holdings are already being cataloged, with access through the archival and manuscripts control (AMC) subfile of the RLIN cataloging database.

The best and largest collection of audiovisual lesbian and gay erotica is located on the West Coast, at the library of the Institute for Advanced Study of Human Sexuality in San Francisco. Under its erstwhile and indefatigable president, Ted McIlvenna, the Institute's filing cabinets and book shelves are packed with films, videos, audiotapes, books, and magazines documenting all sorts of sexual practices, including homosexuality. Graduate students enrolled in the school's doctoral program have the opportunity of a lifetime to peruse rare materials unavailable elsewhere.

Another academic institution, Indiana University's Kinsey Institute for Research in Sex, Gender, and Reproduction, holds a major erotica collection, including materials on homosexuality; internal turmoil, however, forced the closing of its library for several months in 1988 and 1989 (Yee 1988; Wheeler 1988; Gilbert 1988; Associated Press 1989b).

Although most public libraries shy away from collecting erotica, the premier U.S. public research library, the New York Public Library, periodically sends its librarians down the street to the adult bookstores that line Manhatttan's 42nd Street, to search for lesbian and gay magazines. These gems are then carefully microfilmed for posterity, with access through the library's online catalog (cf. Spornick 1988, 3). The library also recently acquired the collection of the International Gay Information Center in New York and is currently processing its holdings. Whether this collection development focus will be maintained, however, is open to question. The recent appointment of Rev. Timothy S. Healy as NYPL President has raised concerns about whether a priest with an anti-gay record is the appropriate choice for that position. As Georgetown University President, he had opposed the recognition of lesbian and gay student organizations. Library workers are so concerned that they are reportedly rushing to microfilm newly acquired lesbian and gay periodicals before Healy comes on board (Solomon 1989; Humm et al. 1989; Steinfels 1989).

A 1988 study of erotica collections at libraries that belong to the Research Libraries Group found that of 22 respondents, most (15 libraries) indicated that the library collected material relating to sex. But only 3 (Brown University, New York Public Library, and Temple University), admitted that erotica constituted a specialty for the library (Spornick 1988).

An enterprising archivist has surveyed special collections librarians about their library's collections on lesbians and gay males. After surveying several dozen lesbian and gay archives, Knowlton (1987) sent questionnaires to 12 traditional archives in many of the same cities, receiving 10 responses. With one exception (Stanford University), these established archives did not collect any gay rights movement records, and 6 of the 10 archives said there were no gay archives in their area.

"GRASS-ROOTS" ARCHIVES

Outside academia, and mostly hidden from academia as Knowlton discovered, a host of community-based archives and libraries have sprung up, empowered by the lesbian and gay movements and fired by feminism and gay liberation. Many reject any ties to academia as restrictive or elitist and leading to loss of community control (Nestle 1979; Timmons 1986; Halfhill 1988; cf. Monahan 1979 and Sitzman 1988). Within the United States, two such archives stand out: the Lesbian Herstory Archives and the International Lesbian and Gay Archives.

Located in an apartment in Manhattan and staffed by dedicated volunteers, the Lesbian Herstory Archives was founded in 1975 by Joan Nestle and Deborah Edel. It is the largest such archive in the United States, and its founders have inspired countless other archives around the country and abroad with their enthusiasm, selflessness, and willingness to share information. Its holdings, which span the globe, are reported in its occasional but detailed newsletters. Periodically the Archives crew goes on the road, with a travelling slide show that captivates audiences around the world (Loeb 1981; see also Bennet 1979; Hodges 1979, 1980; Lehman 1979; Nestle 1979; Schwarz 1979; Sturgis 1979).

On the West Coast, in sunny southern California, the largest community-based gay collection is located at the International Gay and Lesbian Archives in West Hollywood. Its curator, Jim Kepner, began collecting gay ephemera back in 1942 (Steele 1985; see also Anonymous 1986). Forced recently to vacate its premises because of rising rent and courted by various area libraries, the Archives eventually found a home in municipal quarters in West Hollywood (Associated Press 1988; Perkins 1988–1989), where it shares space with a West Coast lesbian archives, the June L. Mazer Lesbian Collection (Whitlock 1989, 16). Another collection, the Baker Memorial Library and Archives at the One Institute of Homophile Studies, is also located in the Los Angeles area; its librarians have begun cataloging the collection (Walker 1988), and its site was recently officially designated as a historic/cultural monument by the City of Los Angeles (Perkins 1989).

In San Francisco and Toronto, active gay archives also exist. The Canadian Gay Archives in Toronto is the more established, with a publication series of monographs and bibliographies, including one on how to set up a gay archives (Fraser & Averill 1983; see also Miller 1980; MacDonald 1984). The San Francisco Bay Area Gay & Lesbian Historical Society has pioneered the collaborative microfilming (by the nearby University of California, Berkeley, Library) of selected Bay Area lesbian and gay titles, an important project to preserve the legacy of lesbians and gays (Anonymous 1989c; Kreitz 1989). Although housed in a private residence, its archival holdings are accessible to researchers (Garber 1988; Koskovich 1988).

A number of archives, including Third World Women's Archives in New York (Anonymous 1984) and the author's Lavender Archives in Costa Mesa, California, focus on the experiences of Third World lesbians and gays in the United States. And the AIDS crisis has created the need for speedy and accurate information about the disease and efforts to combat it (Lesley 1988): an AIDS Library has just been established in Philadelphia (Rose 1989), and an HIV Center in West Hollywood (Anonymous 1989a, 1989b).

Other smaller archives dot the landscape throughout the United States. Despite setbacks, such as burnout or the lack of funding, many survive and continue to collect erotica and community publications.

Outside North America, each western European country boasts at least a major archive or two, and sometimes many more. There is more government support for such archives in western Europe. One good example is in the Netherlands, where the Lesbian Archives (Lesbisch Archief) in Leeuwarden is supported by grants from the city and the province (Anonymous 1987). In Berlin, the world's first Gay Museum has sought to commemorate the Hirschfeld legacy (Martin 1987). In addition, three foundations (two in the Netherlands, one in West Germany) have been set up to preserve erotica and other documents relating to the taboo practise of homosexual pedophilia (Anonymous 1979).

At least three empirical studies have been conducted on the proliferating lesbian and gay archives scene in the U.S. and abroad. The author of this chapter, in an unpublished study in 1984–85, obtained 33 responses to a questionnaire sent to lesbian and gay archives and collections, in both academia and the community. Knowlton (1987) surveyed 40 lesbian and gay archives and received completed responses for 15. Following up on work begun by the late James Fraser, Miller (1987) sent surveys to over 100 collections and archives on the mailing list of the International Association of Lesbian and Gay Archives and Libraries (formed at the Sex and the State Conference in Toronto in 1985) and received completed responses from 37 collections.

Although the questions varied, one striking overall theme emerges from the analysis of the results of all three surveys. These community-based archives are virtually all run by unpaid, volunteer staff, with many if not most sharing private apartment space. Most lack steady, outside funding. Many of these archives are also brand new; Knowlton (1987, 20) discovered that 40% of her responding archives were founded since 1980, with the majority since Stonewall. Most of those responding to Miller's survey indicated they did collect "pornography and erotica."

Like many small businesses, these archives are undercapitalized, and because they depend almost entirely on volunteer help, they run mostly on dedication and energy and are subject to the ups and downs of all voluntary organizations. With the AIDS epidemic causing havoc in the gay community, money to fund research and support for persons with AIDS has of necessity had a higher priority than financial aid for archives. But unless creative efforts are made to provide a more secure base for these archives, many will not survive.

HOMOSEXUALITY ARCHIVES, PORNOGRAPHY, AND POLITICS

In addition to the impact of AIDS, lesbian and gay archives have had to face increasingly repressive legislative climates in both the United States, under former Attorney General Edwin Meese (see

Tsang 1987), and in the United Kingdom under Margaret Thatcher. The same conservative trends have also affected the relatively liberal societies of western Europe, including the Netherlands.

Legitimate concern about child abuse has led to outright bans on erotic or nude depictions of minors, with some states and the U.K. banning mere possession of child pornography. In the United States, the latest attack on free expression comes in the form of the Child Protection and Obscenity Enforcement Act of 1988 (part of Public Law 100–690), passed in the waning hours of the 100th Congress. This blockbuster law, attached to an anti-drug bill, breezed through Congress despite lobbying by such groups as the American Civil Liberties Union and the Media Coalition.

The effect of this new law on libraries and archives remains to be seen. In addition to cumbersome record-keeping requirements, under the law, individuals—including librarians—could be deemed "engaged in the (obscenity) business" by transferring "obscene" books or magazines or selling microform copies; the entire library could also be seized. On March 14, 1989, the American Library Association and eight other organizations filed suit in District Court in Washington, DC in the first legal challenge of the law, in *ALA vs. Thornburgh* ("Censorship" 1989). Two months later, a federal judge threw out as unconstitutional the provisions on recordkeeping and forfeiture of assets before trial (Associated Press 1989a; Geyelin 1989). However, the government subsequently filed an appeal to overturn the decision (Parachini 1989), and the same provisions have already been reintroduced in a Senate bill.

At the state level, more legislatures are heeding the *Final Report* of the U.S. Attorney General's Commission on Pornography (1986) and have banned possession of child pornography. Other state legislatures are expected to do so, especially in the wake of the U.S. Supreme Court's April 1990 decision (Greenhouse 1990), upholding the right of states to outlaw the mere possession of child pornography. California has announced its intention to seek legislation upgrading the penalty for such possession from a misdemeanor to a felony (Camposeco 1990). Archives on homosexuality are especially vulnerable since material already in the collections may violate such state possession statutes. That even established institutions are not immune for prosecutorial excesses is shown by the indictment for child pornography and obscenity pandering of a Cincinnati art museum and its director, who exhibited photographs taken by the late gay photographer, Robert Mapplethorpe (Masnerus 1990).

If the state were to act against homosexuality collections per se, most vulnerable would still be independent or community-based archives. With their highly paid attorneys, established or university-affiliated collections are likely to survive any such legal harassment.

Lesbian and gay archives remain especially vulnerable to police raids or to charges of corruption of minors who use their materials.

Controversies within the lesbian and gay communities over pedophilia and sadomasochism also threaten to split archivists into two or more camps. Lesbian Herstory Archives founder Joan Nestle's speaking engagement in London to promote her book *A Restricted Country* (1987), was pointedly *not* sponsored by the Lesbian Archives and Information Centre in that city, where she was accused of supporting "non-feminist" sex (Bergman 1989). She has deplored the "self hate" that keeps lesbians and gay males separate and bickering among each other (Whitlock 1989). Indeed, the energy and passion that led to the creation and growth of many archives must be diverted from internal squabbling and mobilized toward joint efforts to cement solidarity among lesbians and gays in the face of virulent homophobia and erotophobia.

UNCERTAIN FUTURE

The outlook, then, for lesbians and gay archives is not a particularly optimistic one. Unless the current wave of repressive legislation recedes, and unless the lesbian and gay community can work together to preserve the common herstory and history, more and more collections will go the way of the Institute for Sexual Science in Berlin in 1933. By networking and forming coalitions with existing free speech and civil liberties organizations, this bleak forecast can be—hopefully—made less likely to come to pass.

For a list of existing lesbian and gay archives and collections, consult the *Directory of the International Association of Lesbian and Gay Archives and Libraries* (Miller 1987). For a more up-to-date listing of North American archives and collections, consult the state and national entries in the latest edition of the *Gayellow Pages*, or the listing, *Gay/Lesbian Archives and Libraries in North America*, issued by the American Library Association's Gay and Lesbian Task Force Library Information Clearinghouse (1989). A selected list of periodicals from these archives appears in the Appendix to this chapter.

REFERENCES

Anonymous. 1933. Nazi students raid Institute on Sex: Seize half a ton of scientific information at Dr. Hirschfeld's Berlin establishment. *The New York Times*, May 7: 12.

Anonymous. 1979. Paedophile foundations. *Pan: A Magazine about Boy-Love*, 2 (August): 21. (The foundations cited are: Wolfgang Tomdsek, Postfach 15 20 31, D-8000 Munchen 15, West Germany; Frits Bernard Stichting, 350 Gijsinglaan, 3026 BG Rotterdam, The Netherlands; and Edward Brongersma Stichting, Tetterodeweg 1, Overveen, The Netherlands.)

Anonymous. 1984. Third world women's archives. Asian Lesbians of the East Coast *Newsletter*, 2 (Fall).

Anonymous. 1986. Jim Kepner: Activist, archivist, historian. *The Bulletin* (Long Beach), 3/12, August: 9–11.

Anonymous. 1987. *Ana Blaman Huis.* Leeuwarden, The Netherlands: The House. (Brochure).

Anonymous. 1988. Gay archive launches sexuality collection. *American Libraries*, June: 548.

Anonymous. 1989a. Education as weapon against AIDS. *Los Angeles Herald Examiner*, April 11: A6.

Anonymous. 1989b. LA County Public Library offers HIV information center. *Library Hotline*, 18/13, April 3: 1.

Anonymous. 1989c. Microfilming project underway. The San Francisco Bay Area Gay & Lesbian Historical Society *Newsletter*, 4/4, Summer: 2.

Ash, Lee, and William G. Miller. 1985. *Subject collections.* 6th ed. New York: R. R. Bowker.

Associated Press. 1988. Archive of Gay Literature in need of new home. *The Orange County Register*, November 7: B6; also as Extensive homosexual archives in need of a home. *San Jose Mercury News*, November 7, 1988: 4B.

Associated Press. 1989a. Judge overturns law on child pornography. *The New York Times*, May 18: A20.

Associated Press. 1989b. Kinsey Center embroiled in dispute over director. *The New York Times*, January 24: B13.

Baumann, Melinda. 1988. Sexuality archives comes to Cornell. *Outlines: A Newsletter for Ithaca's Lesbian and Gay Community*, June–August: 10.

Bennet, Paula. 1979. Focus on: The Lesbian Herstory Archives. *Focus*, February–March: 8.

Bergman, Deborah. 1989. Joan Nestle: Making history. *Frontiers*, January 25-February 8: 13.

Camposeco, Maria. 1990. State will seek to make it felony. *The Sacramento Bee*, April 19: A1.

Censorship, not child protection. 1989. *The Washington Post*, March 15: A22.

Conner, Randolph. 1983. A rare library with a wealth of gay/lesbian history. *The Advocate*, 378, October 13: 32–33, 35, 65.

Cornell University. 1989. Collection on human sexuality. June. (one-page announcement).

Directory of special libraries and information centers. 1989. Edited by Brigitte T. Darnay and Holly M. Leighton. 12th ed. Detroit: Gale Research.

Fraser, James A., and Harold A. Averill. 1983. *Organizing an archives: The Canadian Gay Archives experience.* Canadian Gay Archives Publication No. 8. Toronto: Canadian Gay Archives.

Fryer, Peter. 1966. *Private Case—Public scandal.* London: Secker and Warburg.

Garber, Eric. 1988. A visit to the archives. The San Francisco Bay Area Gay & Lesbian Historical Society *Newsletter*, 4/1, Winter: 2.

Gay/lesbian archives and libraries in North America. 1989. Edited by Cal Gough. Rev. ed. Atlanta: GLTF Clearinghouse.

Gayellow pages: USA & Canada . . . 1989. 1988. Edited by Frances Green. 17th ed. New York: Renaissance House.

Geyelin, Milo. 1989. Publishers gain as court strikes down key aspects of a child pornography law. *The Wall Street Journal*, May 18: B9.

Gilbert, Richard. 1988. IU faculty concerned over loss of curators at Kinsey Institute. *Sunday Herald-Times*, October 2.

Greenhouse, Linda. 1990. Justices, 6 to 3, restrict rights to pornography. *The New York Times*, April 19: A1, A16.

Haeberle, Erwin J. 1981. Swastika, pink triangle and yellow star—The destruction of sexology and the persecution of homosexuals in Nazi Germany. *The Journal of Sex Research*, 17/3, August: 270–287.

Halfhill, Robert. 1988. The demise of the gay and lesbian archives. *Gay Community News*, June 19–25: 5. (Letter)

Hodges, Beth. 1979, 1980. Interview with Joan and Deborah of the Lesbian Herstory Archives. *Sinister Wisdom*, 11, Fall: 3–13 and 13, Spring: 101–105.

Humm, Andrew, Eleanor Cooper, and Tom Smith. 1989. Fought gay groups. *The New York Times*, March 31: A14. (Letter)

Kearney, Patrick J. 1981. *The Private Case: An annotated bibliography of the Private Case Erotica Collection in the British (Museum) Library*. London: Jay Landesman.

Knowlton, Elizabeth. 1987. Documenting the gay rights movement. *Provenance: Journal of the Society of Georgia Archivists*, 5/1, Spring: 17–30.

Koskovich, Gerard. 1988. Gay archives are accessible. *San Jose Mercury News*, June 14: 6B. (Letter)

Kreitz, Patricia. 1989. UC-Berkeley preserves rare gay & lesbian serials. *ACRL Women's Studies Newsletter*, 4/1, June: 4.

Lehman, J. Lee. 1979. The Lesbian Herstory Archives. *The Advocate*, April 15: 15.

Lesley, J. Ingrid. 1988. Libraries and the AIDS crisis: Information is the only vaccine. In the *ALA Yearbook of Library and Information Services 1988*. Chicago: American Library Association.

Loeb, Catherine. 1981. Radical archiving: The Lesbian Herstory Archives. *Feminist Collections*, 2/4, Summer.

Loth, David. 1962. *The erotic in literature*. New York: MacFaddeen Books.

MacDonald, Stephen. 1984. Diggers. *The Body Politic*, November: 35–36.

Marston, Brenda. 1988. Women's history archives: Documenting women's lives and women's organizations today. *Feminist Collections*, 10/1, Fall, 5–7.

Martin, Robert K. 1987. In the wake of Eldorado. *New York Native*, 232, September 28: 22–23.

Masnerus, Laura. 1990. The Cincinnati case: What are the issues? What is at stake? *The New York Times*, April 24: B1, B3.

Miller, Alan V. 1980. Canadian gay archives: Keeping it gay but safe. *Gay Insurgent*, 6, Summer: 41–43.

Miller, Alan V., comp. 1987. *Directory of The International Association of Lesbian and Gay Archives and Libraries*. Toronto: The Association. (Includes text of completed survey responses.)

Mitgang, Lee. 1988. Sex archives. *AP News*, March 22: 10:38 am and 10:11 pm PST. (Online data file)

Monahan, Jim. 1979. Considerations in the organization of gay archives. *Gay Insurgent*, 4/5, Spring: 8–10.

Nestle, Joan. 1979. Radical archiving: A lesbian feminist perspective. *Gay Insurgent*, 4/5, Spring: 10–12.

Nestle, Joan. 1987. *A restricted country*. Ithaca NY: Firebrand.

Parachini, Allan. 1989. Administration to fight ruling on child porn statute. *Los Angeles Times*, July 18: VI, 1, 4.

Perkins, Stephen M. 1988–1989. Home at last. *Frontiers*, December 28/January 4: 14.

Perkins, Stephen M. 1989. One gets historical. *Frontiers*, January 11–25: 18.

Potter, Clare. comp./ed. 1986. *The lesbian periodicals index*. Tallahassee, FL: Naiad Press.

Rose, Kim. 1989. AIDS library moves to Philadelphia old city. *Au Courant*, 7/22, April 17: 3, 6.

Schwarz, Judith. 1979. Living herstory. *Off Our Backs*, May: 20.

Sitzman, Glenn L. 1988. Gay archives and university libraries. *Gay Community News*, August 14–20: 5. (Letter)

Solomon, Alisa. 1989. Scholar or bigot? Is Father Healy fit to run our public library? *The Village Voice*, March 28: 11.

Spornick, Charles. 1988. RLG British and American literature bibliographers, survey of collections and collecting practices, erotica: Results of survey. July 7: [5] p. Available from Charles Spornick, Collection Management Librarian, Robert W. Woodruff Library, Emory University, Atlanta, GA 30322.

Steakley, James D. 1985. Biobibliographical introduction. In *The Writings of Dr. Magnus Hirschfeld*. Canadian Gay Archives Publication No. 11. Toronto: Canadian Gay Archives.

Steele, Gary. 1985. Jim Kepner: The making of a pioneer. *Frontiers*, 3/37, January 23–30: [10–11].

Steinfels, Peter. 1989. Library's choice of priest is debated. *The New York Times*, April 2: 14.

Sturgis, Susanna. 1979. Women's night out. *In Our Own Write*, June: 5.

Subject Directory of Special Libraries and Information Centers. 1989. Edited by Brigitte T. Darnay and Holly M. Leighton. 12th ed. Detroit: Gale Research. (Vol. 2: Social Sciences, Humanities and Education Libraries.)

Timmons, Stuart. 1986. The future of the past: Who controls gay history? Special report, gay/lesbian archives. *The Advocate*, 447, May 27: 30–33.

Tsang, Daniel. 1979. The gay press. *Gay Insurgent*, 4/5, Spring: 18–21.

Tsang, Daniel. 1980. Gay press preserved at Michigan. *Gay Insurgent*, 6, Summer: 43–45.

Tsang, Daniel. 1987. Broad new porn laws planned. *Update*, 313, December 23: A1, A3, A14.

United States. Attorney General's Commission on Pornography. 1986. *Final report*. 2 volumes. Washington, DC: U.S. Government Printing Office.

Walker, Bill. 1988. A visit to Los Angeles. The San Francisco Bay Area Gay & Lesbian Historical Society *Newsletter*, 3/4, June: 2.

Wheeler, David L. 1988. Conflict over management leaves Kinsey Institute in turmoil. *The Chronicle of Higher Education*, October 26: A6.

Whitlock, Mary. 1989. Joan Nestle: Raising the collective consciousness. *The News* (Los Angeles), February 3: part 4, 15–16.

Wolff, Charlotte. 1986. *Magnus Hirschfeld: A portrait of a pioneer in sexology*. London: Quartet Books.

Yee, Edward, J. 1988. 3 librarians leave Kinsey Institute. *Indiana Daily Student*, October 3.

Appendix: Selected Periodicals from Lesbian and Gay Archives

Archives, Recherches et Cultures Lesbiennes. 1984– . 3/year. 100 francs/85 francs in France. ARCL, BP 662, 77531 Paris, Cedex 11, France.

Australian Gay Archives Newsletter. 1983– . 4/year. A$5. PO Box 124, Parkville 3052, Australia.

Capri: Zeitschrift für Schwule Geschichte. Irregular. Freunde eines Schwulen Museums in Berlin, Friedrichstrasse 12, 1000 West Berlin 61, West Germany.

Gay Archivist. 1979– . Irregular. Free. Canadian Gay Archives, PO Box 639, Station A, Toronto, ON, Canada M5W 1G2.

Gay Bookworm. 1986– . 12/year. Quatrefoil Library, 1619 Dayton Avenue, St. Paul, MN 55104.

Gerber-Hart Library Newsletter. 1982– . 4/year. Free. Gerber-Hart Library, 3238 N. Sheffield Avenue, Chicago, IL 60657.

Hall-Carpenter News. 1985– . 4/year. Free. Hall-Carpenter Memorial Archives, 67-69 Cowcross Street, London, England EC1M 6BP.

International Gay and Lesbian Archives. *Bulletin.* Irregular. Free. IGLA, PO Box 38100, Hollywood, CA 90038.

Lesbian Archive and Information Centre. *Newsletter.* Irregular. Donation requested: £2–20. LAIC, BCM 7005, London WC1N 3XX, United Kingdom.

Lesbian Herstory Archives Newsletter. 1975– . Irregular. $5/2 issues. LHA, PO Box 1258, New York, NY 10016.

Lesbisch Archivaria. Irregular. Inquire. Lesbisch Archief Leeuwarden, Postbus 4062, 8901 EB Leeuwarden, The Netherlands.

Magnus Hirschfeld Centrum Kommunications. 1981– . 12/year. Magnus Hirschfeld Centrum Library, Borgweg 8, 1000 Hamburg 60, West Germany.

Mitteilungen der Magnus-Hirschfeld-Gesellschaft. 1983– . Irregular. DM6. Magnus-Hirschfeld-Gesellschaft, Gorssbeerenstrasse, 13 a, 1000 Berlin 61, West Germany.

Nyhedsbrev fra Biblioteket. 1984– . 12/year. Bibliotek for Bøsser og Lesbiske, Postbox 1023, DK-1007 Kobenhavn K, Denmark.

San Francisco Bay Area Gay & Lesbian Historical Society. *Newsletter.* 1985– . 4/year. $15 (membership); $6 (low income membership). SFBGALHS Newsletter, PO Box 42126, San Francisco, CA 94142.

Editor's note: An additional excellent resource is the current "Inventory of Publications Identified by and/or Available through the Library Information Clearinghouse of ALA's Gay & Lesbian Task Force," which includes a number of bibliographies both of items recommended for purchase and of items about gays, lesbians, and libraries.

CHAPTER **14**

Access or Censorship? Libraries and Pornography: An Annotated Selective Bibliography

Evelyn Apterbach, Adam Halicki-Conrad, and
Mimi B. Penchansky,
with additions by Martha Cornog

INTRODUCTION

The subject of pornography has numerous ramifications that fall into the broad classes of materials dealing with behavioral or legal aspects. The purpose of this bibliography is to select publications from both areas that relate pornography as a concept to libraries and, by extension, to censorship. Since many listed references include obscenity along with pornography as their topics, a distinction between these two different concepts should be made in order to avoid confusion. The following definitions of both terms are adopted from *Encyclopedia of Crime and Justice* (New York: The Free Press, 1983):

> In the strict sense, *obscene* refers to that which is disgusting, repulsive, vile, offensive, or loathsome. No necessary connection exists between the obscene and the sexual. A portrayal of sex may be obscene, but it need not be, and something may be obscene without having anything to do with sex at all.
>
> *Pornography*, on the other hand, derived from the Greek words for harlot and writing, means in its strict sense, the portrayal of sexual

This bibliography was prepared in connection with the 1987 Institute of the same name held by the Library Association of the City University of New York.

activity. Contemporary usage of the term is somewhat narrower, referring only to portrayals designed to produce sexual arousal. Under either meaning, pornography need not be obscene except by adoption of the controversial proposition that any portrayal of sex is necessarily disgusting.

Legal usage has obliterated the distinction between obscenity and pornography. Legal regulation of pornography has been premised on the assumption that pornography is obscene, and only rarely have forms of obscenity other than pornography been the subject of legal sanctions. Hence, obscenity when used in the law, refers almost always either to pornography or to particular words thought to be offensive because of their sexual connotations. If the assumption that pornography is regulated because it is thought obscene is kept in mind, confusion can be avoided, but failure to appreciate the relationship between the obscene and the pornographic can be question-begging when the issue is why pornography should be regulated and which forms of pornography should be subject to sanctions.

Some of the abstracts in this bibliography were derived from those available in various online databases and existing bibliographies if the compilers considered them sufficiently descriptive of the items listed.

DEFINITIONS

Daily, Jay E. "Erotica." In *Encyclopedia of Library and Information Science.* Edited by Allen Kent and Harold Lancour, vol. 8 (New York: Marcel Dekker, 1980), 164–184.
Daily has written a comprehensive essay defining and distinguishing between erotica and pornography. He provides a history of both with advice on building library collections. It is worth quoting the author's final paragraph:
Intellectual supervision of graphic materials, the old fight of the censors, was waged to prevent the fantasizing that gave such pleasure to so many people. It failed. Now the supervision, it is the belief of the writer, must achieve a different purpose, selecting erotic materials carefully so that no collection is maltreated because of the prejudices, fears, and taboos of the librarian. Nothing about erotica requires us to change rules that require a librarian to know the community he [sic] serves and collect materials of use to the individuals in it, not on a majority basis of those interested but on the basis of a balanced collection that will lead the user on as far as his interest takes him.

Dyal, Robert A. "Is Pornography Good for You?" *Southwestern Journal of Philosophy*, 7 (Fall, 1976), 95–118.
The author argues that the concept of pornography has been confused with that of obscenity and that this lack of differentiation is the source of judicial and other disputes.

Heir, Hilde. "Obscenity, Politics and Pornography." *Journal of Aesthetic Education*, 5 (October, 1971), 77–97.
Pornography is classified as obscene and "inherently objectionable." The author distinguishes between obscenity, which simply offends, and pornography, which glorifies perversion and inhuman activity.

Moroz, George A., II. *Prolegomenon to an Aesthetician's View of "Erotic-Art," "Obscenity," and "Pornography".* Ph.D. Dissertation, University of Illinois, 1979.
The author attempts to clarify the meanings of the following terms—erotic, erotic-art, obscene, obscene-art, pornography, and pornographic. He provides and then analyzes historical definitions of each.

Reed, John P., and Robin S. Reed. "Consensus and Disensus in Pornography Definitions: A Content Analysis." *International Behavioural Scientist,* 5 (September, 1973), 1–12.
The Reeds compare legal and individual definitions of pornography and review federal court definitions from 1870 to 1970.

Ridington, Jillian. "Pornography: What Does the New Research Say?" *Status of Women News,* 8 (Summer, 1983), 9–13.
Ridington examines the problem of defining pornography, especially in research. She surveys some of the present research, its findings, and the theory on which it is based.

Steinem, Gloria. "Erotica and Pornography: A Clear and Present Difference." *Ms.,* 7 (November, 1978), 53 ff.
This article was one of the first in which the distinction was made between "pornography," as pertaining to violence linked to sex, and "erotica," as pertaining to sexual pleasure.

BIBLIOGRAPHIES

Busha, Charles H. "Censorship and Intellectual Freedom: A Bibliography, 1970–1981." *Drexel Library Quarterly,* 18 (Winter, 1982), 101–108.
This bibliography cites 94 books and unpublished library science doctoral dissertations, the majority of which pertain to problems in the United States dealing with censorship, intellectual freedom, legal aspects of freedom of expression, and problems associated with obscenity and pornography.

Byerly, Greg, and Rick Rubin. *Pornography, the Conflict Over Sexually Explicit Materials in the United States: An Annotated Bibliography.* (New York: Garland, 1980).
This selective, annotated bibliography of research materials concentrates on works related primarily to the creation and dissemination of sexually explicit materials in the United States and covers psychological, sociological, religious, philosophical, legal, and popular perspectives on the subject.

Chervenak, Mary Francesca. "Selected Bibliography on Pornography and Violence." *University of Pittsburgh Law Review,* 40 (1979), 652–660.
A selected bibliography gleaned from a number of different sources—including psychology treatises, social science journals, newspaper editorials, and popular magazine articles—in addition to the research reports, studies, surveys, and scientific experiments where one expects to locate such information. The citations are divided into sections: surveys and scientific experiments upon which the 1970 Commission on Obscenity and Pornography based its Report; studies dissenting from the Commission's conclusion that exposure to erotic materials cannot be considered as a factor in the causation of sex crime or sex delinquency; the increasing depiction of violence in various aspects of American culture; violence against women; and the debate between those for and against censorship. These sections are liberally interspersed with commentary by the compiler, who analyzes each issue and point of view, concluding that "the increasing number of psychological experiments and studies demand that the possibility of harmful effects be added to the balance of interests when dealing with censorship and pornography."

"Libraries and the Censorship Issue: A Selected ERIC Bibliography." (Syracuse, NY: ERIC Clearinghouse on Information Resources, 1983). ED NO. 232709.
Books and articles listed discuss libraries and the censorship issue, with emphasis on publications that include views of such groups as the Moral Majority, other religious groups, and teacher organizations. Other emphasized issues include court reactions to the censorship issue, guidelines for forming policies on materials selection and preventing censorship battles in schools, and the basic issue of censorship versus intellectual freedom.

Sellen, Betty-Carol, and Patricia A. Young. *Feminists, Pornography, and the Law: An Annotated Bibliography of Conflict, 1970–1986.* (Hamden, CT: Shoe String Press, 1987).
Writings stemming from and reflecting the antipornography debate of the 1970s and 1980s ("the porn wars") are listed by type of media. Each item has an abstract giving content and point of view. Included are lists of organizations and periodicals, plus a chronology of newspaper articles, 1976–1986. [MC]

Wilson, Carolyn F. *Violence Against Women: An Annotated Bibliography.* (Boston, MA: G. K. Hall, 1981).
Wilson's work is a highly selective, well-annotated bibliography on various forms of violence against women written from a feminist perspective. Pornography is one major section of the work. The bibliographic listings are preceded by a short essay that presents an overview of the relevant historical background, research efforts, and social policy implications of the topic.

LIBRARY COLLECTIONS OF EROTICA

Fitz Hugh Ludlow Memorial Library
P.O. Box 99346
San Francisco, CA 94109
This stored collection includes 600 volumes of drug-related pornography, including manuscripts, maps, pictures, slides, phonorecords, and other media. Only important mail inquiries will be accepted. No interlibrary loan or telephone inquiries, please.

Institute for the Advanced Study of Human Sexuality
1523 Franklin Street
San Francisco, CA 94109
The Institute is a professional graduate school licensed by the State of California to grant masters and doctoral degrees in human sexuality. Associated with the National Sex Forum at the same address, the Institute was established to educate and train professionals interested in sex counseling, therapy, education, or research. The Research Library, with subject emphasis on human sexuality, contains 160,000 books, 110,000 periodicals, 89,000 AV/ films, and 650,000 other media. Many of these items may be classed as erotica and pornography. [Editor's note: Although licensed by the state, the Institute is not accredited by the Western Association of Schools and Colleges.]

Kinsey Institute for Research in Sex, Gender & Reproduction, Inc. Library
Indiana University
416 Morrison Hall
Bloomington, IN 47401
This is one of the greatest and most extensive collections on sexual behavior, erotica, and pornography, comprising over 70,000 volumes, plus cataloged manuscripts, works of art, pictures, phonorecords, audiotapes, slides, and films. The library collects materials on all aspects of sexual activity.

Providence Athenaeum
 251 Benefit Street
 Providence, RI 02903
 This collection of erotica contains 175 uncataloged items, including German imprints as well as many French titles. The emphasis is on the early twentieth century. The *Boston Globe* recently reported the Athenaeum's acquisition of the $20,000 collection of foreign erotica donated by Professor David C. Miller. This collection is dominated by German books, but also includes Russian folklore, French limericks, American Indian mating practices, and ancient Chinese materials.

University of North Carolina
 J. Murrey Atkins Library
 UNCC Station
 Charlotte, NC 28213
 This erotica collection of 100 cataloged items includes scholarly works on sex; classics by such writers as Frank Harris, D. H. Lawrence, and Norman Douglas; and about 40 novels published between 1890 and 1930.

CONCERNING COLLECTIONS AND COLLECTING

Fryer, Peter. "The Private Case: An Annotated Bibliography of the Private Case Erotica Collection in the British (Museum) Library." *New Society* 57 (July, 1981), 158.
 Fryer reviews this "monumental bibliography" compiled by Patrick J. Kearney that lists, annotates, and—due to Kearney's detective flair, his persistence and ingenuity in solving so many of the problems inherent in collections of clandestine books—attributes authorship and publication data not previously available for this collection of 1,920 books long hidden in the British Library. First revealed in 1913, the existence of a secret collection of sexological and pornographic books was finally entered in the General Catalogue in the mid-1960s. There is a "typically colourful and erudite introduction by Gershon Legman, still the world's most plagiarised—because most knowledgeable—authority on the folklore of sex," that provides the background of this collection with "fascinating revelations about the pornography writers and publishers who operated in the days when it took courage as well as greed, or need, to be of their number."

Katz, Bill. "The Pornography Collection." *Library Journal*, 96 (December, 1971), 4060–4066.
 Katz considers the idea of building a pornography collection as a way to explore the various selection problems confronting the librarian. He reviews basic Supreme Court decisions broadening and liberalizing obscenity law and cases involving librarians and dissatisfied library boards.

Keerdoja, Eileen, and Patricia King. "Keepers of the Kinsey Flame." *Newsweek*, 103 (June 18, 1984), 15.
 Appointed as director of the Kinsey Institute for Sex Research in 1982, June Reinisch, a psychobiologist, has changed its orientation from sociological to biomedical and its name to the Kinsey Institute for Research in Sex, Gender & Reproduction. It now allows greater access to its (then) 64,000-volume collection of erotica, the world's largest.

Morgan, Lael. "Psst! A Peek Inside Orange County's Big 'Blue' Library." *Los Angeles.* (December, 1979), 204.
 The author discusses the collection at California State University Library in Fullerton, including the moral and religious aspects of collecting pornography.

Selth, Jefferson P. *Alternative Lifestyles: A Guide to Research Collections on Intentional Communities, Nudism, and Sexual Freedom.* (Hamden, CT: Greenwood Press, 1985).
Selth gives detailed descriptions of 36 research collections. Besides indicating holdings, he provides data about each collection, including a history of the group or institution responsible for the collection, a history of the collection itself, and a general description of the collection.

Wertheimer, Leonard. "Pornography in the Public Library, Are Librarians Ignoring Its Role?" *Canadian Library Journal*, 37 (February, 1980), 21–26.
The author discusses the pros and cons of pornography as an information source, and of its inclusion among library materials. Attitudes towards pornography, particularly those of librarians, are examined, but no conclusions or recommendations are drawn.

HISTORY—CENSORSHIP THROUGH THE AGES

Cotham, Perry C. *Obscenity, Pornography and Censorship.* (Grand Rapids, MI: Baker Book House, 1973).
Cotham asserts that the Biblical and Christian perspectives on pornography, obscenity, and censorship are valuable ones for both viewing and shaping modern American society.

Craig, Alec. "Censorship of Sexual Literature." In *Encyclopedia of Sexual Behavior.* Edited by Albert Ellis and Albert Abarbanel. (New York: Hawthorn, 1961), Volume V, 116–138.
This article presents a legal and historical survey of literary censorship in the United States and Great Britain. Craig concludes that although some censorship is probably unavoidable, "censorship in any form . . . can never be more than a necessary evil." He presents guidelines for censorship designed to protect serious works in any country where freedom is prized.

Dhavan, Rajeev, and Christie Davies, editors. *Censorship and Obscenity.* (Totowa, NJ: Rowman and Littlefield, 1978).
Dhavan and Davies present a varied collection of essays that include views on censorship in Great Britain and the U.S., as well as on the psychology of obscenity and pornography.

Donnelly, Harrison. "Pornography: Setting New Limits." *Editorial Research Reports*, 1 (May 16, 1986), 351 ff.
This review of the subject concerns itself with the current reaction against the apparently more widespread availability of pornography as is evidenced in the distribution of rock porn, X-rated videos, and cable pornography. Legal issues are considered, as is the nature of the objections posed by groups ranging from feminists to fundamentalists.

Ginzburg, Ralph. *An Unhurried View of Erotica.* (New York: Helmsman Press, 1958).
Ginzburg provides an informal and selective review of erotic tales and literature published in England and other countries. He includes passages from early literature.

Goldstein, Michael J., and Harold S. Kant. *Pornography and Sexual Deviance: A Report of the Legal and Behavioral Institute, Beverly Hills, California.* (Berkeley: University of California Press, 1973).
This work grew out of the *Report* of the U.S. Commission on Obscenity and Pornography. Its conclusions, namely that pornography does not contribute to either antisocial or criminal behaviors, rest on empirical data consisting, in the main, of the extensive interviewing of sample populations.

Gordon, George. *Erotic Communication: Studies in Sex, Sin and Censorship.* (New York: Hastings House, 1980).
Gordon's book examines different aspects of sexual communication, including an overview of both the history of pornographic literature and of its censorship. He takes an anecdotal, journalistic approach to the material.

Haight, Anne Lyon, and Chandler B. Grannis. *Banned Books: 387 B.C. to 1978 A.D.* Fourth Edition. (New York: Bowker, 1978).
The volume includes an introductory essay discussing the First Amendment and the legal aspects of censorship, an annotated list of books that have been banned throughout history, and five appendices discussing trends in censorship, important censorship court cases, excerpts from a report of the Commission on Obscenity and Pornography, a list of First Amendment laws and regulations, and a bibliography.

Hughes, Douglas A., editor. *Perspectives on Pornography.* (New York: St. Martins Press, 1970).
This is a collection of essays, published between 1961 and 1969, that present views on pornography from such writers as Susan Sontag and Harry Levin.

Lewis, Felice Flanery. *Literature, Obscenity, and the Law.* (Carbondale: Southern Illinois University Press, 1976).
This historical overview of major works of fiction that were subject to censorship includes such works as *Fanny Hill* and *The Tropic of Cancer*. The author tries to convey the American sexual values that were reflected both in the works themselves and in their censorship.

Meister, Robert. "Vigilante Action Against Pornography: The Symbolic Destruction of Symbols." *Social Text: Theory, Culture, Ideology*, 12 (1985), 3–18.
Meister carefully explores the nature of pornography, erotica, and obscenity and then discusses possible appropriate forms of protest against them. To this end, he distinguishes between censorship that involves real or symbolic destruction of symbols and censorship that involves the real destruction of objects—possibly books or works of art—that are treated as symbols.

Oboler, Eli M. *The Fear of the Word: Censorship and Sex.* (Metuchen, NJ: Scarecrow Press, 1974).
This book discusses censorship and sex throughout the ages. Chapters focus on the bases of censorship, the concept of taboo, the role of words in the control of people's thought, censorship and eros, and the individual and eros.

Opposing Viewpoints: Sources. *Human Sexuality.* (St. Paul, MN: Greenhaven Press, 1986).
This volume includes a section summarizing articles from trade journals for and against pornography. These articles include: "The Campaign Against Pornography: An Overview" by *Newsweek* Staff; "Pornography Fosters Violence Against Women" by Annie Laurie Gaylor and Gina Allen; "Prohibiting Pornography Will Not End Sexual Violence" by Lisa Duggan; "Pornography Reflects Men's Attitudes Toward Women" by John Stoltenberg; "Pornography Does Not Reflect Men's Attitudes Toward Women" by Philip Weiss; "Society Has a Right to Prohibit Pornography" by Kenneth S. Kantzer; "Prohibiting Pornography Would Violate Civil Rights" by Edwin Chemerinsky. The original source articles are cited.

Rist, Ray C., compiler. *The Pornography Controversy: Changing Moral Standards in American Life.* (New Brunswick, NJ: Transaction Books, 1974).
Rist has compiled a collection of essays, all previously published, of various aspects of pornography. Topics covered include views on the moral, legal, and theoretical dimensions of pornography as well as discussions on the research problems related to the subject.

Sontag, Susan. "The Pornographic Imagination" *Partisan Review*, 34 (Spring, 1967), 181–214.
  Sontag asks whether some pornographic texts possess sufficient artistic merit to be considered "literature." She examines *The Story of O* and *The Image* in detail and concludes that they do belong in the literary category.

Sutherland, John. *Offensive Literature: Decensorship in Britain, 1960–1982.* (Totowa, NJ: Barnes & Noble Books, 1983).
  This book is a calendar following a series of events, mainly trials, from 1960 to the present day. The author investigates how Great Britain's "permissive" society has come to terms with prohibited books. The "offensive books" discussed include *The Naked Lunch.*, *Fanny Hill*, *Lady Chatterley's Lover*, and *My Secret Life.*

Thomas, Donald. *A Long Time Burning: The History of Literary Censorship in England.* (New York: Praeger, 1969).
  The book is a history of literary censorship in England from the introduction of printing in 1476 to date. The pertinent topics discussed include laws against obscene literature, liberty vs. licentiousness, expurgations and moral censorship exercised chiefly by booksellers, libraries, publishers, and editors during the period covered. A 200-page appendix contains extracts from little-known publications banned during the past 500 years.

PORNOGRAPHY AND THE LAW

Allain, Alex P. "First and Fourteenth Amendments as They Support Libraries, Librarians, Library Systems, and Library Development." *Women Lawyers Journal*, 60 (Spring, 1974), 55–72.
  Allain recommends that librarians and the public institutions they represent be exempt from criminal obscenity prosecution. He examines the potential effects of *Miller v. California* on libraries and librarians with regard to evaluating collections and acquiring materials. He concludes that presumption of knowledge is unconstitutional.

Copp, David, and Susan Wendell, editors. *Pornography and Censorship.* (Buffalo: Prometheus Books, 1982).
  This book deals with the social, theoretical, and legal questions raised by censoring pornography. It is divided into three parts: philosophical essays, scientific studies, and judicial essays.

Ernst, Morris L., and Alexander Lindey. *The Censor Marches On: Recent Milestones in the Administration of the Obscenity Law in the United States .* (New York: DaCapo Press, 1970).
  Here is an unrevised reprint of a work on the legal history of censorship. First published in 1940, it emphasizes the censorship prevalent in the 1930s, particularly concentrating on the censorship of literary works, cinema, and radio broadcasting.

Ernst, Morris L., and Alan U. Schwartz. *Censorship: The Search for the Obscene.* (New York: Macmillan, 1964).
  The authors present a factual and historical account of censorship and outline the major laws and court cases that have formulated American obscenity law.

Gerber, Albert B. "The Right to Receive and Possess Pornography: An Attorney Foresees the End of Legal Restrictions." *Wilson Library Bulletin*, 44 (February, 1970), 641–644.
  The Supreme Court decision in *Stanley v. Georgia* is interpreted as ending restrictions on possession or acquisition of allegedly pornographic materials.

This does not end censorship problems in several areas, the most significant for librarians being in distribution of such materials to juveniles.

Guccione, Bob. *Pornography & the First Amendment.* Sound Recording. (New York: Encyclopedia Americana/CBS News Audio Resource Library, 1977).
  Bob Guccione was interviewed on "60-Minutes," February 27, 1977.

Kronhausen, Eberhard, and Phyllis Kronhausen. *Pornography and the Law: The Psychology of Erotic Realism and Pornography.* (New York: Ballantine Books, 1959).
  The authors distinguish between hard-core pornography and erotic realism, presenting historical examples, with excerpts. Supreme Court guidelines and "contemporary community standards" are discussed.

Lewis, Felice Flanery. *Literature, Obscenity, and Law.* (Carbondale: Southern Illinois University Press, 1976).
  The author gives some overview of the nature of suppressed literary works, citing passages that drew censorship. Lewis remains in favor of literary freedom, generally opposing book censorship.

Pilpel, Harriet F. "Obscenity and the Constitution." *Publishers Weekly,* (December 10, 1973), 24–27.
  Pilpel avers that librarians and publishers must fight against the restrictions from new obscenity standards imposed by recent Supreme Court decisions. She believes attacks should be made on the constitutionality of most obscenity laws, with no obscenity laws directed against sex.

Rembar, Charles. "Obscenity and the Constitution." *Publishers Weekly,* (January 14, 1974), 77–79.
  Reacting to Harriet Pilpel's Bowker Memorial Lecture cited above, Rembar contends that she, like many civil libertarians, is too pessimistic about the 1973 Supreme Court decisions. Such emotional lectures contribute to an "unwarranted anxiety." He worries that this anxiety will affect not only how authors write, but also how the Supreme Court will decide future cases. There is still more than enough literary freedom in the United States.

Robertson, Geoff. *Obscenity: An Account of Censorship Laws and Their Enforcement in England and Wales.* (London: Weidenfield & Nicolson, 1979).
  Robertson criticizes the British Obscene Publications Act of 1959. He cites the law's inherent threat to civil liberties and presents cases both dryly historical and humorous—a Customs' confiscation of *Fun in Bed*, a book of games for children who are ill. Robertson recommends the law's repeal.

Serebnick, Judith. "The 1973 Burger Court Rulings on Obscenity: Have They Made a Difference?" *Wilson Library Bulletin,* (December, 1975), 304–310.
  The results of a study conducted at 10 medium-sized libraries with 210 librarians regarding the effect that the 1973 Burger Court rulings had on library practice and policy indicate that librarians are aware of the decisions and often exercise self-imposed restraints on materials selected. Such caution indicates a possible repetition of the library activities prevalent during the period of congressional Un-American Activities committees.

Sunderland, Lane V. *Obscenity and the President's Commission.* (Washington, DC: American Enterprise Institute for Public Policy Research, 1975).
  Sunderland, a political scientist, suggests that pornography is, in fact, a threat to the institutions of marriage and the family. He examines the Supreme Court rulings of 1973-1974 on obscenity and presents a careful discussion of the legal issues involved.

Sweet, William. "Schoolbook Controversies." *Editorial Research Reports*, 2 (September 10, 1982), 675 ff.
>Sweet surveys both the issues and the major cases involved in schoolbook censorship in the United States. Growing concern on this issue is reflected in the tripling of complaints registered by the ALA Office of Intellectual Freedom over the years 1979–1981. Most of these complaints involved school library books and concerned issues of sex, profanity, and obscenity.

U.S. Commission on Obscenity and Pornography. *Report of the Commission on Obscenity and Pornography.* (Washington, DC: Government Printing Office, 1970; New York: Bantam, 1970).
>These reports and evidence presented to the first "porn commission" generally indicate that pornography has a neutral or positive effect on its consumers. [MC]

U.S. Department of Justice. Attorney General's Commission on Pornography. *Final Report.* (Washington, DC: Government Printing Office, 1986). The *Final Report* (also known as "The Meese Commission Report") consists in the main of two volumes of testimony and evidence brought before the Commission, which had been charged to "determine the nature, extent and impact on society of pornography in the United States and to make specific recommendations . . . concerning more effective ways in which the spread of pornography could be contained. . . ." Generally, the Commission concluded that pornography has "a predominantly negative behavioral effect."

Wenglin, Barbara. *The Effects of the 1973 Supreme Court Obscenity Ruling on the Public Library.* Master's Thesis, University of Arizona, 1974.
>Wenglin discusses the results of a survey of public libraries conducted to discover whether the five decisions of the Supreme Court altering the legal definition of obscenity resulted in an increase of community censorship of library materials. These decisions placed greater emphasis on local community determination of standards for judging a work obscene. The majority of respondents reported no change in patron concern about library materials or about specific titles since the Supreme Court ruling.

PORNOGRAPHY, CENSORSHIP, AND LIBRARIES

Berninghausen, David K. "Toward an Intellectual Freedom Theory for Users of Libraries." *Drexel Library Quarterly*, 18 (Winter, 1982), 57–81.
>The author considers theories of intellectual freedom for library users, focusing on policies and practices that have developed in publicly supported libraries in the United States during the late twentieth century. He discusses the librarian's role in dealing with problems of censorship and the ALA position on intellectual freedom and censorship.

McShean, Gordon. *Running a Message Parlor: A Librarian's Medium-Rare Memoir About Censorship.* (Palo Alto, CA: Ramparts Press, 1977.
>McShean, once head librarian in a New Mexico public library, offers an autobiographical narrative on his past campaigns against censorship in libraries. Issues discussed include book selection, equal access to materials, and the reactions of other librarians to McShean's activities against censorship.

Molz, Kathleen. "The Public Custody of the High Pornography." *American Scholar*, 36 (Winter, 1966–1967), 93–103.
>The author attempts an interpretation of the librarian's role in the selection of materials of a controversial sexual nature. She discusses the historical background and the influence of contemporary judicial rulings on book selection, advocating literary discrimination in lieu of legal abolition.

Oboler, Eli M. *Defending Intellectual Freedom: The Library and the Censor.* (Westport, CT: Greenwood Press, 1980).

Oboler, a champion of intellectual freedom and the right of all persons to have access to information, covers various aspects of these topics in this collection of essays. Specifically, the chapters include such subjects as: "The Free Mind: Intellectual Freedom's Perils and Prospects," "The Politics of Censorship," "The Fear of Science," "The Young Adult and Intellectual Freedom," "The Etiology of Censorship," "Public Relations and Fighting Censorship," and "The Censorship Battle in a Conservative State." There are also editorials and letters on intellectual freedom, reviews of recent literature on intellectual freedom, and an Intellectual Freedom Creed.

Oboler, Eli M. "Everything You Always Wanted to Know About Censorship (But Were Afraid to Ask) Explained." *American Libraries*, 2 (February, 1971), 194–198.

The author provides the background for the development of censorship of sex writings.

Oboler, Eli M. "'Just Like the Child in the Family': Paternalistic Morality and Censorship." *Library Journal*, 98 (September 1, 1973), 2395–2398).

Oboler employs the philosophical distinctions of private and public morality to analyze the desirability of censorship of pornographic materials. He argues that such censorship constitutes paternalism and requires clear evidence of harm to those being protected before censorship should be imposed.

Oboler, Eli M. "The Politics of Pornography." *Library Journal*, 95 (December 15, 1970), 4225–4228.

Oboler reacts to the U.S. Senate's rejection of the report of the Commission on Obscenity and Pornography.

Shuman, Bruce A. "The Moral Majority and Popular Political Issues." *Drexel Library Quarterly*, 18 (Winter, 1982), 26–33.

In his discussion of librarians and their relations with members of the Moral Majority who seek to censor their collections, Shuman concludes that "it is the librarian's duty to be ready to point out to all self-styled guardians of public morality just what might be gained or lost in revising these rights" (i.e., those granted by the Bill of Rights).

Wertheimer, Leonard. "Pornography in the Public Library, Are Librarians Ignoring Its Role?" *Canadian Library Journal*, 37 (February, 1980), 21–26.

This is an analysis of the emotive connotations of pornography that prevent its routine treatment as ordinary library material. The author outlines the case made respectively for pornography as harmful and as beneficial, and considers the position of the librarian whose policy is to meet user needs. He concludes by stating that it is impossible under present circumstances to treat pornography primarily as a source of information and hence legitimate library material.

White, Howard D. "Library Censorship and the Permissive Minority." *Library Quarterly*, 51 (April, 1981), 192–207.

White re-analyses a nationwide survey of adults conducted in 1970 for the Commission on Obscenity and Pornography to permit new comparisons of the large majority who favored library censorship of "erotica" with the minority who opposed it. The anti-censorship group, younger, better educated, more liberal and permissive, has much in common with the group identified in other studies as users of public libraries.

Woods, L. B. "'For SEX: See Librarian.'" *Library Journal*, 103 (September 1, 1978), 1561–1566.

In this analysis of statistical data gathered by ALA's Office of Intellectual Freedom in a survey of censorship in U.S. libraries, the author shows that censorship is on the increase and that censorship attempts are becoming better organized.

LIBRARIANS' SELF-CENSORSHIP AND SELF-IMAGE

Ball, Phyllis, et al. "An Attack on Ms. West's Attack: Reader Forum."
American Libraries, 13 (September, 1982), 495.
Letters commenting on the Celeste West article in *American Libraries* cited
below, with a response from Ms. West.

Berman, Sanford. "'Inside' Censorship." *Wisconsin Library Bulletin*, 77
(Spring 1981), 21–24.
Berman describes two types of self-censorship by librarians, especially in
relation to materials about sex: pre-selection—not buying materials that are
controversial, small press, or representative of minority viewpoints; and
post-selection—rendering items impossible to access via inadequate cataloging, obscure or confusing shelving, discriminatory service, and meagre signage. [MC]

Bristol, Roger P. "It Takes Courage to Stock Taboos." *Library Journal*, 74
(February 15, 1949), 261–263.
Bristol discusses the content of Kinsey's *Sexual Behavior of the Human Male*
and the language of Mailer's *The Naked and the Dead* with a view to
revealing the problems that librarians face in deciding whether to add controversial books to their collections. He presents the decisions of professional
staff of seven libraries polled about these two works, their reasons for these
decisions, and the method of handling the books, if they were in fact
purchased (open shelf availability, restricting use to adults only, etc.) Bristol's
conclusion is that most librarians are personally more liberal than their
practices.

Ficociello, Tony. "Censorship, Book Selection, and the Marketplace of Ideas."
Top of the News, 41 (Fall, 1984), 33–38.
This essay discusses issues raised in Carol Hole's article, cited below, on
library material selection and censorship. Balancing a library's book collection, controversial issues and materials, moral judgment, and the mission of
librarians are noted.

Flemming, Tom. "Politicians and the Practicing Librarian." *APLA Bulletin*,
43 (November, 1979), 4.
Flemming outlines the Halifax Library Association's opposition in 1979 to
those provisions of Canadian Bill C-21 dealing with obscenity, primarily the
need for the bill to differentiate clearly between public display of salacious
material and free access to publications. Librarians must be involved politically if they are to be professionally effective and they must remember that
the price of freedom is eternal vigilance.

Hole, Carol. "Who Me, Censor?" *Top of the News*, 40 (Winter, 1984),
147–153.
In a humorous and provocative article, the author discusses the many reasons
librarians buy certain books and do not buy others. Whatever we call the
process, it is really censorship involving personal biases.

Hole, Carol. "Yeah, Me Censor: A Response to Various Critics." *Top of the
News*, 41 (Spring, 1985), 236–247.
This essay responds to comments received on Ms. Hole's previous article
expressing her concerns about problems of censorship by librarians as book
selectors. Her discussion covers the American Civil Liberties Union, vulgar
language and inadequate vocabulary, library collections, library material selection, and censors and selectors.

Olson, Lowell E. "Blind Spots in Collection Development." *Top of the News*, 41 (Summer, 1985), 371–376.
This discussion of the librarian's perspective on collection development cites professional "blind spots" in areas of responses to and misinterpretation of information, censorship, identifying and satisfying reader demand, and confusion over the role of the librarian.

Pope, Michael. *Sex and the Undecided Librarian: A Study of Librarians' Opinions on Sexually Oriented Literature.* (Metuchen, NJ: Scarecrow Press, 1974).
The basis for a doctoral dissertation, this study was designed to assess librarians' attitudes towards sexually oriented literature. A range of the degree of censorship exercised was found from the librarians from smaller communities to academic librarians based in larger communities.

Poppel, Norman, and Edwin M. Ashley. "Toward an Understanding of the Censor." *Library Journal*, 111 (July, 1986), 39–43.
The authors identify two types of censors—individuals and representatives of organized groups or crusades. They examine factors that motivate attempts at library censorship as well as the factors that influence librarians who deal with censorship. They advise librarians to understand themselves as well as potential censors, since censorship is a problem that will confront them throughout their careers.

Serebnick, Judith. "Self-Censorship by Librarians: An Analysis of Checklist-Based Research." *Drexel Library Quarterly*, 18 (Winter, 1982), 26–34.
The author analyzes checklist-based research designed to investigate whether particular books, periodicals, and films considered to be controversial by the investigators are owned by certain groups of libraries. The objectives of checklist studies, definitions of self-censorship, compilation of checklists, and interpretation of data are highlighted.

West, Celeste. "The Secret Garden of Censorship: Ourselves." *Library Journal*, 108 (September 1, 1983), 1651–1653.
This essay focuses on self-censorship as applied to the library book selection process, highlighting librarian practices of selection, library collections, censorship and the publishing industry, and self-defense against censorship. Examples of five controversial titles are included.

West, Celeste. "Stalking the Literary-Industrial Complex: A Publishing-Conglomerate Watcher Is More Worried Than Ever." *American Libraries*, 13 (May, 1982), 298–301.
Lamenting the conglomerate takeover of publishing, West castigates the mega-corporation emphasis on selling the greatest number of units for the highest profit. With their concentration on trash because it sells, they are polluting the publishing environment. "Bad books drive out good books." She states: "Good publishing, however, has much to do with art, in all its eccentricity, iconoclasm, and daring." It is up to librarians to enforce the First Amendment diversity guarantees, recognizing that media ecology is too important to be left to the rich.

Woods, L.B., and Claudia Perry Holmes. "The Flak If We Had the *Joy of Sex* Here: Libraries Practice Prior Censorship." *Library Journal*, (September 15, 1982), 1711.
Librarians need honest self-appraisal to examine whether budget and apathy are not self-censorship expedients.

Woods, L.B., and Lucy Salvatore. "Self–Censorship in Collection Development by High School Library Media Specialists." *School Media Quarterly*, 9 (Winter, 1981), 102–108.
The authors describe a nationwide survey of librarians in secondary school library media centers designed to find out how much self-censorship is practiced in collection development. They discuss the results of this survey,

which indicate that librarians do seem to censor voluntarily their acquisitions.

CHILD PORNOGRAPHY

Ahart, Gregory J. "Sexual Exploitation of Children—A Problem of Unknown Magnitude." Report to the Chairman, Subcommittee on Select Education, House Committee on Education and Labor. (Washington, DC: Division of Human Resources, 1982).
The report contains the results of an extensive literature search by the General Accounting Office on the subject of teenage prostitution and child pornography, and federal, state, and local efforts to deal with the problem.

Burgess, Ann Wolbert, and Marieanne Lindeqvist Clark. *Child Pornography and Sex Rings*. (Lexington, MA: Lexington/Heath, 1984).
This comprehensive work by many authors summarizes research on children and adults involved in child pornography, and treatment/rehabilitation issues. Each chapter has a bibliography, and several appendices contain legal case studies and background materials. [MC]

Payton, J. M. "Child Pornography Legislation." *Journal of Family Law*, 17 (1979), 505–543.
The author reviews and analyzes laws on child pornography in the U.S., discussing in detail the Protection of Children Against Sexual Exploitation Act of 1977. He discusses the great increase in state legislation since 1977, indicating that all courts must now comply with the Supreme Court's guidelines on obscenity.

Shrum, Rebecca A., and Richard P. Halgi. "Sexual Victimization: Educating Psychology Majors About an Important Social Problem." *Teaching of Psychology*, 12 (April, 1985), 78–80.
A senior psychology seminar that dealt with recent psychological, sociological, and feminist literature on sexual victimization is described. Major topics addressed were rape, childhood sexual abuse, and incest. The topics of pornography, sexual harassment, and sexual exploitation in the media were also covered.

Slan, Beverly. "Child Sexual Abuse—One Victim Is Too Many." *PTA Today*, 9 (December, 1983-January, 1984), 25–27.
Parents are warned about the dangers of child sexual abuse and child pornography. To recognize potential threats, parents should know their children well, take time to communicate with them, and watch for changes in personality patterns.

Tyler, R.P., and Lore E. Stone "Child Pornography: Perpetuating the Sexual Victimization of Children." *Child Abuse and Neglect: The International Journal*, 9 (1985), 313–318.
The history of child pornography photography is briefly reviewed and the current problem is examined and attributed in part to the profit motive. The authors urge changing child abuse reporting statutes to include photofinishing laboratories.

Wishon, Philip M. *School-Aged Victims of Sexual Abuse: Implications for Educators*. Paper Presented at the Conference of the National Association for the Education of Young Children. (New York: ERIC, 1979), 13 p. ERIC Document No. 181373.
Wishon states that nationwide annual profits from the child pornography industry and female and male child prostitution are in the tens of millions of dollars. The author discusses the educational and sociological ramifications of child sexual abuse in this overview of the problem. He recommends measures

that can assist educators to respond to the needs of child victims and to the concerns of high-risk individuals.

WOMEN AND PORNOGRAPHY

Berry, John. "Drawing the line." *Library Journal,* 104 (November 15, 1979), 2385.
An editorial commenting on the aims and objectives of Women Against Pornography.

Bosmajian, Haig A. "Obscenity, Sexism, and Freedom of Speech." *College English,* 39 (March, 1978), 812–819.
Supreme Court decisions on obscenity are sexist, according to the author. Acceptance of the argument that there is a connection between pornography and antisocial, criminal behavior allows the Court to impose restrictions on such materials. But the criminal acts associated with pornography are committed by men, not women. Therefore, these decisions are effectually determining what adult females can read.

Burstyn, Varda, editor. *Women Against Censorship.* (Vancouver: Douglas and McIntyre, 1985).
The articles in this book are by feminists who oppose censorhip as a means for dealing with pornography. The various authors are concerned that state censorship of pornography will lead to the suppression of civil liberties and limitations on varying forms of sexual expression and activity.

Dworkin, Andrea. *Pornography: Men Possessing Women.* (New York: Perigee Books, 1981).
This book is a major modern work on pornography. Dworkin argues that pornography is not an isolated phenomenon but is deeply rooted in male culture and values.

Ellis, Kate. "I'm Black and Blue from the Rolling Stones and I'm Not Sure How I Feel About It: Pornography and the Feminist Imagination." *Socialist Review,* 14 (May-August, 1984), 103–125.
In this summary of the feminist antipornography movement in the United States, the author discusses the images of pornography and analyzes the theories of Susan Griffin and Andrea Dworkin. In the conclusion, she points out the limitations of the feminist antipornography position and calls for continuing discussions of human sexuality.

Griffin, Susan. *Pornography and Silence: Culture's Revolt Against Nature.* (New York: Harper and Row, 1981).
Griffin offers a feminist analysis indicting the development of pornographic values. She argues that pornography feeds our culture while it is, at the same time, a product of the culture. She sees our fear of and alienation from nature as the source of negative values reflected in pornography. This book enlarges the body of theory relevant to this issue.

Lederer, Laura, editor. *Take Back the Night: Women on Pornography.* (New York: William Morrow, 1980).
This is a pioneer collection of articles by a group of feminists who assert that pornography is about violence against women and about male power. It covers definitions of pornography, its effects on women, the research on pornography, and actions women can take against it.

McCormack, Thelma. "Passionate Protests: Feminists and Censorship." *Canadian Forum,* 59 (March, 1980), 6–8.
McCormack acknowledges that feminist support of censorship and right-wing, anti-sex advocacy of censorship are motivated by different concerns. She concludes, however, that censorship is not the way to deal with pornography.

McKenzie, Elizabeth M. "Librarians and the New Censorship." *Public Library Quarterly*, 71 (Spring/Summer, 1986), 23–34.
  According to McKenzie, most librarians as well as most feminists have long held liberal views on most issues, including freedom of information or free speech. Thus, it is assumed that both groups share an antipathy toward censorship. Theorists of the women's movement have begun redefining the issue of pornography, however, as one of an infringement of women's civil rights, rather than one of free speech. One result of this redefinition is a crop of proposed new ordinances giving women the right to bring a civil suit against the producers and distributors of pornography. These ordinances would include libraries as distributors of pornography. Librarians must familiarize themselves with the feminists' arguments for a new type of censorship in order to understand legal developments that may affect them profoundly. (Based on author's abstract)

Manion, Eileen. "We Objects Object: Pornography and the Women's Movement." *Canadian Journal of Political and Social Theory*, 9 (Winter, 1985), 65–80.
  The author criticizes the "Women Against Pornography" movement. She warns that pro-censorship feminists are making the same mistake as nineteenth-century feminists who, in their concern for women, allied with social purists and became submerged in a repressive social purity movement.

PUBLISHERS ON PORNOGRAPHY

"AAP Joins Playboy in Suit Against Meese Commission." *Publishers Weekly*, (June 20, 1986), p. 14.
  AAP joins *Playboy* in suit charging the Meese Commission on Pornography with intimidating retailers into refusing to carry *Playboy* and other sex-oriented magazines. When constitutional "safeguards are disregarded or violated by government—for whatever reason—the liberty of all Americans is jeopardized."

"As We See It: Hustler's Pornography Not Any Worse Than TV's Violence and Sex." *TV Guide*. (March 19, 1977), A4.

DeCrow, Karen. "Strange Bedfellows." *Penthouse*, 16 (May, 1985), 96.
  Column on feminism and erotic literature.

Dershowitz, Alan M. "Foolish Fig Leaves." *Penthouse*, 16 (February, 1985), 28.
  Column on radical feminists teaming with conservatives to fight pornography.

Dershowitz, Alan M. "Government Waste." *Penthouse*, 17 (September, 1985), 56.
  Column on a "Misdirected investigation into the causes of certain crimes—child abuse, juvenile delinquency, and pornography."

Gelman, David, and Betsy Carter. "From Here to Obscenity." *Newsweek*, 86 (November 17, 1975), 76.
  Article on *Playboy* and pornography.

Hefner, Hugh. "The Blacklist: The Meese Commission Has Become the Tool of Evangelical Terrorists." *Playboy*, 33 (July, 1986), 1.
  Editorial on the Meese pornography commission.

Hefner, Hugh. "Sexual McCarthyism: Senatorial Accusations, Inquisitorial Investigations, Unfounded Conclusions—It's the Same Old Story." *Playboy*, 33 (January, 1985), 58.
  Editorial on pornography and censorship.

Hefner, Hugh. "Sex and the State." *Playboy*, 33 (October, 1986), 53.
Editorial on censorship.
"No More Adults: 7-Eleven Ban Skin Mags." *Time*, 127 (April 21, 1986), 62.
On *Playboy*, *Penthouse*, and pornography.
Prager, Emily. "Baby Socks." *Penthouse*, 16 (March, 1985), 27.
Column on children in pornography.
Sanford, Leda. "Sex in the Seventies." *American Home*, 80 (February, 1977),
46.
Interview with *Penthouse* publisher, Bob Guccione, who comments on pornography.

PORNOGRAPHY AND BEHAVIOR*

There is a large and growing literature on this topic; included
below are a few recent items. Most have bibliographies of additional
research.

Donnerstein, Edward, Daniel Linz, and Steven Penrod. *The Question of Pornography: Research Findings and Policy Implications*. (New York: The
Free Press, 1987).
A scholarly examination of pornography and violence in the media with
respect to antisocial effects and implications for legislation, education, and
public policy. The authors conclude that the violent element has much more
potential for harm that the erotic elements, and recommend media education
programs rather than censorship.
Gubar, Susan, and Joan Hall, editors. *For Adult Users Only; The Dilemma of
Violent Pornography*. (Bloomington, IN: Indiana University Press, 1989).
A series of essays examining violence in pornography from multidisciplinary
perspectives: history, literary criticism, religious studies, ethics, political science, film studies, law, and psychology.
Heilbrun, A.B., and David T. Self. "Erotica Value of Female Distress in
Sexually Explicit Photography." *The Journal of Sex Research*, 24 (February, 1988), 47–57.
The authors report that college males found pornographic pictures of women
in bondage more arousing when the models' faces indicated distress rather
than pleasurable emotion.
Malamuth, Neil M., and Edward Donnerstein. "Letter to the Book Review
Editor." *The Journal of Sex Research*, 23 (May, 1987), 281–283.
The authors reply to Mosher's criticism of *Pornography and Sexual Aggression*. (See Mosher listing, below.)
Malamuth, Neil M., and Edward Donnerstein. *Pornography and Sexual Aggression*. (Orlando, FL: Academic Press, 1984).
A lengthy and complex scholarly summary of much research that collectively
suggests that there may be negative social effects from pornography, particularly violent pornography. All chapters are followed by reference lists.
Marshall, W.L. "The Use of Sexually Explicit Stimuli by Rapists, Child
Molesters, and Nonoffenders." *The Journal of Sex Research*, 25 (May,
1988), 267–288.
A much higher percentage of child molesters and rapists reported using "hard

---

*This section was compiled by Martha Cornog.

core" pornography than did controls. Moreover, about 30% reported using pornography as preparation for committing an offense.

Mosher, Donald E. "Book Review of *Pornography and Sexual Aggression*, by Malamuth and Donnerstein." *The Journal of Sex Research*, 22 (November, 1986), 532–535.

Malamuth and Donnerstein's findings have been used by antipornography groups as evidence of a link between pornography and crime. Mosher is highly critical of this inference and also critical of some of the findings reported in the book.

Scott, Joseph E., and Steven J. Cuvelier. "Sexual Violence in *Playboy* Magazine: A Longitudinal Content Analysis." *The Journal of Sex Research*, 23 (November, 1987), 534–539.

According to this research, the violent element in *Playboy* pictorials and cartoons has always been extremely small and, moreover, has been decreasing since 1978.

Winick, Charles. "A Content Analysis of Sexually Explicit Magazines Sold in an Adult Bookstore." *The Journal of Sex Research*, 21 (May, 1985), 206–210.

Winick found that only about 5% showed bondage themes and about 1% showed sadomasochism themes, while the vast majority showed unclad women or couples involved in sexual activity.

Yaffé, Maurice, and Edward C. Nelson, editors. *The Influence of Pornography on Behaviour*. (London: Academic Press, 1982).

A series of papers from the United Kingdom exploring different facets of pornography in society: free speech/censorship issues; use of explicit visuals in sex education and therapy; erotic art; and a summary of research on pornography and sexual aggression. The latter are deemed "limited, but nonetheless suggestive."

CHAPTER 15

An Annotated Bibliography of Quality Erotica

David Steinberg

INTRODUCTION

This bibliography is an eclectic one. Books of short stories, books of poetry, and lots of photography books. Books that are avowedly feminist, and books by people who would never think of themselves in feminist terms. Books that are highly sexual, books that are impeccably sensual, and books that will appeal to almost any reader interested in the erotic. Books that will delight only a small group of readers, while thought bizarre by many more. And, finally, periodicals that are all of the above.

Essentially, this is a listing of the currently available books and periodicals that I most like and admire. Perhaps for their aesthetic beauty, perhaps for their erotic tenderness. Perhaps for their willingness to explore erotic questions that few people have dared to address publicly and thoughtfully. I certainly feel deep personal appreciation for every writer, artist, poet, photographer, and publisher who offers erotic or sexual work to the public and who, at the same time, acknowledges the issues of erotic sexuality in all their complexity, their psychological depth, their elusive importance. These are the people whose work helps us all to better understand, respect, and clarify our own erotic natures.

We live in a culture that is so confused and frightened by erotic feeling, and by its sexual expression, that it turns all but the most superficial (and therefore the most dishonest) depiction of eroticism into the forbidden, the pathological, the disreputable, the ridiculous. In so doing, it tells every one of us that *we* are forbidden, pathological, disreputable, and ridiculous because at our core we all know that our uniquely defined erotic existence is in no way superficial or trivial—is not a matter of simple fun and games, indulged or denied.

We know, on the contrary, that opening to our deeper sexual and erotic feelings often leaves us terribly vulnerable, open, and unprotected. We know that being sexual raises issues and emotions that are both difficult and exciting to engage—fear, anger, loneliness, intimacy, power, powerlessness, loss of control, loss of self, death, infantile longing, the possibility of being misunderstood, ignored, or rejected, past embarrassments and humiliations, personal worthiness, and the difficulty of truly loving our bodies, ourselves, another person, or of allowing another person to truly love us.

These are powerful issues. And though we seem to be trying as a culture to separate eroticism and sexuality from all this complication, the deeper issues have a way of jumping out at us whenever we engage our sexuality with some depth. (When we make a habit of entering the sexual realm more perfunctorily, we find ourselves facing instead such issues as emptiness, boredom, lack of satisfaction, lack of purpose, emotional isolation, cynicism, and personal doubt.)

The "sexual revolution"—the possibility of vastly broadened sexual understanding and exploration as a result of improved birth control, improved understanding of our psychological processes and the role of sex in those processes, and improved information about the physiology of sexual response and disease—has cast these sex-related issues into the center of our culture, our social psychology, and our politics with increasing urgency over the past 50 years. Even with AIDS and the current antisexual backlash, these issues will not, cannot, go away. We may find ourselves sexually healed in this new era, or we may become more sexually miserable than ever. But the new sexual era is irrevocably upon us. One of the central tasks for our culture over the next few generations, therefore, will be to integrate these far-reaching and (historically speaking) sudden changes into new social, political, psychological, and ethical structures. If we do our work well, they will be structures that bring increased richness, joy, and personal awareness into people's lives with minimal anxiety and grief.

To accomplish this we will need to acknowledge who we are and what we feel as erotic and sexual human beings much more than we have been willing to do to date. We will need to respect our diverse desires and pleasures even when it is difficult to understand why we (or "they") are the way we are. We will even need to learn to enjoy the frightening and chaotic process of discovering what is going on at the core of our erotic identities, since the process of understanding this part of ourselves is likely to take all our lives. Clearly, these are no small tasks. But they are tasks truly worthy of our best efforts and attention.

In the end, I suppose, I have chosen the books and periodicals in this listing because I feel that, in different ways, each of them provides tools that can help us, as individuals and as a culture, to succeed at these difficult undertakings. Each offers a lens beyond the conventional, beyond the cliché, beyond both sexual repression and its alter-ego, pornography. Of course, this makes each of these works controversial as well. The people who most fear their erotic natures insist that the process of discovery be halted, that the fertile but disturbing erotic issues be stuffed back into repressive darkness, where they have been causing misery and confusion for hundreds of years. These people condemn any work that deals with erotic sexuality in a straightforward and unapologetic manner. And even among those who are friendlier to their erotic feelings, coming face to face with erotic expressions that lie outside their personal experience or understanding often provokes stern criticism. These people all too often condemn any work whose erotic point of view is substantially different from their own.

But this is precisely the reason materials of this sort need to be more widely known and distributed. Exposure to new realms of erotic expression brings understanding to replace prejudice and information to replace stereotyping ignorance. And all new material, whether in form or content, allows us to expand our individual erotic horizons beyond the stultifying limitations most of us have suffered all our lives.

If the writers and artists who expose their erotic energies to public view are heroes of sorts, then so too are those of you who are willing to risk criticism and misunderstanding to help make this body of creative, thoughtful, conscientious, provocative work available to waiting readers.

ANNOTATED BIBLIOGRAPHY

Bad Attitude: A Lesbian Sex Magazine. (Jo Smith and Donna Turley, editors, P.O. Box 110, Cambridge, MA 02139, three times per year, $10/year [individuals], $20/year [institutions]).
   An attractively produced journal of lesbian fiction, poetry, and imaginative photography. The journal's title echoes "what women who take their sexuality into their own hands (so to speak) are told that they have."

The Ballad of Sexual Dependency, Nan Goldin. (Aperture, 1986, 144 pages, hardbound, $39.95, 0-89381-236-6, LC 86-070154).
   This powerful volume of moving, disturbing, often brutal color photographs reaches below surface aesthetics to probe the complex and contradictory roots of sexual desire. The individual photographs, many of which are powerful images in themselves, serve primarily as elements of Goldin's intensely personal exploration of her sexuality. This difficult and complex work is as untidy, unpredictable, and engaging as sex itself.

Beneath This Calm Exterior, David Steinberg. (Red Alder Books, P.O. Box 2992, Santa Cruz, CA 95063, 1982, 96 pages, perfectbound, $8.00, 0-914906-03-9).

A collection of quietly personal sensual and sexual poetry, including a long section of "Touchpoems" exploring the connections between sex, desire, intimacy, fear, surrender, trust, and changing concepts of male roles and masculinity.

Bizzaro in Love: A Comic Lesbian Sex Fantasy. Jan Stafford. (Cheap Shots Publications, 227-A Vicente, San Francisco, CA 94127, 1986, 56 pages, saddle-stitched, $7.95).

An outrageously funny, sexy series of short vignettes in which the heroine falls into an unending series of absurd, impossible, and delightfully enticing sexual adventures. Stafford's playfulness and her tongue-in-cheek hyperbolic descriptions make this fling into sexual wonderland an utter delight.

Black Book, Robert Mapplethorpe. (St. Martin's Press, 1986, 108 pages, hardbound, $40.00, 0-312-08302-5, LC 86-13050).

This beautiful collection of oversized portraits of black men transcends Mapplethorpe's fascination with high-fashion glamor imagery to offer a rich, predominantly erotic, collection of evocative male nudes. The duotone photographs, splendidly reproduced, demonstrate convincingly that the neglected male body can be as fertile a source of erotic nude imagery as that of the female.

Breath Marks in the Wind: A Book of Erotic Poetry and Illustrations, Deborah Eve Grayson and Linda F. Shotz. (Breath Marks/I.D.F., Inc., P.O. Box 292204, Ft. Lauderdale, FL 33329, 1988, 80 pages, hardbound, $19.95, perfectbound, $14.95).

A lovely book of sensually erotic poems paired with pencil drawings that are at once soft and sexual. Grayson's poetry speaks simply and directly of the subtleties of sexual play and desire while Shotz's drawings provide a delightfully flowing, tender, yet explicit visual exploration of the same sensual, even spiritual, mood.

Caught Looking: Feminism, Pornography and Censorship, edited by Kate Ellis, Beth Jaker, Nan D. Hunter, Barbara O'Dair, and Abby Tallmer. (Real Comet Press, 3131 Western Ave, #410, Seattle, WA 98121, 1988, 96 pages, illustrated, perfectbound, $9.95, 0-941104-23-0, LC 87-32122).

A collection of feminist writing on the issues of pornography, censorship, and sexuality, set against an elaborate, almost chaotic, potpourri of sexually explicit imagery dating from the 1890s to the present. The writing presents thoughtful, prosexual, feminist perspectives on the issues of pornography and sexual imagery—perspectives that fully appreciate the complexity, depth, and contradictions of sexual feeling and desire. The photographs, most of which are quite explicit, have been selected as examples of nonexploitive sexual imagery from both public and private sources. The mode of this book is confrontative rather that aesthetic, rebellious rather than artistic. A thought-provoking, sexy, heart-warming, mind-boggling work.

Collectors Photography. (Jeff Dunas, editor, 9021 Melrose Avenue, #301, Los Angeles, CA 90069, bi-monthly, $30/year, ISSN 0896-9043).

This increasingly popular journal of photography, devoted to the female nude, is conventional in its concept of female beauty and, to my mind, overly taken with the iconography of glamor and fashion. However, the quality, imagination, and breadth of the photography itself, and the interviews in which the photographers discuss their goals and techniques, make this an interesting magazine of erotic photography that pushes beyond the established clichés of commercial pornography. Contemporary work, both color and black-and-white, is mixed with examinations of historically relevant photographers. Portfolios are by women and men both famous and obscure.

Dance Photographs, by Lois Greenfield. (Photo Review, 301 Hill Avenue, Langhorne, PA 19047, 1987, 24 pages, saddle-stitched, $10.00).
This little catalog of a photo exhibit at Philadelphia's University of the Arts contains some of the most wonderfully erotic dance photography I have ever seen. The images of leaping, arched, usually clothed men and women comprise a sexy (but not sexual) hymn to movement, to the form and exuberance of the human body and to the excitement and beauty of uninhibited physical expression. Joyous, beautiful, imaginative, and inspiring, this book is an impeccable gem.

Deep Down: The New Sensual Writing by Women, edited by Laura Chester. (Faber and Faber, 1988, 342 pages, hardbound, $17.95, 0-571-12957-9, LC 87-33202).
An exceptionally literary, sexy, thoughtful, and complex collection of women's erotic writing. The 150 poems and (usually short) prose pieces by 71 writers include a wonderful and diverse celebration of sexuality as well as perceptive and unsimplified explorations of many of the more painful facets of women's sexual experience. Many well-known contemporary feminist writers—including Marge Piercy, Joyce Carol Oates, Ntozake Shange, Mary Mackey, Deena Metzger, Sharon Olds, Susan Griffin, and Alice Walker—are represented. I find this the richest collection of women's erotic writing published to date.

Delta of Venus, Anaïs Nin. (Harcourt, Brace, Jovanovich, 1986, 276 pages, paperback, $5.95, 0-15-625277-5).
Little Birds, Anaïs Nin. (Harcourt, Brace, Jovanovich, 1986, 168 pages, paperback, $4.95, 0-15-652798-7).
Anaïs Nin's erotic short stories, written in the 1930s as a lark for a private patron who paid her and Henry Miller $1 per page for their work, are actually worthwhile erotic ventures—subtle, literary, playful, and complex—despite the author's refusal to take them seriously.

Dreams of the Woman Who Loved Sex: A Collection, Tee Corinne. (Banned Books, P.O. Box 33280, Austin, TX 78764, 1987, 142 pages, perfect-bound, $7.95, 0-934411-05-0, LC 87-20216).
A collection of erotic writing "especially for women who love women," demonstrating that Corinne is a fine and sensitive writer as well as an accomplished photographer. The book includes a short novella ("Passion is a Forest Fire Between Us"), 31 very short poems, and the delightful title story in which "The Woman in Love" and "Desire" engage in an archetypal pas-de-deux that goes right to the heart of the feelings, dilemmas, and choices involved in acknowledging sexual attraction.

Erotic by Nature: A Celebration of Life, of Love, and of Our Wonderful Bodies, edited by David Steinberg. (Shakti Press/Red Alder Books, P.O. Box 2249, Berkeley, CA 94702, 1988, 224 pages, hardbound, $35.00, 0-933211-03-1, LC 87-26426).
This collection of 122 duotone photographs, 17 drawings, 15 short stories, and 38 poems is my own attempt to present a variety of both visual and written erotic material that is not only arousing, but also honest, serious, playful, and full of emotional warmth—work that honors women, men, and the wonder of sex itself. Drawing from the work of 36 women and 25 men, ages 30 to 73, the book presents a wide variety of sensual and sexual erotic perspectives ranging from the familiar to the novel, from the conventional to the daring, from light-hearted play to confrontation of the deepest aspects of personal identity and interpersonal connection.

The Erotic Comedies, Marco Vassi. (The Permanent Press, Noyac Road, Sag Harbor, NY 11963, 1981, 224 pages, perfectbound, $16.95, 0-932966-20-9, paperback, $8.95, 0-932966-21-7).
This collection of a dozen "erotic fables for radical minds" and seven "essays on the erotic experience" is the only available anthology of one of the most

perceptive and talented writers of sexual fiction. Vassi's sexual imagination, dry wit, reverent appreciation of the ironies of sexual existence in an antisexual culture, and his willingness to connect sexuality to fundamental questions of human existence, infuse his work with a wonderful combination of outrageous sexuality and metaphysical exploration. A unique and important book.

Erotic Photography: An Exhibition, Demarais Studio Press Staff. (Demarais Studio Press, 64 Lawn Park Avenue, Trenton, NJ 08648, 1981, 102 pages, perfectbound, $12.95, 0-9607462-1-8, LC 81-70902).
A creative and imaginative collection of black-and-white photographs by 85 photographers, selected from submissions to a national competition. The imagery here avoids the common clichés, offering instead a wide variety of interesting photographic and erotic perspectives.

Field Guide to Outdoor Erotica, edited by Rob Moore. (Solstice Press, P.O. Box 9223, Moscow, ID, 1988, 176 pages, perfectbound, $9.95, 0-932722-11-3).
A collection of 29 short stories and poems by 11 women and 5 men, all of which take place in the grand outdoors. While the writing as a whole is hardly great literature, the stories are intentionally nonsexist, sensual, often imaginative, always friendly, and often deliciously sexual as well. The outdoor theme, and the fact that the publisher and many of the contributors are Idahoans, give this book a rural flavor that is a nice break from the urbanity of most of the new erotics.

Fleshfire: Love Poems, Lili Bita. (Lyra Press, 5901 S.W. 51 Street, Miami, FL 33155, 1984, 80 pages, perfectbound).
A rich collection of poems filled with fierce eros from the Greek-born poet and actress. One of the few available books of quality poetry that is erotic in its focus from beginning to end.

Graffiti for the Johns of Heaven, James Broughton. (Syzygy Press, P.O. Box 183, Mill Valley, CA 94942, 1982, 80 pages, perfectbound, $6.00, 0-9608372-1-3).
Ecstasies: Poems, 1975–1983, James Broughton. (Syzygy Press, P.O. Box 183, Mill Valley, CA 94942, 1983, 128 pages, perfectbound, $7.00, 0-9608372-2-1).
Two books offering a delightfully impish, playful, irreverent, and deep-reaching appreciation of the miracle of sex from this 73-year-old gay poet. Broughton's whimsical but determined affirmation of joyful wonder, in sex as in life, is a holy celebration of the life-force itself.

Herotica: A Collection of Women's Erotic Fiction, edited by Susie Bright. (Down There Press, P.O. Box 2086, Burlingame, CA 94010, 1988, 160 pages, perfectbound, $8.50, 0-940208-11-3, LC 88-12293).
A wonderful new collection of 21 short stories by previously unknown women writers ranging "from fantastic to autobiographical, nostalgic to pressing, quick and dirty to philosophical and maddening." The unapologetic purpose of the book is to turn women on, and editor Susie Bright has both the liveliness and the good sense to know that this involves nonexploitive "sleaze" as well as tenderness, the forbidden as well as material within the accepted boundaries of political or emotional rectitude. An important addition to the growing body of quality erotic fiction.

High Desire, Leslie Simon. (Wingbow Press, P.O. Box 2249, Berkeley, CA 94702, 1983, 80 pages, perfectbound, $4.95, 0-914728-41-5).
An eloquent look at the complexity of sexual emotions through a combination of poems and short prose segments. Simon is a strong, sexual woman who is willing both to affirm the power of her sexuality and to confront her pain as a woman pursuing love and sex in these times of changing roles, images, and expectations.

Ladies' Own Erotica, The Kensington Ladies' Erotica Society. (Ten Speed Press, 1984, 240 pages, illustrated, perfectbound, $8.95, 0-89815-127-9).
Look Homeward Erotica, The Kensington Ladies' Erotica Society. (Ten Speed Press, 1986, 240 pages, illustrated, perfectbound, $8.95, 0-89815-195-3).
Two collections of erotic short stories and occasional poems by a group of "women over forty" who began meeting together to examine where their erotic lives had gotten derailed, and who decided to write out their own erotic fantasies as a way of reinvigorating that part of their lives. The stories, full of ease and emotional warmth, if lacking in sexual heat, are an enjoyable, non-confrontative stroll through a delicate and gentle erotic garden.

The Leading Edge: An Anthology of Lesbian Sexual Fiction, edited by Lady Winston. (Lace Publications, P.O. Box 10037, Denver, CO 80210, 1987, 228 pages, illustrated, perfectbound, $9.95, 0-917597-09-05).
A sexy and diverse collection of well-written lesbian short stories and poems from 20 contributors, including Dorothy Allison, Pat Califia, Chocolate Waters, Artemis OakGrove, Jewelle Gomez, and Noretta Koertge.

Libido: the Journal of Sex and Sensibility. (Marianna Beck and Jack Hofferkamp, editors, P.O. Box 146721, Chicago, IL 60614, quarterly, $20/year).
A new journal of erotic writing (prose, poetry, interviews, essays), photography and illustration, with the feel of a fine literary quarterly. Its purpose is to "explore the erogenous zones of a new sexual age." While the editors are still defining what they want this new magazine to be, their perspective is unequivocally positive, playful, experimental, and imaginative, as well as being distinctively midwestern in contrast to the coastal perspectives of most new erotics. *Libido* has quickly managed to build a network of skilled writers, thinkers, photographers, and artists who bring a wide variety of interesting thoughts and beautiful, provocative images to its pages.

Macho Sluts, Pat Califia. (Alyson Publications, 40 Plympton Street, Boston, MA 02118, 1988, trade paper, $8.95, 1-55583-115-X).
This long-overdue collection of sexual stories by the controversial thinker and writer is an important addition to the widening spectrum of new erotica. The power of Califia's imagery and the depth of her sexual insight—the connections she draws between sex and such fundamental issues as life, death, power, desire, gender, pain and pleasure—make her writing uniquely provocative to both mind and body. These stories offer a seductive excursion into radical sexuality for those who are willing to go well beyond the boundaries of conventional sexual imagination.

Men Loving Themselves: Images of Male Self-Sexuality, Jack Morin. (Down There Press, P.O. Box 2086, Burlingame, CA 94010, 1980, 102 pages, perfectbound, $15.00, 0-9602324-5-1, LC 80-52942).
A joyous and sensitive collection of photographs of men masturbating. The book offers separate photographic portfolios of each of its nine subjects, with a statement from each man giving his personal perspective on masturbation, as well as an overview by photographer/psychotherapist Morin. This book is both a powerful collection of sexual male nude photography and an effective celebration of masturbation itself.

Naked Landscape, John Swannell. (Quartet Books, 27/29 Goodge Street, London, W1P 1FD, 1986, 132 pages, hardbound, $50.00, 0-7043-2609-4).
This beautiful produced, oversized collection of 59 duotone photographs is a study of female nudes in various natural settings. Swannell's use of the female form against trees, rocks, driftwood, grasses, lakes and forests—some in extreme close-up, some from great distance—evokes much mystery and deeply erotic sensuality. The superb quality of the photographic reproductions adds to the aesthetic impact of this lovely, subtle, and moving book.

The Nature of Desire, Duane Michals. (Twelvetrees Press, c/o Twin Palms Publishers, 2400 N. Lake Avenue, Altadena, CA 91001, 112 pages, hardbound, $40.00, 0-942642-23-6).
In this attractive collection of handwritten poems and quietly erotic gravure photographs, Michals offers a delicate and intensely personal exploration of his own, often unrequited, erotic longings, principally for other men. While not all of the images are explicitly erotic, the book as a whole has a definite gently, erotic focus.

Obsession, Bob Carlos Clarke. (Quartet Books, 27/29 Goodge Street, London, W1P 1FD, 1981, 164 pages, hardbound, $29.50, 0-7043-2298-6, perfect-bound, 1984, $17.95, 0-7043-3472-0).
This collection of surreal, often glamorous, sometimes violent, tinted photographs uses symbolic images of women from mainstream erotic culture as the basis for a flowing dreamscape of subconscious erotic iconography. Clarke's erotic imagination, his presentation of conventional symbols in unconventional juxtapositions, and the effectiveness of his eerie tinting technique raise his images above simple manipulations of cultural clichés to erotic explorations of real complexity and depth.

On Our Backs: Entertainment for the Adventurous Lesbian. (Susie Bright, editor, 526 Castro Street, San Francisco, CA 94114, quarterly, $19/year, ISSN 0890-2224).
Outrageously lusty and delightfully irreverent, this journal of lesbian fun and games offers short stories, photography, occasional poems, and regular feature columns of information and opinion for lesbians of all persuasions. Criticized by some as "pornographic," this magazine is actually a courageous vehicle encouraging lesbian women to acknowledge and honor the power and true personal parameters of their sexual desire and practice, beyond the limitations imposed by conventional, patriarchal, or supposedly progressive political propriety. The playful, provocative, and thoughtful perspectives of this explicitly feminist magazine cut important new ground for all who would celebrate the sanctity of sex taken on its own terms.

Photographs: 1931–1955, George Platt Lynes. (Twelvetrees Press, c/o Twin Palms Publishers, 2400 N. Lake Avenue, Altadena, CA 91001, 1981, 132 pages, hardbound, $45.00, 0-942642-01-5).
This lovely, oversized collection of duotone reproductions emphasizes Lynes' surreal, mythological, and directly erotic sensual nudes, both male and female. The mixed imagery connects erotic images from the conscious realm to the subconscious roots of eroticism in the worlds of dream and symbol. A beautifully erotic collection of Lynes' pathfinding work.

Pleasures: Women Write Erotica, edited by Lonnie Barbach. (Doubleday, 1984, 264 pages, hardbound, $14.95, 0-385-18811-0, LC 84-5922; paperback, Bantam, 1985, 304 pages, $7.95, 0-553-25449-9, LC 85-42550).
Erotic Interludes: Tales Told by Women, Lonnie Barbach. (Doubleday, 1986, 288 pages, hardbound, $15.95, 0-385-23319-1, LC 86-6232; perfectbound, Harper and Row, 1987, $6.95, 0-06-097110-X).
Two collections of women's sexual stories that have become best sellers and demonstrated the mass-market potential of quality erotic fiction. The two books present a wide variety of women's sexual perspectives, mostly in slick journalistic style, but with occasional ventures into less polished and more literary modes. *Pleasures* is a collection of supposedly true stories; *Erotic Interludes* a compilation of fantasies. Both emphasize sexual heat over emotional warmth and, despite their sometimes annoying infatuation with men of wealth and power, offer effective sexual entertainment to women and men alike.

Rapture, Ron Raffaelli. (Chatsworth Press, 9135 Alabama Avenue, #B, Chatsworth, CA 91311, 1983, perfectbound, $14.95, 0-917181-01-8).
Passions, Ron Raffaelli. (Chatsworth Press, 9135 Alabama Avenue, #B, Chatsworth, CA 91311, 1989, 144 pages, $19.95).
Rapture is a playful celebration of human sexuality offering 13 widely varied sexual fantasies, each pursued in its own photo esssay. It is a book of imaginative and artful photography, probably the friendliest, most sex-positive collection of sexual photography to be collected in book form. Raffaelli is the most accomplished sexual photographer whose work is commercially available, and his love and reverence for sex infuses this collection of highly explicit sexual imagery with infectious good cheer. *Passions,* the newest collection of Raffaelli photography, was released in 1989.

Robert Mapplethorpe, edited by Richard Marshall. (New York Graphic Society Books, 1988, 216 pages, hardbound, $50.00. 0-8212-1728-3; perfectbound, Whitney Museum of American Art, 0-87427-060-X).
This book presents the photographs from Mapplethorpe's 1988 retrospective exhibit at New York's Whitney Museum of American Art. The photos are quite similar in tone and content to those that have provoked such strong erotophobic criticism as they toured nationally in 1990. Eroticism is not the only focus of these photographs, but the erotic and sexual content of many of the images is striking and direct, ranging from aesthetically stunning male and female nudes to graphic depictions of gay S/M scenes that are almost painful to look at. This is certainly the most sexually provocative of the books of Mapplethorpe's work. That these more difficult photos were included in the work shown at a prestigious museum, and that they are now recorded in a book of this fine quality, is documentation of significant sexual/artistic progress, despite the reactionary controversy they have also inspired.

Sexual Magic: The S/M Photographs, Michael A. Rosen. (Shaynew Press, P.O. Box 11719, San Francisco, CA 94101, 1986, 72 pages, perfectbound, $25.00, 0-936705-69-8, LC 85-90537).
This striking collection of S/M photography emphasizes and visually documents the intimacy, intensity, and playfulness of sadomasochism. The photographs of actual S/M scenes—heterosexual, lesbian, and gay—offer concrete, honest, emotionally powerful images in contrast to the stereotypical misinformation of mainstream media. Mixed with the photographs are short but informative statements on S/M by several people who appear in the book. This is a controversial and confrontative book, and many of the images will be difficult for some readers; but the emotional quality and complexity of the interactions that Rosen captures is extraordinary, regardless of how one feels about S/M.

Skin Deep, Helene Guetary and Patrice Casanova. (Grove Press, 1984, 108 pages, $24.95, 0-394-53812-9).
A striking photographic essay, emphasizing archetypal form and imagery, movement, dramatic gesture, and vivid use of color in costuming and body paint.

Twelve Months of Rapture, Harriet Moore. (Collection of 12 oversized prints, limited edition, available from the artist, 717 14th Avenue, San Francisco, CA 94118, $150.00).
An engaging collection of fierce, sexually explicit line prints, one for each month of the year, printed on fine paper and collected in an unbound portfolio. Moore's sexual imagery is intense, fiery, and explosive, with the energy almost spinning off the page. An unusual sexual perspective from this 67-year-old artist and sculptor.

Word Alchemy, Lenore Kandel. (Grove Press, 96 pages, perfectbound, $2.45, 0-394-17303-1).
This is the only book of poetry still in print by the author of *The Love Book*, the volume of sexual poetry that provoked two separate obscenity trials during the 1960s. Kandel is one of the most profound contemporary writers of sexual poetry. Her work combines deep spirituality and openly lustful desire into a magical blend that affirms sexuality as one of the deepest and most holy aspects of our existence. Her reverent vision and her rich imagery make the erotic aspect of this book a pure delight.

The World of Jan Saudek: Photographs and Stories. (Aperture, 1983, 144 pages, hardbound, $35.00, 0-89381-116-5, LC 82-73758).
An intriguing collection of powerful, often surreal, images in both color and black and white, by the Czech photographer. While the themes of this book go far beyond the erotic, the great majority of Saudek's photographs have strong, if extremely unconventional, erotic appeal. His combinations of nude and clothed figures—adults, adolescents, children, women, and men—some visually attractive, some practically grotesque—confront the reader's aesthetic and erotic assumptions on both conscious and unconscious levels. A moving, seductive, and often disturbing work.

The X-Rated Videotape Guide, Robert H. Rimmer, revised edition. (Harmony Books, 1986, 662 pages, illustrated, perfectbound, $16.95, 0-517-56058-5, LC 85-27062).
While this is not an erotic book in itself, it deserves mention here as the best consumer's guide to X-rated videotapes. Rimmer reviews, rates, and gives "plot" summaries for 1,300 sex videos, with brief supplemental listings for 2,840 more. His short descriptions of the content of the films, actors, directors, and coded notations on the types of sex depicted offer viewers of sexual videos a better than random chance of matching their sexual tastes with those of the videos. Rimmer himself is both critical and appreciative of the X-rated film industry: critical of its low-quality productions and its trivialization of sex, and appreciative of the current availability of sexually explicit material for the enjoyment of men, women, and couples alike.

Yantras of Womanlove: Diagrams of Energy, photographs by Tee Corrinne, text by Jacqueline Lapidus. (Naiad Press, P.O. Box 10543, Tallahassee, FL 32302, 1982, 64 pages, perfectbound, $6.95, 0-930044-30-4).
A fascinating and imaginative collection of multiplied, mirrored, often solarized photographic images of lesbian couples, individual women, and close-ups of women's genitals. A unique photographic exposition of lesbian desire, and an elaborate visual celebration of the richly textured beauty of female genitals.

Yellow Pears, Smooth as Silk, Rochelle Lynn Holt. (Ragnarok Press, c/o Merging Media, 516 Gallows Hill Road, Cranford, NJ 07016, 1977, four pages with one 45 rpm record, $2.00).
This six-part prosepoem offers a liquid, dreamlike progression of sensual images that follows the erotic dance of two women as they approach and seduce each other, slowly and quietly. Holt's style, reminiscent of the novels of Anaïs Nin, takes the reader onto an ocean of rich, subconscious imagery. The enclosed record provides an opportunity to hear the author read her work. An obscure treat.

Yellow Silk: Journal of Erotic Arts. (Lily Pond, editor, P.O. Box 6374, Albany, CA 94706, quarterly, $20/year [individuals], $24/year [libraries], ISSN 0736-9212).
The most widely distributed and best known of the new erotic periodicals, this journal offers well-written poetry and prose, as well as quality sensual artwork, in a format that is consistently aesthetic and appealing. The magazine is more concerned with its artistic quality than with its erotic content. Consequently, the eroticism of its material is often extremely diffuse and

only occasionally sexual. It has become an important vehicle for establishing new legitimacy for and recognition of quietly erotic work, and occasionally publishes extraordinary sexual pieces as well.

Yoni: Lesbian Erotica. (B. Fibbs, editor, P.O. Box 19316, Oakland, CA 94619, quarterly, $13/year).
A simply produced, yet aesthetic journal, offering lesbian short stories, poems, photography, and commentary. Softer in tone than many of the other lesbian journals.

Editor's note: I believe that most academic and public libraries should also have in their collections some of the "classic" erotica/pornography, particularly those works that inspired the great censorship court cases: *Lady Chatterley's Lover*, Miller's *Tropics, Fanny Hill*, etc. See Walter Kendrick's *The Secret Museum* (New York: Viking Penguin, 1987) for titles and background information.

CHAPTER 16

A Connoisseur's Selection of X-Rated Videotapes for the Library

Robert H. Rimmer

EDITOR'S INTRODUCTION   by Martha Cornog

Videotapes are becoming an increasingly popular addition to circulating collections in libraries. Many libraries acquire both classic and popular, first-run films for lending. And just as many librarians cannot avoid noticing that many films well-reviewed by critics, and hence presumably eligible for adding to a "quality" collection, are more or less sexually explicit, for example *Last Tango in Paris* or *Pretty Baby*.

It is only a small mental jump from here to considering quality erotic films on videotape for the library collection. Realistically, few librarians may choose to go this route at present, but many may want to keep their options open, particularly if reviews are available to help assess "quality."

Until recently, comparative reviews of erotic or adult films have been few and far between. Sources have been there—several books on the history of erotic films plus a regular column in *Screw* magazine—but consulting these sources requires a certain amount of digging plus a degree of convention flouting. Hence, librarians who might be receptive to adding "a few good films about sex" probably know very little about what is available.

This chapter is designed to raise a little consciousness about possibilities. As you will see, erotic films are not all of the sleazy-audience-in-raincoats variety. Some are not designed as entertainment at all but for educational or therapeutic purposes. As Rimmer, best known for his many utopian novels on sexual relationships, points out, several hundred out of the thousands of adult films on videotape *are* worth seeing once, and some of these deserve repeated viewings.

Below, Rimmer has annotated in lively style some 60+ erotic films that are suitable as "classics" for consideration in library collections. While his selection is designed for a variety of tastes, many will appeal to women and couples. Whether or not you as librarian reader use his ratings as selection criteria, you may find your preconceptions about adult films modified. And whether or not you buy or rent any of the films (for the library or for yourself), you should certainly consider Rimmer's book on erotic videotapes, *The X-Rated Videotape Guide*, for the reference collection and some of the books he cites for circulation.

AUTHOR'S INTRODUCTION   by Robert H. Rimmer

Many people wonder why the author of *The Harrad Experiment, Proposition 31*, and many other novels proposing alternative life styles (all relatively conservative by 1980s standards, and novels that many libraries have on their shelves) ever started reviewing "porno" films. I answer in some detail in my book, *The X-Rated Videotape Guide* (1986), but essentially it comes down to the fact that I believe we would have a healthier society if our religions exalted human sexuality and encouraged the joyous visual depiction of men and women making love. If we made sex itself a sacrament instead of degrading it, we could create an environment where it was really possible to define "sick sex." Sick sex certainly does not include human nudity or seeing from early childhood the wonder of caring, loving human copulation. If anyone reads the 3,000 reviews I have written on adult films, they'll quickly get the message. I think 85% of them belong in the category of sick sex or are just boring to watch.

However, I wouldn't censor any X-rated film unless it combine sex and violence. Most X-rated tapes don't, but hundreds of R-rated films do; nor do X-rated tapes offer child pornography (which in a sane society shouldn't exclude the sight of teenagers naked or playing together naked but now legally does). My feeling is that in a sexually sane society, sick sex videos would be ignored or would appeal to only those on the fringe. But among the 1,000 or so adult films that are available on tape, about 500 *are* worth seeing once, and there are some that deserve repeated viewings. (Keep in mind also that rentals of adult films at video stores in the 1980s exceeded 50 million rentals annually and hundreds of millions of dollars.)

I have reviewed both the best and the worst of the so-called adult films, and I'm constantly "discovering" tapes that for one reason or another deserve my Collector's Choice rating. The following annotated listing includes 60+ of those videotapes that I think many libraries could have available on an "adults only" basis for people who wish either to discover what an adult film is like or to learn more about their own sexuality by watching others make love. In aggregate, they cover every aspect of human sexuality on videotape. Whenever possible, I have given the date that the film or shot-on-video tape was made and the original distributor. An up-to-date address listing of the distributors is available in the forthcoming Sundance edition of *The X-Rated Videotape Guide* (see the reference at end of chapter), with 750 reviews that do not appear in the Crown edition. But for convenience in ordering, I would suggest that General Video, with offices in most of the major cities, is a reliable wholesaler who handles or can obtain all these tapes. Their headquarters address is General Video of America, 3700 Kelley Avenue, Cleveland, OH 44114. They also have offices in Denver; Baltimore; Phoenix; Cherry Hill, NJ; Livonia, MI; Chicago; Canton, MA; San Francisco; and North Hollywood. Also, Great Pictures, Inc., 150-50 Coolidge Avenue, Jamaica, NY 11432, advises me that they can supply any adult film ever made.

Another survey of adult films, which will supplement my *X-Rated Videotape Guide* in the adult section of libraries, is a book by Jim Holliday, *Only the Best*, which reviews Jim's choice of the 100 best adult films produced between 1970 and 1985. This is obtainable along with a tape showing excerpts from some of these films from Cal Vista, 6649 Odessa St., Van Nuys, CA 91406.

Finally, librarians will be interested to know that the Kinsey Institute at the University of Indiana, which has the largest collection of "stag films" anywhere, is slowly building a tape library of adult films produced between 1970 and the present.

CONNOISSEUR'S SELECTION

Alice in Wonderland. 1975, Xtra-Vision.
There's both an X-rated and an R-rated version of this tape, which is a laughing, musical version of *Alice*, featuring many of Lewis Carroll's characters, including Alice, in amusing sexual encounters.

American Babylon. 1984, VCA.
A small cast of good actors and a director with imagination lend class and surrealism to this story of a suburban menage à quatre.

Angela, The Fireworks Woman. 1975 VCA.
In one of the few sexvids to mix sex and religion, a young man becomes a priest to atone for his love for his sister Angela. Naturally, amour triumphs over celibacy. Excellent cinematography and a believable story and background.

Autobiography of a Flea. 1976, Mitchell Brothers.
A beautifully costumed version of a famous and amusing seventeenth-century pornographic story; the "flea" lives on a lovely, vacuous young woman and an occasional man and narrates their dalliances.

Behind the Green Door. 1975, Mitchell Brothers.
Next to *Deep Throat*, probably the most famous porno film ever made, about a young woman kidnapped, taken to a sex club, and subjected to every imaginable variety of sex. Among the first sex films of high quality, plot and cinematography. The film features Marilyn Chambers, who at the time was the Ivory Snow soap box model.

Behind the Green Door, The Sequel. 1986, Mitchell Brothers.
The sequel is in name only, and the fact that it takes place in the same sex club. The star, Eliza Florez, was page to Senator Orrin Hatch and made this porno film to protest against the Republican party and Edwin Meese for "hacking away at the Constitution" and First Amendment rights. All sex in the film follows "safe sex" techniques, often in a silly, humorous way.

The Big Switch. 1985, Catalina Video.
While a standard convention of adult film is the inevitable bisexual sequence, this has always been a lesbian, or girl/girl, encounter. This is probably the first sexvid that introduces bisexual men who have oral and anal sex with each and also make love with the women.

Blond Ambition. 1981, Quality.
A hilarious spoof of the young-show-girls-from-the-West-make-it-in-New-York theme, with the ingenue obligingly starring in an X-rated *Gone with the Wind*. The well-integrated story, plot, and dialogue would make a marvelously funny Broadway musical.

Cafe Flesh. 1982, VCA.
A porno cult movie about the world after the first nuclear war, in which the tiny percentage of the population who can still feel sexual pleasure are required by law to put on sex shows for the mass of "sex negatives." Clever photography and good acting.

Caligula. 1980, Penthouse Films.
Bob Guccione, chief factotum of *Penthouse* magazine, poured $15 million into this X-rated film. It was criticized for its relentless series of decapitations and disembowelings as well as sick sex, but it can't compare with the "reality," as described by Suetonius in his *Lives of the Twelve Caesars.*

The Dancers. 1982, VCX.
A well acted and really funny story of four male strippers (not gay) barnstorming around the country to make a living and their encounters with local women. Entirely heterosexual.

Deep Throat. 1972, Arrow.
Linda Lovelace, who later claimed she was forced to appear in pornos, stars as the now infamous woman who can't reach orgasm until she discovers that her clitoris is in her throat. This sometimes very funny film added a new word to our sexual vocabulary and grossed $50 million or more on a cost of probably less than $50 thousand.

The Devil and Miss Jones. 1972, Arrow.
A virgin spinster commits suicide to escape her sexual compulsions and before entering Hell is granted a reprieve to experience the totally lustful life she has missed. A porno classic that reflects the director's Catholic conscience.

Diversions. 1979, Great Pictures, Inc.
A British-made chronicle of a young woman's fantasies, running the gamut through romatic sex, bisex, much kinky sex, and some sadistic sex. Well put together and sometimes humorous.

Educating Julie. 1984, Heritage Video Ltd.
  A British-made introduction to the nudist way of life in England, France, and the United States. In the story, Julie is given a university assignment to write a thesis on nudism. Nicely photographed. Available from E.G.L. Enterprises, 700 Robinson Road, Topinga, CA 90027.

Fallen Angels. 1986, Vestron.
  An R-rated documentary on the porno industry, which gives the viewer an inside look at, and discussion with, several porno stars and directors. The thrust of the tape is antiporn, but in the process of trying to reveal the seamy side of porn, it becomes pornographic itself.

Famous Smokers, Volumes 1 and 2. Wonderful World of Video.
  A three-hour collection of black-and-white 8mm and 16mm "stag films" (accompanied by songs of the times) that were young males' introduction to sex from the 1930s to 1950s.

A Guide to Making Love. 1973, Vestron.
  A low-keyed "how to do it" sex film covering sexual exercises, sexual arousal, sex toys, stripping, and kinds of kissing, plus sexual positions in soft-focus without too much genital exposure.

The Harrad Experiment, 1973, Lightning Video.
  R-rated and based partially on my book of the same name about a college in which serial cohabitation with sexual and emotional intimacy is promoted and supported by the curriculum. Nicely romantic and well acted but does not deal with the idea of group marriage proposed in the book.

Hot Desires. 1986, VCA.
  An amusing, sophisticated slice of life film made in France, with much of the same humor as *Cousin Cousine* and *Get Out Your Handkerchiefs and Cry*. A French husband and wife, both of whom are secretly having an affair, independently invite their lovers to a lodge they own in the Swiss Alps, each thinking they have the place to themselves. Keeping their lovers and their spouses unaware of each other creates amusing and titillating sequences.

In All the Right Places. 1986, Video.
  An adult film with a couples orientation that tells an amusing story about two lonely single people, man and woman, who buy the same sex book in a paperback store, read it separately, and wish it were happening to them. They finally meet each other and read the final chapter together.

In Love. 1983, VCA.
  A romantic, happy-ever-after tale of an extramarital love affair that persists over 15 years and finally conquers all. Good dialogue, character development, and realistic sex, photographed with loving warmth. Hopefully, this film marks the start of a long-awaited "new wave" of adult films.

Le Sex Shop. 1973.
  This R-rated movie in French with subtitles tells an amusing story about the owner of a bookstore that is going bankrupt until he turns it into a "dirty bookstore," after which he is inundated with far-out customers and nearly ruins his marriage.

Love Theatre. 1985, VCA.
  A German-made video that offers all the sex you'll find in American-made sexvids but with a much more sophisticated sense of humor. The story involves a troupe of actors and actresses traveling in a bus through Europe and stopping in small towns and at the estate of a wealthy count, where they provide various dramatic performances that involve the actors and the audience.

Love You. 1980, Caballero.
John Derek (husband of Bo) directed this believable story about two couples who spend a weekend on a deserted island off the coast of California and get into group sex. Loving and caring ambience; most couples watching will be fascinated.

Males in Motion. 1985, Ambassador Video.
A one-hour tape featuring eight male strippers, peeling and strutting in a variety of fascinating erotic styles. No women and no sex, but this one reverses the usual equation of woman equals sex object.

Miss September (Whatever Happened to Her?). 1973, Great American Pictures.
A wealthy man hires a detective to locate the woman of his dreams, a beautiful and likeable college grad pin-up girl. Through the search, the detective also falls in love with her. The star, Tina Russell (who died of cancer in 1981), wrote several books, one about her ethics and the sexual philosophy that she put into practice as an actress.

Mondo Magic. 1985, Magnum.
There's no explicit sex in this; it's an around-the-world trip about the sexual practices of primitive people that you never read about in *National Geographic*.

Not a Love Story. 1980, Canadian Film Board; Great American Pictures on General Video.
This film proves that you can't explore pornography without becoming pornographic. It's a documentary about the X-rated industry, produced and financed by the National Film Board of Canada (Toronto), which provoked much pro and con discussion.

Nothing to Hide. 1982, Cal Vista.
The characters are similar to Lenny and George in Steinbeck's *Of Mice and Men*. A Don Juan is confronted with the success of his socially backward best-buddy, who meets the girl of his dreams and—despite his shyness with women—finally marries her. This one proves that porno films can cover all the explicit sex bases and still be entertaining.

Old, Borrowed, and Stag. 1975, Video-X-Pix.
A 1½ hour collection of scenes edited from at least a dozen "stag films," plus animated stag cartoons and newsreels, all in black and white and dating back to the early 1900s. Most of this sexvid is joyously naive compared with modern-day adult films. For more about stag films, read *Dirty Movies (1915–1970)* by Al Di Lauro and Gerald Rubin (Chelsea House, 1976).

The Opening of Misty Beethoven. 1975, General Video.
A retelling of the Pygmalion myth with a sex twist: a (male) sex expert and brothel keeper try to make a top society hooker out of a Paris whore. The film contains much sophisticated humor and climaxes in a long sequence of romantic sex-making.

Passage Through Pamela. 1985, VCA.
The very attractive "Pamela" is a South American transsexual, who made the film to pay for her male-to-female sex change operation. In the film, Pamela is a top Argentinian female model who is hired by a New York modelling agency. The owner of the agency, a woman, doesn't learn that Pamela is a transsexual—with a penis—until they are about to make love.

The Passion Within. 1986, Masterpiece. The story of a woman executive, divorced, hoping to find true love, but who attracts men who are married or who want no marital commitments. She finally is "conned" by a man who reads her diary and caters to her emotions to bed her, but then happily falls in love with her. The sex scenes are not only sensuous and erotic, but believable and reveal the characters of the people making love.

Pretty Peaches. 1978, Astro.
A sexy, funny film about a happy-go-lucky female victim à la Candide. In an unforgettable sequence, the heroine gets an enema to cure her amnesia.

Punishment of Anne. 1979, Highbridge Entertainment.
This is a sadomasochistic classic, if depiction of pain and horror can become a classic. Exquisitely and erotically photographed in Paris.

Raw Talent. 1984, VCA.
A young, tough short order cook wants to be a legitimate actor but falls into the hands of a just-as-tough lady who makes porno films. Produced by a woman, the film has a strong story line and good acting. (I have worked with the star, Jerry Butler—real name: Paul Seiderman—on his autobiography; see Butler, 1989, in References).

Raw Talent II. 1986, VCA.
A continuation of the story of the actor and the porno film producer who is determined to ruin him. The sequel is as good or better than the original.

Reel People 1 & 2. 1984, Arrow.
These are two separate tapes produced by Anthony Spinelli, one of the top porno directors and producers, using average Americans (not porno stars) who were willing to do a "one time" vignette revealing their own sexual desires and peccadillos.

Reproduction of Life. 1981, Mastervision.
A sex education film (without live people) that can be viewed by teenagers and their parents. The first segment shows a kitten being born. In the second, drawings in motion explain all aspects of human sexuality. The third segment describes the influence of prenatal development on the human fetus.

Ribald Tales of Canterbury. 1985, Caballero.
A very clever, nicely costumed and acted sexvid that features stories from Chaucer's *Canterbury Tales.*

Rising Star. 1986, Caballero.
A well acted, almost slice-of-life film that begins in Athens and ends in porno land. The hero tries to rise in the world, but falls in love with a hooker, and joins her in becoming a porno star. It features Jack Wrangler, a handsome bisexual, who tells about his love for Margaret Whiting (a famous 1940s singer) and his gay life in his autobiography *The Jack Wrangler Story* (St. Martin's Press, 1984).

Roommates. 1982, Video-X-Pix.
This fascinating film interweaves the sex lives of three women roommates in New York City with their personal triumphs and failures. One of the best adult films ever made, with superb acting and explicit and beautifully honest sex scenes.

Sailing into Ecstasy. 1986, CDI Home Video.
Another film for couples, although the director occasionally goes overboard in deference to sexvid conventions. This is a story about a woman who loves her husband but has never had an orgasm with him and daydreams about (or enjoys in reality, you're not sure which) more exciting lovers. In a "happy ending," she finally has an orgasm with her husband.

The Secret World of Erotic Art. 1986, Vestron.
Every library should have this survey of erotic art, which is based on Bradley Smith's coffee-table size books, *Erotic Art of the Masters* and *20th Century Erotic Art.*

Sensational Janine. 1979, Caballero.
It is London, 1910, and a young woman tells about her introduction to sex in her mother's boardinghouse. Earthy and warmly funny, this small classic evokes an era.

Sexual Freedom in Denmark. 1986, Rainbow.
This film was originally released to adult theaters in the 1970s. It was shocking then, and, for millions of Americans, it still is. The title is a bit of a misnomer, but Denmark has sex education, plus no restrictions on consensual sex from age 15. Even in the 1970s, Danish schools were far ahead of the U.S. in the 1980s.

She Comes in Color. 1986, Persuasion.
A sexvid with a very volatile extended sex scene in which the lovers paint each other's bodies in colors while making love.

Shocking Asia. 1980, Magnum.
A documentary film that explores strange sexual cults, rituals, and sex practices in Malaysia, China, India, and Japan. It concludes with an explicit sex change operation performed by a Professor Rattman, who presumably specializes in these operations for transsexuals who arrive from all over the world.

Skinny Dipping. n.d., Naturists.
This is one of several tapes offered by the Naturists (P.O. Box 132, Oshkosh, WI 54902). It takes you on a tour of nude beaches and resorts all over the U.S. and the Caribbean.

Sodom and Gomorrah. 1977, Mitchell Brothers.
Supposedly the biggest budgeted adult film ever made (until *Caligula*), this is the only adult film that I know of with a Biblical story line. Many of the sequences offer kinky sex, and some border on the sadistic.

Sometime Sweet Susan. 1975, VCA.
A very well told story about a schizoid woman with multiple personalities and her encounter with a psychologist. Good acting, good editing, excellent dialogue, and some really warm, loving sex.

Suzie Superstar. 1983, Cal Vista.
A melodrama about a female rock star, her band, and several lecherous no-good Mafia types. Good story, good acting, and nice cinematography. The star, Shauna Grant—whose real name is Coleen Applegate—was the subject of a PBS documentary, "Diary of a Porn Star."

Taboo 1-6. 1983–1988, Standard Video.
A superior sexvid sequence of six 1½ hour tapes of continuous sex, dealing generally with incest throughout a complicated plot.

Taboo American Style, Parts 1-4. 1985, VCA.
Four separate 1½ hour tapes chronicling the sex life of a wealthy family in Connecticut and offering incest as well as more conventional sex in a sort of sexvid soap opera.

Talk Dirty to Me. 1983, Caballero.
According to *Screw* magazine, the best porno film ever made. The film tells the story of a successful cocksman and his buddy, who is so shy he can hardly talk to a woman. No kinky sex or bisexuality and several funny sequences.

Three A.M. 1975, Cal Vista.
A believably acted story that ends in tragedy, about the love triangle of a married couple and the wife's sister. Contains an erotic bisexual scene featuring Georgina Spelvin, one of the most famous porno actresses, plus loving and caring heterosex.

Traci Lords' Fantasies. 1986, Caballero.
One of the last films that Traci Lords made before it was discovered that she began making pornos when she was only 15. To avoid prosecution, the distributors withdrew all of her films made during a three-year period, costing them millions of dollars. During her porno career, Traci Lords earned at least $150,000 a year and her films are collector's items. The story line involves a young woman's introduction into sex and her joy with sexmaking,

lots of it kinky, under the guidance of a smooth Parisian libertine. This one is available because Traci was 18 when it was made.

Virginia. 1983, Caballero.
Warm and romantic cinematography and good dialogue and editing mark this chronicle of a young woman's attraction to her "father" and of her father's romances. The ending is a letdown, however.

Wet Rainbow. 1974, Arrow.
An intimate little story about adultery, with a lesbian sequence involving the wife and the other woman that has made it a sexvid classic. With Harry Reems and Georgina Spelvin, famous porno actors of the 1970s.

Wickerman. 1973, Media.
This R-rated, beautifully photographed and well-acted film is an erotic tour de force about an imaginary pagan island off the coast of modern-day Scotland. The ending leaves viewers gasping at its shocking denial of Christianity, but also keeps them entranced all the way through.

FILM DISTRIBUTORS AND COMPANIES

Femmes Distribution (Film Distributor).
588 Broadway, Suite 1110
New York, NY 10012
This is the address of Candida Royale, a well-known porno star in the late 1970s who went into the production and direction of adult films with her husband, Per Siostedt. Their films are aimed at the women and couples market, with sex that is explicit, but always believable and caring. Titles include *Femmes 1 and 2* and the Star Director Series of films directed by women porno stars. The Star Director Series includes *Rites of Passion*, in which Tantric sex is explored visually; *A Taste of Ambrosia*; and *Sensual Escape*. Write for further information.

Focus International (Film Distributor).
14 Oregon Drive
Huntington Station, NY 11746
Offers many educational videotapes explaining all aspects of human sexuality, including the EDCOA Series of Sexual Counseling. Write for catalog.

Institute for Advanced Study of Human Sexuality (Film Distributor).
1523 Franklin Street
San Francisco, CA 94109
Their catalog offers many videotapes explaining and revealing all aspects of human sexuality.

RM International Films, Inc. (Film Company).
P.O. Box 3748
Hollywood, CA 90078
This is the address of Russ Meyer, who along with David Friedman (once chief factotum of the adult film industry) became very wealthy in the late 1940s and through the 1960s by making and distributing what became known as "tits and ass" (T&A) movies—no male genitals showing and no explicit sex. Russ Meyer movies feature his obsession with "big boobs" and often are sexually violent.
   The early porno business is thoroughly covered in *Sinema* by Kenneth Turan and Stephen F. Zito (New York, Praeger, 1975). Russ Meyer films, which include *Beyond the Valley of the Dolls, Vixen, Up Lorna*, and many others, are sold direct by him. See reviews in the *X-Rated Videotape Guide*.

REFERENCES

Butler, Jerry. 1989. *Raw Talent*. Buffalo, NY: Prometheus Books. (This autobiography of a top porno film star, who has appeared in 400 or more adult films, is the only book available that gives a detailed inside look at the adult film industry. It was co-written with Robert H. Rimmer and Catherine Tavel. Available in an attractive hardcover edition with nonsexual photos.)

Rimmer, Robert H. 1986. *The X-Rated Videotape Guide*. Revised and updated edition. New York: Crown/Harmony. (A 4th and 5th edition have been published in 1988 and 1990 by Sundance Associates, P.O. Box 18709, Los Angeles, CA 90007. Together, these three editions review 3,000 X-rated films produced between 1970 and 1990.)

CHAPTER 17

For Sex, See Librarian: Reprise

Timothy Perper

So, when all is said and done, what lessons have we learned from these sometimes meticulous, sometimes impassioned, and sometimes librarianly essays on libraries, erotica, and pornography? As a non-librarian, but as a sex researcher for many years and former Book Review Editor and Associate Editor of *The Journal of Sex Research*, I am struck by several interrelated issues. Furthermore, when—as Martha Cornog's husband—I watched this book take form, I was also struck by how diversity in opinion and viewpoint steadily converged towards the themes of *censorship* and of the obvious *concern* felt about it by so many librarians. They range from the contributors to this book to other librarians who, like Louis Feipel back in 1922, have written feelingly about the *troubles* occasioned by books on sexuality. Let us consider in depth these themes—censorship, concern, and trouble—if only to provide one individual's opinions about the issues this book raises.

But I must confess my biases openly. I believe in books, their preservation, and the hope they embody. So by definition, I defend diversity in writing and publishing, not uniformity or unanimity. Furthermore, I defend diversity in reading or, if you prefer, the right to read.

I also believe in education. Not lodged solely in the perusal of books, education nonetheless requires books. Perhaps in ancient times, verbal transmission of knowledge and wisdom sufficed, but no longer. However, with that thought, one reaches the first of many issues evoked by the essays in this book. It concerns education and the right to read, but it also concerns an American feeling—*distrust* might be a better word—about mere "book larnin.'"

MALE AND FEMALE: GENDER, SEX, AND LEARNING

For the "practical man"—an individual as rare as the man of *moyen sensibilité*, but who still provides a cultural archetype around which swirl a complex set of beliefs about practicality, commonsense, and hard work—book-larnin' is an inferior sort of learning compared to knowledge attained through experience with the world. "One learns by doing, not by reading," runs the slogan, applied to everything from carpentry to salesmanship. It is the educational ethic of the "self-made man," who, in the old days, never went to college (and proud of it, too!) or who, today, can hardly wait to finish college in order to "go out and make money" and who treats a college degree as only a piece of paper necessary for success in business. For such men, book-larnin' has something feminine in it, to be eschewed and avoided.

The corollary in fact, as well as in American myth, was that books and book-larnin' were domains of women, either as teachers or as librarians. In traditional America, with its sharp role distinctions, elementary school education and librarianship were the two primary fields in which a woman could openly seek intellectual development and education. When Lee Alexander Stone, the physician and humanist quoted in Chapter 1, wrote his 1922 letter to Dorothy on her twelfth birthday, he said:

> Read good books, and think deeply over what you read. You will find that when all have failed to please you and your soul is tired and hungry for sympathy that joy may be found between the covers of a well-written book. . . . Vow to be more than a parlor ornament. (Stone 1922, viii)

It was radical advice, not so much in recommending books as solace for the soul (it sounds as if he himself found such solace in books!), but in his telling Dorothy that she should *think deeply*. In Dorothy's day, a superficial knowledge of books was treated as ornamental in women, for her society deeply felt that women should be mothers and housewives for whom books were not needed. So ever since Mary Wollstonecraft's (1792/1967) *A Vindication of the Rights of Woman*, education for women has been a central goal of feminism.

However, much in the debate about women's education, learning, and social role reminds one of the battle of the sexes. If the librarians who tended the books—and literacy itself—in a new America were women, we must recall that part of the ideal of women's association with book-larnin' was that the practical, rough-hewn brawny men of America needed something to *refine* them—and *that* could be provided only by a leavening of reading. This point is charmingly but tellingly made in Christopher Morley's *Parnassus on Wheels* (1917/1983) and *The Haunted Bookshop* (1919/1983), with its slightly nutty itinerant book pedlar Roger Mifflin, the rebellious Helen McGill, who takes over Mifflin's traveling book van, and Miss Titania Chapman, who is transformed from a silly, flighty rich-girl-gone-slumming to a serious person simply because she starts to read. Yet, by contrast, one is reminded of L. Frank Baum's immensely popular Oz books, written before World War I and continued after Baum by Ruth Plumly Thompson and others up to the World War II period. The girls of Oz—Dorothy, Trot, Betsy, and even Ozma—are continuously planning parties and outings, never immersing themselves in a "well-written book." And in Baum's image of the ideal college, Professor Wogglebug's institute, one merely swallows a pill to learn all there is to know about a topic, so as not to take time out from collegiate sports. Satire? Yes, but Baum's Oz captures on a popular culture level the stereotypes and prejudices of his time: education is suspect for all, men and women.

Against this anti-intellectual vision, there emerged a practical, if not ideal solution for women who refused the role of party-giving parlor ornament: to obtain an education for elementary school teaching or for librarianship. From this anchor point they could nurture a faith that books and the education they contain are not only a positive good, but also a necessary bulwark against brawling violence—and rough, open sexuality.

And there was no question, in the educated tradition that was emerging with the late 19th and early 20th century librarians and school teachers, that sexuality was *not* a topic one brought into the home. In part, the anti-sexuality of early 20th century America was reactive, and an effort was made to suppress a prior tradition of redlight districting, tenderloin development, gambling, drinking, and "general vice." Furthermore, the tenderloin and its sexuality belonged to uneducated *men*, self-made perhaps, but for whom sexuality was as common as the nearest whore.[1]

Thus, in a very real sense, libraries are *already* about sex. Librarianship, both as a body of knowledge and as a profession with roots in early 20th century America, has been centrally concerned with preventing sexually explicit materials—"smut," as they used to say—from spreading too far. Its entry into the library had become a *symbol* of social degradation that could spread from "out there" to we ourselves, and could have destroyed what we wanted for our own futures. Sexuality thus represented chaos, disorder, and violence for those who sought to elevate themselves from the gutter. As a symbol, then, sexuality indeed had no place in the library.

Even today, there remains a strong sense that sex endangers the library in a deeper sense of undermining its ethos and its very purpose. (See the replies Cornog obtained when asking libraries about their *Playboy* subscriptions, Chapter 10.) The issue begins by asking, "What will those crude men, brutes that they are, do with such materials?" and ends by concluding that the only solution is to eliminate *Playboy*, or at least hide it away (in microform, for example). As a nonlibrarian, I would have thought it more reasonable to solve the problem by eliminating the particular men who destroy library property, but my "solution" misses the point: sexuality materials in the library attract the "wrong sort" of person, against whom traditions of American education were once in virtually life-and-death struggle. And *this* problem is not merely "practical," if by that, one means subject to straightforward technical solutions like calling the security guard. Instead, the problem is of symbol and meaning: it is a question of *place*. Does sex, with its appeal to the prurient interests of crude men, have a place in the library, that Elm Street house of culture (Molz 1966–1967, 103)? The answer has been absolute, at least for many librarians: "No."

Furthermore, this ethos is clearly gendered, in the sense that it is identifiably a counter to male sexuality. If, contrary to facts and myths, American libraries were typically masculine institutions, one can easily imagine the (male) librarian saying to the man mentioned in Chapter 10 who used *Playboy* as a masturbation aid, "Hey, jerkoff, get your own copy for that. This here is *library* property!" This voice of male authority says that masturbating to the library's copy of *Playboy* is wrong because the magazine is ruined for others, not that masturbation itself is wrong. We all do that, runs the underlying thought, but not with someone else's property.

Likewise, if we imagine for argument's sake that the public would rise up to a man and a woman if they found that libraries stocked sexually prurient materials (later, I argue that the American public would do no such thing), their target would be material that aroused men, not women. No one in the library community or elsewhere seems to care one whit that the romances, gothics, and Harlequins, with their ever-so-suggestive heaving bosoms and half-draped women on the covers, might stimulate sexual, romantic, and erotic fantasies and actions in women. It is *male* sexuality that is deemed unpleasantly crucial in the debate, even if this view of maleness completely misunderstands male sexual arousal.

But is this image of male sexuality, as violent, brutal, and socially dangerous, sufficiently true-to-fact to warrant *retaining* the library's traditional anti-sexuality stance? On one hand, the view that male sexuality is dangerous, while female sexuality is harmless, is grounded in a combination of 19th century feminine virtue triumphant, a patriarchal view of the passionlessness of women,[2] and in simple fear and dislike of heterosexual intimacy. Again, we are in the domain of symbols and meanings, not observationally verifiable facts, when one asserts that the gothic novel is harmless, although it depicts a woman's barely draped bosom, whereas a similar bosom photographed by a "man's magazine" is harmful. If, again, for argument's sake, one assumes that visual depictions of women's bosoms cause untrammeled sexual impulses in men (later, I argue that they do not arouse men sexually but merely focus sexual arousal on a convenient image), then we must conclude that if *Playboy* has to go, then so do the gothics.

Fundamentally, then, the debate about the propriety and dangers of sexuality in the library center not on the facts of sexual arousal, but on how those facts have been given *meaning* by librarianship itself and by the larger culture external to the library. In one component of those multifaceted traditions and cultures, it is a truth universally acknowledged that male sexuality is dangerous and polluting, whereas female sexuality is harmless and essentially innocent (or childlike, if one prefers that word for this cultural viewpoint). Accordingly and paradoxically, the debate about sexuality in the library revolves around two seemingly contradictory assertions: the library is *not* "about" sex, because sex has no place in the library; and yet the library *is* profoundly "about" sex, because by eliminating it the library and librarians prove themselves the pure guardians of High Culture. Either way, sex is not trivial to librarianship.

But They Won't Like It

If librarians are exercised about sex, so too is the public. For aside from whatever agendas various public groups may have, librarians have ideas and visions of how the "public" will respond to knowing that the library has sex books. These two components of public reaction—one actually held by various public groups and the other thought to be held by the public by librarians—are not necessarily the same. Nonetheless, they converge towards the same point: in the librarian's mind, "they" won't like it, and they *will* do something about it.

Yet one can wonder if the no longer monolithic "public" cares very much about library holdings in a world that has been saturated with sexual discourse at every turn. To be sure, particular individuals and groups object to sexually explicit materials, but one senses that sometimes librarians' rhetoric about public outcry over sex is overdone. It is not clear that the public at large cares very much about the traditions and ethos of librarianship, or even knows enough about them to recognize how controversial it is for a library to possess, say, *The Complete Book of Erotic Art* (see below). The typical librarygoer is more likely to say, "Hey, look at that! Neat. I didn't know that library had that," than to say, "Oh, dear, what a violation of library traditions for them to have bought this book." Nor do the would-be individual censors know or care much about the traditions of librarianship when they come up to the reference desk and demand angrily that "that piece of smut be removed from the library forthwith." The would-be censors are acting within their own ethical/moral traditions, which do not necessarily correspond to those within librarianship. Indeed, when library patrons demand that a book be removed because of its sexual content, they assume that the library does *not* share their vision of a morally perfect world. Indeed, that is why they are complaining.

So it is unclear to what extent librarians' references to public objections about sex materials are a projection of *library* traditions onto a largely indifferent and ignorant public (perhaps in the optimistic hope that the public *does* care, at least about *something* the library does), or an overgeneralization of the motives of those patrons who do demand a book be removed, or even the librarian's personal identification with an imagined public that shares the librarian's tastes. It is doubtful indeed if the public at large would rise up in outrage and outcry against a library that subscribes to *Playboy*, or *Hustler*, or *Gay Community News*. A few irate and perhaps politically powerful citizens might band together to call themselves "United Citizens for Decency in the Library," and thereby claim universal public support, but what faction today, of *any* sort, can claim to have "universal" public support?

Thus, whether or not "they" don't like it, the issue of sexuality materials in the library remains largely a problem within librarianship. It cannot be solved by shifting the ground to an allegedly universal or even widespread *public* sense of what libraries should and should not acquire. (Even if—contrary to observable reality—the public did universally object to sexually explicit materials, a library still might have the librarianly responsibility to stock and make accessible works on sex.)

However, the insistence with which the question of public reaction is raised, and the speed and thoroughness of librarians' reactions to such threats suggests that a private wish is hidden behind the expressed fear of public reaction. Perhaps some librarians wish that the public would put a stop to this naughtiness, either by preventing librarians from buying books about sex or by forcing them to keep such books under lock and key. Still, against that possibility, one can oppose another. May it not be time for libraries to *be* a bit naughty? By doing so, all of us—librarians, educators, people of good will—can bring some morality and respect into the field of sexuality. By giving sexuality a place of honor in a library, sexuality is no longer beset by horrors of imagination, myth, and fear, but becomes subject to conscious, thoughtful, and serious consideration, just like any other part of human life and experience.

Ultimately, to me, a nonlibrarian, that is the hope offered by including sexuality materials in the library. It becomes a subject about which we can educate ourselves and others, and about which we can learn to be civilized and decent, rather than being unruly stupid people who destroy books and ruin them for others, say, by masturbating with the library's copy of *Playboy*. It is not an overnight solution, nor does it promise instant remediation, but it is preferable to censorship and ignorance. Of course, I have colleagues who would say that I espouse the view that *education redeems sexuality*, but that critique would miss a point. Sexuality is a natural function and needs no redeeming. But sexual *habits* may well require redeeming, and sexual ignorance assuredly requires not merely redeeming, but remedial action. Not street-level action, but action that alters the myths and realities of sexual crudity by replacing them with socially institutionalized and socially recognized forms of learning.

In that educational effort, libraries can potentially play an enormous role by replacing ignorance with information; contempt for sex with respect for the immense thought and feeling that has entered the books written about sex; hatred for sexual variation with tolerance for human differences and needs; fear with understanding and the caution that knowledge brings; anxiety with calm reassurance. In this, the Library is more than a mere repository of books and more than the Middletown Book Disbursement Center of a previous chapter. Within it can lodge a sense of respect for books and education, including the books that show how human sexuality works. Once sexuality is included between the covers of a book, it becomes something exterior to the bedroom and the privacy of fantasy, normal or pathological. It becomes a culturally legitimated subject, because now it is a topic heading in the catalog. The Library speaks now to say, "Here, be calm. Read and think deeply about what you have read."

AND YET . . . A MEDLEY OF OBJECTIONS

Yet these ideas seem vaguely utopian. They are not thereby made incompatible with the ideals of librarianship, but still they seem to lack the hard edge of reality. Am I in fact suggesting that if libraries expanded their sexuality collections rape would thereby stop? That smut would become prettier if kept on a library shelf? That teenage pregnancies would dwindle? That abortion would cease being a complex and difficult topic? That if the Elm Street Library bought the Kinsey reports or the work of sexual utopian Wilheim Reich, men and women would join hands in a loving peaceable kingdom of goodwill and respect?

Hardly. One cannot expect mere availability of books to work social miracles. But one *can* expect them slowly to erode ignorance and replace hate and fear. And assuredly, if the books on sexuality continue to be sequestered, then far worse social evils can arise, for example, the unprincipled power of censorship run mad. Start with sex, move to politics and religion: a formula for total social oppression. The Nazis made a special point of burning Magnus Hirschfeld's library when the Nazi street gangs broke into his Institute for Sexology in 1933 (Haeberle 1982). And so it is well worthwhile to examine the counter arguments, explicit and implicit, that can and have been made against the open policies I am urging for sexuality materials.

Likewise, it is worthwhile to make a few concrete suggestions for how ideals for library policies might be enacted if there is sufficient will to do so. If the 1980s and 1990s are the Media Decades (as opposed to the Me Decade of the 1970s), then I feel that libraries can make far more use of the media than they perhaps have. For example, consider a nationwide, regional, state, or local library effort one might call the "PUZZLED ABOUT AIDS? VISIT YOUR LOCAL LIBRARY!" campaign, which one envisions as an exhibit, or series of exhibits, showing books, pamphlets, reprints, and other material, psychological, social, and medical, about AIDS and its prevention, as well as a series of library-sponsored talks. Here assuredly is an opportunity for librarians to make the media and the public aware that "WE CARE ENOUGH TO INFORM YOU," to invent a slogan. It is certainly news that a town library—known for cookbooks, works on gardening, and the long-dead classics—would so actively seek to inform the public about a "controversial" topic. One can hear the press conference now:

> *Reporter:* What made you in the library decide to overcome taboos about this topic?

> *Library Spokesperson:* We feel that libraries are very well equipped to bring information to the public. After all, isn't that what libraries are for? They have books, don't they?

Good publicity for the local, regional, and state libraries and library systems, especially when one recalls that if controversy breaks loose ("Local Pastor Demands Library Stop AIDS Education Campaign," reads a possible headline), then all the better: it brings *more* people to the library, not less.

Such possibilities generalize. "PUZZLED ABOUT ABORTION? VISIT YOUR LOCAL LIBRARY!" Puzzled about pregnancy? About homosexuality? Do you want to know what is "normal," and what to do about it? Visit your local library. And what about pornography? Not hard, provided there is will enough within the library community at large to put together a traveling erotica exhibit that could, once again, be the focal point for a series of public lectures and discussions about aspects of the pornography and erotica debate. One would have no trouble accumulating the print material for such an exhibit, even if insurance and security arrangements might be complex and expensive. Still, one can imagine a display case containing a few "Tijuana bibles," those eight-page, badly printed pieces of anonymous erotica, and a title "Remember These? Erotica in the Old Days." Again, one can imagine the conversation:

> *Woman: Popeye?* Doing that? (Turns to her husband.) Have *you* seen these before?

> *Man:* Ah, no, I mean . . . no, actually, that was before my time.

> *Woman:* Miserable drawing. You mean they turned people *on?*

> *Man:* I guess so. I don't know. Ah, maybe. Um.

One can never be too sure of how people will react—and, in this case, it will probably be with a combination of amazement at the genuinely silly drawing and situations, and thoughtful consideration of what *modern* erotica might—or should—be like.

To be sure, there are legal issues, and assuredly a serious question about individuals under 18 attending such an exhibit. But if the material represents the range of genuine American erotica, one can be sure that the American adult public will generally react with good will and amused interest. After all, didn't the American public help *create* this stuff? So why should they object?

And, with that question, the sound of low grumbling can be heard. Soon it rises to a dull roar, or at least *some* would say it is that loud. These are the voices of objection and doubt mentioned briefly above, and to which we must now turn in careful attention.

Repairing Society?

An assumption underlies the idea that libraries ought to purchase sexuality materials and make them available to a wide public. It is that one purpose of the Library is educational, and that real libraries, to the extent they strive for and embody the ideal of (capital letter) Library, should try to fill in where the schools have failed, where parents have denied or dismissed sex, or where the usual media vehicles have presented incomplete and misleading information. But one can challenge this assumption and, with the challenge, reach other ideologies for how real libraries ought to treat sexuality-related materials.

One viewpoint—that of the "practical man," perhaps—is that libraries have better things to do than repair the failures of *other* portions of American society. "Yes," runs this viewpoint, "we help out the schools and the parents who send their children to us, and we help out adults who might visit the library seeking information about any matter we do deal with. However, fundamentally libraries are not equipped—by the training of their personnel or by their professional standards—to become educators in sexuality. That is the business of teachers who receive special training, often at the graduate level, to learn how and what to teach. It is also the business of school boards, comprised of teachers and parents working together, which set the standards of the curriculum and determine what the children in our community should learn. Finally, it is the business of physicians and of the medical community to determine what information should be placed before the public, and not the library's concern."

One problem with this viewpoint—obviously I disagree with it—is that it defines the library's purposes in negatives, as what it is *not*. When taken in the context of sexuality, such a viewpoint boils down to a less high-sounding paraphrase: "We do not want to teach sexuality and are delighted that it isn't our problem." Any library adopting such a viewpoint joins other sources of trouble and difficulty in American society as hindering, not promoting, learning and truth about *all* subjects, as well as arenas of emotional and social difficulty, such as sexuality.

Nor is this objection in the least tied to problems with a perhaps fanciful description of how libraries might put together educational campaigns about AIDS or even a display of erotica. Although these objections might arise in the context of a specific proposal, they reach far beyond specifics to the idea that libraries are merely warehouses, rather like the Middletown Book Disbursement Center, instead of being organized and carefully designed *collections*. "Take it or leave it," growls this practical man, "it ain't my problem." No matter how common such an attitude may be in America, it is certainly not the basis for librarianship. Truth inheres in more than merely having boxes of books, because truth is an active, not passive, concept: if one wants knowledge to spread, one does not hide it away.

Morality

Yet, the moment one writes the word *truth*, one encounters another, perhaps deeper objection to the "sex-educational" function I described above. Once again, the objection transcends the specifics of any given proposal about how libraries might achieve such goals, and seeks to lodge the ideals of librarianship in a specific moral view of sexuality. Like the voice of the "practical man," this voice too sounds high-principled: "Ah," it says, "you hit the nail on the head when you say 'truth.' Indeed, the truth about sexuality is not in the ugliness of pornography, old and new, nor in the filth of degraded, stupid words long deemed unprintable, not in the near-criminal exploitation of sexuality for the purposes of transient lust and virtually masturbatory pleasure, but in the truths of Love, and Family, and Responsibility, in brief, in that now-so-easily-laughed-at word, Morality. If by 'education,' you mean teaching our community the truths of loving sexuality, in the context of conjugal bonding between men and women, then Yes, I believe out library should have a section on sexuality. But, if by 'education,' you mean teaching our readers the dirty stuff, the gutter language, the stupidities of meaningless nudity and careless adulteries, then No, I am not in favor of sexuality in the library. There is enough filth in the world without more filth finding a home among the great books."

This viewpoint at least says what a library should be, rather than expressing only *no's* and *won'ts*. But there are some problems. First, this position takes its stand on one morality alone. Most often, that morality is homophobic and heterosexist, and denies the personal validity of any sexual expression except the one it mandates: *My sexual morality is the only way, and if you have another, then you are wrong.* This position brooks no tolerance, no variation, and no discourse on the range of behavior people have enacted with pleasure and satisfaction. It is literally narrow-minded.

Second, if building a library collection on the basis of a single morality is acceptable, then, by that very logic, we in pluralistic America should have *many* different kinds of libraries, each championing one and only one viewpoint and censoring all the rest. For the C-word is the dirty word lingering below the high-sounding, moralizing voice of the "softly anti-sex collection" stance I have just paraphrased: "I, the Librarian, make a moral judgement about what is True and Good, and I damn and censor the rest."

Taste, Good and Otherwise

An on-going attraction to this censoring viewpoint probably troubles at least some librarians about the widespread sexuality of modern literature and the mass media. "That"—and here this librarian points to a magazine, a best-seller, a gothic, a sex manual—"that *is* filth, and even though I'm supposed to tolerate it these days—"

But the low growling has become louder. Someone is eager to interrupt.

"I certainly am," says a new voice. "I am a Literary Critic, and it is my area to discuss such matters. But, before doing so, I must raise a question to you who are writing this." Here, the Literary Critic's voice takes on a cunning tone. "Who, exactly, are these people whom you are paraphrasing? Is it not merely that most famous of devices, The Straw Man, who speaks? Not a cousin to the Scarecrow of Oz, yet The Straw Man too is unreal, and you have introduced him, and his friend, The Straw Woman, only as a trick, a rhetorical sleight of hand whereby you will now proceed to Demolish the Straw People—in brief, present arguments wrong and fallacious on their fact and yet seemingly imbued with truth because objections to them have been shunted off to The Straw People and demolished. But we, taught by the canons of Literary Criticism, know better! We detect your trick!"

Alas, my critical—and cynical—friend. The voices that speak here (only some of whom are librarians) are neither straw men nor women, but are real people, composed into a few voices, to be sure, but which still represent the real diversity of doubts and uncertainties about sexuality and libraries. Nor shall we demolish them, for the objections these voices raise are deep and difficult, not a matter of a few swipes of rhetoric. Instead—

"Do you mind if I continue?" asks the first voice. "Because I have a question for this Literary Critic. It is *your* cadre of folk that have made the problems, what with your defenses in court and in magazines of all this modern junk! Why, you people have called the most outrageous books great writing, from *The Story of O* back to *Jurgen* in the old days! How can *you* speak, when your academic and journalist colleagues support all this stuff?"

"Only some of us do," replies the Literary Critic. "I, for example—"

"So you *agree* with me?" the first voice responds in amazement.

The Literary Critic nods. "My colleagues call me old-fashioned, and stodgy, and some even call me a moralizing old coot. But, my friends, there are Standards, and We Must Uphold Them!"

"Well said," agrees the first voice enthusiastically. "Take me, for example, I'm supposed to tolerate all this filthy junk, but I will not. In fact, I hate it, with its easy-going approach to a topic that was for me—and it still should be this way—deeply painful when I was growing up and is deeply troubling to me morally and emotionally as an adult. The words *penis* and *vagina* and *cunnilingus* are all too easily said these days, and it shouldn't be that way. They are words that physicians should use, not everyday people—"

"I suppose," interrupts the Literary Critic, "that you find words like *cock* and *pussy* objectionable too?"

"I assuredly do. They are vulgar, and not nice words. We should keep for the doctors, psychiatrists, ivory-tower scholars, and professors a carefully locked cabinet of medical and social scientific sexuality works, but, for everyone else, sexuality *should* be a morally difficult and troubling area, not an arena for the casual misuse of medical words nor the language of the gutter."

"I agree," joins in the Literary Critic.

But we must interrupt this enthusiastic brawl. Who says that libraries are supposed to keep only one *kind* of book about sex? Who amongst the essayists in this volume is claiming that if a library purchases selected videotapes about sex, it must therefore rid its collection of works of morality, religion, philosophy, and criticism? The point I am making is that a library sexuality collection should be *balanced*, that it must contain more than a single viewpoint about *anything*. In brief, the library's holdings must be *representative* of what has been written about sexuality, even when individual books offend or anger people who hold to other opinions.

"Huh," grunts the Literary Critic, "we thought you meant getting rid of the great works of morality—"

No, that is not what I am saying, for that, once again, is the C-word. My stance is against censorship, *no matter of what.*

But What About the Barbarians?

"Well," adds a quieter voice, almost timid in comparison to the bumptiousness of the others, "at Centerville Library, we try not to be censors. We even tried keeping an updated collection on sex, but it was no end of trouble. We believe in making books available, but the vandalism was more than we could handle. After all, you can't keep a security guard peering over every carrell, or put magnetic tape into every copy of *Playboy* or even *The New York Times Sunday Magazine*. Why, they even tear out the pages of the Sears catalogue to get the bra ads! Some of them are barbarians. So we decided that since we needed the money for other purchases, we just wouldn't buy more sex materials."

But a question: did your library also get rid of *The New York Times Sunday Magazine* and the Sears catalogue when it eliminated *Playboy*?

"No, but . . ."

The oddest problem about this librarianly voice is that it points *selectively* to sexuality materials when it discusses vandalism. I once assigned an article in a research journal to a class, and was bewildered when the students reported that "the library didn't have it." Out of the question, I thought. I know the library receives *Nature*. And so it did, but not the assigned article—because someone had neatly sliced it out of the bound volume. Whereupon, I promised the librarians to notify them in advance about such assignments, so they could put the needed material on reserve.

This essay is not the place for advice on how to protect sexuality collections (see Chapter 11). Instead, my point is that vandalism is not restricted to sexuality materials, and that any security protocols developed for protecting the general collection can be enhanced when it comes to sexuality books. But even so, there are deeper issues raised when someone from the library community speaks about vandalism. These issues appear to concern technical aspects of security protocols and the like, but upon analysis they become matters of politics, power, and ultimately censorship.

I can illustrate how a discussion of the "security issue" becomes a discussion and angry debate about politics and power by returning to the idea of a library display case containing sexuality materials. Let us imagine that we suggest such a case as a *security measure*, envisioning it as a flat locked case, containing books and other materials that adults can easily see. Such a technique, I suggest, would serve two purposes at once: library patrons know the books are in the library but that they cannot be stolen, destroyed, or vandalized. Indeed, it might make an excellent additional point to handle part of the sex collection this way, for the display would say "We have and we protect these books."

Now, let us ask if such a solution really settles the library's problem, or if this display case—which certainly protects the books against vandals—does not bring to the surface underlying and far more real problems. If the latter, we can then conclude that discussion of vandalism can sometimes be a disguised way of talking about other issues, which we wish to bring to light. So, we ask the librarian: Does that solve the problem?

"No," says the librarian, "I really don't think so. Wouldn't the display case be a red flag for the censors? I'm pretty sure they would come down hard on us or Library Board, if *we* put out such a display!"

But, one can argue, that depends on what is put on display. If one recalls the word *balance*, there seems to be a solution, although, once more, the solution only serves to reveal that something else is going on in this debate about security. Imagine, for example, that this display case contains the library's precious illustrated copy of the *Kama Sutra*, a 1950's "nudie" magazine, a few titles of the "Sex Slaves of the Astro-Mutants" variety, the Kronhausen's *Complete Book of Erotic Art* (1978) or perhaps Michael Grant and Antonia Mulas' 1982 *Eros in Pompeii, plus* several selected books expressing anti-pornography positions, such as Susan Griffin's radical feminist *Pornography and Silence: Culture's Revenge Against Nature* (1981) and editor Tom Minnery's 1986 *Pornography: A Human Tragedy*, published by *Christianity Today*. The impression created by such a display is *not* that the library favors one position over another, but that the library contains a variety of works expressing a variety of opinions on an important and controversial topic. No local censor could then attack the library for putting sex into that cabinet, and the issue would be defused, at least partly.

But, I suggest, only partly. It would become *strongly* controversial within the library itself as to what goes into the display case. One side would argue loudly that the "display gives the wrong impression" if it contains that 1950's nudie magazine or if it shows erotic art. "That looks as if we *favor* the stuff!" runs the objection. "If you want a display like that, make sure it's against porn!"

Yet that viewpoint would soon be at cross-purposes with itself when it came to choosing which anti-pornography material to include. Should it be the feminist critiques or the Christian ones? Since these usually contradict each other in most other ways, picking one or the other seems to give "the wrong impression" once again. "Why, it would look like the library is against Christianity if we didn't have Minnery's book!" "And it would be anti-woman if it didn't have Griffin!" "Why not both?" "Because we disagree about *why*!"

The practical solution is simple enough. Include a representative sample of all of it, as well as brief typed descriptions of the various combatants' view of what went into the display. Let the public read how the different factions on the library staff and board argued amongst themselves, and make the debate itself public. Let the public know that Pastor A opposed the inclusion of the nudie magazine as well as Griffin's book; let the public know that Feminist B opposed the inclusion of the nudie magazine but objected to Minnery's sexism; let the public know that Historian C agreed with Pastor A *and* with Feminist B but wanted the nudie magazine included anyway. *Let the public know, and then let the public decide.*

In this, the library is still performing its major function, at least insofar as the Intellectual Freedom tradition has it. The different sides are represented, you hear their voices, and now you make up your mind in the traditions of American democracy. However, as the debate escalates, it becomes clearer that each side wants this display case *for its own purposes*, and that none of these purposes is genuinely educational in the Jeffersonian sense of an educated populace making educated decisions. Instead, the issue has become that of *power*, in specific, the power to influence people's thinking by presenting them with only one view, only one position, and only one opinion. That is the essence of censorship, and ultimately its purpose: to attain power for one faction while suppressing the ideas of the rest.

But let us include one additional book: Alan Soble's 1986 *Pornography: Marxism, Feminism, and the Future of Sexuality*, with its Marxist argument that an ideal socialist or communist society would tolerate pornography because that society would be fully egalitarian in all ways, sexuality included. With *that*, the choice has become either to include it all or to suppress it all. The diversity is too great to remain the property of a local battle between local factions; and it is all too clear that if one suppresses one view—Soble's Marxist analysis, say—then the purpose *is* censorship and power, not education, and certainly not education in the sense of Jeffersonian democracy.

Oddly, then, the problem of guarding a library's sexuality collection becomes genuinely politicized, for the question arises of *What is one guarding the collection against?* The usual answer—vandalism and the barbarians—is only the tip of an iceberg, because librarians all too easily speak selectively about the vandalism of sexuality materials. Furthermore, as the device of discussing the sexuality display case shows, the more real, underlying issues are of censorship and power, of presenting only one view and actively suppressing the others. Thus we see the barbarians fading into the distance, to be replaced by very real, very modern political concerns.

Technical solutions to preventing vandalism are simple, if perhaps expensive, and are not fraught with ideological baggage. But another aspect of security soon emerges, of protecting the library itself from becoming the battleground for implacably opposed social forces that will cheerfully use the library as one more theater of war. Against that, no system of anti-theft devices will work, because the issue is *not* the occasional vandal who rips up *Playboy*, slices articles from *Nature*, or steals *Forbes Magazine*. Instead, we are concerned with a different sort of barbarian—those who would suppress diversity in the name of attaining social and political power for their own faction. And it is for that reason that the combatants in the war over the display case would *refuse* to have their correspondence included in the display: "It's none of their business," runs the voice of this new sort of barbarian. "*We* decide, not them out *there!*"

A Generalization

In each of these arguments—indifference, morality, taste, and politics/vandalism—as well as in further arguments to come, the objection to sexuality materials has the same form. The objector makes a statement about sexuality, and concludes that "therefore" the library should not have sexuality materials. Thus, the indifferent "practical man" says that sexuality is the business of educators and physicians (true at least in part); "therefore" the library should not deal with sex. The moralist says that sexuality is morally complex, and that "therefore" the library should not have sexually explicit materials. The conservative aesthetician says that much of sexuality is not pretty, and that "therefore" the library must not have it. Finally, the political debater says that sexuality is controversial and that "therefore" the library must not involve itself except as it supports the debater's own side. Yet, when compared side by side, these arguments make no sense.

In logic, such arguments are called *non sequiturs*, from the Latin "it does not follow." Someone interested in proving a different point could reverse each argument and conclude that the library *should* "therefore" purchase sexuality materials and make them accessible to a broad public. Thus, if educators and physicians deal with sex, as they sometimes do, then "therefore" the library should help out. If sexuality is morally complex, then "therefore" the library should contain as much as possible that clarifies the complexities. If sexuality can have its ugly side, then the library "therefore" should contain discussions of both its ugliness and its beauty. And if sexuality is controversial, then the library "therefore" has a responsibility, in a pluralistic and democratic society, of presenting all sides of the controversy so that the public can decide for itself.

To the undecided listener, the question is which of these "therefores" is correct. Since they reach opposite conclusions, clearly they cannot both simultaneously be true! But which is it? Furthermore, in public or committee debates, the undecided listener goes away convinced that "it's all a matter of definition," or that "all they did was argue about logic." No decisions are reached, and the arguments become sterile.

But they need not do so, and for two reasons. The first is that arguments against sexuality (which are, I feel, the far worse offenders against logic) are nearly always built backwards, from the *presupposition* that sexuality is ugly, bad, or distasteful, to the argument itself that libraries must have nothing to do with it. Yet, if I am opposed to something, I can always argue in this (illogical) way. For example, assume that I am staunchly opposed to gardening, and that I wish to root this quirk in what sounds like good logic. "Gardening," I assert, "wastes one's time better spent in other matters, such as polishing the brass andirons, and therefore the library should not have a collection of gardening books." Obviously, the argument is spurious, if not downright silly. My tastes, decisions about my life, domestic aesthetics, and hierarchy of values about andirons and rosebushes are all simply irrelevant to what a public and social institution, like a library, should do.

The anti-sexuality stance would object, of course. "That's a ridiculous comparison. Sex is so much more important than polishing brass andirons or even gardening!" Perhaps so, but *if* so, then does it not follow that libraries should have at least as much material on sexuality as they do on gardening?

Second, arguments that run "X is true about sex and therefore the library should not have books on sex" provide no integral connection between the predicate—that sex can be morally complex, can be ugly, can be a political problem—and the conclusion. These arguments make as little sense as someone arguing against a gardening collection "because it is more important to polish the andirons." By contrast, however, the argument that libraries should have sexuality collections openly available *does* make an integral connections between its parts. That connection comes from the principles of librarianship itself: the concept that libraries are collections of knowledge about topics of concern. If educators and physicians are concerned about sex, it follows that libraries *should* contain sexuality materials because it is part of the function of libraries to provide information that people want, patients and students included. That is what libraries are for—just as it follows that if the community contains ardent gardeners then the library should have an extensive gardening collection.

But, Really, Libraries Are Just Supermarkets

Yet here too an objection can be raised, which, unlike the previous arguments, does make an integral connection between the purposes of the library and the nature of its holdings. This viewpoint sees the library not in the exalted sense of being a repository of knowledge, but merely as a service institution for a particular local clientele.

"You can talk all you want about ideals," this objection runs, "but in this world, the bottom line is who wants what. Our library's clientele simply isn't interested in sex books, and we feel we exist to provide our main clientele with what they want. So we have cookbooks, gardening books, a collection of romance novels, several shelves of how-to-get-rich-in-real-estate books, plus mail order catalogues and a scattering of the classics like Milton, so we look good to the local English teachers. That's what libraries are *really* for, and you can forget this *ideals of librarianship* stuff."

I doubt if this attitude is often expressed in as hardboiled a fashion, but at least some individuals within librarianship do hold the view that libraries are really supermarkets and that they must maintain collections that meet the profile of use their clientele generates, just as real supermarkets stock high-salt, high-fat, junk food.

But there is a hidden flaw here as well. Have you ever noticed how well sex materials sell in supermarkets, mail order catalogues, and bookstores? Our local convenience store, part of a large chain, has a small collection of over-the-counter medications, locked in a cabinet. On top, unlocked, is a condom display. It is right next to the sandwich counter. Increasingly, mail order firms are offering "intimate lingerie," not as sleaze in the back of "nudie" magazines, but next to housewares, plastic clocks in the form of smiling chipmunks, and electronic doorchimes that play "Bridge Over the River Kwai." Our local video shop has a selection marked "X-rated" adjacent to "Adventure." And our local "fine" bookstores—also chain booksellers—all have sections on *Sex*, typically among the Psychology/Self-Help books.

So one can reply to this marketing-oriented critic: "Don't hardboil *me*. You know full well that sex sells and sells very well. So why don't you have any?"

Once again, an argument that appears to make sense falls apart at the first critical examination. Once again the answer is an embarrassed pause and a retreat to one of the other arguments already discussed, e.g., taste.

And, "Well, no one ever asks for it. They just *don't*."

And no small wonder, either. For many decades, librarians have carefully built the public image of the library as a place that does not deal with sexuality, nor contain sexuality materials. In the library literature, librarians have repeated to each other a dozen or more arguments—all fundamentally flawed, I am saying—why sexuality materials should not be introduced in libraries. The arguments have grown so familiar, I suspect, that they no longer seem illogical, e.g., that because sex is controversial, it should be *excluded* from the library. All these are lessons the public, I suggest, has learned and learned *well*. In plain English, the last place many Americans would look for information about sex is the library. Public image, long nurtured by librarians, and repetitions of the same arguments by librarians to each other, have both interacted to yield the same result. Of course many library patrons don't ask about sex! They know the rules very well!

WHAT SHOULD THE AMERICAN LIBRARY CONTAIN?

It is clear, I hope, that I am arguing strongly that libraries must make the effort to overcome these problems of history and public image. And yet, what ought the library to contain?

Perhaps a major objection to the idea that libraries should contain thorough and balanced sexuality collections is that there are simply too few good books on sex. This argument is more complex than the preceding, if only because it accepts the possibility that libraries should have sex books. But it also raises issues of history, symbol, and quality. Accordingly, this objection cannot be eliminated simply by listing books on sex given high ratings by experts. Although such bibliographies are essential, they alone are not sufficient to explore the nuances of the quantity/quality argument.

It is useful to recall that part of librarianship's emphasis on "good books" arose as a reaction in the late 19th and early 20th centuries against what was then perceived as vice rampant. Earlier, I suggested that one consequence was the emergence of the censoring mentality in librarianship, which suppressed sexuality materials seen as conducive to vice and sexual immorality. But another consequence of this early trend in librarianship was a simultaneous emphasis on *good* books, works that uplifted the reader, as well as educating or entertaining.

Thus it was not merely in the suppression of rough, brawling sexuality that this new wave in morality found its strengths, but also in an ideal that books necessarily must be uplifting. It was one reason why early library architecture is of the grand school: columns, portals, marble floors. Such libraries were not merely collections of books on shelves, but were monuments to a precious belief: that if your town had a library, then assuredly you were a better person—or, perhaps, belonged to a better *class* of persons—than the dirty cattlemen, miners, trappers, and hunters who came first. The library symbolized the emergence of civilization and culture in America, at least in the minds of its early library founders.

Furthermore, this ideal of civilization and culture was practical and optimistic (if not too demanding, lest it frighten off those to whom book-larnin' was suspect as a feminine frill; see above). Accordingly, the characteristics of a "good book" were not merely literary excellence, and particularly not if excellence was judged on European models of *haute culture* à la Baudelaire, Swinburne, or even Kipling. Instead, a genuinely American voice was emerging, in the popularity, for example, of O. Henry and Mark Twain, as sardonic, wry, practical, and with pretensions of gentility. Likewise, in women's writing—and women novelists in the 19th century were far more widely read than male novelists—the novel held out its heroine as a person who vanquished her internal and external adversaries, to emerge a better person (see Nina Baym 1978, for a detailed discussion). In this, writing and reading had a purpose beyond entertainment and beyond leisure, a characteristic still true of American readers in their predeliction for self-help and how-to books. Thus, a cookbook is not merely a collection of recipes; it tells the reader how to be a *better* cook. Though not the only hallmark of American writing, nonetheless it is characteristic of much American writing, and therefore of reading, that it should be educational, useful, practical, down-to-earth, and commonsensical, in brief, "American." ("What good is poetry?" asks the student, thus paraphrasing a genuinely American ethos.)

Sex Books as Good Books

Given these characteristics of the "good book," it is not surprising that American readers and librarians have looked askance at "sex books." If their purpose is pleasure, what "value" do they have? One cannot use them to build bridges, repair stairs, cook meatloaves, or even tinker with the toaster when it refuses to work. Instead, many focus on *internal* experience—like poetry!—and on the body as an entity in its own right. When one hears the phrase "curl up in bed with a good book," one does not complete the idea by adding "and with my lover!"

So it is hardly surprising that when sexuality books *did* begin to appear on the American book scene, from the middle 1960s onwards, they powerfully emphasized practicality. There is an entire subgenre of such books that tell one *how to* have a better sex life and thereby *communicate* with one's partner. "How to" is attached to a purpose ("communication"), thereby justifying the book's existence: one can learn good things from it. Its purpose is *not* pleasure, and indeed many such books explain in endless detail just how difficult it is "to

learn how to communicate with one's partner." Sexologist and writer
Arno Karlen calls such books "owner's manuals," and indeed in some
of these books one expects to see a wiring diagram of the genitalia,
with a boxed-in sidebar entitled "Trouble-shooting." (See Sussman
1965 for a parody of such sex manuals.)

Moreover, such works tend strongly to emphasize the goal of
sexuality as "loving communication." Again, we hear an echo of the
American notion of what a "good book" is—and it must have a Clear
Moral Purpose. One does not enjoy sex so much as *employs* it in the
service of another goal, which—by an ironic and probably unconscious twist—is often called "spontaneous loving communication."

Another subgenre, also hugely popular, is the how-to-find-the-
ideal-mate group. Characteristically written by women for women,
this tradebook subgenre typically includes material on how to make
oneself attractive to the man of one's choice, how to let him know
you are interested, how to keep him interested, how to balance career
and the search for a mate, and so on. Once again, the style is a
how-to practicality adjoined to the moralizing goal of "forming a
committed relationship," a modern euphemism for marriage or something that will become marriage.

Few such books are written for men, but one of the exceptions
illustrates the point quite well. It is Eric Weber's 1970 *How to Pick
Up Girls* (New York: Symphony Press), with its subtitle "Discover
exactly how to meet beautiful women. In bars, buses, trains—even on
the street! The fool proof [sic] guide to meeting women without a
formal introduction." Women angered by being treated as objects by
men will find the subtitle infuriating, but it is important to examine
its prose as much as its sexism. The emphasis is on *how to* do
something, with the guarantee that the method is "fool proof."

Likewise, Joyce Jillson's 1984 *The Fine Art of Flirting* (New
York: Simon & Schuster) has a cover illustration of a woman's hand
dropping a handkerchief next to a handsome young man wearing
formal dress, and says on the cover "The one and only complete
guide—for would-be flirts of *all* sexes. Learn how to Fascinate, Titil-
late, Captivate, and Be Great at Love's Most Amusing Sport." Surely,
that set of claims covers every American base possible, from *how-to*,
to being *complete*, even to *sports*!

So, in no way is this practical, commensensical, "fix-the-damn-
thing-it-doesn't-work" viewpoint restricted to the few books written
by men like Eric Weber. Indeed, one can argue that the how-to
approach has its numerical home in books written by and for women,
concerning "how to" find a husband and "how to" be attractive. In
that, the genre is strikingly and obviously American. No foolishness
about love poetry in this stuff!

By contrast—and one is tempted to say, *And what did you
expect?*—books by real writers can be marvelously written, and can be

equally American in their humor. Helen Brown Norden's 1936 *The Hussy's Handbook* (New York: Farrar & Rinehart) is a collection of sardonic, witty essays, e.g., about "Men: and what to do about them." James Thurber and E.B. White's 1929 *Is Sex Necessary? Or Why You Feel the Way You Do* (New York: Harper & Row, 1975) is one of America's classics, in part because, in Twain-like irony, it satirizes all concerned.

If one expanded this list, the conclusion would only grow stronger. Many American books on sex heavily emphasize one or another feature of the "good book," either as how-tos for achieving a "good purpose," such as marriage or communication, or as satiric, which also achieves a "good purpose," at least as Americans see such things, of preventing us from taking ourselves too seriously. Moreover, in recent years, trade book publishers have gone to great lengths in titling and advertising to make sure the readers *know* that they are examining a "good book": it will teach you things you need to know and it will be hard to learn them. And not far in the background the grandfather of them all beams approvingly: Dale Carnegie's *How to Win Friends and Influence People*, published in 1936.

There then follows a criterion for assessing a book in this genre. If it is published by an established trade book house, if its titling and advertising refers to "how to communicate" or "the problems of communicating," it is guaranteed to be a "good book." Trade book houses will not risk anything else, and will insist that such books follow very closely existing formulas for American nonfiction. The book may also be trivial, derivative, badly written, and generally of no greater significance than any other book in this genre, but it will assuredly be a "good book." In fact, such books could be put right next to the cookbooks and the gardening collection, for that is what they often are: harmless recapitulations of accepted wisdom, repetitive in content and uninteresting in style. In brief, nothing to worry about even if the word *sex* appears in the title.

From Euphemism to "Explicit Enough"

Again, an objection arises. "But such books are not sexually explicit. I'm not even sure why you're talking about them at all, because surely *they* do not cause the problem in libraries. What have they to do with pornography?"

But recall that broadly the topic is *sex*. Trade books on how to find the perfect mate, especially when written by women for women, presume a knowledge of an unspoken but collective lexicon of meanings, in which, for example, the phrase "committed relationship" refers to a *sexual* relationship, and in which the concept of "letting him know you are interested" means sexually interested, and not interested merely in going to the movies with him. These books specialize in sexual euphemism, and they have brought it to a high art. They are *explicitly* works of erotica precisely because they are *implicitly* about sex.

To be sure, these how-to books deal with sex somewhat euphemistically, often in the context of love and marriage. And in that sense, they, like "erotica," deal with the emotions and strategies of sex and love without necessarily including photographs of nude couples in various forms of coital embrace.

Furthermore, one can cavil at the word *explicit*. It sounds clear enough, but how explicit *is* explicit when it comes to characterizing a book, say, as erotica or as pornography? If the cover of a gothic novel shows a woman whose dress is open between her breasts, but one cannot see her nipples, is the depiction "explicit"? Suffice it to say that it is *explicit enough* to discharge its function of communicating the content of the book to the potential reader.

Similarly, the social setting of today's language makes it explicit enough to infer the content of a book called *Smart Women, Foolish Choices*. In a coded and euphemizing language, the title tells you that the book is *not* about women who decide to cook pork chops when their husbands like hamburgers. And if you are uncertain, the subtitle will tell you: *Finding the Right Man/Avoiding the Wrong Ones* (Connell Cowen and Melvyn Kinder, Clarkson Potter, 1985). Thus euphemism has a marketing function of making such books acceptable to a reading public and to librarians as well, where more explicit titling might work the reverse. But we should not be fooled by the marketing soft-sell: these are works about sex. They are not different in kind from the *Joy of Sex* (one of the most famous how-tos of them all) but in degree.

. . . And on to Explicit Sex . . .

Euphemistic titling has another function as well. It divides sexuality into three parts: the euphemistic discourse of books like *Smart Women, Foolish Choices*; material that is vaguely acceptable, if somewhat explicit; and all the rest, which convention and morality sweeps into a little pile and labels "dirt." If, simultaneously, we held a small meter, marked "Social Value and Usefulness (Conventional Scale)," over these piles, it would read in the green—"OK!"—for the euphemistic books; in the yellow—"Doubtful! Be Careful!"—over the second group; and slam-bang in the red—"Yip! Yip! Yip! Danger! Useless! Bad Books!"—over the rest.

So one has no choice but to ask a question. Can one have quality books that are sexually explicit? And, furthermore, what exactly *is* in that third pile, over which the meter is so upset?

... And from Explicit Sex to Quality ...

Most readers, from librarians to the general public, hold to a model of sexuality books that corresponds roughly to what I have just outlined. Sexuality comes in only three forms: euphemism, marginally acceptable material, and dirt. In a sense, librarians historically have been partly responsible for the continuation into the 1980s and 1990s of this tripartite division, because they have not brought works to the public's attention that do *not* fall into any of these categories or, if they do, so puzzle conventional morality and taste that the meter reads "Overload. Check Batteries." These are often *very* high quality books, and yet . . .

Once more there arise voices of objection and doubt, for the word *quality* is itself among the great euphemisms of the field of sexuality and books. Some librarians and readers believe that libraries should contain books about sex and of sex (e.g., sexual fiction) but are puzzled about what is available. That voice says, "We face the realities of limited budgets, anti-prurient library boards and colleagues, and the prudes for whom *anything* with sex in the title is bad. How can we, nonsexologists, judge a book's quality?"

And instantly a second voice breaks in. "Yes," it says, "that is the question, quality! I feel that if the library contains a sex collection, assuredly it must be of high quality!"

Beware of the word "quality," for it can be used to support diametrically opposed opinions. The first comment above says, "We know there's junk out there. How do we tell the dross from the gold?" But the second voice does not *really* want the library to seek out sexuality materials, and has used the loose and slippery notion of "quality" to do an end-run around the pro-sex-collection viewpoint to condemn everything he or she does not like personally or morally, or finds repulsive or frightening. "Well, for me," continues the second voice, "the notion of quality eliminates most pornography, and who knows, really *knows*, about the rest?"

A LIST OF QUALITY WORKS ON SEXUALITY

The following list, and the descriptions that come after, are based on some years as Book Review Editor of *The Journal of Sex Research*. (For discussion of review sources, bibliographies, and selection tools for both nonfiction and fiction works about sexuality, see the Appendix to this chapter.) The first list would probably be considered first-rate by most sexology experts, and can be called a *minimal* or *core* listing of books a library should possess. The nonexpert, especially someone befuddled by media silence on sexuality works (and not assisted by the library's deny and avoid strategies), may find much that is surprising in the core list and in the descriptions following. In 1990, it is rather as if that meter's programming were out of date.

The Boston Women's Health Book Collective. *Our Bodies, Ourselves.* (Rev. ed. Simon & Schuster, 1976).
An epoch-making book, and a darling of the censors. Despite them, this book is essential for its straightforward discussions of health and sex.

Brecher, Edward M. and Consumer Reports Books (eds.). *Love, Sex, and Aging.* (Little, Brown, 1984).
Already a classic; sympathetic and helpful.

Brownmiller, Susan, *Against Our Will: Men, Women, and Rape.* (Bantam/Simon & Schuster, 1975).
Epoch-making in forming the modern, feminist view of rape.

Comfort, Alex (ed.). *The Joy of Sex.* (Crown, 1972).
Many imitators, but few surpass it. First-rate graphics and writing, and very little of the sex-is-a-machine viewpoint.

de Beauvoir, Simone, *The Second Sex.* (Vintage/Random House, 1952).
An all-time classic, deeply thoughtful.

Firestone, Shulamith. *The Dialectic of Sex.* (Bantam/Morrow, 1970).
With Brownmiller and Friedan, one of the classics of feminist thinking about sex.

Freud, Sigmund. *Three Essays on the Theory of Sexuality.* (Basic Books, 1962).
Dates of the essays vary; these are from the Standard Edition of Freud. Dense, difficult; but here we find Freud's basic ideas about sexuality, repression, the superego, and so on.

Friedan, Betty. *The Feminine Mystique.* (Dell/Norton, 1962).
Another landmark of modern feminist thought.

Hite, Shere. *The Hite Report: A Nationwide Study on Female Sexuality.* (Macmillan, 1976). *The Hite Report on Male Sexuality* (Knopf, 1981).
Often criticized by researchers as flawed, the Hite Reports contain material found nowhere else, particularly their direct quotations from Hite's respondents.

Kaplan, Helen Singer. *The New Sex Therapy.* (Brunner, Mazel, 1974).
Together with Masters and Johnson's books, the basis of modern sex therapy. Clinical, thoughtful, and professional, and yet deeply sympathetic.

Kinsey, Alfred C., Wardell B. Pomeroy, and Clyde E. Martin. *Sexual Behavior in the Human Male.* (Saunders, 1948).

Kinsey, Alfred C., Wardell B. Pomeroy, Clyde E. Martin, and Paul H. Gebhard. *Sexual Behavior in the Human Female.* (Saunders, 1953).
This and the preceding are the "Kinsey Reports." They are irreplaceable, and are still the only works many people think of when they talk of sex research or about "serious" works in sexuality.

Luker, Kristin. *Abortion and the Politics of Motherhood.* (University of California Press, 1984).
Indispensable.

Marcus, Steven. *The Other Victorians.* (New American Library/Basic Books, 1964).
Despite its seeming focus on a bygone era, *The Other Victorians* remains one of the major works in the study of pornography and pornographers. In it, Marcus coined the term "pornotopia."

Marcuse, Herbert. *Eros and Civilization.* (Beacon, 1955).
Contains some of the theoretical underpinning for the sexual revolution of the 1960s and later.

Masters, William H. and Virginia E. Johnson. *Human Sexual Response.* (Little, Brown, 1966). *Human Sexual Inadequacy.* (Little, Brown, 1970).
When people ask "Do you have Masters and Johnson," these are the books they mean. Indispensable.

McWhirter, David P. and Andrew P. Mattison. *The Male Couple.* (Prentice-Hall, 1984).
The psychiatrist/psychologist author team present a developmental model of how gay men enter and build relationships. Well received in the field; sympathetic and thoughtful.

Mead, Margaret. *Male and Female.* (Morrow, 1949).
The great anthropologist's most complete theoretical work on sexuality. Her *Coming of Age in Samoa* (Morrow, 1928) and *Sex and Temperament in Three Primitive Societies* (Morrow, 1963) are perhaps better known. A library should possess all three.

Reich, Wilhelm. *The Sexual Revolution.* (Noonday Press/Farrar, Straus, & Cudahy, 1945).
In the years since his death, Reich has gained a fair following. This book summarizes his thinking quite well.

Russell, Lord Bertrand. *Marriage and Morals.* (Horace Liveright, 1929; many editions since then).
Russell's still provocative analysis of the failures of marriage as an institution, and his philosophical suggestions for its improvement. A classic.

U.S. Department of Justice. *Attorney General's Commission on Pornography Final Report, Volumes 1 and 2.* (United States Government Printing Office, 1986).
The "Meese Report" on pornography. Indispensable.

Vatsyayana. *Kama Sutra.*
The edition entitled *Kama Sutra of Vatsyayana,* translated from the original Sanskrit by S.C. Upadhyaya, and published by Taraporevala's Treasure House of Books, Bombay, India (1961; Reprinted 1963) is beautifully printed and illustrated. If a library is fortunate enough to possess this edition, it should be kept safe and a second copy provided to readers and browsers. The illustrations include photographs (half-tones) and line drawings taken from classic Indian erotic art, including the temple at Khajuraho.

Three other highly productive and respected authors must be mentioned in a core listing, although their work is not as well known to the general public, and to librarians, as it should be. These are Vern Bullough, Robert T. Francoeur, and John Money.

Bullough, Vern. *Sexual Variance in Society and History.* (University of Chicago Press, 1976).

Bullough, Vern and James Brundage. *Sexual Practices in the Medieval Church.* (Prometheus, 1982).

Bullough, Vern and Bonnie Bullough. *Women and Prostitution.* (Prometheus, 1987).
Readers of this volume will recognize Bullough as the author of Chapter 6, "Research and Archival Value of Erotica/Pornography."

Francoeur, Robert T. *Utopian Motherhood: New Trends in Human Reproduction.* (Doubleday, 1970).

Francoeur, Robert T. *Eve's New Rib: Twenty Faces of Sex, Marriage, and Family.* (Harcourt Brace Jovanovich, 1972).

Francoeur, Anna K. and Robert T. Francoeur. *Hot & Cool Sex: Cultures in Conflict.* (Harcourt Brace Jovanovich, 1974).
   Utopian Motherhood is an important effort to bridge the ethical gap between Aldous Huxley's inhuman images of test-tube babies in *Brave New World* and the newly emerging techniques for artificial insemination and the like. *Eve's New Rib* and *Hot & Cool Sex* are likewise ethical and moral explorations of the new sexual and emotional responsibilities and pleasures associated with changes in American family and sexual lifestyles. The issues these books raise are still very much alive in 1990. Francoeur is also editor of *Taking Sides: Clashing Views on Controversial Issues in Human Sexuality, 2nd Edition* (Dushkin, 1989), a collection of popular articles on crucial issues. It is highly recommended for its balance of viewpoints.

Money, John and Anke A. Ehrhardt. *Man & Woman, Boy & Girl: The Differentiation and Dimorphism of Gender Identity from Conception to Maturity.* (Johns Hopkins University, 1972).

Money, John. *The Destroying Angel: Sex, Fitness & Food in the Legacy of Degeneracy Theory, Graham Crackers, Kellogg's Corn Flakes & American Health History.* (Prometheus, 1985).

Money, John. *Lovemaps: Clinical Concepts of Sexual/Erotic Health and Pathology, Paraphilia, and Gender Transposition in Childhood, Adolescence, and Maturity.* (Irvington, 1986).
   Money's characteristically long subtitles serve as content summaries. *Man & Woman, Boy & Girl* is no longer up-to-date in its biological detail, but no better source can be found for modern sexological ideas about gender and sexual differentiation. *The Destroying Angel* is a biohistorical analysis of American sexual fads and fancies, including the development of "healthy food," such as Kellogg's Corn Flakes, as anti-aphrodisiacs. It is a must for an Americana collection. *Lovemaps* provides an invaluable update on *Man & Woman, Boy & Girl,* as well as discussing Money's concept of a lifelong pattern of sexuoerotic turn-on, the *lovemap.* Money's books are written for the lay reader, and will be understandable to most library-goers.

Supporting Works

Readers familiar with the extraordinary range and variation in books on sexuality will quickly point out that this list omits many excellent and important works and authors. Others, believing that "sex books" fall into three neat piles, will perhaps be surprised how extensively and seriously sexuality has been treated, in both nonfiction and fiction, since the days the "morality meter" was programmed. Accordingly, it is worthwhile to include some further comments on a selected list of additional books.

One topic notably absent from the core list is lesbianism. *The Lesbian Issue: Essays from Signs* (Estelle B. Freedman, Barbara C. Gelpi, Susan L. Johnson, and Kathleen Weston, University of Chicago, 1985) contains essays from the scholarly journal *Signs: Journal of Women and Culture in Society* and can be used as a valuable source for materials. Likewise, *The Women's Review of Books,* published at the Wellesley College Center for Research on Women, Wellesley, MA, contains long and thoughtful reviews of works about women's sexuality, including lesbianism. Although a subscription to

Signs might be more relevant to an academic library, a wider reading public will probably find *The Women's Review of Books* interesting and significant.

A book that achieved some fame and notoriety among lesbian writers and critics is the strikingly-titled *Lesbian Nuns: Breaking Silence* (Rosemary Curb and Nancy Manahan, eds., Naiad Press, 1985). Since the work attracted some media attention, library patrons may ask about it. It is a deeply moving and troubling account of lesbian women in the Catholic Church, and is guaranteed to stir up many emotions among readers—and among anti-sex critics of a library's sex holdings.

Male homosexuality too has been the subject of much writing. The scholarly *Journal of Homosexuality* (Haworth) covers both male and female homosexuality, although perhaps fewer lesbian authors contribute than do gay researchers. Physician Richard Green's 1987 *The "Sissy Boy Syndrome" and the Development of Homosexuality* (Yale University Press) describes a longitudinal study of boys whose behavior labelled them as "sissies" (e.g., a desire to wear girl's clothing, and repudiation of the rougher boy's sports), and discusses how such behavior predicts adult homosexual orientation. *Homosexualities: A Study of Diversity Among Men and Women*, by Alan P. Bell and Martin S. Weinberg (1978; Simon & Schuster) is a controversial, but fascinating, study of a sample of homosexual men and women, that covers lifestyle, sexual experience, social adjustment and the like. It was a landmark study. An excellent, if quirkily arranged, bibliography compiled by Wayne R. Dynes (*Homosexuality: A Research Guide* 1987; Garland) contains in over 850 pages a series of annotations about books, magazines, periodicals and other material from the United States and elsewhere. Much of the material it describes would interest the general reader.

Additional areas of interest include the history of sexuality, e.g., the work of Bullough, Francoeur, and Money, already mentioned. However, a number of popularly written histories also exist, such as Morton Hunt's *The Natural History of Love* (Knopf, 1959), Reay Tannahill's delightfully chatty *Sex in History* (Stein & Day, 1980), and Wayland Young's serious, thoughtful, and provocative *Eros Denied: Sex in Western Society* (Grove Press, 1964).

Library patrons with interests in religion also have a variety of works to select from, including Michael V. Fox's very scholarly, yet fascinating *The Song of Songs and the Ancient Egyptian Love Songs* (University of Wisconsin Press, 1985). Fox derives the Biblical Song of Songs from sources in Egypt, all moving in their poetry and feeling. Rachel Biale's *Women and Jewish Law: An Exploration of Women's Issues in Halakhic Sources* (Schocken, 1984) will also interest some readers. Richard Ginder's impassioned book on Roman Catholic anti-sexuality, *Binding with Briars: Sex and Sin in the Cath-*

olic Church (Prentice-Hall, 1975), presents a viewpoint that cannot be denied an audience, even if the reader disagrees with it. Finally, there is Leo Steinberg's sensitive and fascinating discussion of depictions of *The Sexuality of Christ in Renaissance Art and in Modern Oblivion* (Random House, 1983). Handsomely illustrated, though only in half-tones, Steinberg's book documents beyond doubt that in Renaissance times Christ was thought to have a sexual personhood. The illustrations will surprise people who feel that everyone always treated Christ as *anti*-sexual.

In popular culture, surely a crucial purchase is by Gershon Legman, whose essay in Chapter 2 graces this volume. *Rationale of the Dirty Joke, Volumes 1 and 2* (Volume 1: Grove Press, 1968; Volume 2: *No Laughing Matter*, Breaking Point, 1975) is powerfully written and even dauntingly intellectual, because for Legman, there is nothing funny in the dirty joke. Yet why do we laugh—or cringe? The casual reader may be interested only in the jokes themselves; however, a straying eye looking for more "good stuff" will encounter the text and its relentless effort to understand—truly to *understand*—why such jokes sometimes amuse, often offend, and usually touch unconscious and subconscious urges the conscious mind might wish to deny. A major work by the foremost scholar in the field—and an opinionated, fascinating stylist as well.

Perhaps the finest treatment of sexuality in the modern film is *Dark Romance: Sexuality in the Horror Film* (David J. Hogan, McFarland, 1986). Hogan's thesis, well-presented and convincing, is that the horror film, particularly the slasher flick, carries powerful *anti*-sexual messages lodged in a visual milieu of violence and fear. Richard Wortley's *Erotic Movies* (Crescent/Crown, 1975) contains many color and half-tone stills from the history of erotic film, and is lightened by a faintly sardonic style. Because they are illustrated, both must be protected against vandals, whether those who destroy sexually explicit materials for their own sexual uses or who loathe sexuality and want to destroy it forever and for all.

That possibility rises with even more force when considering sexuality and the visual arts, for example, *The Pin-Up: A Modest History* (Mark Gabor, Bell, 1972). Oversized and illustrated beautifully in color and half-tone, *The Pin-Up* is a classic to be protected for its artwork and for its view of a genuinely American pastime: putting up photographs and drawings of pretty women in some very unlikely places. The frontispiece is the most famous pin-up of all: Marilyn Monroe's 1951 nude calendar photo. Likewise to be protected against vandals of whatever stripe is Alan Watts and Eliot Elisofon's magnificently photographed *Erotic Spirituality: The Vision of Konarak* (Collier Macmillan, 1971). Konarak, together with Khajuraho, are among the most famous temples in India that possess erotic carvings, and this book, with Steinberg's book on Renaissance images of Christ's sexuality, provides a visually convincing proof of the close connections between embodied sexuality and spirituality. Here we see no mortification of the flesh and denial; instead, in sexual union is felt to exist spirituality itself.

In a world perhaps different from our own, Steinberg's *Sexuality of Christ*, Wortley's *Erotic Movies*, Gabor's *The Pin-Up*, the Vatsysyana/Upadhyaya *Kama Sutra*, and Watts/Elisofon's *Erotic Spirituality* would be part of a genuinely beautiful visual display for a library lobby. It is a sign of our times, regressive and darkening, that the idea seems so remote, so silly, so dangerous.

Other books have achieved classic status by virtue of their history or age. Sir Richard Burton's 19th century translation of *The Perfumed Garden of the Shaykh Nefzawi* is one example (titles and spellings for this classic of Arab sexology vary with edition), as is the early 17th century *Lives of Fair & Gallant Ladies* by the Seigneur de Brantôme. (Our edition is Liveright, 1933). Chatty, gossipy, and remarkably tolerant, de Brantôme's book lacks the vicious cattiness of, say, Suetonius or even Ovid—who, together with Catullus, should be added to that display case in the lobby. Perhaps we shall need *two* display cases?

Other works of undeniable historical importance include Havelock Ellis' *Studies in the Psychology of Sex* (in 7 volumes, F.A. Davis, 1928). Magnus Hirschfeld's work may interest a gay readership, since Hirschfeld was openly homosexual and a supporter of gay rights in pre-Hitler Germany (e.g., *Sexual Anomalies and Perversions*, 2nd ed., a summary of the great German sexologist's early works by Norman Haire, Encyclopedaedic Press of London, 1952; other editions of Hirschfeld's work also exist). The Nazis burned his books. Legend has it that Th. H. Van de Velde's *Ideal Marriage: Its Physiology and Technique, Revised Edition* (Random House, 1926; also in different editions) is the all-time best seller among marriage manuals, and our edition lists some 50 printings between 1941 and 1974.

Two comprehensive, somewhat theoretical works are Paul Robinson's *The Modernization of Sex: Havelock Ellis, Alfred Kinsey, William Masters and Virginia Johnson* (Harper & Row, 1976) and Michel Foucault's *The History of Sexuality, Volume 1: An Introduction* (Pantheon, 1978). Robinson discusses how beliefs and ideas of their times and personalities entered the work of four recent major writers in sexuality, and Foucault's book, less a "history" of sexuality than its "story" (in French, *histoire* can mean either or both), has produced something of an intellectual coterie of followers. Both aim at intellectual readers, and as *Library Journal* might say, they are suitable for academic libraries. But who can tell? Why are we so quick to put down the intellectual interests of public library patrons?

To be singled out for special treatment is Richard von Krafft-Ebing's *Psychopathia Sexualis with Especial Reference to the An-*

tipathic Sexual Instinct: A Medico-Forensic Study (various editions). Krafft-Ebing—whose name is easily misspelled—was a late 19th century German physician who sought to prove that sexual psychopathologies are caused by nervous degeneration, and he illustrated his work with deliberately grisly accounts of some quite strange forms of behavior. It is the sort of book that a sensitive person would find quite disturbing, partly for its grinding insistence on proving that sexuality is susceptible to "degeneration." Moreover, its gruesomeness was designed to produce horror, fear, and disgust in order to make the reader shy—if not downright terrified!—of anything even remotely sexual. One can suggest that it played a large, if little remarked role in shaping American anti-sexuality sentiment. Money's *The Destroying Angel*, already mentioned, provides a necessary balancing viewpoint, because Money's sardonic, enlightening, and readable history of "degeneracy theory" explains a great deal about American anti-sexual feeling and activism. Especially fascinating are historical details of how Graham and Kellogg invented Graham Crackers and Corn Flakes as aids for attaining sexual purity and abstinence.

Another historically important book, if only because it triggered powerful censorship, is Richard Payne Knight's 1786 *A Discourse on the Worship of Priapus* . . . (oversized, reprint edition, University Books, 1974; the full title runs on for half a page). It was Knight's thesis that priapus worship (penis worship) was characteristic not only of ancient Rome, but also of southern Europe in Knight's own time. The engraved illustrations seem to make his point.

Several interesting books on Greek and Roman erotic art exist, including the handsomely illustrated *Sex or Symbol: Erotic Images of Greece and Rome* (Catharine Johns, University of Texas Press, 1982) and *Eros in Pompeii: The Secret Rooms of the National Museum of Naples* (text by Michael Grant, photographs by Antonia Mulas, Bonanza Books, 1982). A very different perspective on Greek art is contained in Eva C. Keuls' *The Reign of the Phallus: Sexual Politics in Ancient Athens* (Harper & Row, 1985). She argues that what today we see as the "erotic art" of the ancient Greeks was in fact the political manifestation of an emerging patriarchal power in Athens. Her book too is copiously illustrated in half-tones.

Perhaps the most important books on modern erotic art are edited by Drs. Phyllis and Eberhard Kronhausen, including *The Complete Book of Erotic Art: Erotic Art Volumes 1 and 2* (Bell, 1978). Additional examples of erotic art are contained in Ove Brusendorff and Poul Henningsen's five-volume *A History of Eroticism* (published in the U.S. by Lyle Stuart, 1961; original from Thaning & Appels Forlag, Copenhagen). Unfortunately, the volumes are small, and reductions in size make some of the illustrations difficult to see.

These books of erotic art are mainstream, in the sense that they contain works by the "great" graphic and plastic artists of world history (e.g., Picasso; the unknown sculptors of Khajuraho and Konarak). However, there exist far less mainstream forms. Several examples will suffice, for each would appeal more, perhaps, to libraries that have strong art holdings than to general libraries. Two involve the so-called "underground comix," of which Gilbert Shelton's work is one example. (See page 6; the "x" is the usual spelling adopted by the artists themselves.)

One artist is S. Clay Wilson, whose extraordinary images of sex and violence are not so much sadomasochism or titillating but deeply felt expressions of an intrinsic war between the sexes, in which pirates battle lesbians, "Ruby the Dyke and her six perverted sisters stomp the fags" (Wilson's own title), and Star-Eyed Stella is the openly hostile victim of evil, drooling men and demons. These images are not for everyone—I am tempted to say they are not for the faint-hearted—but they are an important part of a genuinely American realization of what "really" goes on between the sexes.[3] (See *Radical America Komiks*, Radical America, 1969; *Bent*, no publisher, 1971; *Zap Comix* nos. 2, 4, 5, 6, Apex Novelties, 1968, 1969, 1970, 1973; *Zap Comix* no. 7, Print Mint, 1974; *Zap Comix* no. 8, Print Mint/Apex Novelties, 1975.)

The second is Lawrence Welz, whose comix series *Cherry Poptart*, and later *Cherry (née Poptart)*, depict the irrepressibly explicit and gleeful sexuality of Cherry. Particularly striking is Welz' image of Cherry as the Statue of Liberty, holding a vibrator instead of a torch. In contrast to Wilson's powerful, virtually expressionistic images, Welz' view is sardonic and light. In one marvelous parody of the horror flick, a group of teenagers is beset by a drooling, chainsaw-wielding monster, whom they finally blow away with an amazing collection of shotguns, attack rifles, and pistols. It is a wonderful commentary on the horror genre, and the revenge of the teen victim (*Cherry Poptart* nos. 1 & 2, Last Gasp, 1982, 1985; *Cherry* nos. 3–9 Last Gasp, 1986–1990).

In general, underground comix artists deal openly with sex, sometimes satirically, sometimes erotically, and sometimes deliberately shockingly (see Mark James Estren's *A History of Underground Comics*, Ronin Publishing Co., 1974/1986, for a brief illustrated history). Other examples include the ebulliently sexual early work of R. Crumb; the late Dave Sheridan's meticulous pen-and-ink drawings, done alone and in collaboration with Gilbert Shelton and Paul Mavrides; the haunting eroticism of Richard Corben's strongly cinematographic images, and the highly varied, often satiric and often feminist-political work of women artists like Trina, Lee Marrs, and Patricia Moodian among others of the Women's Cartoonist's Collective.

Less "underground," but certainly not mainstream either, is the work of Lynda Barry, whose unpretty and not-too-bright characters fight the war between the sexes with a savage and pathetic underhandedness that cuts close to home. Among gay cartoonists, noteworthy are Alison Bechdel and Gerald Conelan, whose characters struggle with relationships, political issues, and sexual dilemmas—all portrayed with sympathetic humor. Here indeed is an integral part of American art and culture that must not be relegated to the corrugated storage boxes of an "alternative" collection before being finally disposed of in the dumpster back near the library's parking lot, after the staff of the alternative collection has met a similar end.[4]

Two excellent books that do not fit easily into pigeonholes are Dorothy Tennov's *Love and Limerence: The Experience of Being in Love* (Stein & Day, 1979) and editor Carole Vance's *Pleasure and Danger: Exploring Female Sexuality* (Routledge & Kegan Paul, 1984). Tennov's book put the easily misspelled word *limerence* into the language; it was called *lovesickness* once, and is a form of acute anxiety, depression, and obsession all rolled into one. Anyone who has suffered through "unrequited love" will find *Love and Limerence* genuinely helpful. Carole Vance's edited collection also achieved some fame as the record of a feminist conference about sexuality. The essays, ranging from scholarly through impassioned, are all written with an immediacy and a clarity that makes this book particularly valuable.

A number of books focusing on men are also available. Some noteworthy examples include *The Kahn Report on Sexual Preferences*, by Sandra Kahn and Jean Davis (1981; St. Martin's Press), which is a discussion of how men and women express their own sexual preferences and (mis)perceive each other's preferences, and contains descriptions of how people try to communicate with each other. *Men and Abortion: Lessons, Losses and Love*, by Arthur B. Shostak and Gary McLouth with Lynn Seng (1984; Praeger) addresses the rarely discussed topic of how men feel when the woman decides to abort the man's child. It is troubling, painful, and hopeful all at once; no easy answers emerge. Warren Farrell's *Why Men Are The Way They Are: The Male-Female Dynamic* (1986; McGraw-Hill) is a provocative analysis of men's sexuality and of why they respond to women sometimes lovingly, sometimes angrily. It is unusual in its emphasis on sociology and economics, rather than on psychology.

What of the so-called "pop sex" books? Trade books, many of them, and with quite a range in importance and usefulness. *The G-Spot* (Alice Kahn Ladas, Beverly Whipple, and John D. Perry, Holt, Rinehart and Winston, 1982) not only put a phrase in the language but came to summarize a sense of potential limitlessness in female sexuality that characterized the late 1970s (when the research on the Grafenberg spot was done). Its place on the best-seller lists, plus its careful attention to what was and was not known, make it an important purchase. Carol Cassell's *Swept Away: Why Women Fear Their Own Sexuality* (Simon and Schuster, 1984) is a serious and sensitive attempt to explain aspects of femininity that trouble women. It too is highly recommended.

Another fine tradebook is Arno Karlen's *Threesomes: Studies in Sex, Power, and Intimacy* (Beech Tree Books/Morrow, 1988). It is the only serious study of the menage à trois, one of the commonest sexual fantasies and, as a reality, an increasing part of many individual's sexuality, at least occasionally. In *Threesomes*, Karlen examines in detail the lives of people who have had sexual encounters with two other people, sometimes as a years-long lifestyle and sometimes briefly. Clearly, the topic fascinates many people, and *Threesomes*, readable, thoughtful, sensitive, is precisely what such readers want. The problem is how libraries can put such a book into those readers' hands.

A large number of books discuss the biological and medical aspects of sexuality, many highly specialized. These are omitted here since they would be of little interest to general library-goers. However, several popularly written trade books on the biological bases of sex can be recommended. One is James D. Weinrich's *Sexual Landscapes: Why We Are What We Are, Why We Love Whom We Love* (Scribner's, 1987), which combines sociobiology, psychology, and sociology in an effort to answer the questions in the title. It is provocative and well-written. Helen Fisher's *The Sex Contract: The Evolution of Human Behavior* (Morrow, 1982) is an anthropologist's effort to understand modern human sexuality in light of its evolutionary history. It too is provocative and well written. Here I may mention my own *Sex Signals: The Biology of Love* (ISI Press, 1985), an analysis of how men and women meet, fall in love, and try to communicate emotional and sexual interest in light of human biological and social history. One reviewer called it a "complex" book, yet its descriptions of flirtation and the bar scene may interest some readers.

Unfortunately, I do not have the space to deal further with psychology or sociology. For anthropology, however, a sufficiently curious situation exists that some comments are warranted.

For many years, "anthropological" works on sexuality were widely if covertly disseminated, often under the rubric of "curious sexual customs of the savages." Modern anthropologists eschew such exploitation, and some very valuable anthropological work on sexuality now exists. An elegantly illustrated example is Edgar Gregersen's *Sexual Practices* (Franklin Watts, 1983). Among classic works are Mead's books, cited previously, Brontislaw Malinowski's *Sex and Repression in Savage Society* (1914–1922; there are numerous later editions, e.g., Meridian Books, 1955); Frank Beach's *Human Sexuality in Four Perspectives* (Johns Hopkins University Press, 1977);

Clellan S. Ford and Frank A. Beach's *Patterns of Sexual Behavior* (Harper & Brothers, 1951); and Robert C. Suggs' *Marquesan Sexual Behavior* (Harcourt, Brace & World, 1966). The anthropological literature on sexuality grew healthily during the 1970s and 1980s: Sherry B. Ortner and Harriet Whitehead's *Sexual Meanings: The Cultural Construction of Gender and Sexuality* (Cambridge University Press, 1981) has become a classic in the so-called "constructionist/symbolist" interpretation of sexuality. *Self, Sex, and Gender in Cross-Cultural Fieldwork* (Tony Larry Whitehead and Mary Ellen Conaway, eds., University of Illinois Press, 1986) will give a reader a flavor of modern anthropological sex research. It is a far cry from the finely produced, privately issued *Sexual Relations of Mankind* by Paolo Mantegazza (Falstaff Press, 1932), printed on tinted paper and with a " . . . COVER DESIGN . . . carefully reproduced to retain the exquisite original coloring of the painting BY WILLIAM BLAKE" (upper case original).

Yet, if we return to that lobby display case, here too is a delicate, but clear example of how matters have changed since 1932. This edition of Mantegazza's work says on the title page, "Of this edition a limited number have been privately issued by the anthropological branch of the Falstaff Press for exclusive subscription of adult students of anthropology." And next to it, in that imagined lobby display case, let us set a work published 55 years later: Suzanne G. Frayser and Thomas J. Whitby's invaluable *Studies in Human Sexuality: A Selected Guide* (Libraries Unlimited, 1987). It contains 627 numbered and annotated references to papers and books, and has a combined author and title index of 18 printed pages. Frayser and Whitby's bibliography does not say on *its* title page, " . . . privately issued for the adult student of anthropology . . ."

. . . And From Quality Back to Reality

That is progress, of course, and yet . . .

La plus ça change. Granting that these books all have genuine value, how many librarian readers can say that they have seen all or most of them, or that their library has copies of all or most? True, sexuality librarianship is its own specialty, so some might be unfamiliar. But how many large public or academic libraries own a majority?

There is the problem. If a library possesses only both Kinsey reports plus one Masters and Johnson, are there not still people who feel that such "dirt"—their word, not mine!—should forthwith be removed? How can a library then build a collection of the solid, serious, often beautifully printed and illustrated works that exist today, a half-century or more after Falstaff Press placed its cautious warning on the title page?

And, again, what of that display case? When shall we see books on sexuality presented openly and displayed as the library's proud possessions, not hidden away as dirt, filth, and garbage? *We are no longer dealing with raggedy smut.* Indeed, such "smut" has become the prized possessions of archivally oriented libraries. But nonetheless, I suspect that it will take time—who knows? Another half-century?—before it is widespread library practice to exhibit publicly the books about sex and erotica that have only very briefly been summarized.

CONTAGION AND CONTAMINATION

Once again, we are forced to examine the anti-sex collection viewpoints that I paraphrase throughout this essay. But now another aspect of that attitude requires scrutiny: the idea that by having books of "filth"—again, their word—somehow the "higher" purposes of the library are subverted. (This, after all, is what is meant to "dirty" something.) It is as if sexuality, even between the covers of these undoubtedly high quality books, can still reach out and, if uncontrolled by moral fervor, poison and contaminate the library goers. Now, no one in their right mind believes that books containing explicit descriptions of sex literally exude poisonous vapors that corrode the quality of the other books like acid rain. Instead, in the notion of contamination by proximity is the apprehensive belief, even total conviction, that sexuality materials are dangerous to the soft and susceptible mind of the reader.

And here too voices arise, one speaking of a traditional America that is fading, and the other speaking of something else that I feel is far more dangerous than the putative evils of sexuality books. The first voice is frail, not because it is timid, but because it is elderly. "Ah, sex"—and perhaps a woman speaks—"I see you are still as fascinated as we were. But we treated sex differently then; it wasn't as open as it is now, and we treated it with respect. I am surprised and distressed to see sex everywhere, and it would seem wrong for a library to put sex so far forward." And an elderly man's voice adds, "I agree. Sex just doesn't belong in the public library."

In these voices echos a fading American tradition. Its passage puzzles and saddens many older people, for they do not see what has caused the changes. So, while one respects these voices, one must still remember other aspects of the culture to which they belong. In that culture, it was an undoubted item of faith that the women's place was in her home as wife and mother, and that normatively her career options were restricted to being her husband's auxiliary at company gatherings. Furthermore, her sexuality was circumscribed by the "feminine mystique" that gave Friedan the name for her 1962 book, and by what later feminist writers have called "patriarchal" oppression of women's sexuality. No longer the 19th century idea of female sexual passionlessness, nonetheless 20th century conservative traditions place female sexuality strongly (normatively, *solely*) in marriage, and with its flourishing dependent on a husband's love. Otherwise, it had no value or was even immoral. Clearly, this value system is at hopeless odds with the beliefs and experiences of millions of younger American women.

Then, too, in that culture it was an undoubted item of faith that children were essentially pure and innocent, if mischievous, an image captured perfectly in "Dennis the Menace." Tow-haired little boys and curly-haired little girls made faces at the teacher and played with toys; none of them dreamed, as Calvin does in the modern cartoon strip, "Calvin and Hobbes," of blowing up his school in a fighter bomber attack run. And if children were sexual, then conservative tradition could either only laugh and deny, or punish the child because even if that tradition had its child-molesters, it also had protective mechanisms to shield the adult while denying that exploitation could occur. "Oh, Uncle Louis is like that," the voice explained as Uncle Louis planted a wet kiss on his twelve-year-old niece's mouth and fondled her developing breasts. "He doesn't mean anything by it."

And perhaps even more importantly, within that culture of American sexual denial pornography itself developed. In a world in which sex was either "dirty" or "pure," i.e., marital, no legitimate outlets existed for sexual interests not directly tied to family moralities. Officially, no married woman could even *think* of an extramarital affair, although some women had them; and if a married man wanted a sexual "adventure," it could only be with a prostitute, although in unofficial reality, some married men had long-term sexual relationships with "other women." Likewise, sex for the unmarried, young or old, did not "officially" exist. In this world, pornography had a unique place, not morally but sociologically: it was an illicit but widespread outlet for men locked into marital and sexual relationships that were, for them, as repressive as they were for women, or who had not even marital sexuality. Inevitably there arose the badly made stag film, the "blue movie" of American film history; novelty items like the ice-cube tray that made ice cubes in the form of penises or breasts, the "take-a-drink-and-she-strips" glasses that revealed a nude woman as the fluid level in the glass dropped, or the badly carved statuettes that "my cousin got in Japan during the Korean War" that showed men and women in various forms of copulatory activity; and finally the books of pornography themselves, sold under the counter and showing badly exposed photographs of prostitutes naked on motel beds, bored-looking models posing for "nude art magazines," and hack-written tales of *Nurses on a Spree.*[5]

Today, these items are primarily of historical or scholarly interest, for by present-day standards of graphic production, most are very poorly done. And if modern libraries could put together the display case of erotica discussed previously, the exhibition would produce more amused laughter than arousal. These items are *culture-* and *history-specific* in their content, style, and production values. Indeed, the nonsexologist might wonder exactly what these items meant to consumers in a bygone America. To the sexologist, however, the answer is this: they broke *then* existing taboos about sexuality, in history-specific ways, and served as focal images of alternatives to marital and duty-bound sexuality. When men, say, *laughed* at penis-shaped ice-cubes, it was the laughter of relief and a moment of spontaneity that transcended the rules of official, marital sexuality.

But hidden under the sexual repressions of both men and women was more than the overloaded and over-loud laughter of relief. In the jerkily twisted fantasies of masturbation was something that John Money, in *Lovemaps*, calls *vandalized*—a distortion of simple, direct erotic arousal into complex fantasies of sexual revenge, helplessness, and often vindictive fury.[6] It can very plausibly be argued that these are the psychologically inevitable sequellae to sexual repression. Contrary to conventional moral wisdom, attempts to suppress sexuality most often merely redirect its explicit imagery towards contexts that combine the original eroticism with images of repression, guilt, shame, and fear. The result can be a sexualized fantasy of angry revenge, expressed in symbols of either power or helplessness, and not the replacement of sexual images with other, less erotic imagery. In this, pornography—either of the traditional nudie "art magazine" type or in its newer exemplars—merely serves to focus *already existing* sexual feelings on a specific visual or written depiction. One result, often stressed by researchers on pornography, is that individual preferences in pornography are extremely narrow and highly idiosyncratic. Summarizing his field work in a Washington, DC adult bookstore, anthropologist Jack McIlver Weatherford observed:

> Working in the Pink Pussy [Weatherford's name for the adult book store], I was surprised to learn that many of the men to whom I doled out all those quarters each night [for peep shows] expressed a dislike for pornography in general although they sought one variety of it in particular. The man who could not have an orgasm without looking at big breasts ignored everything else in the store. Another, who fantasized about blond pubic hair, showed no interest in big breasts unless they happened to be on a woman who also had blond pubic hair. The man who liked pictures of transvestites thought that the customer who bought pictures of young men was sick, and the men who liked bondage had no common interest with the men who wanted the soft-core magazines. Often it seemed that the men who liked to read written stories had little interest in the picture magazines. Each man had a narrow range of fantasy and showed interest only in the precise kind of pornography that sustained this fantasy;

as far as he was concerned, the rest was trash. There were no
connoisseurs of pornography as a whole, no little old men in raincoats who got equal thrills from bondage, incest, and interracial
rape. Even within the extreme monotony of pornography, there was
a marked specialization of fetishes and fantasies that kept the users
separate and isolated in their . . . pleasures.

Pornography is a fetish, or a collection of fetishes. As such it is
simply a very explicit aid to fantasy and thereby to masturbation.
(Weatherford 1986, 45)

Probably the great majority of sexologists would agree with this
assessment.

Accordingly, any form of visual and written pornography has its
roots both in the details of a specific period of history (e.g., the
1940s, say), and in the psychology of individual sexual development
(wherein one individual comes to prefer blond pubic hair while
another prefers transvestites). It has no universal origin in degeneration, in immorality rampant, in social collapse imminent or otherwise, or in a universal tendency among male users of pornography to
see women degraded or harmed. It is as varied as sexuality itself,
because for its aficionados, it serves unique and personal sexual ends.

But once again one can very plausibly argue that pornography as
a social-historical phenomenon is an outgrowth of other social-historical phenomena, most notably a widespread tradition in America to
treat sexuality with suspicion, distrust, and even dislike, and to
vandalize its expressions when they appear, say, in adolescence. Under these social repressions, sexuality does not disappear, but becomes fetishized and reappears wearing strange, idiosyncratic, and
even bizarre clothing. Thus, paradoxically, we in part owe pornography to the traditions that sought to suppress sexuality except in the
service of family and morality, in brief, in the very traditions of
conservative America that themselves find pornography so abhorrent.

A Return to the Old Ways?

But here rises another voice, which, if youngish, nonetheless also
speaks of tradition. "Well, be that as it may," this voice says, "for I
am not convinced by your argument. I am a traditionalist, and I
believe in traditional American virtue. Maybe there are no little old
men in raincoats individually, but *collectively* they are all dirty and
together they represent an evil that must be suppressed. And do not
be misled! Our traditional ways are not dying at all, because some of
us want to preserve our traditions as the surest guide and bedrock of
American morality."

But in these voices, we do not hear genuine experience with older
American sexual traditions, nor knowledge of the complexities of
sexuality in a modern America. Instead, we hear an *imitation* of those

traditions designed with very modern social and political goals. All too often, such self-proclaimed "traditionalists" can work a cynical political manipulation of present-day discontents, such as concern over pornography, in order to create social and political solutions in which *they* have the power. "Elect me!" cries the voice. "I stand for traditional American virtue!" But is this politician's eye on morality, or on the cash register? It is easy to rise to power with the votes and support of trusting people, only to fall when one is found stealing from the collection box.

And the fact is that America has changed, that sexuality is no longer what it once was, and that therefore libraries must also function in a changed America. It does not matter if sexologists believe—and with good reason—that sexually repressive times lead to the recrudescence of sexuality in exactly the forms originally found so abhorrent. Instead, it is certain that we can never return to those old days of "innocence," of the "platonic" love affair with the shy young girl or boy next door, or to Norman Rockwell idealizations of a past that had its own nasty problems, like the Great Depression. A younger generation, born after World War II, after the Korean War, after Vietnam; born after oral contraception had been introduced in 1961; born after Supreme Court decisions rendered older definitions of *obscenity* obsolete; in brief, those born after what is too simply called the "sexual revolution" simply *cannot* reconstruct the old America. For many such people, sex is an open part of life, and they simply cannot envision a time when one could be arrested and prosecuted for possessing a photograph of a nude woman and man or information about contraception.

And so too is rendered obsolete a part of the myth of the American library, that it is the proper domain of gentility, purity, and moral superiority over people who actually enjoy sex sufficiently to want to read about its history, biology, psychology, sociology, or anthropology—or in fiction. Today, there is no possibility that some horde of pornography aficionados might tramp from the Pink Pussy to the library and demand in gravelly voices that the library stock their favorite and unique blend of blond pubic hair, transvestite boys, and incest. Whatever their needs are, and from whatever origin those needs arose, adult bookstores and adult zoning ordinances supply them. Few libraries serve such a clientele, although some collect such works. Instead, libraries serve another clientele, either in actuality or potentially: a group of readers nurtured on material written in the opening atmosphere that followed World War II and that has increasingly prevailed in the decades that came after. That clientele is younger, better educated, and more sophisticated than any library population has ever been, and it cares very little for sweeping moral arguments about why sex is dirty.

Accordingly, today there is no reason why a library should not have a balanced and clearly labelled collection of works *on* sexuality and *of* sexuality. If we do not sequester books on house painting lest crazies drink cans of paint, why are we worried about the pathogenic and contaminating influences of works on sex?

Social Evil

And here we reach the penultimate voice to speak against sexuality materials in the library. "Oho," this voice says, "now you've gotten it. Sure, you're right, most of us are modern, most of us are sane, and not too many of us are habitués of stores like the Pink Pussy. A little titillation doesn't hurt us, not even the naked ladies in *Playboy* or in your Indian temples. Why, even those sex vids can be fun, you know, if they are used right. But, I admit that I *am* worried about what happens when sexually explicit materials fall into the wrong hands. Doesn't crime follow after that? Doesn't rape increase when sexually explicit materials are available? Isn't that what the studies show?"

In this position, we hear an apprehensive echo of the older idea that sexually explicit materials, of whatever sort, can exude poisonous moral vapors that can endanger the reader's mind. But other themes are also present. One is a jovial assertion of self-health—"I'm OK"— followed by a seemingly worried assertion about *them*—"They're *not* OK." Another is the typically vague reference to "studies" that show that porn causes rape—or at least that is what the speaker thinks they show.

Now, one cannot set aside this voice by laughing away the potential dangers of rape or sexual violence. Indeed, it has been a major component of many books on pornography to hint that exactly such a causal relationship is well established in sexology. But I know of no studies of any sort whatsoever that indicate that sexuality materials in the *library* contribute to sexual crime. Furthermore, there is no area in sex research that is *less* certain than the widely believed correlation between sexual crimes of violence and pornography.[7] There is much impassioned moral rhetoric, some from the so-called "far right," some from feminist writers, and even some from the federal government. There is a growing sense in sexology that when images of physical violence are appended to sexual images, the violence as such can lead to attitudes of indifference to rape (Donnerstein, Linz, & Penrod 1987), but depictions of sexuality alone do not appear to do so. However, for some people, including some librarians, there is no need to prove any connection between pornography and rape. Such people already believe that sexuality can be dangerous and evil.

So, for one group of critics of sexually explicit materials, it suffices to reassure them that most books on sex—euphemistic, erotic, scholarly, popular, or even pornographic—are relatively harmless compared to depictions of sexual violence and even violence in general. Their concern is genuinely about violence and harm, and they can easily generalize from personal experience that sexually explicit materials have little effect other than producing transient sexual arousal.

But for a second set of critics who speak of the "harm" caused by sexually explicit materials, there is a hidden agenda that transcends such reassurances. And *that* agenda is very dangerous.

CENSORSHIP AND POWER

Imagine, for a moment, taking seriously the idea that sexuality books in a library would increase rape and physical abuse of women. Certainly, that would be a convincing argument to many people for eliminating or reducing a library's sexuality holdings and for making further purchases in sexuality areas only with the greatest caution. (This was the argument that the library patron at the Ellensburg Public Library used against Isaac Asimov's *Robots of Dawn*; see Chapter 1.)

But a moment of commonsense must intervene. Do you mean to assert that rapists go to the *library* before attacking women? Do you mean that an innocent young man sees Masters and Johnson in the public library and decides to lurk in alleyways to find women? Perhaps that is the explanation! All these rapists—their problem is that they *read!*

And here, with a sudden nasty twist, one aspect of the "porn causes rape" argument is revealed for something other than what it seems. That argument asserts that sexual fantasies, engendered in one's own mind but *without* the assistance of *Playboy*, *Hustler*, or *The Pearl*, are not alone sufficient to cause a man to rape. Instead, the argument claims that *the words and pictures* this man finds in books are needed to trigger rape. This assertion we easily recognize, perhaps with a bitter smile, for it is the traditional cry of the bookburner and the censor: *Books are dangerous. The printed word and picture are dangerous.* (See Carole Vance's brief analysis of the recent attack on the National Endowment for the Arts for funding "offensive" and "indecent" work; Vance 1989). Mutated through time, always this view surfaces by associating the worst moral crimes—rape, in our present era—with the *real* enemy being attacked: books and learning.

Accordingly, the "pornography is dangerous because it leads to rape" argument collapses not merely for lack of empirical support. It collapses for a far more important reason: it asserts that the unaided mind is never evil, never harmful, never dangerous, never pathological, unless it has been *made* evil by books. Unassisted, a man's mind can neither plan nor execute a rape, but give him *books* and he can enact evil. And then the books are burned.

But is the target here the miserable devil who rapes a woman or is it the devils the censors believe lurk in books or pictures? To the censor, the real crime, deserving the auto-da-fé, is not rape, but publishing freely and disseminating freely the products of the printing press and the photolithograph machine. The firebrand that lights the auto-da-fé also lights the fires under the books.

Now, for some people, burning the books of sexuality would not be a great loss. For them, materials written on sexuality represent either incomprehensible medico-physiological jargon, or quickie-cheapo popular novels, or are otherwise pure pornography—not that this view could be altered by a visit to the libraries where sexuality has been an underrepresented and restricted topic! Yet, if that is the problem, then the solution is not difficult: I believe that *all* libraries should have adequate, reasonable, and even thorough collections on sexuality.

"Well," interrupts another voice, the last one to object, "I do *not*. Your intellectualizing about knowledge is irrelevant. There are rules and they exist to be obeyed. It does not matter if you say these are excellent works. The most important rule of all is that sex does not belong in the library. It is as simple as that. There is no argument or discussion. The answer is *No*."

Ultimately, that is the issue: the power to censor. Such power does not question; it does not explore; it does not think. It says *No* and it acts: the books are burned. Yet, hidden within the censor's argument of moral and political power is something else, something less reasoned, something less rule-abiding. . . *fear*.

Many who uphold this argument do so not in hatred of books and pictures, even of naked women, but in fear and terror. Such fears are genuine, not the product of evil media manipulation. But so too were fears of witches real in their time. The profound problem is that the fear is misplaced and misconnected. If, in the screaming enthusiasm of the audience to an auto-da-fé we hear the voice of terror, in the softer but no less dangerous voices of those who would ban sexuality we also hear the voice of terror. Internal fears of sex as ugly and frightening, vandalized, distorted, and warped through ignorance and shame, connect to external fears, like the fear of rapists, and find a victim in the books and pictures that fear and terror say were to blame. But a *false* cause has been erected by fear when the books—or witches—are burned. The real causes remain, and fuel the terror and the fires of the witchburners; ignorance, oppression, mistreatment, and willful stupidity.

For the censor, the terror is that books and pictures have immensely more power than the unaided and unassisted mind. And *that* is the poison the bookburners and witchburners see exuding from the sexuality books. They fear the *power* of books far more than they fear rape.

And still another image arises. In this fear of books and pictures about sex is always the insistence that these books have evil, not good influence. No one discusses how a young man went to the library once, his mind troubled with fantasies he did not understand, fantasies of sexual violence and hatred, and there he found a book that described sexual fantasies, not in terror or nightmare, but simply, directly, scientifically. Perhaps that young man relaxed a bit that day, and perhaps the next he sought help. But the idea that sexual books and pictures can *cure* is never to forefront in the mind of those who fear sexuality, and for whom all books and pictures about sexuality need to be hidden away, lest their putative danger pollute and contaminate the innocent.

Through censorship, and through the library's strategies of denial and avoidance, how many deeply troubled people have been refused access to the cool, simple, and direct voices of those who have studied sexuality, or of those for whom it is not a danger and who write cheerfully about its pleasures? I insist that for every rapist not born in the halls of a *censored* library, there are thousands of men and women who have remained troubled and in pain in the halls of that same censored library.

It does not distill so easily, that books either kill or cure. They, like people, are complex. But I choose to take my side with the books themselves, openly displayed, openly available, clearly catalogued and referenced, than with the miserable terrors of the bookburners and the censors. I choose the ideal of the library where nestle together the great philosophers, the great novelists, the great artists, and the great works on sex. And, if no library's holdings can contain only Plato, Milton, Sartre, and Michelangelo, then too no library can contain only Masters and Johnson or Kinsey. Who is to say where the cures and the knowledge lie hidden? Sometimes in the great, but sometimes in the less great too. But I assert that a far greater evil, a darkness of *mind*, lit only by the executioner's fire and echoing only with screams, lurks at the threshold of the marble pillars of the library when one says "Well, I don't think the library should have sex books . . ."

The Library, and all real libraries, should and must. In no other way can the true power of books—to educate and illuminate—be brought to dawn.

ENDNOTES

1. Pete Dexter's novel, *Deadwood* (1986) captures the whoring, brawling masculinity of the American frontier. Another excellent example is contained in Louise Dickinson Rich's *We Took to the Woods* (1942), the story of how she and her husband lived in Maine for many years. She recounts (pp. 272–278) a neighbor's story of being a boy in Maine in the early 1900s, when one day he found himself driving the coach belonging to Aunt Hat, the madam, as they paraded up to the fairground. When the fairground gate proved locked, Aunt Hat yells, "Open up these gates, you sons of bitches! Here comes Aunt Hat and all her whores!" (p. 277). Not a story of today. . . .

2. References to the considerable literature on this topic can be found in Perper (1989), Perper & Weis (1987), and Perper (1985). The *locus classicus* is perhaps Cott (1978).

3. At the 1973 Obscenity trial of *Zap Comix* no. 4 in New York City, writer Steven Marks testified that he had used earlier R. Crumb strips in the Humanities course that he had taught at Columbia University, and would have used some of S. Clay Wilson's visions of Hell if he had been teaching Dante when *Zap* no. 4 came out (Estren 1987, 231).

4. For libraries wishing to collect American radical ephemera, Ivan Stang's 1988 *High Weirdness by Mail: A Directory of the Fringe: Mad Prophets, Crackpots, Kooks & True Visionaries* (Simon & Schuster) provides addresses, prices, and sardonic commentaries on a wide menu of American fringy publications. It covers some, though not all, of the "oddball" sex publications, which are not pornographic so much as they are genuinely unclassifiable mixtures of sexually explicit material, radical politics, personal rants, and weird graphics. The book itself would offend no one, but assuredly some of the publications it cites would. It is therefore a valuable purchase on several counts.

5. Space does not permit analysis here of pornography itself nor of the now huge literature about pornography. To the layperson, contact with actual hardcore pornography can be very frightening, partly because much pornography deals with *vandalized* sexual needs, which can bring the reader very close to the deep psychoses and paraphilias of the writers and their audiences. Tragically, public discussion of pornography most often uses it for its explicit *moral* shock value, wherein the anti-pornography presenter or writer is trying to frighten the audience into hysterical anti-sexuality, much the way Krafft-Ebing used his case histories in *Psychopathia Sexualis*. From the standpoint of treatment and therapeutic modalities, such presentations are unforgivable, because they invoke the audience's hatred and loathing for what is merely a form of psychopathology to be dealt with by professionals. Accordingly, since it in fact takes considerable psychological and sociological sophistication and professional training to deal with the themes of pornography, I have omitted their discussion in this essay as taking me too far from the subject matter at hand.

6. Descriptions of some of these fantasies may be found in Nancy Friday's 1973 *My Secret Garden: Women's Sexual Fantasies*, in her 1980 *Men in Love: Men's Sexual Fantasies: The Triumph of Love Over Rage*, and in William J. Slattery's 1975 *The Erotic Imagination: Sexual Fantasies of the Adult Male*. Much written on sexual fantasy is of the "ain't it awful" school, and represents a countervailing rage more than analysis of content or of sociological psychological function. A significant exception is psychiatrist Robert J. Stoller's 1985 *Observing the Erotic Imagination*.

7. **Editor's Note:** See the works cited in the "Pornography and Behavior" section of Chapter 14, "Access or Censorship? Libraries and Pornography: An Annotated Selective Bibliography," particularly the exchange between Mosher (1986) and Malamuth & Donnerstein (1987) about Malamuth and Donnerstein's 1984 book, *Pornography and Sexual Aggression.* Nor is the more recent Donnerstein, Linz, & Penrod book (1987) a simple indictment of pornography. Still more recent research by Padgett, Brislin-Slütz, & Neal (1989) produced no correlation whatsoever between exposure to nonviolent pornography and negative attitudes towards women or women's issues.

REFERENCES

Baym, Nina. 1978. *Woman's fiction.* Ithaca, NY: Cornell University Press.

Cott, Nancy F. 1978. Passionlessness: An interpretation of Victorian sexual ideology, 1790–1850. *Signs,* 4:219–236.

Dexter, Pete. 1986. *Deadwood.* New York: Random House.

Donnerstein, Edward, Daniel Linz, and Steven Penrod. 1987. *The question of pornography: Research findings and policy implications.* New York: The Free Press.

Estren, Mark James. 1987. *A history of underground comics.* Berkeley, CA: Ronin Publishing.

Friday, Nancy. 1973. *My secret garden.* New York: Trident Press.

Friday, Nancy. 1980. *Men in love.* New York: Delacorte.

Haeberle, Erwin J. 1982. The Jewish contribution to the development of sexology. *The Journal of Sex Research,* 18:305–323.

Malamuth, Neil M., and Edward Donnerstein. 1984. *Pornography and sexual aggression.* Orlando, FL: Academic Press.

Malamuth, Neil M., and Edward Donnerstein. 1987. Letter to the Book Review Editor. *The Journal of Sex Research,* 23:281–283.

Molz, Kathleen. 1966–1967. The public custody of the high pornography. *American Scholar,* Winter:93–103.

Morley, Christopher. 1917/1983. *Parnassus on wheels.* New York: Avon.

Morley, Christopher. 1919/1983. *The haunted bookshop.* New York: Avon.

Mosher, Donald E. 1986. Book review of *Pornography and sexual aggression,* by Neil M. Malamuth and Edward Donnerstein. *The Journal of Sex Research,* 22:532–535.

Padgett, Vernon R., Jr., Jo Ann Brislin-Slütz, and James A. Neal. 1989. Pornography, erotica, and attitudes towards women: The effects of repeated exposure. *The Journal of Sex Research,* 26:479–491.

Perper, Timothy. 1985. *Sex signals: The biology of love.* Philadelphia: ISI Press.

Perper, Timothy. 1989. Theories and observations on sexual selection and female choice in human beings. *Medical Anthropology,* 11:409–454.

Perper, Timothy, and David L. Weis. 1987. Proceptive and rejective strategies of U.S. and Canadian college women. *The Journal of Sex Research,* 23:455–480.

Rich, Louise Dickinson. 1942. *We took to the woods.* New York: Grosset & Dunlap.

Slattery, William J. 1975. *The erotic imagination.* Chicago: Regnery.

Stoller, Robert J. 1985. *Observing the erotic imagination*. New Haven: Yale University Press.

Stone, Lee Alexander. 1922. *Sex searchlights and sane sex ethics*. Chicago: Science Publishing Company.

Sussman, Gerald. 1965. *The official sex manual: A modern approach to the art and techniques of coginus*. New York: Putnam's Sons.

Vance, Carole S. 1989. The war on culture. *Art in America*, September:39–45.

Weatherford, Jack McIlver. 1986. *Porn row*. New York: Arbor House.

Editor's Appendix: Book Selection in Sexuality

Finding reviews of either erotica or nonfiction materials about sexuality is not usually simple. There are sources, however, although some a bit off the beaten track.

For erotica, see Chapter 15, "An Annotated Bibliography of Quality Erotica," by David Steinberg, for some recommended currently available items. For other materials, check out excerpts, advertisements, and reviews appearing in *Yellow Silk* and *Libido* (see addresses given by Steinberg in Chapter 15) and *Eidos* (Brush Hill Press, Inc., Box 96, Boston MA 02137-0096). The Sexuality Library, 1210 Valencia Street, San Francisco, CA 94110, carries a small selection of erotica books and videos, and its catalog provides annotations.

For gay and lesbian erotica, two mail order concerns offer lengthy selections of items described in minicatalogs and flyers:

Giovanni's Room
Mail Order Department
345 South 12th Street
Philadelphia, PA 19107

Lambda Rising
1625 Connecticut Avenue, NW
Washington, DC 20009

A somewhat better situation exists with nonfiction. During the 1970s and early 1980s, writing popular sex books was a growth industry, and produced its share of ephemeral trivia and even misinformation. (Courtesy and perhaps the libel laws prohibit me from giving examples here.) Fortunately, during these years *Library Journal* was publishing many capsule reviews of sex works. Unfortunately, *LJ* has not kept up that practice; however, *LJ, Choice,* and *Kirkus* all cover some current material. But the best source of reviews is the excellent *SIECUS Report*. Also helpful but with far fewer reviews per issue are *Archives of Sexual Behavior, Journal of Sex Education and Therapy,* and *The Journal of Sex Research.* The *Women's Review of Books* is essential for feminist and lesbian topics. For both gay and lesbian works, Lambda Rising and Giovanni's Room catalogs carry annotations for scholarly and popular nonfiction as well as erotica.

For serious collection development in nonfiction sexuality materials, however, the best guides are the many bibliographies—in book form, as journal articles, and as brief publications. The compilation below, while not exhaustive, contains many major lists. For smaller public libraries, the SIECUS bibliographies will provide adequate guidance.

Brewer, Joan Scherer, and Rod W. Wright. *Sex Research: Bibliographies from the Institute for Sex Research.* (Phoenix, AZ: Oryx Press, 1979).
This is a selected, unannotated compilation of some of the many bibliographies put out by the Institute (now the Kinsey Institute); over 4,000 books and articles are covered. It complements the Frayser and Whitby book in containing older materials.

Campbell, Patty. *Sex Guides: Books and Films about Sexuality for Young Adults.* (New York: Garland, 1986).
This is a narrative, critical review of the "teen sex manual," covering the history of the genre and providing core collection lists for public and secondary school libraries.

Dynes, Wayne R. *Homosexuality: A Research Guide.* (New York: Garland, 1987).
Nearly 5,000 books and articles are included in this comprehensive annotated bibliography. Most articles are from the scholarly literature or the gay press.

Frayser, Suzanne G., and Thomas J. Whitby. *Studies in Human Sexuality: A Selected Guide.* (Littleton, CO: Libraries Unlimited, 1987).
Each of the more than 600 books listed in this bibliography of sex research has a 300-word (or longer) abstract. Most items are from 1970–1987. This is a very valuable tool for university and research libraries.

Jenkins, Christine. "Heartthrobs & Heartbreaks: A Guide to Young Adult Books with Gay Themes." *Out/Look*, 1(3) (Fall, 1988), 82–92.
Jenkins lists and annotates 41 young adult novels with gay characters or themes, published from 1969–1986 in the U.S. In an introductory essay, she discusses to what extent these novels reflect gay stereotypes and gay realities.

SantaVicca, Edmund F. "Acquired Immune Deficiency Syndrome (AIDS): An Annotated Bibliography for Librarians." *Reference Services Review*, 16 (Winter, 1987), 45–67.
Every public, academic, and school library should use this article as an acquisitions aid. It includes books, organizational and governmental publications, serials, databases, audiovisuals, pamphlets, and organizations.

Sex Research: Early Literature from Statistics to Erotica. 120 reels of microfilm, plus bibliographic guide and indexes. (Woodbridge, CT: Research Publications, 1981).
This microfilm collection of actual texts includes about 1,000 titles published between 1700 and 1860 and covering erotica, sexual behavior, law, medicine, and women's studies.

Y-A Hotline: An Alert to Matters Concerning Young Adults. Issue 29/30, c. January, 1988. "Super double issue of sex ed materials." (Available from School of Library Service, Dalhousie University, Halifax, NS B3H 4H8, Canada.)
This compilation includes articles, audiovisuals, and fiction and nonfiction books, all with reviews or abstracts, about providing sex education to young adults.

SIECUS Bibliographies

The Sex Information and Education Council of the U.S. (SIECUS) compiles and updates regularly a number of useful bibliographies. All contain addresses of sources and are available for a small fee from SIECUS, 32 Washington Place, New York, NY 10003.

AIDS and Safer Sex Education.
Books, curricula, reports, audiovisuals, organizations, and hotlines.

Audiovisuals for Sexuality Professionals: A Selected Bibliography, and *Audiovisuals for Sexuality Professionals: An Addendum to a Selected Bibliography.*
Films, filmstrips, videos, and slide programs.

Bibliography of Religious Publications on Sex Education and Sexuality.
Largely materials from denominational presses.

Child Sexual Abuse Education and Prevention: A Selected Bibliography of Materials for Sale.
Books, pamphlets, curricula, and audiovisuals currently available from various sources.

Human Sexuality: A Bibliography for Everyone.
Books and booklets divided into categories according to intended audience.

Human Sexuality: A Selected Bibliography for Professionals.
Books for sex educators, counselors, and researchers.

Sexuality and Disability: A Bibliography of Resources Available for Purchase.
Books and booklets currently available from various sources, categorized by type of disability.

Sexuality and Family Life Education: An Annotated Bibliography of Curricula for Sale.
Books and booklets currently available from a variety of sources.

Sexuality Periodicals for Professionals: A SIECUS Bibliography.
Mostly professional and scholarly journals.

Index

Compiled by Estella Bradley